As the Ash Fell

AJ Powers

Editing by: Talia Philips
Additional editing by: Christi Eisenberg & Jerian Powers
Cover design by: AJ Powers
Stock Photography: Public Domain Pictures @
Pixabay.com
Cover title font: Candal
ISBN: 1511874120
ISBN-13: 978-1511874120

DEDICATION

To my Creator and King.

To my loving wife and editor, Talia. I owe you a great deal of gratitude for your constant encouragement and constructive feedback. You not only helped me to become a better writer but a better person. I love you.

To my daughters and son who inspire me each day.

ACKNOWLEDGMENTS

To my mom, Shelia. To my father, Bill, and my step-mom, Jerian. Thanks for the encouragement and excitement.

To the talented J.T. O'Connell, who pushes me to hone my craft and has always offered great feedback on every piece I've written. Thank you!

To my best friends, Phil and Geoff. Thanks for the countless hours of humorous conversations (some of which end up in my writing) and for the memories that will last a lifetime. I truly appreciate your friendship.

To Christi and Richard, thank you for your constant encouragement and genuine excitement for my endeavors. Your friendship means more to me than I can ever articulate.

To my brother Mark, my good friend Jon, as well as Joe and Amy Alton, for being great resources for medical trauma.

A special thanks to Adam Francis of Equip 2 Endure (www.equip2endure.com) for the great survival resources and for one of my favorite quotes about being prepared.

Lastly, but certainly not least, a heart-felt thanks to those who read an advanced copy of this book. Your feedback and critiques were invaluable, and as a result this book is better for it. I appreciate you taking time out of your busy schedules to read my first novel.

Chapter 1

It was getting late. Though the sky was hazy—it was always hazy—he could see faint colors just above the horizon. He checked his watch. It was nearly 6:00. He had already been on his feet for fourteen hours, and it was about a two and a half hour hike back home.

Another goose egg, Clay thought to himself. Discouraged, weary, and exhausted, he climbed down from his perch in the tree and began the trek home. He started to speculate why it had been so long since he had seen deer in his favorite hunting hideaway. Over the last two years that location had consistently provided him a doe or two each month, and it wasn't hard to figure out why. It was a bit of an oasis just outside of a cave where a small stream trickled into a slightly larger one. The water was some of the purest he'd seen since the ash fell; it was naturally filtered as it seeped through the cracks in the rocks from the hills above. The small wooded area was only about

500 yards from the interstate, yet you'd never know it was there if you were looking from the road.

Though it was nicely hidden away, it was risky to fire a rifle so close to the highway. Even though the days of lane changes and gridlocked traffic were long gone, it was still commonly used by travelers on foot. He could shave forty-five minutes off his journey if he used the highway, but Clay rarely did. The hip-high overgrowth in the median and the decayed vehicles that pockmarked the road made it easy for bandits to ambush travelers. Or worse, Screamers could easily be concealed, waiting to kill merely for the thrill of it. The convenience of the road was seldom worth the risk.

Nearly thirty minutes into his journey, Clay heard a noise. It was faint, but unmistakable—a tree branch cracking. He instinctively stopped and crouched down low, partially hiding himself behind a twisted mess that may have once been called a shrub. His vantage point near the top of a hill allowed him a clear view of the field from where he thought the sound originated. Clay wasn't sure if it was from a man or beast. Lately it seemed difficult to distinguish a difference between the two. He slowly raised his Ruger Scout, looked through the optics, and scanned the field. He noticed some movement right at the edge of a tree line. Daylight was fading, but the distinctive silhouette was obvious.

Yes!

A doe and her fawn were feeding in the field just in front of the trees. They were about 200 yards away; he needed to get closer. His hefty .308 was more than enough bullet for the distance, but he didn't trust himself. With the exception of some powdered eggs and a stale breakfast bar when he woke up, he hadn't eaten all day. His body was weak, his hands shaky, and his aim would be anything but true. The wind from the approaching storm wasn't helping matters either.

He carefully removed his backpack and placed it beneath the bush that had been providing his cover. Staying low, he crept forward, moving quietly into a better position. As he came to a stop, he reacquired his target. The animals were still grazing, steadily making their way across the field. As he went prone, he felt some leaves crunch beneath his stomach. The sound was barely audible to him, but loud enough to cause the fawn to look up in his direction.

No, he thought to himself, *you didn't hear that.*

The baby looked over at its mother who was not the least bit fazed by her surroundings as she continued to munch on what little she could find to eat. After a moment, the fawn began to graze again, following in the footsteps of the doe.

Clay reached into his pocket and retrieved a velvet bag with a few bullets inside. He opened the bag and pulled a few rounds close to the opening, but left them inside. Because the magazine for his rifle had broken several months back, and he had yet to find a replacement, Clay had to keep extra cartridges nearby for a quick, manual reload.

He clicked the safety off and took aim. He tracked the doe through his scope as it moved; unfocused blades of grass danced around the bottom of his sight picture from the increasing wind which was fortunately blowing in his face. His breathing was shaky and his head cloudy. Clay took a deep breath, slowly exhaling through his mouth. He moved the crosshairs just behind the shoulder and breathed in once more. After expelling half the air in his lungs, he held his breath and pulled the trigger.

The first thing Clay heard after the deafening shot was the cries and moans from the doe as it attempted to stand. His shot was far from perfect and the animal was going to suffer. He shook his head and smacked his forehead with his fist as he laid on the ground. "Nice shooting, Clay," he said in a hushed, sarcastic tone.

He felt awful, but there was nothing he could do. He wanted to run down and finish off the suffering animal, but he quickly dismissed the idea. The sound released from the sixteen inch barrel was substantial, and anyone within a couple of miles would have heard it. Though most people wouldn't be running towards a powerful gunshot like that, there were always a few nutjobs wandering around who might, perhaps somebody with more firepower. It wasn't safe. So he waited.

Clay pulled the bolt back, spitting out the shell onto the ground a few feet away. He patted around, found the ejected brass case, and stuffed it into a pocket. Grabbing a new round from the bag, he chambered the bullet and closed the bolt.

Looking through the scope, he contemplated taking another shot from where he was, but decided it would only further expose his location. It could also end up being another lousy shot, furthering the animal's agony and possibly ruining some of the meat.

The doe's cries and snorts continued for about ten minutes before there was silence. Clay stayed put another ten minutes as he kept an eye out for signs of other people. He saw no indication of danger so he approached the doe. He towered over the lifeless body; blood had splattered in every direction as the animal kicked and jolted around in a hopeless attempt to flee. *Sorry, girl,* he thought to himself as he bent down and grabbed the hind legs to drag it into the woods. Not far. Just enough that he would be hard to spot by any potential passersby.

The temperature had dropped many degrees since he left the creek. Puffs of his exerted breath could now be seen as Clay field dressed the animal. His fingers were starting to numb, and his efforts were becoming painful. Tired, hungry, and uncomfortably cold, he felt vulnerable and was eager to leave.

An hour had passed; the light was all but gone. He still had the neck, and shoulders to harvest, but there was no time—he had to move out. Clay had no chance of making it home now, so he decided to stay at the cabin for the night. Walking through Normandy Creek in the darkness was not a risk he was willing to take.

Clay stuffed the last bit of meat into an insulated bag, collected his pack from the bush, and headed off for the cabin. He was chilled to the bone. His tattered jacket provided little in the way of protection from the wind, and he had forgotten his gloves. He feared winter was coming early this year. The winters were long and harsh, not something he ever thought he would experience in Texas. And it seemed that each year it came sooner and stayed longer—like an unwanted house guest. But for tonight, it would actually benefit him greatly. It would keep the meat from spoiling.

He reached the cabin without incident and felt a wave of relief rush through his body. The cabin was in a rustic house in a relatively undeveloped area. It wasn't quite the country, but the neighboring houses weren't so close that the inhabitants could have heard one another singing in the shower each morning. Clay often thought it would have been nice to live there when things were still normal: mowing the lawn; firing up the barbecue pit for the big game; watching the kids chase lizards. What a life! But Clay quickly pushed thoughts like these out of his head—thinking of the past was just too much to bear at times.

Clay entered the garage through a side door and stumbled his way over to a heavy-duty floor mat towards the rear of the garage. He lifted it up revealing a floor door to a small underground shelter hidden beneath—the cabin. He opened the door and descended a few steps before closing it behind him allowing the mat to fall back into place, hunching his 6'2" frame to avoid hitting his head on the ceiling. He left the bag of meat at the top of the steps and made his way down to the shelter.

He fished around in his backpack and found his flashlight. The light was dim—virtually ineffective—so he pulled a small crank out of the side of the flashlight and began winding it like a fishing reel. Gradually, the light got brighter; the beam danced around the room as he wound it.

He tossed his pack onto a cot towards the back wall and walked over to some boxes stacked in the corner. The room wasn't much bigger than a jail cell, about ten feet deep and six feet wide, and it had a musty smell that would stay with him for hours after leaving. It was far from warm, and it was not uncommon to have a rodent or insect wake him. Despite the lack of comfortable accommodations, it was a home away from home. It was safe, and when he left supplies there, he always found them when he returned.

He retrieved a candle from the boxes and placed it on a small bedside table and lit the wick with a match from his pack. The room went dark after he turned his flashlight off. The faint flicker from the candle was the only thing preventing total darkness.

Clay warmed his hands over the tiny flame, repeatedly making fists in an effort to get his blood circulating again. Using a small pocket knife, he speared a couple of thin strips of venison and began rotating them over the flame. It took a while to cook, but it was well worth it. The taste was indescribably good, and the precious energy it provided, albeit just a little, was much needed. He followed it down with some water and a hard candy he found beneath a table at Rita's Diner earlier. He didn't care much for peppermint, but he wasn't about to complain about the rare treat.

He lay down on the cot and pulled an itchy blanket up to his stomach. Despite his exhaustion, Clay had a hard time falling asleep. He reached into the front pocket of his pack and pulled out an MP3 player and ear buds. Shortly after, classical music overpowered reality. Chopin was on stage for the night, and, as always, he performed flawlessly. Sleep finally came.

When Clay's eyes opened again, it felt as if he had only slept a few minutes. He watched as light danced around the ceiling for several seconds before he looked at the candle. It was several inches shorter than when he fell asleep. He wasn't sure if the candle provided any actual heat, but the soft glow of the wax light and the occasional floating ember offered him a creature comfort that was few and far between.

He sat up and swung his feet over the side of the cot, making fists with his toes on the cheap, small rug. He let out a big yawn and stretched his arms over his head. Clay felt well rested, which surprised him given that he had only four, maybe five, hours of sleep, if he had to guess.

Inside his bag was a granola bar. It was stale. Very stale. Most every food that had a barcode no longer held the consistency or texture it once had, but it was a small boost of energy for the rest of his journey home. He drank the last few gulps of water in his bottle and tossed it back into the pack. He had not planned on staying at the cabin for the night and had not brought enough water. He usually kept a few extra bottles and some canned goods in the cabin, but he had gone through those a couple weeks back and had never restocked his supplies. He made a mental note to drop some things off the next time he was out that way.

He laced up his shoes and slung his pack over his shoulder. Grabbing his rifle, he took a quick glance towards the stairs as if to memorize the short, straight path. He leaned over the table and with a quick puff of air the candle's flame vanished and the room fell as dark as a moonless night. Cautiously, he walked towards the stairs and reached his hand out to feel for the doorway. As he made his way to the top of the steps, he could feel the temperature drop. It wasn't much, but it answered his question about the candle providing warmth.

He pushed up on the door, and light flooded the stairwell as if a dam had burst from above. He quickly turned his head and squeezed his eyes shut, completely unprepared for the solar onslaught. His eyes eventually adjusted, and the world once again faded to a drab, grey tone that was only bright in comparison to the dungeon he had slept in.

How long did I sleep? he asked himself.

He reached into his pocket and pulled out an old pocket watch that once belonged to his father, his grandfather before that.

"Nine-thirty!" he said in astonishment. He wouldn't have guessed it was a minute past seven.

On one hand, he needed the rest and it wasn't often he was able to pass out for nearly twelve hours. On the other hand, though, it was still cold outside, he knew it would be warming up which would increase the risk of the meat spoiling. Not to mention he had missed the ideal time to travel on the road—a short span of time after which the Screamers had already retired for the night but before most people would be out and about for the day. The fewer encounters during travel, the better.

Clay set out hoping there wouldn't be any setbacks that would prevent him getting the meat home in a timely manner. He recalled a time when he was delayed six hours while a group of bandits waited to meet up with another group. He had stopped for a few minutes allowing himself to rest, but by the time he got back on the move, he had to quickly find cover. There were easily twenty-five of them, and once the other group arrived, they had to be fifty strong. Fortunately, he had no time-sensitive cargo, and he could just wait them out.

Since he missed his short window to travel on the road, he would have to pass through Normandy Creek. The threat of Screamers was no longer there, but he always hated that route. He had yet to walk through without seeing some remnants of a brutal, ritualistic sacrifice hanging from a tree or lying lifeless in the leaves. Each time it was something different. As if every murdering spree was unique, like a sadistic snowflake. This time was no exception. He came across bloodied clothes half buried beneath some leaves and grass sending a chill down his spine that was not from the temperatures outside.

He crouched down and searched through the worn out khakis and flannel shirt. Nothing. He did a quick search around the area and found three 9MM cases. It looked like whoever owned these clothes didn't go down without a fight though Clay doubted the man's fate would have been any different either way.

At first, he thought the shells were nickel plated brass, but upon closer inspection, Clay realized they were zinc plated steel and Berdan primed as well; they would be useless to him. He dropped them back to the forest floor and continued on. He said a silent prayer for the recently departed soul and happily left the area.

Reaching the top of a hill, he could see home. He always felt relieved to see it soaring in the sky like a tower of hope in a world of despair. Even though it was just a couple of miles away, it would still take him more than an hour to get home. Cautiously, he would go up and down side streets at random to lose any potential tails that might be tracking him from afar. It was inconvenient, especially after long journeys, but it had become standard operations security (OPSEC) to ensure nobody knew where his home was.

Satisfied with his evasive maneuvers, Clay made the final approach.

Chapter 2

Home. It was a sixteen story building once owned by one of the biggest banks in the country, though Clay liked to think he had assumed ownership. Nobody had contested that fact so far. The building was modern, mostly made up of glass. It was the second tallest building in the area with a few nearby buildings that were half as tall creating a nice little urban jungle with Clay living right in the center.

He circled around to the back of the building where there was an entrance to an underground parking garage. The entrance was discreet. In fact, it almost looked as if it was where delivery trucks might have unloaded except there were parking spaces inside, each with an assigned name. Making sure no one had followed him, Clay walked down the ramp. Next to the large garage door was a maintenance door with a large padlock. Break-ins were common, and it was the fourth lock he had installed already this year. After all, a locked door must be protecting something valuable. It wasn't hard to find new latches, but installing them was an exhausting job when they had to be drilled by hand into a metal door. The latest one seemed to be doing the trick. Scrapes and dings adorned the door near the lock, but no one had broken in. Yet. He discovered two men trying to break in one evening a few months back. Clay drew his weapon; the men were unarmed other than the rock they were using to try and smash the lock. The man holding the rock started towards him, shouting profanity. Clay thought for sure he was going to have to shoot him, but then the other man was able to calm his friend down and led him away without incident. Perhaps if Clay had just been holding a pistol or one of the clunky post-ban double barrel 12 gauge shotguns, the men would have responded more aggressively. But staring down the barrel of an AR-15, especially after the ash fell, was akin to stepping in front of a Sherman tank. Clay had considered giving them some food. It looked as if they hadn't eaten anything of real nutritional value in quite some time. But he had decided not to. Give a mouse a cookie...Still, he felt guilty and wished he could track them down to give them something. That was months ago though, and the reality was they were probably dead now.

Clay opened the door just enough to slide through and then quickly latched it. He hung the padlock on a little hook just inside, grabbed a doorstop, and wedged it under the door.

On the far side of the garage, a series of tarps hung from the wall, covering a stretch of about thirty feet with paint buckets, ladders, and other tools carefully strewn about nearby. Clay walked over to a specific spot on the wall and lifted the tarp, revealing a door just behind. It was by no means secure—that was what the padlock and door wedge were for—but of all the people who had been able to get into the garage, nobody had discovered what was behind the tarp. For all intents and purposes, that tarp was there to keep the painters from making a mess on the wall years and years before.

Clay walked through and quietly shut the door behind him, once again placing a wedge beneath the door. It acted as the deadbolt on the door when everyone was home. He began his ascent up the stairs.

As he reached the first floor landing, he stepped around a large pile of debris in front of the door. It didn't take long after moving in to realize that they needed a way to block the stairwell doors on the first few floors. Even if someone was able to knock the door off its hinges, they wouldn't get through the blockade behind it. They had effectively made the garage the single point of entry to the home and it was fairly well disguised. Clay wasn't sure if it was truly an effective means or just luck.

He climbed up the last flight of stairs; he had barely broken a sweat. To him, it was as common as walking to the end of the driveway and back. He stopped in front of a door with the faded label *Level 16* stenciled in paint. He knocked quickly on the door three times, then two hard pounds spaced about a half second apart. Within a few moments, he heard small feet fast approaching the door.

"What's the password?" a high pitched voice said from the other side.

"There isn't one," Clay replied.

The handle turned, and the door slowly opened. Peeking from behind was a bright-eyed boy, seven years of age.

"Clay!" he shouted. "Did you get any food?"

"You betcha," Clay responded and held up the bag of meat.

The boy, overfilled with excitement, ran down the long hallway screaming "Clay's home!"

Clay walked down the hallway with considerably less gusto than the boy. It was good to be home, but he just couldn't match that kid's enthusiasm. Tyler was *always* smiling and joyful, a rare sight in such a dreadful world.

Before he could get down to the end of the hallway, Clay heard more feet fast approaching. "Clay!" two young girls shouted in unison as they rounded the corner and headed straight for him.

"Hey girls!" he said as he put an arm each around their shoulders and squeezed them tight. "Did you miss me?"

They both nodded.

"Paige drew a picture for you," one girl said.

"Sarah! I wanted to surprise him!" Paige said with disappointment.

"Oops, I forgot," Sarah replied.

"I'm sure it's beautiful, Paige, I can't wait to see it," Clay said, nudging them forward to continue down the hall.

The two girls walked at a fast pace, and Clay trailed behind. He turned the corner and walked to the end of that hallway eventually reaching the lobby of an old law firm. Parkland & Howell was written in fancy brass letters across the wall behind a receptionist's desk. The floor was a nice light oak, though it was in need of a good cleaning. Fake potted plants were carefully placed throughout, but all of the furniture that wasn't bolted to the floor had been moved to other rooms.

"Where's Megan?" Clay asked Paige.

"I think she's in the kitchen."

Clay walked over to an executive conference room just off the lobby. He unlocked and opened the door, quickly dropping his pack and rifle off before locking back up.

He made his way to the break room, which was now their kitchen. Though the faucets didn't work, the counter space and cabinets made it an obvious choice for a kitchen. The linoleum tile also helped with cleaning up the frequent spills. There was a fridge next to the sink and a freezer chest in the corner on the opposite side of the room. They had carried the freezer chest up from the ninth floor from a research lab. It was the only residential one they could find, the other ones on the floor would consume too much power, not to mention would have been nearly impossible to carry up the stairs.

Megan was dicing fresh carrots next to a bowl of rehydrating peas. At first, it was odd to mix dehydrated vegetables with fresh, garden grown ones, but they quickly realized the days of being picky about what they ate were long over. Now, it was just second nature to combine whatever they could to make a dish as palatable as possible.

"Smells delicious," Clay said.

She turned around and gave him a look—the kind of look any sister would give when their younger brother said something stupid. "There's nothing to smell yet," she said as she continued chopping.

Clay put his arm around her and gave her a hug.

"I was worried about you, Clayton," she said with frustration in her tone. She ran her fingers through her short black hair and sighed with relief. "You gotta stop doing that to me, I was up all night." Megan blew a strand of hair out of her face and continued chopping.

While it wasn't uncommon for him to be gone several days at a time, he rarely stayed out overnight without advanced warning. Though she was irritated, Clay could see the tension dissipate as her shoulders lowered and her chopping became more fluid and relaxed. He was home, and that's all that mattered.

"Peace offering?" Clay said with a smile as he held up the venison.

She looked over with a smile. "Venison?" she asked with a hopeful look.

He nodded.

"Sweet!" she said excitedly

"Want to put it in the stew?" Clay asked.

"Either that or we're having meat stew without the meat," she said half-jokingly, realizing had Clay not come home with the venison her statement would have been true.

Clay placed the venison into the freezer. It was nearly empty except for some frozen vegetables, a few pounds of hog, and some concentrated juice mixes. That freezer held the "overflow" of meat and veggies, while the freezer above the fridge had most of the food for a given week or two. Clay was happy to have venison to add to the overflow. He would need at least another deer, a hog or two, and some other smaller game to fill the compartment to the top for winter. That was always his goal, but he had yet to achieve it.

"We had to turn on the heater last night," she turned back to look at him. "Batteries drained in less than a half hour this time. I think the solar panel is broken again."

Clay let out a deep sigh. It seemed like he was fixing that thing every week. He would have to find some replacement parts soon. He would check with his friend Vlad—a trader working out of a small community named Liberty Township—the next time he was out that way, which would likely be tomorrow.

"Charlie is working on getting the banks recharged right now," she added.

"All right," Clay said wearily. He was ready to eat and rest, but there was work to be done. "I'll go take care of it in a minute."

Clay walked out of the kitchen and past a bathroom which had become their cooking room. He had rigged up a makeshift stove for Megan. Sitting atop a small table was a two burner propane grill, the kind once used on a campout. They also had a small oven that would sit on top of the burners when needed.

The hood was merely some ventilation ducts that fed up to the bathroom's exhaust fan that Clay had rigged to run on a nine volt battery. Though the makeshift bake room worked well, their ever dwindling resources—of both propane and batteries—prevented it from being used more often. It was only used to *cook* food, never to reheat.

Lona, the eldest of the ten children Clay and Megan had 'adopted', was preparing a stock for the stew.

"Hey Lona," Clay said casually.

"Hi," she responded with little emotion as she stirred the contents inside the pot.

Lona had a lot of scars from the past. Some he knew about, others were too deep for her to reveal. He wondered sometimes if she even remembered what they were. The mind has a way of blocking out horrific memories, but the impressions they once made will linger. She was a good kid, though, and even though she rarely smiled, when she did the room would light up as if the power was back on. If she were his daughter—and in his mind, she essentially was—he would be sure to clean his shotgun in the open whenever she had a date. Though he didn't figure he'd have to worry about that anytime soon.

He continued down the hallway and heard a buzzing sound coming from the end of the hallway. As he got closer, he started to hear panting. He reached the door and popped his head through.

"Hey dude," Clay said.

"Hey Clay!" Charlie said before puffing for another breath as he pedaled on a stationary bike.

Charlie was just six years old when Clay found him in a ransacked pharmacy, clinging to his mother's motionless body. It was less than a year after Yellowstone erupted, and most of the population had started making their way to the various FEMA camps around the country. It was around that time that the rule of law really began to decline, and areas started to fall under the control of the group with the biggest guns.

He didn't talk for nearly three months, but ever since then, he hadn't stopped. Charlie looked up to Clay like an older brother and even a father figure. Having just turned thirteen, Charlie was the second oldest of all the kids, just a few weeks younger than Lona. Charlie was a hard worker and never complained, no matter how tough or boring the task. He even wanted more responsibility which he asked for on a daily basis.

"Just charging the batteries. The switch cut the power last night while we were using the heater so I am just charging them back up," he said pausing every couple of words to suck in more oxygen.

Clay realized it was his day to charge the battery bank. The family had a daily rotation of who would be responsible for charging the batteries should the need arise. Because of the constant lack of direct sunlight, the solar panels on the roof—when functioning properly—were only really enough to power the fridge, freezer, and a few USB devices. Anything more, though, and someone would usually have to supplement the power on the stationary bike that operated like a dynamo or the batteries would quickly drain.

"Thanks for covering my shift," Clay said, giving Charlie a pat on the shoulder.

"Just...doing...my part," he gasped as he wiped his forehead with his arm.

Charlie had been on the bike for three hours already. He was exhausted, but more than that he was bored. Unlike Charlie, Clay didn't mind the boredom. In fact, he welcomed it. Being able to take a couple hours without challenging his mind did him a lot of good. Though, more often than not, thoughts of daunting tasks in the near future would creep in and disturb his quiet time.

Clay looked over at a little meter and saw that the bank—a little over a dozen car batteries daisy chained together—was nearly two-thirds of the way charged.

"Hey, I gotta run up to the roof and fix the solar panel. I might need some help. You interested?"

Charlie's eyes lit up with joy. "Sure!" he said with a crack in his voice before disappointment colored his words, "but, the batteries aren't charged yet."

"Don't worry about that. I'll finish up later tonight. It's my day anyway."

"Okay," Charlie replied with a smile.

"I need to do a few things and grab some tools. I'll meet you up on the roof in about fifteen minutes?"

"You got it," Charlie said and sped up his pedaling in the meantime.

Clay made his way back to the conference room and grabbed the backpack and rifle and headed to the armory. The armory was once a server room for the firm's network. The door to the room was concealed by a soda machine. It was on wheels and easy to push aside. After unlocking the door and walking in, Clay flipped on a dim LED lamp that coated the room in a thin film of light. It was just enough to see, but hardly used any energy.

He had converted some of the server racks into gun racks. This was where he kept all of their firearms except for the ones he and Megan always had on them. He put the Scout rifle back in its place on the rack and traded it out for his LaRue AR-15, which he carried with him if he didn't need another long gun at the time.

Several five gallon buckets surrounded a table that served as Clay's reloading station, each containing various shell casings. He reached into his pocket and fished out the .308 brass case from when he shot the deer and tossed it into one of the buckets. He loved to reload bullets before the eruption, but now, when it was more of an essential than a hobby, he still found it to be relaxing; it was another opportunity for productive quiet time.

He inspected his inventory. He was running dry on most bullets. His powder and primer supply was also dwindling but not nearly as much. He still had quite a few factory loads left and at least twice as many reloads. He would be fine for the winter at least, but finding more bullets would need to move up on his priority list soon.

Clay looked up and saw a picture taped to the wall. It was a photo of him with his mother before the car accident—the one that ultimately caused her death. It was taken on his twelfth birthday when she had taken him to pick out some rollerblades. Clay had four sisters and no brothers. Spending time with his mom one-on-one was very rare, even on birthdays.

They both looked so happy in the picture. Clay was holding up his new skates while she crouched down next to him. He could still remember the joy he felt on that day. But every time he looked at the picture now, all he felt was guilt. Not even three years later his mom was dead.

"Take care of your sisters." His mom's last words echoed in his memory.

It was a task he had failed.

Chapter 3

Clay climbed the stairs and walked out to the roof. Charlie was already there playing tag with Blake and Courtney, siblings who had just joined the group last month. Erica and Maya were enjoying the swings on the jungle gym. It was well worth the three months it took Clay to piece together. The children loved it. It was important to Clay that he provide ways for the kids to be entertained, to have fun, and most importantly, to just be kids. Life was already hard enough for them. They had all lost their parents, most by way of death but a few were abandoned. Clay couldn't understand how anyone could just leave their children back when things were relatively normal, let alone in a world like this. He tried not to think about it too much; he always got angry when he did. It was hard for kids to be kids anymore. There were no governments to keep commerce rolling, no law enforcement to keep evildoers in check. The world was a pit, and kids we forced to grow up fast.

Clay did everything in his power to keep that from happening to these kids—his kids—which is why he was dreading the coming conversation.

Charlie saw Clay walking over to the solar panel. He said something to Blake and then darted over to Clay.

"Oh, Clay," Charlie said, his apology heard in the awkward chuckle in his voice, "Blake and Courtney looked bored, so I, uh, thought I would play with them. Ya know, to help them fit in," he stammered.

"You know, Charlie, you don't have to always act so grown up. It's okay to be a kid." Clay said.

"I guess," he murmured, "but I know I can be more help to you if you would just let me."

"You *are* a big help, Charlie, to both Megan and me." Hesitantly, he began the conversation he didn't want to have. "But you want a gun, don't you?" Clay said, already knowing the answer.

Charlie had been hinting at this for the past few months. He wanted a gun. It wasn't because Charlie was eager to shoot a bad guy or try and impress the other kids. Having a gun meant trust, responsibility, and duty. It also meant sacrifice. He would have to give up much of his time to work for the family. He would also have to be willing to put himself at great risk in order to protect the family. It was a terrible burden to lay on the shoulders of a thirteen-year-old boy—a burden Clay knew from personal experience.

"You're still a little young, Charlie," Clay continued.

"Geoff was the same age as me when he joined us, and you gave him a gun."

Four years ago, Clay was first introduced to Geoff Sackenheim when they both had their guns pointed at each other. Clay had surprised Geoff as he walked into an abandoned—or so he thought—arcade and startled him as he slept, causing a brief standoff. From that point, they became good friends. Clay was only sixteen himself, so the age difference wasn't all that much. Geoff had been a great contributor to the family, and his presence was still missed.

"You're forgetting that Geoff already knew how to use a gun," Clay said as he knelt down and started loosening some screws on the under part of the solar panel.

"Yeah, so would I, if you would teach me."

Clay was silent.

"How old were you when your dad taught you how to shoot?"

Clay thought about it and realized Charlie had him in check. "Well, I guess around the time I was five, maybe six."

Charlie gave him a look of envy.

"Times were different back then, Charlie."

"Yeah, people were nicer. They weren't trying to kill you, which is why I need to know how to defend this family," Charlie's face was serious, his eyes displaying a wisdom most adults lacked. "Clay, you might go out one morning and never come back..."

When did this kid grow up? Clay thought to himself.

Charlie continued, "I didn't have a dad to teach me those things, even before all this happened. If you die, then who will teach me? Who will teach Blake and Tyler?"

Checkmate.

"Plus," he added under his breath, "I won't abandon the family like Geoff did."

"Hey!" Clay barked at him, "Geoff did *not* abandon the family. He has a wife. *She's* his family now and his responsibility. There's nothing wrong with that. In fact, that's what he ought to do, even in an upside down world like this."

Charlie shrugged, "He isn't even old enough to smoke."

"Takes more of a man to be a husband than to smoke a cigarette; age has nothing to do with it."

Clay knew that this was more than just Geoff "abandoning" the family; it was Geoff abandoning Charlie. Even though Charlie and Clay were close, Charlie grew that much closer to Geoff in the two years he lived with them. Charlie knew that hurt before, and he had felt its sting again. Geoff had come by a few times since he left, and each time Charlie would retreat into his room or the rooftop to avoid him.

Clay continued to work on the panel, occasionally asking Charlie for help and explaining each step along the way so that Charlie could learn. It only took about twenty minutes to fix, and it was back to charging the bank. He knew the next storm that blew through would probably break it again, but for the time being it was fully operational.

"I'll think about it," Clay said ruefully. He knew there really wasn't anything to think about. Charlie was right and that frustrated him. Clay *had* to grow up when he was only thirteen, and he was doing everything in his power to keep that weight from landing on Charlie. But it was going to happen, whether Clay liked it or not. Charlie was capable, willing, and responsible.

"And what does that mean?"

"It means," Clay paused and thought best how to answer, "soon, Charlie. It means, soon."

Charlie smiled.

"In the meantime, you keep on being a kid because those days are coming to a close."

Charlie gave him a salute and went back to play tag with the others. Clay collected his tools and made his way back downstairs. His stomach was in knots thinking of Charlie having to defend the family. Taking a man's life never got easier for Clay; he just learned to ignore the hesitation when it came time to do so.

As Clay was walking towards the lobby, he heard a familiar voice.

"Da-da!"

"Beth!" Clay shouted and crouched down to pick up his little girl as she clumsily ran to him.

Bethany wasn't even two. She was only six months old when she became part of the family. She melted Clay's heart, and he would do anything for her. Sometimes, though, he was overwhelmed with how much she reminded him of his youngest sister Colleen. He missed her. He missed all of them.

He picked her up and she leaned in, giving Clay a kiss. "Someone took a long nap this morning," Megan said standing in the doorway of the kitchen.

Bethany started sucking her thumb and looked over at Megan, giving her a subtle nod of agreement, not really knowing what she was acknowledging.

"Lunch will be ready in a few," Megan added.

Clay inclined his head, telling Megan he had heard her and returned to the front conference room. He laid down on his bed for a few minutes and tried to clear his mind. He could hear muffled screams and laughter from outside as Megan wrangled the children for lunch. Those children were everything to Clay, as if they were his own blood. But he was tired, and sometimes he just wanted to be able to get away from it all. He hated that such selfish desires would flash through his thoughts, even if for just a moment.

His thoughts were interrupted with a quick knock on the glass door. He looked over and saw Paige waving him to come out for lunch.

"Be right there," he answered.

She skipped across the lobby towards the hallway and disappeared into the kitchen with the rest of the kids. Clay eventually mustered enough energy to get to his feet and follow her.

After lunch, Clay spent the rest of the afternoon and evening doing various little chores around the house and getting ready for another trip. He hated being gone so much in a single week, but he'd told Vlad that he would stop by every couple of weeks until winter hit. Clay was waiting for a few key items Vlad promised to hold for him if they came in. But Vlad was a businessman and wouldn't hold on to such high-valued items for long.

Back in the conference room, Clay inventoried the goods he planned to use for bartering with various merchants in Liberty. He regretted that he was unable to take the time needed to properly skin yesterday's deer—the pelt would have fetched a decent price.

*In a perfect world...*The thought made him chuckle.

He was cataloging his items on a small sheet of paper when he heard a soft knock on the door. Megan was standing in the doorway holding two plastic cups. "Heading to Liberty?" she asked.

"Yeah, it's about that time. Been almost three weeks. Not gonna be too many more opportunities before winter hits."

"You think he will have any antibiotics?" she asked with a gleam of hope in her eyes.

Clay shrugged. "Dunno. Hope so. It *is* a little late in the year, though. Most people see the temps start to drop and hang on to their pills like a life preserver."

They were both quiet as Clay started to pack his bag with the items he planned to trade.

"We're not going to have enough food this winter, are we?" Megan said, breaking the silence. She immediately regretted saying that, knowing very well that Clay was already stressing to find a solution to that problem.

Last winter had been brutal. They had all but run out of food and had begun rationing what was left. At one point, the kids were down to less than a thousand calories a day. Clay and Megan both took a little less than that. Clay was able to snare some rabbits and bag a coyote. The feral canine tasted awful but kept them alive. With winter just a month or so out and three more mouths to feed, they really needed a jolt to their reserves. The deer Clay had just killed would help, but he would need at least one or two more of those, a couple of hogs, and a slew of fruits and vegetables to make things comfortable for the winter.

He sighed and closed his eyes for a minute, as if to try and escape the question. "We'll make it; we always do," he said with uncertainty in his voice. He took a deep breath and looked at her with a genuine smile and said, "We'll be all right," this time with much greater confidence in his voice.

She smiled warmly. Even if she knew he couldn't promise such things, she always felt reassured by his confidence.

He looked over at the cups. Each cup was filled halfway with lemonade and a couple of cubes of ice. "What are the drinks for?" he asked before realization sunk in.

"Today is..." her voice trailed off, her glossy eyes looked away from Clay as she tried to fight back the tears.

"Michelle's birthday," Clay finished her sentence as he took one of the cups from her.

She wiped away a few tears from her eyes. "It would have been her sweet sixteen." Megan reached up to twirl her hair—a habit she developed at a young age to deal with stress. But three months ago, she cropped her long locks leaving the only real length to hang above her eyes. Megan cut her hair to ease the time required for personal maintenance, but Clay could tell it was a sacrifice she regretted at times. When her fingers found no hair to twist, Megan breathed in deeply and slowly exhaled. "I miss her, Clay. I miss them *all*. Mom. Dad. Michelle. Emily...Colleen," she began to cry. "I just wish I knew why all of this happened..." She trailed off.

The loss of all their siblings had been hard, but Michelle's death was particularly difficult. The first winter they were in the office building Michelle had fallen ill with pneumonia. Megan was able to diagnose it, but without antibiotics and a genuinely warm place to sleep, they knew she wasn't going to make it. Despite the grim prognosis, Michelle pulled through. It was truly a miracle. Then, not even two weeks after the thaw, she took a tumble down the steps while playing with some of the other kids and died instantly. Just like that, after a winter of fighting for her life and prevailing, she was gone.

Clay put his hand on Megan's shoulder and gave her a reassuring squeeze. They sipped on lemonade made with individual portion packets—Michelle's favorite—and reminisced about their family—both past and present.

Megan looked down at her watch, "Well, I better get the kids ready for bed."

Clay raised his cup, "Happy birthday, Michelle."

She clanked her cup to his, and they both finished their drinks. Megan held out her cup to collect Clay's for washing. She gave him a hug and said, "I love you, brother. Glad you're home safe...for now, anyway."

Clay smiled. In such a cold, treacherous world, it was nice to have someone who worried about him.

Megan left the room, shouting for the kids to get ready for bed. Clay saw the boys all dart away from her like she was kryptonite. It was a nightly ritual for them, not one Megan particularly cared for.

Clay had to get a few things from the armory specifically for Vlad. It was against his better judgement to offer such coveted items for trade, but Clay was in need. He had bartered with his friend enough in the past to know which items Vlad would be unable to refuse, and if Vlad had what Clay desired, he wanted to be prepared for an even trade.

As Clay walked down the hallway, he heard Megan reading to the children. It was the same routine every night: read a passage from the book of Psalms and then a chapter from whatever novel they were reading. This month they were reading *The Adventures of Huckleberry Finn*.

Clay listened as Megan finished the chapter and then said good night to all the kids. They all closed their eyes right away as if to fall asleep on command, but the whispers and giggles began as soon as both the adults walked out the door.

The room was completely dark, so Clay used a flashlight to make his way back out to the halls. Megan preferred the soft glow of a candle over the bright, sterile beam of the flashlight but never mentioned that to Clay.

"Goodnight, sis."

Megan hugged him, "Night, Clay. Be safe! We will see you in two days, right?"

"Yep."

Megan disappeared into her room as Clay slipped into the armory to retrieve the items he'd decided to trade. He returned to his room, climbed into bed, and flipped on his e-reader. Though he didn't have that much time to dedicate to reading, he always enjoyed the few stolen moments he found, especially with his current book *The Remaking.* Clay wasn't quite sure why he had never read *The Remaking* before the tremors began, but he was glad to have the entertainment.

After an hour, Clay forced himself to put the book down mid-chapter and go to sleep. His departure time would not wait for sunrise.

Chapter 4

The alarm shrieked callously, forcing Clay to scramble for the off button. He was convinced that it was, in fact, the most aggravating sound in the world. Effective, but aggravating. His eyes finally focused on the digital readout; it was 4:08. He must have been more exhausted than he realized if it took him eight minutes to notice the sound.

The glow of a waning electric lantern secured to the ceiling with a piece of paracord provided just enough light for Clay to dress. The fading gleam lasted just enough time for Clay to finish getting ready. He picked up his pack and rifle and headed for the kitchen.

Sitting on top of the freezer chest was a plastic bag with a few fruits and vegetables from their small rooftop greenhouse to use for trade. The potting shed wasn't very impressive looking, but it worked well enough and kept residual ash off the plants during the storms.

As he grabbed the bag, he noticed a note Megan had left him: *Portioned some of the venison and hog meat to take. Don't forget your pack in the fridge.*

Like a mother getting her kids ready for school, Megan would often put together a travel pack for Clay. When she didn't, Clay would typically forget and only eat what he could pick or kill out in the field. Quick trips, such as the one he was about to begin, spared little time to hunt and gather, and Clay was grateful that Megan had thought of this ahead of time.

He grabbed everything from the kitchen and quietly made his way to the stairwell, careful not to disturb the sleeping children. Any loud sounds would easily echo throughout the floor, especially when there were no ambient sounds to muffle it, so Clay carefully closed the landing door and began his journey.

By the time he reached the last flight of stairs, his body had fully awakened, and he was ready for the daylong journey. His restful sleep had revitalized him, and he was optimistic that his energy would last despite the additional weight of all the extra goods he planned to trade.

Before he exited the garage, Clay did a double check of his guns and gear, ensuring he had everything he needed for the trip. He racked the slide on his Sig Sauer P225 then holstered it. After powering up the EoTech, he yanked on the charging handle of the AR-15, chambering the first round. Ready to go, he walked outside and promptly closed and locked the door. He gave the padlock a couple of tugs to ensure it had engaged.

The frost on the grass was evidence of just how cold it had gotten last night, though it didn't seem like the temperature had dropped quite as low as the night before. He moved slower and more cautiously for the first hour. Though it was getting late for the Screamers to be out, he knew a couple would still be wandering around. A heartless shriek cut through the morning stillness, confirming Clay's suspicions. It was a good distance away—far enough that he wasn't overly concerned but close enough to make the hair on his neck stand and the grip on his rifle tighten.

Dawn approached and the murky landscape began to illuminate. The total darkness cast from the moonless night—moonlit nights had become extinct—was quite nerve-racking. Though the sun was never very pronounced, its light was welcomed. Clay always felt relief once the sun was up.

As the morning drew on, he scavenged a couple of buildings that were along the way. He had already searched them several months earlier, so they were mostly empty. He did, however, find an old cane. He wasn't sure if he just overlooked it the last time he was in the building or if perhaps somebody recently left it behind after seeking refuge for the night. In any event, it was his now. It needed a good cleaning but still maintained its integrity. It would bring a decent trade.

He made a short detour to the cabin to replenish some of the supplies he had consumed when staying there the other night. He took the opportunity to rest for a minute while sipping on some water. The added weight from his trades was taking a harder toll on his body than he anticipated, and he wanted to stay put. But he forced himself to move out anyway.

As always, he stayed off the major roads and did his best to steer clear of even small side streets, though that was often unavoidable. He sometimes wondered if he was being overly cautious in taking the extra travel time to avoid the highways but quickly dismissed such notions as laziness. There were just too many tactical disadvantages to traveling on the roads, especially alone.

Screamers were not the only threat he had to worry about. After seven punishing years, those who were still alive grew more desperate by the day. Doctors—those who once took an oath to do no harm—wouldn't think twice before putting a .357 sized hole in someone for a few morsels of food. People who made a living helping less fortunate now preyed on them. It was sad, Clay often thought, to see such hopelessness in humanity. Yet, most of the people he ran into during his travels were either aggressive, or, more often than not, they looked utterly defeated. At first, Clay gave people the benefit of the doubt, but experience eventually taught him to be far more skeptical of *anyone* he didn't know. Trust had to be earned.

Clay passed a burned out city bus on one of the side streets he took. It meant Liberty Township was just over five miles away. The sight of the charred public transportation always gave him a burst of energy that helped him pick up the pace.

The day's journey was overall smooth. He didn't see another soul the entire trip, which was ideal. He preferred keeping to himself, or if he was going to meet someone new, doing so inside a place like Liberty. But that never stopped him from helping someone in need, which is why there were ten kids back at home depending on him. Being an orphan himself, Clay had a soft spot for children walking around these deserted cities. He would never turn away a kid with nowhere to go.

With little daylight left, Clay could see the small town up ahead. He would be there just after sunset. His pace had slowed once again, but he wasn't worried about any negative encounters at that point.

Screamers weren't too active in that particular area. Liberty was well guarded, and the Screamers had discovered that first-hand on several occasions in the past. They eventually learned their lesson.

Clay arrived at the long driveway leading to the gated community just after sunset as he had expected. As always, there were two guards posted at the gate. "Welcome to Liberty Township," an older gentleman said from behind a wrought iron gate. Another man stood a few feet away cradling an SKS. "What brings you here this evening?"

Clay took the last few steps and stopped just in front of the gate. "I am here to do some trading," he said.

"Name?"

"Clay Whitaker."

The man pulled up a clipboard and flipped through some pages. He put his finger on one of the pages and slowly slid it down the sheet, coming to an abrupt stop. "Ah, Mr. Whitaker. Yes, come right in. Better hurry; it's gettin' to be closing time," he said as he glanced at his watch.

Without saying a word, the other man slung his rifle over his shoulder and then unlocked the gate. Clay walked in and thanked them both before heading straight for Vlad's.

Liberty Township used to be an upscale subdivision filled with large, high-quality houses that would have easily fetched millions back in the day. The houses were anywhere from five to seven thousand square feet perched on five acre lots, Clay guessed. There were about fifty in the community, and quite a few were either converted to shops or split into multiple houses. The neighborhood's community center had been transformed into the town hall, and fairly decent additional housing had been constructed on vacant areas of the land. Nothing like the shanties most communities showcased.

The neighborhood mostly consisted of outsiders—people who couldn't have afforded the annual taxes, let alone the mortgage that went with it. After the first winter, more than half of the population of the community had died, leaving a rather large void in skills and trade. The following year, they carefully—and limitedly—brought more people in to help build and secure the neighborhood. The following spring, they officially became their own little town. Now, most of the folks that call Liberty Township their home had never stepped foot in the subdivision prior to the eruptions.

A couple of families that lived there had been there for a decade before the eruptions. Barry Shelton, the mayor, bought the first house constructed on the site back in 1994. Shelton was a tall man with a strong southern accent, he was the stereotypical Texan, right down to the boots and scorpion bolo tie. He was a kind man. Clay had only met him once, but Shelton had given Clay the "welcomed guest" status within the community. Such a status allowed Clay to come and go at any time without being disarmed. It was a status Clay preferred since he made a point to never willingly give up his guns.

After a ten minute walk, Clay arrived at Vlad's house and headed straight to the garage where he ran his shop. The sign said closed, but Clay knew better. He knocked on the door. Nothing. He pounded harder. A moment passed, then he heard footsteps.

"We are closed!" Vlad said with a thick Russian accent.

"Just open the door, Boris," Clay said with a smile.

He could hear Vlad laughing on the other side. The door popped open. "I told you, do not call me that name," the man said as he shook Clay's hand.

Vlad and Clay met after the first winter and had been doing business ever since. Clay started by trading his surplus ammo and pre-ban magazines. As time passed, though, those items became rarer and Clay's stock dwindled. He was down to his personal stock now, and he didn't much like the thought of trading that away. But on occasion, it was something he had to do.

They spent a few minutes catching up over a drink while Olesya tidied up around the store. She straightened some of the shelf items and swept up dirt stamped in by the customers. A few minutes later, she went upstairs to the loft apartment above the garage.

"How's she holding up?" Clay asked quietly.

Vlad took a drink and sighed. "She does not speak much anymore," Vlad's eyes welled up, "but she is tough girl. She will be ok."

"How about you?"

He nodded. "I am okay. Some nights are harder than others, but I get through. I still have my Olesya, and for that, I am grateful."

They were silent for a couple of minutes while they finished their drinks. Clay wasn't sure what words of comfort he could offer to his good friend. Clay had suffered loss several times before, but he recognized that there was something different about losing a spouse. It was a pain he was glad he had not experienced.

They finished their drinks and then got down to business. Vlad walked over to a steel cabinet and unlocked it with a key. He pulled out a brown paper bag and set it on the counter. Clay looked inside. A gleeful look crossed his face like a kid on Christmas morning.

A trust between the two men had formed over the years which allowed both of them to extend benefits to each other that were hard to come by— benefits that included setting aside a couple of bottles of antibiotics for weeks until they could be picked up.

Clay pulled two bottles out of the bag and saw they were both amoxicillin. It was marketed as fish antibiotics, but evidently the majority of fish antibiotics were the exact same as those sold in pharmacies—so long as the pills didn't contain additional ingredients that gave fish shinier, healthier scales. It had been available on the internet with no prescription and for a reasonable price. Of course, with health insurance and no need for the pills unless someone was ill, most people didn't buy them unless they were preparing for a rainy day... or had sick fish.

Clay reached into his bag and pulled out three PMags, each loaded with 30 rounds, and handed them to Vlad.

Vlad removed one of the bullets and inspected it more closely. He ran his thumb over the green painted tip and then looked at the back of the shell casing. "Lake City? Green tip? These are factory load, yes?"

Clay nodded. "Yeah, I don't have many of those left. They are probably worth more than what I am getting, but I know you're good for it," Clay said.

He wasn't trying to hassle the Russian, but Clay had a point. Factory loaded ammunition was a coveted commodity. Everyone wanted it, and very few people had it. That particular type of ammunition, XM855, was a light armor piercing round with more than enough power to punch a hole through a quarter inch of steel. After they were banned from civilian purchase, remaining supplies dried up in a hurry.

"How about this," Vlad said walking back to the cabinet to retrieve a box. "A man came to me few weeks ago for a trade. He gave me this." Vlad handed Clay the box.

Hornady V-Max bullets, .224 diameter; an incredible find.

"I will throw these in to deal, but I want half back. *Loaded*," he added.

Clay would have agreed on half for Vlad, but he knew it was still a lopsided deal. Bullets weren't easy to come by, but brass, primers, and powder were just as difficult, if not more so. Since Clay had three-quarters of the components, it was only reasonable that Vlad got a quarter back. They settled on it, and Clay shopped around for a few more minutes. He was excited to find some Lithium AA batteries he could use in his EoTech. He had wanted some ever since the alkaline batteries leaked and made a mess of everything. Thankfully, the EoTech survived—a testament to its quality.

Vlad also had a hydration bladder for sale. The darn thing was brand-new, still had the company tag tied to it. Carrying multiple bottles of water was inefficient and also quite loud when the plastic bottles bounced off each other. The bladder would be a nice addition to Clay's travel supplies.

Vlad preferred trading weapons, medicine, and nonperishable items, so he really never had much in the way of food. He did, however, have a couple of cans of deviled ham. It was a gamble to buy since the expiration date was about three years past due. Even though the can was not bloated—a clear indication of spoilage—it was never a guarantee it would be safe to eat. Clay took the chance. Though fresh food was always better tasting, having a preserved food to take on long trips was a welcomed treasure.

With only a few more items left to trade, Clay brought his order to a close so he could hit up a few stores on his way out in the morning. Megan would kill him if he didn't find some fresher food than pasty canned ham.

"I assume you need room for night, yes?" Vlad asked.

"You assume correctly."

The main house on the property was a hotel of sorts run by Vlad, which is why he and Olesya stayed in the apartment above the garage. Vlad always gave Clay a room for the night—no charge. He was a very gracious host, at least to Clay.

Clay walked out of the garage and heard Vlad lock up behind him. He walked into the house and spotted a few men playing poker at the dining room table by candle light. They asked if he wanted to join, but Clay politely declined and headed straight to his room.

Vlad had done some work to the house to split larger rooms into multiple smaller rooms. This time around, Clay had gotten a room smaller than the cabin; however, it was relatively warm, dry, and the bed was very comfortable. It was perfect.

After nearly thirty miles on foot, Clay was exhausted and had no trouble falling asleep.

Chapter 5

Clay's room didn't have any windows, so he had no idea what time it was when he woke up. He had slept so soundly—as he always did at Casa de Bezrukov. Looking at his watch, he saw that it was quarter 'til seven. He was in good shape. After visiting a few shops, Clay planned to head straight home; no scavenging, no detours, just a straight shot home.

He hadn't unpacked anything when he got to the room, so Clay just put his shoes on and made the bed; he always felt it was the least he could do. On his way out, he stopped by Vlad's complimentary water station to fill up his new hydration bladder. He stuck it in his pack and ran the extended straw over his shoulder. He gave it a test; it worked perfectly.

Clay stopped by the shop to thank his host once again, but Vlad was busy haggling with another customer over some binoculars. Clay just gave him a simple wave.

"Safe travels, my friend," Vlad interrupted himself.

Clay made his rounds to the other shops in town. His first stop was Roses Are Blue. It was operated by a young woman around Clay's age named Rose. The shop was one of his favorite stops in town. She always had an abundance of herbs, spices, and essential oils. And from time to time, she had some fruit and vegetable plants. The vibrant colors in her shop and the attached greenhouse made the world feel alive again. It was nice change of pace. Plus, Rose was quite attractive. Her black hair was punctuated with blue streaks. Though she joked that her color was natural, Clay wondered how she was getting ahold of the blue hair dye.

Other than a small potted aloe plant, Rose didn't have much that interested Clay. If properly maintained, Rose said the plant would easily grow to ten times its current size. Clay thought it would be a nice addition to their own garden. Rose also had a small bottle of lavender oil that Megan would have loved, but Clay didn't have anything worth the trade. Rose mentioned a couple of things she needed so he could keep a lookout. *Maybe next time,* he thought.

Next, he swung by a shop called Short Stop— which was ironic because Clay could spend hours in there sifting through the inventory. It was like the Wal-Mart of the little town; it had a little bit of everything. Short Stop distributed the locally grown food for the community farmers who didn't have their own stores, so fresh produce was usually available. Clay got a half dozen ears of corn, two tomatoes, and a five pound sack of beans. He also finagled a box of bandages out of the deal.

He had planned to visit a few other stores but had run out of items to barter. On his way out of town, Clay stopped by the bulletin board for some updates. Placed in the middle of a large gazebo in the center of town, the bulletin board alerted the townspeople of news flowing in from the outside. People would tell Mayor Shelton things they heard or saw, and he would work with a few other folks to put up relevant, reliable stories. They had a small section for rumors or unconfirmed reports, but the mayor preferred facts over speculation.

There wasn't much new since the last time Clay had stopped by. Only one new note posted, and it was substantial. Clay read it carefully:

Outbreak in Megora FEMA camp 7C. It appears to be some sort of advanced flu strain with an extremely high rate of fatalities—nearly 90%. Medical examiners are suspecting a mutated strain of H1N1, but they are unable to confirm. More than 80% of the camp's population has been infected. The camp is now all but abandoned. Do not, under any circumstances, come in contact with those from Megora Camp.

It went on to explain in detail what a citizen of Liberty Township should do if they encounter someone from that camp or anyone who appears to be ill with the flu.

FEMA camps were the federal government's response following the eruptions after nearly two-thirds of the continental US was declared a disaster zone. They set up regional camps across the country, but only half of them were ever brought to a fully operational state. Each regional zone was broken up into a dozen or more campsites with about fifteen to twenty miles between each. This would allow them to work together as one united camp, but separated enough to prevent outbreaks, such as the flu, from spreading to too many people. It didn't work. Camp

7C was not the first to be lost to disease, nor would it be the last.

Clay was saddened by that news. Those camps had anywhere from 25,000 – 35,000 people. If it was indeed true, most of them were dead now. The families affected by it were in his prayers. How many more camps were there? How many people had died in them? Just before the major news outlets went off the air, Clay had heard the director of Homeland Security say it was estimated that 36% of the American population had died. That was roughly eight months after the eruption. A combination of ongoing seismic activity, civil unrest, starvation, and additional eruptions worldwide continued to hamper relief efforts. He had noticed a steady decline of people on the road in the past two years. He imagined that the nationwide death toll had long passed the 50% mark; it was more likely near 70% or 80%. Epidemics such as the one that hit Camp 7C only made survival harder.

There had been sporadic messages from the federal government for a little while following the collapse: promises of aid, encouraging tales of the government hard at work actively rebuilding what had been destroyed. For many, the messages brought hope, but it had been nearly three years since the last message was received. Like so many others, Clay had given up hope in the government and knew he was on his own.

As he left Liberty, Clay stopped and chatted with the gatekeeper about what he read on the bulletin board and then headed out. When he got about a half a mile away, he remembered that he had forgotten to get the parts he needed for his solar panel. He had been so enamored by the antibiotics and the hydration pack—even the batteries—that he hadn't even looked to see if Vlad had the parts in stock. Clay was mad at himself for forgetting but knew that with what he had gotten, he probably wouldn't have done things differently anyhow.

It was a little after 8:00A.M. If the trip went smoothly, he would easily make it home by nightfall, if not a little earlier. Things seldom went smoothly, though, and Clay readied himself for rough travels.

About halfway through the trip, Clay had to cross over a large highway that spanned nearly fifty yards. It was almost always the worst few minutes of the trip. As he was preparing to dash across the road, he noticed a few rugged looking guys walk on to the asphalt on the opposite side. They were searching through some of the abandoned cars scattered around the road. Even though crossing the highway was always dangerous, Clay had chosen this particular spot due to the long North/South sightlines and very few hiding spots. Even the most ideal spots were never guaranteed coverage.

The scavengers took a break after searching through a trailer. One of them sat on the trunk of a car while the others sat on the pavement. They drank some water and munched on food while they joked back and forth. Clay considered just continuing down the highway and crossing elsewhere, but he knew that no other spot along that entire road provided such protection as this. He would have to wait it out.

After a short time, the men continued their search through a few more cars. Bearing no fruit from their efforts, they continued down the highway, ignoring the rest of the cars. Clay waited until they were mere specks on the horizon. Making himself as small and quick as possible, he darted to the other side of the highway without incident. After he got a safe distance away from the road, he checked his watch. He had lost about half an hour; overall, no real harm done.

Clay walked parallel with the highway but kept hidden from view as much as he could. He stayed at least a quarter mile away from the road but still used mile markers and exit signs as a guide to keep his bearings. Passing exit 254, Clay calculated he was about three hours from home when something caught his eye.

No way! he thought in disbelief. No more than forty yards in front of him was a massive buck; he thought it was the biggest he had ever seen. Unbelievable! He could spend an entire day hunting for anything to eat without so much as seeing fresh tracks, and yet, when he had no intention to hunt, he came across this trophy buck.

The buck was alone eating some berries from a bush. Clay ever so slowly raised his AR-15. He took a few deep breaths and exhaled slowly to lower his heart rate. The shot would not be as easy as it would be with the .308. He was much closer than the last deer, but the 5.56 millimeter round didn't pack near the same punch. Fortunately, he had some soft point bullets loaded in the magazine and considered going for the standard shot. But his gut was telling him that round would still go right through the buck and he would run off. He didn't want to shoot it a half dozen times as it pranced away, ruining precious meat or even spoiling the whole lot by puncturing its bowels.

He finally settled the holographic sight on the animal's head. Headshots were typically avoided by most hunters, but with a bullet so small and such a close shot, Clay felt it was his best option. He took another deep breath in, but before he could exhale, he heard a woman's scream come from the highway. Clay whipped his head around, then turned back just in time to watch the deer bolt. Without hesitation, Clay ran towards the highway. He approached the road cautiously and heard voices cursing and laughing. As he got closer, it became overwhelmingly clear.

Screamers.

Instinct told him to flee, but his conscience demanded he stay. He knew he wouldn't sleep for months if he ran away and allowed an innocent woman to suffer the violent pleasures of the Screamers.

"Please, let me go!" she begged. "I didn't do anything, and I don't have anything."

Her cries for mercy only amused them. It was as if the more their victims begged, the more satisfaction they got out of the kill. The lady didn't have much time left. Staying low, Clay ran behind an overturned tractor trailer. His concealed position gave him a clear line of sight to the attack; his suspicions were confirmed: Screamers; three of them.

There were many tales about what the screamers looked like. Since they almost exclusively came out after dark, very few people ever got a good look at them. Those that did seldom walked away to talk about it. The rumors of their appearance, however, were surprisingly accurate. Their skin was covered in tribal tattoos, their heads shaven except for short Mohawks, and piercings covered their faces.

Then there was the body armor. Their bodies were protected by Kevlar vests, and other makeshift armor shrouded their arms and legs. Where they had obtained such tactical equipment was anyone's guess, but it further enhanced the fear.

One man was shirtless, had only a few tattoos and no visible piercings. A stark contrast to the other two men who fit the Screamer stereotype perfectly. Clay found the whole thing strange. He wondered if this was some sort of hazing ritual, like a rite of passage for a new recruit.

More than anything, their daytime appearance perplexed Clay. It wasn't even dusk yet; it was still late afternoon. *What are they doing out so early?* he questioned. Perhaps they were allowing the recruit to see his kill in all its gruesomeness so that he wouldn't miss a single gory detail that seemed to feed their merciless hearts.

He stopped trying to figure out the why and began psyching himself up for the how. He knew he was about to take a man's life; justified or not, it always made him feel sick afterwards. His heart was pounding, his mind racing.

The woman continued to beg, her voice filled with terror. Clay crouched down as he moved behind a car. He stealthily slid down the side of the sedan and then peeked over the trunk. The two men with vests flanked either side of the shirtless man. They both had machetes, and the one had a six-shooter in an old leather pouch.

"It's time, brother," the man with the gun said to the recruit. "Feed your flesh!"

The men in the vests began to scream the terrible sound that Clay so often heard in the distance. Those screams, he realized, were the prologue to a grisly murder. The man in the middle remained silent, as if he had not yet earned the right to scream.

Clay stood up and took aim at the man on the right—the one armed with the pistol. Just as the shirtless man raised a baseball bat, Clay fired a single shot, striking the armed man in the chest. The vest did its job and prevented the soft point bullet from penetrating, but no doubt broke a few ribs in the process. The man stumbled backwards several feet before falling to the ground, screaming in pain.

The other two men jumped back and looked at their wounded friend in confusion. Clay set his sights on the man in the middle and applied pressure on the trigger until he felt resistance. He was ready to unleash a more devastating shot in the blink of an eye—though he hoped he wouldn't have to. Clay had the advantage; he was mostly covered by the car in front of him, and his targets were unarmed—those still standing anyway.

"Maybe y'all should just walk away," Clay shouted while keeping his sights trained on the shirtless man.

The recruit looked at the man on the left for confirmation. He simply nodded. The recruit turned back to the woman with a sinister grin.

"Don't do it," Clay said under his breath.

The man raised his bat once again. Before he could get his arms over his head, Clay had dispatched two more bullets. The first was a perfect hit right around his heart, the second went a bit high and to the side, striking his shoulder. The recruit was dead before he hit the ground. Clay rapidly transitioned his attention to the third man—the only one left uninjured. The Screamer stared at Clay with hatred and fear in his eyes. He slowly helped his wounded friend to his feet, never breaking eye contact with Clay.

"Go on now," Clay said, "or I'm gonna start aiming a bit higher."

Both men glared at Clay, a challenge in their eyes; however, after a few moments, they backed away from the girl and began to jog away.

Clay's stomach was in knots. It had been around six months since he had shot another man, and he wasn't even certain he had killed that one. There was no doubt this time around. Though the man he shot was lying on the asphalt behind a car, Clay could see the pool of blood growing beyond the fender. He swallowed the bile that had crept up his throat and pulled himself together. Clay rose to his feet and approached the woman, his weapon still pressed into his shoulder until he could assess their safety. A soft whimpering grew louder as Clay approached the woman. *At least she is still alive.* He first saw the recruit's body on the ground; the man wasn't moving. Confident there were no more threats, he lowered his rifle and walked around the front of the car.

Clay saw her leaning up against the car door. She was staring down at the pavement refusing to look at him. Her dark black hair was disheveled and matted as it dangled in front of her face like curtains shielding her from danger. She was holding her left knee. She continued to whimper as she reached up to wipe tears from her eyes. The pool of blood from her attacker had reached the cuff of her pants and began to saturate the cloth. She hadn't even noticed.

Clay approached slowly and stuck out his hand, "My name is Clay."

She looked up slightly and saw the dead body in front of her. She stared at it for a moment before she looked up at Clay. Instinctively, she leaned away from him, a subtle gesture of distrust. Clay didn't blame her for that.

"It's okay. I want to help," he said, softening his voice.

She looked at the lifeless man again, then back at Clay. "I'm Kelsey," she said with a beautiful, soft voice, her strong southern accent ringing through.

Clay was charmed by her beauty. He was captivated by her green eyes and dark, long lashes. She had the faintest hint of freckles on her cheeks near her nose, and Clay wondered if they were brighter when her face was freshly washed. Her radiant presence distracted him from the dangerous situation they faced. He forced himself to focus. It was no time to be sidetracked.

She looked down at her knee and then back up at him. "I don't think I can walk," she said, wincing as she tried to flex her knee.

"Let me help you up," Clay said as he stuck his hand out. "We should have left five minutes ago. These guys don't retreat; they regroup."

Kelsey shuddered at the thought of seeing their ghastly faces again. "Okay," she said as she nodded and reached for his hand. Clay helped her to her feet, and the movement made her gasp in pain.

Her knee was starting to swell. Clay was immediately aware they would have to seek shelter for the night. Both home and the cabin were too far away, but they were only about two miles from his hunting grounds in the woods. The cave would be their best bet. Clay had explored it when he first found the sacred spot, and he knew it was pretty deep; at least 1,500 feet with several turns. It would provide them a safe shelter as they waited for morning.

The two hobbled off the road and towards the tree line. Clay had switched his rifle for his pistol so he could more easily support Kelsey, but after a mile, Kelsey asked if they could rest. It was against Clay's better judgment, but he conceded. They found a large rock for Kelsey to sit on and she grimaced as she sat down, doing her best to stifle her cries. Clay handed her the straw from his hydration pack. She looked at him as if he had read her mind. A small smile began to play at the corners of her lips accentuating her soft dimples and round cheeks. She took the straw and drank deeply from the pack, only pausing once for some air.

"Thanks," she said as she wiped her mouth with her sleeve.

Clay found himself lost in her deep, green eyes again. Even though he had just met her and they were being chased by a pack of ravenous psychopaths, he struggled to maintain focus on the problems at hand. Kelsey noticed the glances of admiration and blushed a little, though it was hidden beneath a layer of dirt and scrapes.

"Okay," Kelsey said after only a moment, hoping to redirect Clay's attention from her. She hopped off the rock onto her good leg. "I think I'm ready."

Their pace had significantly slowed. Kelsey was giving it all she had, but each step she took was excruciating, and Clay could see it on her face. They were about half a mile away from the cave when they heard the screams in the distance. There was only about twenty minutes left of sunlight, and they still had some distance to travel; the odds were not in their favor. Clay stopped and looked at Kelsey.

"What?" she asked.

He holstered his pistol and reached down, placing one arm behind her knees. He scooped her up and without saying a word, began to walk at a fast pace, Kelsey in his arms. After a few minutes, Clay's pace increased to a jog. It was difficult, but he tried to be as light on his feet as he could. The crunch of dead leaves beneath each of his steps quietly echoed around them, but hopefully the Screamers were far enough away that they wouldn't hear.

Clay's breathing became labored. Even though Kelsey couldn't have been an ounce over 110 pounds, his exhaustion from the day's hike made each step increasingly more difficult. The repetitive hits from the muzzle of his rifle against his leg had gone from annoying to painful, but he didn't let that show. On a couple of occasions, Clay caught Kelsey closing her eyes and smiling ever so slightly. He hadn't realized just how poetic the evening had become. A damsel in distress. A heroic rescue. A daring escape. It was the scene from a romantic novel, not a day in post-apocalyptic America.

The screams in the distance had faded. It sounded like the vicious night dwellers had gone a different direction, but there was a good chance the group split up and could still be tracking Clay and Kelsey. The sight of the cave a few hundred yards away eased his perturbation, which was all the more reason he needed to stay alert. He couldn't let his guard down. He gradually returned to a walking pace as they approached the cave.

"I think we'll be safe here for the night."

Kelsey gave a sigh of relief. "Thank you," she said.

Chapter 6

Clay returned Kelsey to her feet, careful not to hurt her in the process, and he supported her as they limped their way through the cave. Once the light from the entrance had faded, Clay turned on his flashlight. After a few minutes, the cave narrowed, becoming only wide enough for the trickling stream.

"I guess this is the end of the line," Clay said as he helped Kelsey to the ground.

"I'll take it," she said, brushing a stray strand of hair from of her face.

Clay placed his pack on the ground and cracked a chem light. After a few good shakes, the light intensified, giving off a bright but soft green glow. He set it on the ground just in front of Kelsey.

"We need to get a fire going. I am going to go collect some tinder and wood." He paused for a moment as he wrestled with what he was about to do next. "I know this is probably a stupid question to ask, but do you know how to use a gun?"

Kelsey smiled as she recalled a fond memory. She had a beautiful smile. "Yeah, my grandfather taught me when I was pretty young. I haven't shot one in a while, but I think I can remember how if I need to."

He hesitated, red flags flying inside his head. It went against every fiber of his being to give his gun to someone he just met, but his gut was overriding all concern. He knew if something happened to him while he was outside, she would be completely defenseless. If someone found and killed him, it wouldn't take long for them to find her. He didn't want her to be prey, again.

He withdrew the gun from the holster and handed it to her. "There's a round already chambered. There's no safety, and it's double action. If you see someone other than me, all you have to do is aim and squeeze."

She took the gun from him, and he immediately noticed a level of respect she had for firearms in the way she handled it. She pointed the gun towards the ground and made sure to keep her finger off the trigger. Clay appreciated the proper protocol being followed. Accidents can kill, especially in a world without advanced medical treatment.

"Be back in a little bit," he said and headed down the tunnel with his flashlight and rifle.

As Clay walked, he felt for his magazine pouch. Whether fleeing from bandits or just hiking through the woods, experience told him his mags could become dislodged at any point. His compulsion to check his pouch regularly—especially before entering unknown or dangerous situations—became almost an obsession. The three spare mags were snugly contained in the pouch as they should be. With the magazine already in his rifle—minus the three rounds from the earlier encounter with the Screamers—Clay knew he had exactly 117 shots total. He wasn't sure if that was sufficient should the Screamers find their camp. It would be best if he never had to find out.

But Clay's more immediate concern was provisions for the night, so he returned his attention to gathering some sticks and twigs. He even snatched a few crayfish out of the stream; he was now carrying his catch in his sock. He looked around for a little longer but couldn't find anything of use for the night. With darkness overtaking the sky, Clay returned to the cave.

"Clay?" Kelsey said with a hint of panic in her voice. "Is that you, Clay?" She had the gun at the ready.

"Yeah, it's me," he said as he shined the light on his face and then back down at the ground.

Relieved, she placed the gun down on the ground by her side. It wasn't that she hated guns; she just wasn't familiar enough with them to feel comfortable handling them. She was always afraid she would accidentally shoot somebody.

Kelsey had started collecting the rocks that she could reach from where she sat and had begun constructing a fire pit. As if they had discussed the plan already, Clay placed the sticks and kindling on the ground next to her fixture and searched for a few more stones to finish the enclosure. Most of them were wet from the nearby stream, but that didn't matter. After he completed the fire pit, he carefully placed the kindling inside the stones.

Clay always kept some survival supplies in his pack in case he found himself in a situation just like this. There wasn't much, but what was there would be crucial to staying alive for the night, especially once the cold set in. He looked around in the pocket for a few moments and came back with a nine volt battery and a sandwich bag containing steel wool.

"What is that?" Kelsey asked curiously.

"Our heat for the night."

She was confused.

Clay pulled a large chunk of the steel wool out of the bag—along with some dried tinder—and carefully positioned it under the neatly arranged kindling. He pressed the battery terminals up to the tuft of wool, and once the connection had been made, the wool near the battery began to glow. The hot, metal fibers quickly ignited the dried tinder. A few moments later, the fire had spread to the twigs and dry grass Clay had collected outside. Within seconds, the kindling was fully engulfed, and Clay started adding some larger sticks every few minutes until it became a slow and steady burn.

The sight of the fire alleviated much of the anxiety plaguing both of them. Kelsey clapped her hands quickly, but quietly, and cheered him on. "My hero," she added.

Hoping the light from the fire wasn't bright enough to reveal his blushing, Clay responded, "And I have dinner." He picked up the sock with the crayfish.

Her eyes got big when she saw the soiled, dripping wet sock dangling in front of his face. "Ooookaaaaay?" she said, a smile visible through her perplexed expression.

"What can I say? I spare no expense." He untied the sock and showed her the contents inside. He looked for something to cook the crayfish in but to no avail. Then he got an idea. He unzipped his bag again and pulled out the can of deviled ham. "May I interest you in a devilishly delightful appetizer?" he said as he waved the can.

She chuckled at his lame pun. "Sounds delicious."

He opened the can with his knife and was relieved to find the contents inside had not spoiled. It was far less appetizing than he remembered, but that could be because it was three years past the sell-by date. Maybe it was because he was ten the last time he had eaten it. Either way, it was food, and they were grateful to have it. They spread it on a few stale crackers and devoured it all in mere moments.

After their snack, Clay filled the can with water and placed it on the fire. Once the water was boiling, he tossed the crayfish inside. Cooking quicker than he had expected; the crayfish turned red after only a couple of minutes. He dumped them out onto a smooth stone and separated them—there were five in all. He gave Kelsey three and kept two for himself. Neither of them had eaten crayfish before, or craw daddies, as Kelsey called them. Clay felt foolish that he had never thought to collect them in the past, especially with how many times he had been there to hunt.

They clumsily figured out how to eat them and were both shocked by the taste; the creek food was delicious. All the more reason why Clay was annoyed that he hadn't been utilizing the resource all along. He tossed Kelsey the last bottle of water from his pack, and she sipped it slowly.

As dinner came to a close, reality snuck back into the conversation. "So, did they hurt your knee?" Clay asked.

Kelsey looked down at her leg; she was in the middle of drinking some water when he asked. She placed the cap on the water and set it down. "Actually, no," she replied. "A few years ago my knee got bashed pretty good. Most of the time it's fine. I can usually run on it with no problem, but every now and then—if I step the wrong way—it'll buckle on me. It can swell up pretty bad," she said as she gently rubbed it with her hand. "I'll be fine in a few days."

"Well, I'm just glad I was nearby," he said as he looked into her eyes, a smile painted across his face. She flashed a quick grin and then took another sip of water.

Clay noticed she was keeping her guard up. Given the circumstances, he understood why. He was a little surprised with how forward he had been, though. He knew he was flirting with her—maybe even laying it on a little thick at times—and hoped it wasn't making her uncomfortable. But this was uncharted territory for him. Since he was forced to mature past his thirteen years so quickly after the earth exploded, the thought of a romantic relationship had never been a priority. He found himself far too busy, overwhelmed, or sorrowful to think about anything as trivial as a girlfriend. That and the average woman he ran into didn't exactly spark romantic desires. With the exception of the blue-haired Rose, he couldn't recall anyone he had met recently that he had been remotely attracted to. But Kelsey wasn't just attractive; she was stunning. And as she sat across from him, the flickering orange glow of the campfire illuminating her face, he wondered, *Could this be love?* Clay tried to shrug off the absurd notion.

"What brings you out this way? Do you live nearby?" she asked.

"I was actually heading back from a trading post a bit north of here."

"Liberty Township?" she asked.

"You know the place?"

"I was just there myself, actually. Small world, I guess. Was looking for some meds but no luck."

Clay contemplated offering her one of the bottles he had in his bag. These days that'd be the equivalent of a hundred long stem roses and a colossal box of chocolates. But he knew he couldn't make such a grand gesture at the expense of his family and quickly dismissed the idea.

"Somebody sick?" he asked.

"No. Just looking to trade them."

Clay was relieved. He would have felt really guilty if she had a sick loved one in need, while he had two bottles sitting just a few feet away with no immediate need for them. As much as he already liked this girl, he didn't know her, and he had his own family to worry about back home.

"So, where are ya from?" he asked her.

She was reluctant to tell him, but she realized she wasn't about to get home without his help—if he was willing to help, that is. "I live on a ranch about twenty miles southwest of here, I think. Not quite sure where we are."

"We're pretty close to Woodridge exit 256, I think."

"Okay. So yeah, pretty close to twenty miles," she said.

Clay knew it was going to take at least another two solid days of walking with that bum knee to get her back home. It wasn't going to be easy, and he could already hear Megan chewing him out for being gone longer than expected. He didn't blame her for that, though. Oh, how life would be easier if he could just call her to let her know he was going to be delayed. Instead, she would probably be up all night worrying about whether or not her little brother was ever coming home. He hated that he put her through that kind of worry so frequently, but it was just part of life nowadays.

"So is this a family farm or something?"

"Nah," she said as she tossed the shell of her last crayfish into the fire and licked her fingers. "It's owned by a man named Watson. Me and my—" she paused abruptly, like she was startled. Clay looked behind him almost expecting to see someone approaching, then back at her. "Sorry. Thought I heard something. Anyway, my sister, Dakota and I stumbled across the ranch, and he let us stay."

"Sounds like a nice guy."

"Yeah, he is," Kelsey said, but her face, for a brief moment, suggested otherwise.

Clay could tell she was getting a little uncomfortable. He switched topics, and they began talking about some of their favorite movies. It wasn't surprising that they were on opposite ends of the spectrum. Clay was more into the action and sci-fi movies while Kelsey preferred the dramas and chick flicks, though she admitted she liked watching a good action flick from time to time. She'd kill for the chance to watch a movie, even a foreign film. It had been years since she watched television.

As much as Clay hated to close down the conversation, it was getting late and he knew they had a long couple of days ahead of them. He pulled out a Mylar survival blanket from his pack. He unfolded it, shook it a few times, and then draped it over her. It was intended for two people, and she was keenly aware of the excessive material.

Kelsey hesitated for a moment. She didn't want to speak up, but felt obligated—it was the least she could do for him. "There's plenty of space if you want to share." Though Kelsey didn't intend for there to be any underlying message with the statement, she knew it could be taken that way.

He wrestled with that idea. On one hand, they would certainly benefit from having two bodies beneath the blanket to keep warm. On the other, he was twenty, his adrenaline had spiked, and she was beautiful. He didn't trust himself in that situation, and that would open up a massive can of worms he couldn't deal with right now. Not to mention, he knew it would be wrong.

"That's all right. You go ahead and get some rest. I am actually pretty comfy temperature-wise, I don't think I'll need a blanket. Plus, I kick in my sleep anyway. I would hate to make that leg any worse," he said adding a nervous laugh.

Kelsey could see the internal struggle. She felt both relieved and respected with the decision. Just about any other guy would have tried to take advantage of the situation the instant she offered. When Clay didn't, she realized that he was unlike any other man she had met. It comforted her to know that there were still some good men left in the world. But despite her prayers for such a man to come into her life, she wouldn't allow it to be someone as goodhearted as Clay.

Eventually Kelsey drifted to sleep, but Clay was wide awake. Sleep was held at bay from the adrenaline spike, and his mind was racing with feelings about the woman sleeping just a few feet away. In addition to that, he *was* cold and just couldn't get comfortable enough to doze. He watched the hours pass on his watch, and before long, it was almost time to begin the next leg of their journey. At that point, falling asleep would do more harm than good.

Kelsey began to stir, her breathing becoming more controlled and less involuntary.

"Morning," Clay said just above a whisper in case she hadn't actually woken up.

She lay there in silence for a moment. "Mornin'," she finally replied with a hoarse voice, her eyes still closed.

The entrance to the cave was far enough back that none of the morning light could reach them, not that there was really any light at that time of the morning anyhow. The fire had all but burned out. Only small pockets of glowing embers and an occasional popping sound remained. Clay wound up the flashlight and turned it on. Though her eyes were already shut, Kelsey squeezed them tighter and rolled over, turning away from the potent light source.

"It's almost six," he told her in a hushed voice. "We should get going."

Kelsey wanted to contend that it was too early, but she knew how slow she was going to move; every minute would have an impact. Without protest, she sat up and began to fold up the Mylar blanket and placed it back in the bag. Clay doused the charred wood with the water from the can that had been their crayfish pot. It hissed and hurled smoke into his face causing him to cough. Before they left, he filled the hydration pack and the two empty bottles he had with water from the stream.

Using a compass, they began their trek. They eased into the journey for the first couple of miles, moving slowly and carefully. Though Kelsey had slept through the night, her knee was still quite tender and stiff from sleeping on the hard ground. He gave her a couple of ibuprofen for the swelling just before they left, but it was having little effect.

Clay wasn't sure how he was going to make it. Fatigue had already started to harass his body, and they had at least another thirteen hours of traveling ahead of them. Sometimes he wished that he didn't get so worked up from killing, that it didn't cause him to become so unsettled. On the other hand, he feared the day when he no longer was affected by taking the life of another person.

About six hours into the journey, they decided to take a rest inside a large electronics store. They squeezed in through a half-open automatic door that had been partially knocked off its track and walked cautiously across the pillaged store, keeping alert for any threats.

Aisle shelves were bare. Several had been toppled over in a panicked rush to take all that could be carried or carted off—as if having fifty copies of the latest military shooter would put food on the table during the apocalypse. Since the collapse, Clay had walked through a number of stores just like this, and they all looked the same. He remained perplexed as to why getting a new flat screen or tablet computer was on anyone's list of priorities after what had happened. Sure, there were various snack foods and sodas near the cash registers for the obligatory impulse buy, but why would anyone waste their time and resources on getting electronic entertainment during such a crisis?

Those types of stores did sell one item in particular that still had a bit of value, though. Unfortunately, they were also the number one targeted item immediately following the social unrest. Cell phones. Prior to the fall of cellular communication, most people snatched them for the face value—after all, one needs to have the latest and greatest smartphone to ring in the end of the world—however, the real value was inside. Gold. Due to its conduction properties, small amounts of gold were often used in phones. Clay once heard that approximately 1,000 cell phones contained an ounce of gold. He wasn't sure if that was accurate or not, but there was still a demand for them if you knew the right trader. Vlad would buy them, and Clay had been saving up what he found for the last year. He had seventeen so far and was waiting to get to twenty-five before trading them to Vlad. They wouldn't yield him much—a few small items or a gram of silver perhaps—but it was something.

Clay and Kelsey walked to the rear of the sales floor and through an open doorway. The door had long been kicked off its hinges as the store was looted. The stockroom was a massive area with a concrete slab floor, unfinished walls, and a corrugated metal roof. Never intended to be seen by the customers, the room was built for function, rather than aesthetics. As expected, the shelves were emptied, boxes and other garbage strewn about as if a tornado had ripped through. One of the loading dock doors was open, providing a reasonable amount of light for them to sit down and eat in a relatively sheltered area.

Kelsey sat down at a small round table in the far corner of the room and enjoyed another helping of crackers while Clay looked around for anything of use. He found a half empty box of ballpoint pens and some paperclips. Neither had any real trade value, but back home pens were still a high-in-demand product for the arts and crafts room.

Finding nothing else, Clay pulled up a chair and sat across from Kelsey who was taking small bites out of each cracker to make them last just a bit longer. She handed the last three to Clay who gladly accepted and popped an entire cracker into his mouth.

"So, how old is your sister?" Clay asked with a mouthful of food.

"She's almost three," Kelsey said with smile thinking about her. "She's a sweet girl."

Clay got ready to ask her a question then thought better of it, "What happened to your mom?" he asked anyway.

Kelsey's reaction was indifferent to the question, catching Clay off guard. "She died shortly after Dakota was born."

Clay frowned. Complications during pregnancy and delivery had become more common for women. The unexpectedly high mortality rate during birth complications in the past seven years was a grim reminder of just how critical even simple procedures such as blood transfusions and cesareans were— procedures that almost everyone in developed nations took for granted.

"Sorry to hear that. I know what that's like," he said with a somber tone.

"What about you?" Kelsey asked, "Got any family at home? A wife? Kids?" she asked realizing that he would have barely been a teenager beforehand.

Clay wasn't sure how much he should read into that question. Was she prodding about a wife or girlfriend because she was interested in him? Or was it just small talk? He was bothered that he scrutinized every question like that, especially when she had not really given him any reason to believe she was interested. "My sister and I take care of some kids who also lost their parents. We're kind of like a post-apocalyptic orphanage," he said with a chuckle.

She smiled at him, not realizing just how many kids he was talking about. Regardless, she was impressed with his maturity. "Just the one sister?" she followed up.

Grief washed across Clay's face before he forced a weak smile, "Yeah, it's just me and her, now."

Kelsey picked up on his hint. She felt guilty for bringing it up. "Well, I think it's really great what you and your sister are doing. Not many folks in the world are willing to help out a strangers' kids...Not many folks would have stopped to save me, either," she said as she started to reach across the table for his hand, but quickly withdrew once she realized it. "You're a good man, Clay," she said, hoping he hadn't noticed the absent-minded gesture.

They finished up with lunch and did a quick check of supplies. They would have to be conservative with their water intake but should have enough to make it the rest of the way, even if they didn't find any streams or water sources along the way.

They went out through the large bay door. Clay jumped off the loading dock then helped Kelsey down. Parked just a few yards away was a tractor-trailer. Clay searched the cab for anything of value. Nothing.

Though more populated areas like this were more likely to turn up some goods, Clay's lack of sleep and Kelsey's injury made it too dangerous for them to stick around and search the area. They could easily be targeted given their physical and mental state, so they moved on.

Clay's body ached from head to toe, and he had developed a nasty headache. He tried not to show that he was in pain. He didn't need Kelsey worrying about him being able to get her home safely.

The two talked quietly throughout the day, learning more about each other's past, making sure to only talk about life *before* the world went belly up. Kelsey talked about school, her obsession with penguins, and her undying love for a good hot fudge sundae. Clay talked about the various sports he played, fishing, shooting, and his favorite band. He talked a little about Megan, but kept the topic more positive in nature.

Despite being injured and exhausted, they were able to travel a bit further than Clay had anticipated. The sun started to set; they had to find shelter. The two made their way back towards the highway to get their bearings. They only had about eight more miles to go, according to Kelsey.

A few hundred yards off the highway was an old apartment complex. The buildings themselves had not been in all that great of shape prior to the eruptions, let alone after Mother Nature had pummeled the world. However, it did provide some refuge and would do just fine for the night.

The air inside was stale and reeked of death— most likely an unfortunate animal, or so Clay hoped. Cockroaches and other critters scurried along the floor and walls providing a rather creepy ambience. The apartment had four levels, and Clay had decided it was going to be best to stay on the second floor. That way, they were high enough so that nobody could smash a window and be in the room before they realized what was going on. But low enough that if someone *did* come into the apartment, they could make a quick escape out the window. Though the thought of jumping out a second story window with her hurt knee made Kelsey cringe.

Clay cleared each room on the lower floor. The apartments were plundered and lifeless like most buildings in the city. The second floor was the same. He didn't bother checking the other floors because he wasn't as concerned with people above hearing them; their movement would echo on the floors below alerting Clay and Kelsey to their presence. They stopped at the end of the long hallway on the second floor, the furthest apartment from the stairwell, and Clay cleared the final room before helping Kelsey inside.

The apartment was cramped; a small living area and kitchenette made up the room just inside the door. A short hallway lead to a nearly jail-sized bedroom with the bathroom just across the hall. The room had a twin-sized bed in one corner; the mattress slumped halfway off the bed. A few feet away from the bed was a crib. Clay shuddered as he began to wonder what happened to this family. Did they make it out of the city before everything imploded? Judging by the remaining clothes scattered across the floor, it was just a mother and her daughter. Perhaps they made it to one of the camps. He then wondered if they did, was it one of the ones hit with the flu or attacked by mobs? Every place Clay visited had a story to tell; he hated that his curious mind always wanted to know more.

Clay lifted the mattress back onto the box springs, and Kelsey sat down, letting out a sigh of relief as she gingerly bent over to take off her shoes. She pushed herself back on the bed and leaned up against the wall closing her eyes. Even though the building smelled awful and the presence of bugs and rodents was overwhelming, it felt safe—at least, more so than camping outside.

Clay went out to look around the apartment a bit more thoroughly. He first stopped by the bathroom and looked for any sort of medication. He found a pair of tweezers and an unopened toothbrush in the medicine cabinet. Below the sink, he found a nearly empty bottle of rubbing alcohol. He thoroughly searched around the toilet, including inside the tank. "Be thorough in everything you do," his father used to tell him. It was true whether playing football or searching a moldy old dilapidated apartment for supplies. Though nothing had ever turned up inside toilet tanks, it never stopped him from looking.

He searched the rest of the apartment as thoroughly, but found little of value. He discovered a packet of taco seasoning and felt as if he had just found gold. The thought of having seasoned venison made his mouth water. He stuffed it into his pocket and walked back to the bedroom. Kelsey had fallen asleep against the wall. He helped lay her down on the mattress and covered her with the Mylar blanket. He grabbed a blanket off the floor and gave it several good shakes, expelling an enormous amount of dust and debris, before placing it onto her for added warmth.

"Thanks," she barely managed to say before drifting back to sleep.

Clay took off his shoes and cleared a spot to lay down on the floor. He found a pillowcase and stuffed it with some of the clothing from the floor. He found one of the baby's quilts and laid down. With his head on a lumpy pillow and his upper body covered by a small blanket. Clay actually felt somewhat comfortable, even relaxed, and thought he might be able to fall asleep. The scurrying creatures, curious about the two life-forms that had abruptly entered their world, made sure that didn't happen.

Morning finally came. Clay thought he might have slept two or three hours, but he wasn't sure. It had gotten much colder inside than he was anticipating. The cave with the fire was considerably warmer than inside the dingy apartment. With a little luck, he would be sleeping in the comfort of his own bed tonight.

They left about the same time as the day before. It was still dark, but evidence of the night was being chased away by the sun as it began painting the sky near the horizon. Kelsey's knee was quite bruised, but a touch less swollen than yesterday, though the pain hadn't improved much. Just walking down the stairs was a time consuming challenge. Clay couldn't afford to be out another night. He knew if he didn't return, Megan would assume the worst and probably come looking for him, even though he had repeatedly told her never to do that.

Hours began to feel like days to the two weary souls. Clay couldn't remember a more daunting challenge to tackle—even when he and his family had to flee their house, eventually finding refuge at their current home. Clay's legs became wobbly, his vision fuzzy. He and Kelsey had finished what was left in the hydration pack a few hours before and were both in need of a drink. Besides the aching knee, Kelsey seemed to be holding up okay. Clay attributed his weakened state to sleep deprivation over the past two nights. Something Kelsey had also noticed.

"You okay?" she asked with a look of concern.

It took a few seconds for Clay to respond, "Yeah, I'm fine. Just tired," he said with a slight slur.

Kelsey thought about asking to stop and rest, more for his sake than hers, but they were almost to the ranch, and stopping might do more harm than good at that point. Ahead of them was a slight incline. Though it would be barely noticeable to Clay on any other day, the small slope might as well have been a mountain. Each step seemed harder than the last. Kelsey, bad knee and all, reached the top before Clay. She stared out ahead, then turned and looked back at Clay.

"We're here," she said through an exhale.

Chapter 7

Seeing the ranch renewed what little energy Clay had left, and his pace began to quicken. The ranch was incredible. Similar to Liberty—although not as grand—it was fenced in with a gate at the end of the driveway. About a hundred yards behind the gate was a large, rustic looking farmhouse, complete with a wraparound deck and vast bay windows. It was a snapshot from history—with the exception of the dozen or so solar panels on the roof.

Several hundred yards to the side of the house were numerous smaller, more crudely built shanties. Each one had a door, a few small windows, and a metal chimney coming from the roof. Clearly built in a hurry and without power tools, the dwellings were a lot less impressive than the main house. But they were tucked away from the dangers outside the gate, and that made them very appealing, even to Clay.

Off in the distance, he saw a large barn and some stables. Animals grazed throughout the fields—it looked to be a mixture of cows and goats with perhaps a couple of sheep—it was hard to see from that distance. As they got closer, Clay could see people moving about—somebody fixing a broken wagon; another replacing some shingles on a roof; a cluster of women talking amongst themselves as they watched their little ones play on some handmade playground equipment. It was nice to see the existence of another place like Liberty.

As Clay and Kelsey approached the gate, the man standing guard recognized her right away. "Kelsey!" the young guard shouted as he waved at her. "I'm so glad to see you. Jeremy was about to send me and a few others out to track you down," he said with relief, clearly not wanting to wander around outside the gates for too long. The guard then looked over at Clay and stared him down in an act of intimidation. "Who's your friend?"

Kelsey, in no mood for small talk, quickly shot back, "Just open the gate, Derrick. He's with me."

"I'll need to take that rifle," the guard said.

"Sorry. That ain't happening," Clay said as he watched the kid eyeballing his LaRue, something the guard probably hadn't seen in over a decade.

"Then you *ain't* coming in," he said with a sneer.

"Derrick, quit acting like you're the law around here and let us in. This man saved my life!"

"Sorry, Kelsey. He isn't coming in unless he gives me that rif—"

"It's okay, Derrick," an older man said as he approached the gate. "You may let them in."

Clay heard Kelsey mumble something under her breath but didn't catch the words.

"Oh, Mr. Watson. He is armed with a fancy looking rifle. I didn't think it would be smart to let him in."

"You are wise to be apprehensive, but I'll take it from here. Thank you, Derrick."

The guard unlocked the gate and stepped aside. He shot Clay a glare as they passed through.

Watson was an older man who looked every bit the part of a Texas rancher. His hair and stubble—in stark contrast with his tan complexion from years spent in the sun—were nearly white with hints of the dark brown from his youth. He wore a flannel shirt and a worn-out pair of jeans held up by a handmade leather belt sporting an appropriately large Texas buckle. Hanging from the belt was a Colt Single Action Army—better known as the Peacemaker. All that seemed to be missing was a cowboy hat.

Watson looked at Kelsey and noticed her limp. "Kelsey, I am so relieved to see you back safe and sound. Why don't you two come back to my place? I'll have Doc take a look at your leg."

"That's okay," Kelsey said. "I just need to rest; I'll be fine."

"I insist," Watson said, gesturing towards the house. "I'll see to it Doc takes good care of you."

Kelsey conceded, and they started walking towards Watson's house. Clay could feel the eyes of the town upon them, watching from afar as they hobbled their way to the house. Out of nowhere, a man came up and greeted Kelsey. He seemed quite concerned with her wellbeing and bombarded her with questions about the injury. Clay assumed it was the doctor.

"I'm fine, Jeremy," Kelsey said to the worried man.

As they approached the house, Clay saw another man was standing on the porch with his hands in his pockets as if he was waiting for an order.

"Matthew, fetch some water for Kelsey and her guest, would ya please?" Watson asked the man waiting for them.

"Yes sir, Mr. Watson," he said and walked inside.

Clay and Kelsey followed Watson through the front door and sat down on a couch in the living room. Matthew returned with the water and set it down on a coffee table just in front of them. Clay picked up the glass and was astounded at how clear the water was. He took a sip, then guzzled the entire thing down. It was even more refreshing than it looked.

As Watson took his seat on the other side of the table from Clay and Kelsey, he asked Matthew to retrieve the doctor. Seemingly unseen, Jeremy, who had been so interested in Kelsey before, stood stiffly behind Watson's chair with his arms crossed. His muscular physique and stone-cold stare were a complete departure from his look of concern when they arrived. It was almost as if he broke character to make sure Kelsey was okay, then immediately resumed his role as Watson's muscle. Something about Jeremy's buzz cut, soul patch, and the way he stood made Clay think former military. He made Clay nervous, but that was the point.

Watson leaned into the chair and rested a hand on his knee. He raised his glass to his mouth and took a long sip. After wiping his mouth, he ran his hand down the length of his white beard. He seemed lost in thought.

"So, what happened?" Watson asked eventually, but quickly continued, "Oh, I am sorry, where are my manners? My name is Jake Watson." He reached out his hand.

Clay introduced himself and shook Watson's hand.

"Pleasure to meet you, Mr. Whitaker," Watson responded, his attention already directed towards Kelsey, an unspoken invitation to answer.

Kelsey explained, keeping the details to a minimum, recalling the major events of the past few days. Watson seemed genuinely concerned about what would have happened had Clay not intervened.

The front door opened, and Matthew returned with the doctor. He was carrying a small leather bag like the ones doctors who made house calls used to carry. The doctor examined Kelsey's knee while she finished recalling her journey with Clay.

"She gonna be okay, doc?" Watson asked.

"Yeah, I don't think it's too serious, but she needs to be off her feet with some ice. Here," he reached into the bag and pulled out a long expired bottle of ibuprofen. "The swelling is pretty bad. Take four of these now. I'll bring you another four later on. You should also stay off the leg for a couple of days, at least."

Kelsey took the pills, tossed them in her mouth, and then finished the glass of water. She acknowledged the doctor's orders. Matthew and the doctor helped her to her feet.

"Hey, Clay," she said as she got her arm over Matthew's shoulder, "thanks for everything. I hope we run into each other again soon."

Clay smiled and nodded, "Yeah, I would like that."

Watson watched as the three left before he turned back to Clay. "Well now, that's a mighty fine piece of hardware you've got there," he gestured towards the AR-15. "How'd a boy like you get your hands on a LaRue OBR? Didn't think any of those existed anymore."

Watson was referring to the "Safe & Smart Firearms Act"—a bill that was rammed through the House and Senate in record timing that outlawed all current semi-automatic rifles of certain calibers, improperly labeling them as assault rifles, to be promptly destroyed. Citizens were required to turn in any rifle described in the bill. Those who quickly handed over their weapons were given vouchers for "Smart-Gun" substitutes. Police were issued warrants for the arrests of those who didn't voluntarily turn their firearms in. Those people who resisted the trade lost their guns anyway, and in several incidents, lost their lives.

The smart gun was intentionally designed to be cumbersome and less tactical. Using computer chips and biometric scanners, the gun could only have up to five registered operators. An operator had to submit a passport photo, fingerprints, and written consent of the firearm owner to the ATF in order to be whitelisted for use of that particular gun. It did not have a detachable magazine; all rounds were manually loaded from above with a maximum of seven; and the computer would force a minimum of one second between each shot. Those guns were significantly inferior to other firearms. After the eruption, however, they were most effectively used as clubs.

Clay lifted his rifle up a bit and looked down at it. "My father was in law enforcement for a little while."

"Oh yeah? My brother was a cop up in Denton County. His department fought to keep their personal rifles as well, but the mayor and sheriff didn't see eye to eye with them and forced them to turn 'em in anyway."

"I was just eleven at the time, but I remember seeing stories like that all over the news. I overheard my father tell a colleague that he thought America had died that day," Clay said.

All Watson could do was nod. Indeed, it seemed that America had died before her destruction had come.

"So, what would I have to give to get that rifle from ya?" Watson asked half-jokingly.

"Your life if you try to take it from me," Clay said with a subtle grin.

Watson laughed heartily. "You got some gumption in your shorts, boy, I'll give you that," he said, highlighting his Texas accent.

Clay chuckled, but with far less gusto than Watson. "Well, I need to be going," he said as he slowly got himself off the couch; his muscles ached relentlessly.

"Now, I can't in good conscience send a young man out two hours before dark, especially after what you did for Kelsey out there. I have several rooms upstairs you could stay in. There's a clean, warm bed. You can take a hot bath and relax yourself some, and then head out first thing in the morning. Whatch'ya say?"

Clay was split on the decision. After all, the offer was tempting, especially the bath, but he needed to get home. "While I do appreciate the hospitality, Mr. Watson—"

"Please," Watson interjected, "call me Jake."

"Okay," Clay replied, "Jake. That's very kind of you, but I have things I must tend to."

"Well, how about this," Watson said looking back at the man standing next to him. "Let Jeremy here take you home. Got a couple of ponies in the stable that need some exercise anyway."

After mentally weighing the pros and cons of Watson's offer, Clay conceded. It was not something he would normally agree to—not so shortly after meeting someone—but his fatigue overruled his overly cautious nature.

"Before you go," Watson said holding up his index finger and walked into the other room for a moment. He rummaged through the refrigerator and returned with a quart of milk.

Clay's eyes widened; he thought he was hallucinating. He hadn't seen fresh milk in ages. The last glass of milk he had was almost two years ago, and it started as a powder. He looked up at Watson who had a smile on his face.

"Take it," he said.

Clay, unsure how to respond to such generosity, hesitated.

"It's the least I can do. After what you did for Kelsey and all—traveling all this way to see her home safely..."

Clay took the bottle from him and stared at it in disbelief. "Thank you," was all he could say.

"Now, you best be gettin' on. Jeremy will take you wherever ya need to go."

Jeremy wrangled the horses from the stable while Clay stood on the front porch. He longingly stared at the bottle, now beading with condensation, just begging for Clay's indulgence. He decided to wait. He wanted Megan to have the first taste; it would be his peace offering for being a couple days late.

The door opened again, and Watson came back out to see Clay off. "Also," he said as if he was finishing a thought from the conversation earlier, "we have all sorts of food and goods for trade in our store," he pointed towards a small barn across the field. "I know I probably won't be able to get you to part with that rifle, but we can always use some more ammo," he said gesturing towards Clay's magazine pouch, "and I'm always interested in seeing what other folks have for trade. Come on by anytime; the door is open."

"I think I'll take you up on that sometime," Clay said and shook Watson's hand.

When he heard the galloping horses fast approaching, Clay slung his pack over his shoulder, gave a quick wave to Watson, and got on the horse. He had never ridden one before and found it to be unpleasant. The physical exhaustion from the previous couple of days probably contributed a fair bit to the discomfort. After a few miles, he started to pick up on some cues, and with a little instruction from Jeremy, he was able to comfortably ride the remainder of the way. Clay quickly became envious of those with horses.

Dusk was imminent as they approached the city. About two miles from home, Clay gently pulled back on the reins, bringing his horse to a stop in a small field. "Whoa, boy." Dismounting, Clay explained to Jeremy, "I can make my way on foot from here."

Jeremy stopped a few feet in front of him and gave a puzzled look. His expression quickly shifted to indifference as he took the reins from Clay and immediately moved out, offering a lazy "Good luck" as they parted.

As Clay began walking in a direction away from his home; he was glad he had thought better of riding the horse into the city. His exhaustion made the last couple miles home seem like an impossible journey, but his family's safety was his main priority—and keeping their location secret was vital to maintaining security.

When Clay checked over his shoulder and could no longer see Jeremy, he ducked into a patch of trees and headed towards home.

It took him another forty-five minutes to reach the garage. His relief to be home was short-lived when he remembered the sixteen flights of stairs awaiting him. His muscles screamed just thinking about it. Having to stop every couple of floors to catch his breath, climbing the steps was a twenty minute ordeal. It was reminiscent of the first few weeks after they moved in, before his body had become accustomed to the ascent.

Home at last. He looked at his watch; it was a little past eight. The kids weren't in bed yet, so he went to bang on the door to be let in. As if he was holding a twenty pound weight, he swung his arm up to knock. Before he could touch the door, he heard the handle on the other side twist, and the door opened. Megan stood there, her arms crossed with a stare that could kill.

"Why do you insist on putting me through this every time you go out?" she asked as they walked down the hallway.

Clay didn't have it in him to argue with her and remained silent except for the occasional "I'm sorry." She continued accosting him about the lack of sleep she'd had the past two nights—something Clay could relate to tenfold, but knew she had no sympathy to offer.

Megan was still talking, but Clay wasn't processing her words. He felt lightheaded and just wanted to get some sleep. Each time he tried to speak up, she cut him off.

They walked into the lobby, and Clay cut her off midsentence. "Megan, just shut up for one second, would ya?"

They stopped walking; Megan was silent. She gave him a scowling look of incredulity. With her hands on her hips and a clenched jaw, her brown eyes—unlike the baby blues typical in his family—pierced him like daggers. Clay would have been as good as dead if he hadn't had a plan. He reached into his pack and pulled the bottle of milk out. She froze, her anger immediately dissolved. He imagined her expression was similar to how he must have looked back in Watson's living room. Her mouth dropped open.

"Is that...?" she trailed off.

Clay nodded. "Farm fresh," he added.

Her eyes were as big as the Texas sky. Suddenly, all the worrying, the anger, the hurt feelings were gone as she grabbed the bottle from his hand. She twisted the lid off, and the snapping pop of the metal lid was like angels playing the harp. She put the bottle up to her mouth, and then looked over at him as if to have permission.

"Go on."

She took several generous gulps, draining nearly a quarter of the bottle. She slowly pulled it away, a whitish mustache left behind. She closed her eyes and sighed with delight. "That," she paused for several seconds, "was like drinking paradise."

Clay took a couple of smaller sips. Since it was raw milk, it tasted a bit different, but he couldn't remember a drink ever tasting so good in his life. He wanted more, but didn't want to take that away from the kids. He knew he would be returning to Watson's anyhow.

Megan went to take another swig then suddenly stopped. "Oh, the kids!" she said, embarrassed she had nearly forgotten them. She turned to head towards the children's room where they were getting ready for bed. Clay didn't budge.

She stopped after a few feet, "Are you coming?"

He wanted to. He couldn't imagine how their faces would light up drinking such bliss, but he probably wouldn't even make it to the other side of the building before collapsing. With his energy now completely depleted, it was time for sleep. He would have to hear the details from Megan in the morning.

"You go on. Tell them to enjoy," he said and turned to go into his room.

He shut the door and closed the blinds on the windows facing the lobby. He placed his rifle on the conference table along with his vest, then tossed his bag over by the bed. He took off his shoes, noticing just how ragged they had become: full of holes, the shoestrings fraying in several spots. He couldn't remember the last time he found a "new" pair.

Despite his brain's desire to decompress from the past several days, his body won out, and he fell asleep mere moments after his head hit the pillow.

Chapter 8

Clay woke to laughter and shrieks muffled by the glass separating his room from the lobby. The crippling pain in his head prevented him from getting up. Dehydration had set in long before he and Kelsey reached the ranch, and he hadn't had anything to drink since the few sips of milk. His mouth felt as dry as the Sahara, and his lips were badly chapped. He stayed in bed for nearly an hour trying to convince himself to go get something to drink, but the thought of walking to the kitchen with all the screams and shrieks was not a pleasant one. And just like that, as if she heard his silent cry for help, Clay heard Megan's footsteps walking across the lobby to his room.

The door opened, and she came in holding a cup, "Good morning, brother. It's about time you woke up."

He gave her a dirty look. *Show some compassion, woman. I haven't slept in days,* he thought to himself.

She handed him the cup, and he drank it down without pausing to breathe.

Before he could ask, she handed him some pills. "Here, this will help with your head."

"How did you know?" Clay said in bewilderment.

"Clayton, what have I been doing pretty much every free moment I have had since Mom died?"

Clay nodded, knowing where she was going with her question.

"I've read all of Dad's medical books, like, three or four times."

Clay and Megan lost their mom ten months after the eruption. Once the pharmacies ran out of her medicine, it was just a matter of time; there was no way to save her. Their dad had not returned home, and they suspected he never would. He had gone out to the West Coast to assist in the relief efforts following the initial earthquakes that ravaged many of the major cities. He was still there when Yellowstone erupted. Clay and Megan were left in charge of their sisters Michelle, Alyssa, and Colleen.

Megan took it upon herself to increase her first aid knowledge with some of their father's medical books that he had collected over the years. As their father prepared to make the switch from police to paramedic, Megan watched and listened to him as he studied. She actually had planned to become a paramedic herself after graduating high school and had already been equipped to handle some basic medical situations.

That knowledge—those books—proved to be invaluable to the group's survival. She embraced the responsibility, and after doing CPR on Tyler a few years ago, she made everyone take a basic first aid course after their tenth birthday—a course complete with pictures, diagrams, and first aid dummies.

Megan was a bit of a geek when it came to presentations but seldom had a reason to make them anymore. So, when she found an excuse to do it, she went all out.

"I could see you were dehydrated when you got home, but I could also see that you were going to be too stubborn to stay up for another hour while I helped you rehydrate. You weren't complaining of a headache at the time, or acting too dizzy, so I figured you weren't *that* bad. I decided to let you get some sleep. I checked on you throughout the day, and at one point, you did actually take a few drinks of water before spilling what was left as you fell back to sleep."

Clay shook his head as if to loosen the cobwebs, "Wow, I don't remember that at all. In fact I—" Clay paused for a moment and gave her a muddled look. "Wait, did you say all day?"

"Yeah?"

"Today isn't Wednesday?"

"Nope," Megan said, "it's most definitely Thursday. You slept all day and night."

Clay was staggered, but it made sense. With the exception of the splitting headache, he actually felt pretty good. Well rested, even. He thanked her for the medicine, tossed them in his mouth, and drank the small amount of fluid—mostly backwash—that remained in the cup.

"Ah, crap!" Frustration steeped in Clay's voice, "I didn't go to the library yesterday," he said as he placed his hands on top of his head.

Clay visited a nearby library every Wednesday from eleven to noon. Anytime he or Megan came across children abandoned or orphaned, they told the children when and where to meet up in the event they needed a place to stay. Clay had started doing that a few months after he moved the family into the building. That way, if kids ever found themselves unable to survive alone, they knew they could always go to the library and join Clay's family. It was a sort of neutral ground that allowed Clay to help those in need without giving away their home address.

The library had been condemned, along with several other nearby buildings. Prior to the eruption, the whole area was being rezoned for a new community of condominiums. Bulldozers and other construction equipment sat around rusting and fading away like so many other things in the world.

Clay felt awful. He hadn't missed an appointment since he came up with the idea. Even though no one had ever met up with him, he felt like the one time he didn't go would be the first time someone would show up. It also gave him an opportunity to have some quiet time with his thoughts. He used it as time for prayer and reading his Bible.

"Clayton?" Megan inquired calmly, bringing Clay back to their conversation. "It's okay. Charlie and I went. Nobody showed up."

He was relieved. He hated the thought of some poor kid looking for help only to find an empty library.

"Speaking of Charlie," Megan said hesitantly, "he asked me if you had said anything to me about training."

Clay sighed deeply, "Yeah, I figured he might bring that up."

"He's mature enough," she said. "I hate the idea as much as you do, but he's ready. Don't wait too long."

She said nothing more and walked out. Clay stayed in bed for another hour or so until his grumbling stomach no longer tolerated his semi-vegetative state. He finally rose to his feet and stumbled from his room to the kitchen for some breakfast.

Breakfast was venison sausage patties, one of Clay's favorites. He scarfed them down and was already working on his third glass of water. A combination of the medicine and fluids had made some of the tension in his head ease, and Clay started to feel normal again. He told Megan what he had gotten from Vlad's while she ate her breakfast, which had long gone cold while she got all of the kids fed. She was thrilled—even about the hydration pack— much to his surprise. She knew that Clay pushed himself to the breaking point far too often, and many of those times it was because he wasn't properly hydrated. At least this way, Megan knew he'd be heading out with a decent amount to drink. The tinge of guilt he had felt since he traded for it disappeared.

Charlie walked into the kitchen. "Hey, Clay!"

"Morning, dude. What are you up to?"

Charlie poured himself a glass of water. "Oh, nothing much. One of the links on the swings broke, so I fixed that for the kids."

Clay couldn't help but laugh. Charlie reminded him of the kid in *Home Alone* when he bought some plastic army men at the grocery store and made sure the cashier knew they were "for the kids."

"Well, it sounds like you're a busy man today. Do you think you can squeeze me in around *2:30*?"

"I think I can pencil you in," he said as he walked out of the room.

Clay shook his head and asked Megan, "How does he even know phrases like that?"

Megan laughed as she took the last bite of breakfast. "Must be all the books he reads."

As Megan cleared the table and washed the dishes, Clay explained to her why he had been late.

He told her about Kelsey, the Screamers, and Watson's ranch with the trading opportunities there and how it might even cut down on the frequency of visits to Liberty. Megan was happy that Clay could reduce the long trips to Liberty, but seemed more excited with the prospect of having a regular source of fresh dairy.

"Aren't you glad I was late?" Clay joked.

She smiled at him as she dried the last plate. "All is forgiven, little brother."

Afterwards, Clay got to work on some small repairs around the house. He had Charlie help him for a couple of the more routine tasks. Claiming he just needed help, Clay used the opportunities for teaching Charlie. He was a quick learner, and after seeing things done only once or twice, he would know the task as if he had been doing it for years. Charlie's ability to retain knowledge was impressive.

Clay had finished the repairs so he decided to spend some time with the kids. He hadn't seen them much over the past week, and he tried to make up for lost time. He played some games with them, then read a few storybooks. He pulled out an old guitar that had once belonged to his father and played some music he had written. The kids danced around the room with glee, enjoying every strum Clay delivered.

After several of the kids had gone down for their afternoon nap, Clay went looking for Charlie again. Alone in the arts and crafts room, Charlie was sitting in a beanbag chair reading an adventure novel.

"Got a sec?" Clay asked.

Charlie dog-eared the page he was on and closed the book. He followed Clay down the long hall and ended up in front of the armory door. Charlie looked at him with bright eyes; he knew what it meant.

Though most of the kids knew where the armory was, Clay typically did not allow them inside.

"Four, twenty-nine, six," Clay said as he spun the padlock dial right to left to right. He unlocked and opened the door.

"Wow!" was all Charlie could say when they walked in. He looked around at the various firearms hanging from old server racks or leaning up against the wall. "So cool!" he said, still in awe.

Clay chuckled. There were quite a few guns in there, but only half as many as he had started with. A couple years into survival, he traded off most of the redundant calibers. He practically gave away his Five-Seven because there was almost no chance of finding ammo for it. Two years ago, he had to trade one that carried a lot of sentiment—his Colt M1911 that his great-grandfather had been issued during World War II. That was one of the hardest trades he had ever made, but Simon—the owner of Short Stop—gave him an incredible deal for the .45 caliber pistol. The trade fed the family for nearly a month.

"Where'd you get them all?" Charlie asked when he finally found his words.

"My father, mostly. A few I found or traded for."

"Boy, your dad sure liked guns!"

"He did indeed," Clay said with a smile. "I remember the very first time he took me deer hunting. I didn't want to go."

"Why not?" Charlie asked.

Clay shook his head and laughed, "Well, I didn't want to get up that early. Plus I'd miss watching my Saturday morning cartoons."

Charlie nodded as if he understood the serious business that was Saturday morning television. He was only five years old when the tremors hit, but like most kids, cartoons had already become a daily ritual.

"I remember complaining about it as he woke me up at five in the morning. But once we got outside and started walking, I just looked up and gazed at the stars. And just like that," Clay snapped his finger, "my attitude did a one-eighty, and I let myself enjoy the opportunity to bond with my father. I grew to appreciate those times. Being in a house with my mom and four sisters, my dad and I were severely outnumbered."

Charlie knew that feeling. Including Clay, the boys living in the tower were outnumbered two-to-one. "So, did you get one?" Charlie asked with enthusiasm.

Clay shook his head, "Nope. We were in a tree stand and up comes this big ol' deer—a buck, at least eight points. I swear, I had the thing right in my sights, but I missed him by a mile. I thought I had let my dad down, but he just looked at me and smiled, then said," Clay deepened his voice mimicking his dad's, "'That was a great try. I know you'll get him next time.'"

Charlie looked at him with eagerness to hear the end of the story, "Well? Did you get him?"

Clay nodded. "The very next time we went out. My dad told me it was the same buck. I didn't think it was, but I still like to think maybe he was right."

Like he was listening to his favorite author tell a tale, Charlie was genuinely interested in hearing about Clay's past and was hanging on every word he had to say. To Charlie, it was the same opportunity for bonding that Clay had with his father.

Charlie's focus eventually turned to the firearms in the room. He asked about the different guns so Clay went through them all, telling him the name, caliber, and how he had acquired it.

"What about that one?" Charlie asked, pointing to a small rifle over on the reloading bench.

Clay walked over and picked it up, "This is an M1 Carbine." He unfolded the stock and made sure the chamber was clear. "This used to belong to my great-grandfather. He used this very gun to fight the Nazis in World War II. He was a paratrooper."

Charlie looked at him quizzically, "What's a paratrooper?"

"Paratroopers were soldiers who would go into battle by jumping out of airplanes. He was part of a group called the 101st Airborne, one of the most well-known divisions of the United States Armed Forces."

"Whoa!" Charlie replied enthusiastically.

"This gun," Clay said holding the rifle up, "was what he carried in almost every battle. It's small and light. The stock folds to make it even smaller...He used this to defend his country, and now *you* will have it to defend your family."

Charlie lit up like the Fourth of July, a grin from ear to ear. He leaned in close and examined the rifle from muzzle to buttplate. "This is mine?" he asked.

Clay nodded.

After showing Charlie a bit more about the gun, Clay went over the four golden rules to shooting. "Keep your finger off the trigger until you are ready to fire; never point at anything you don't intend to shoot; know your target and beyond; and treat every gun as if it was loaded."

Clay paused for a moment and channeled his father's stern voice again. "And remember, there's no such thing as firearm accidents, only negligence."

Charlie listened and repeated the rules after Clay finished speaking.

"You ready to go to the range?"

"Oh yeah!" Charlie squealed, letting the kid in him slip through his mature façade.

Less than a half mile away was an indoor shooting range. Clay was particularly excited to find it when they moved in. Most of the brass had been picked clean, but he dug out several pounds of lead from the backstop that he was able to trade. Clay usually went there once a year to make sure all the guns remained properly sighted. The structure was built to muffle the sound of the shots, and unless someone was relatively close by, no one would hear the shooting. It was a lot safer than target practice outside.

It only took about ten minutes to get there. Charlie, trying to keep his excitement in check, had to force himself to walk and not run. They walked around back to a small alley and got in through the rear entrance—the front had been boarded up by the owners before being abandoned. Clay shut the door and tied one end of a bungee cord around the handle, then stretched the other end of the cord to a nearby eye-hook anchored into the cinderblock wall.

Charlie was wide-eyed as he looked around the retail section of the store for a few minutes. There wasn't much left to scavenge, mostly superfluous items that really had no value in their present day world. *But still,* Charlie thought, *how incredible is this place?*

He followed Clay through a couple of doors, and they found themselves in the rifle bays. Clay set up some old cans on a makeshift platform he had made from a couple of sawhorses and cardboard the first time he visited.

"My father first taught me how to shoot with a .22 long rifle. However, it was hard to find that ammo *before* the eruption, let alone after. So, now we only hunt small game with .22; we train with the real deal," he said as he tapped the side of the M1's stock.

Clay once again went over the safety instructions, and then he explained how to use the sights, load the magazine, and charge the weapon. He handed Charlie the rifle and a magazine. Charlie clumsily put the magazine into the rifle and yanked back on the bolt. Clay watched carefully and ensured Charlie followed the safety protocols he had explained earlier; he did well.

Charlie raised the rifle and tilted his head behind the peep sight. As expected, he stuck his right elbow out so that it was nearly horizontal. For whatever reason, it was the default position most shooters had. Even Clay still fought the urge at times.

"Pull that elbow in," Clay said as he demonstrated the proper stance. "Keep that elbow in as close to your body as you can. Remember, someday your targets might be shooting back at you. Make yourself as small of a target to hit as you can."

Charlie made the proper adjustment and once again took aim; he closed one eye and lined up his target. He pulled the trigger and sent one of the cans flying through the air.

"Nice shot, Charlie!"

"Thanks," Charlie replied with a nervous laugh.

Clay looked at him, then at the cans. The second one was lying on the floor a few feet back. "You weren't aiming for that one, were you?" he asked.

"No."

Clay laughed. "Well, we'll pretend you were," he said and patted Charlie on the shoulder.

Clay critiqued a few things he noticed and answered Charlie's questions. Charlie shot again, this time grazing the first can. It danced around on the cardboard then dropped to the floor. Charlie's follow-up shot was a direct hit to the third can, then the fourth. He paused for a moment and looked at Clay with a smile. He continued to the fifth can, narrowly missing it.

"Remember what I said, just slow down and squeeze the trigger. Don't pull it."

The fifth can went spiraling into the air like an out of control rocket. Charlie then set his sights on the sixth can. He squeezed the trigger, and the sixth can exploded, sending expired cream of mushroom flying through the air. Charlie stepped back in disbelief; his jaw dropped.

"Did you know that was gonna happen?" Charlie asked excitedly.

Clay smiled.

"What about the food, though?"

"That can was bloated—something I found a few weeks ago. Shouldn't eat food from a bloated can. You'll get very, *very* sick."

Charlie made another mental note of Clay's advice.

He had Charlie remove the magazine from the M1 and clear the action. They walked down the range, moved the table to fifty yards, and set the cans back up. Charlie took down all six targets in just seven rounds. He was a natural. Since Charlie was comfortable with the M1 carbine, Clay had him move on to the AR-15. Even though that was Clay's rifle, he wanted Charlie to know how to shoot any and all guns. Whether they found another one in the future or if Charlie suddenly inherited Clay's, it was a skill he needed to have. Charlie's training would encourage proficiency with all of the firearms Clay owned.

Intimidated by the much louder boom and the slightly heavier recoil, Charlie was a bit reluctant at first, but after a few rounds he felt comfortable with it. The holographic sights made aiming a cinch.

"I like that one better," Charlie told Clay as he pointed to the M1 Carbine.

"Hey, ya can't go wrong with a classic," Clay said as he put the AR down. He pulled the Scout from the sling over his shoulder. "Now *this* one is going to have the most kick of all."

Much to Clay's surprise, Charlie really liked the Scout. It was a superb design to have such a small rifle shoot a .308 with minimal recoil. Clay wanted Charlie to be familiar with it, but only allowed him to shoot five rounds—Clay's inventory in that caliber was thin as it was.

"That was so awesome!" he said to Clay.

After rifles, they moved on to pistols. Clay had given him the Smith & Wesson bodyguard, a compact .380 that was good for a beginner. Charlie struggled with the pistol the most, but was competent enough to use it as a fallback weapon. They would work on it more after winter.

Clay and Charlie collected the ejected brass and made their way home just before nightfall. Charlie was eager to tell the other kids all about his natural talent as a marksman. An honorary paratrooper, Clay called him.

As night drew on, Clay set up a table in the kitchen and turned on a lantern. Megan took advantage of the light and started reading. Much to Clay's surprise, it was a fiction, not one of her medical books.

Clay showed Charlie how to fieldstrip the M1 and walked him through proper cleaning. He had Charlie wipe down the bolt while he worked on the receiver.

"What's it like to kill someone?" Charlie asked out of nowhere, a tinge of trepidation in his voice.

Clay was a bit taken aback by the blunt question. He pondered how to best answer before finally saying, "Charlie, I'm not going to sugarcoat it. It's one of the worst feelings I've ever experienced." Clay sighed deeply as he carefully chose the next words to say. "In all likelihood, you will find yourself in a position at some point where you will need to decide: kill or be killed. Unfortunately, it's the world we live in now."

Charlie looked down, his excitement which had shone throughout the day had diminished. It was replaced with a solemn understanding of what his new responsibilities entailed.

"I've killed many men before, Charlie. To this day, I get sick each time I am forced to pull the trigger." Clay lowered his head, ashamed to continue, "But each time, I notice that trigger gets easier and easier to pull."

Charlie's expression was blank as he stared at the disassembled rifle on the table, unsure of how to respond.

Clay continued, "My dad once told me a story about an Indian Chief talking to his grandson. The Chief had said, 'Inside every man is a battle—a battle between two wolves: one evil; the other good.' His grandson then asked, 'Which wolf wins?' to which the chief simply replied, 'The one that you feed.'"

Charlie was quiet as the tale Clay recited sank in. He polished the bolt with a rag, wiping away the excess solvent.

"Don't feed the evil wolf, Charlie. You will be tempted in so many ways to do so, but that's not who we are. That's not who *you* are. Don't ever let it win," Clay said with a firm yet affectionate tone.

"Yes sir," Charlie said and went back to cleaning.

Midnight had rolled around. Charlie had gone to bed while Clay finished cleaning the guns. The following day, Clay would give Charlie the M1 with an empty magazine, tasking him to carry it around for a week while Clay paid close attention to his safety procedures. If all went well, Clay was planning on giving Charlie ammo and promoting him to one of the defenders of the home.

Megan called it a night and retired to her bedroom, which was a long closet that had once housed a copy machine and some office supplies. Clay gathered the guns and put them back in the armory. As he was heading to bed, he got lightheaded for a moment and leaned against the wall. He thought he was about to faint when he heard the rattling, and felt the vibrations tumble through the drywall. It was a tremor. Probably not much above a three-pointer, but enough to feel. That was the third one in the last month. There had been an increase in quake activity in the last year. He had no idea whether or not that meant anything bad—there were no longer geologists on TV speculating what it meant for the future—but each time it happened, he was less and less comfortable with sleeping 150 feet in the air.

Chapter 9

Clay was once again gathering items to barter. He was headed to Watson's this time, and was glad that he had found some tools behind a bench at an old mechanic's shop last week. Hand tools were always in demand and were among the most valuable items to trade. It was fortunate timing to find such rare items since his trade was for a special occasion.

Bethany was turning two, and per Megan's birthday tradition for the children, Bethany got to choose the birthday meal. Typically, birthday meals fell short of Megan's expectations—this was especially the case with Lona's request for beef stroganoff—but regardless of how it looked or tasted, it always brought back fond memories for those who could recall having the meals in the past. Having been born after the eruption, Bethany had never tasted food cooked with all of the proper ingredients. After carefully scanning each page of a cookbook for over an hour, the birthday girl picked macaroni and cheese. The dish was like a beacon for kids, even those who had never tasted it before. Ordinarily, such a dish would be in the disaster zone for Megan, but with Watson having the majority of the ingredients available for trade, it would likely be an exquisite meal for the family to enjoy.

Megan, in an effort to educate the kids as best she could despite the circumstances, had just finished telling them about the Model-T and the substantial impact the first line-assembled vehicle had on the world. Most of the younger children's eyes had glazed over, but a few of the older ones remained interested, asking questions and talking about it later in conversation. Megan had had no plans to be a teacher, but knew the importance of providing an education for the kids, regardless of whether or not the world would ever return to a normal state.

Afterwards, the kids all zoomed by Clay as he was locking up his room, each one saying "Hi!" as they passed in a frenzy to get up the stairs to the roof for as much playtime as they could squeeze in before winter hit.

"Everyone has to wear a jacket!" Megan shouted as she walked towards Clay.

It was late August, and the afternoon highs barely climbed out of the 50's. It was looking likely that the first snow would happen by mid-September, then it was all downhill from there until about May.

"Here's what I need," Megan said casually as she turned her attention to Clay and handed him a list of ingredients, as if she was just sending him to the supermarket. "If he has it, get it," she said, ultimately giving him no room to argue.

Clay looked at the list. The dairy wouldn't likely be a problem, but he didn't know what else Watson might have. "I'll do my best," he said, then folded the piece of paper and stuffed it into his pocket.

He gave Megan a heads-up that he might be a day or two late. With winter fast approaching, the window to scavenge was nearly closed. Clay hadn't ventured down to Watson's area all that much, and he had noticed several potential spots as he escorted Kelsey home. Even though most places had been picked clean years ago, Clay had a knack for finding goods that others overlooked. He attributed it to his thoroughness.

After saying goodbye to Clay, Megan went up to the roof to tend to the garden and keep an eye on the kids during recess. She very much enjoyed working in the garden; it felt more like a hobby than a chore, which brought some sense of normalcy to her life. It took her mind off of being a mother to ten, the family doctor, chef, seamstress, maid, and all the other roles she filled after modern conveniences ceased to exist. Gardening was a pastime for her; something she'd done with her mother; a connection to her childhood.

Clay walked down the hall to Charlie's room. Besides earning a gun, Charlie's recent promotion awarded him some other perks, such as his own bedroom with no bedtime. Though his room was right next to the other kids, he still had privacy and an area to call his own.

Clay walked into the room and saw Charlie reading; the kid was a bookworm most days. His M1 was leaning up against the wall within arm's reach, per Clay's instruction.

Charlie looked up. "Hey Clay. Are you heading out?" he asked.

"Yep, shouldn't be gone more than a couple days, maybe not even that." Clay reached into his pocket and pulled out two loaded magazines. "Here. Just in case."

The kid in Charlie wanted to smile, but the young man he was becoming suppressed it. Over the last week, Clay had stressed the point that having a gun was not a game, but rather a responsibility. Charlie was always serious when it came to anything about guns. So much so that Clay had to tell him to relax just the day before. Charlie had only known firearms to be an important, life-saving tool in a brutal world; he never really experienced the recreational aspect of them.

Charlie took the magazines from Clay and placed one into the gun and the other in the cargo pocket of his pants. He gave Clay a nod. "I won't let you down!"

"I know you won't," Clay said. "And remember," he continued, "don't chamber that round unless you need to, understand?"

"Yes sir."

"Good. You are the man of the house while I'm gone. Keep everyone safe. I'll be back soon." Clay looked down and saw that Charlie was reading *Ender's Game*, "Oh man, I remember the first time I read that one; I couldn't put it down."

Charlie's serious demeanor lifted, and he smiled, "It's really good so far, I like Ender."

And what kid his age wouldn't? Ender, although just a boy, lived the dream that most kids had: be the best soldier there ever was. The book encouraged tactical thinking and strategy as much as, if not more than, weaponry and combat. Ender constantly found himself in situations that really made the reader think. And, with any luck, it would cause Charlie to be more strategic and less confrontational than instinct encouraged. Become a scalpel instead of a broadsword.

Charlie returned to reading as Clay walked out and headed to the kitchen to grab a little bit of food and fill up his hydration pack. As always, Megan had a small care package waiting for him. He grabbed that and was on his way.

Watson's farm was a comfortable fourteen miles away, a more desirable four hour trek compared to the full day's journey to reach Liberty. Clay wasn't sure what Watson had to trade, but he knew he wasn't going to find fresh dairy anywhere else. Vlad's unique inventory—along with the pleasure of visiting the small community—would ensure Clay's continued business. But more mundane trading would likely go to Watson.

Clay looked down at his watch as he approached the gate: three hours and forty-five minutes; he made good time.

"Howdy," Clay said as he stepped up to the gate.

"Hi there," the guard said, searching his brain to recall Clay's name.

It had been over a week since he and Kelsey had limped their way to the ranch. Clay could see that the guard couldn't remember who he was.

"I'm Clay. I think we met a little over a week ago. I helped Kelsey get back home."

The light switch flipped in the young man's mind, and everything came to the forefront of his head. "Oh yeah, that's right! Duh! Sorry about that, Clay. We get a lot of people that come and try to trade here. Believe it or not, we're very selective about who we do business with."

"Oh?" Clay responded. It wasn't altogether surprising to hear that. Most communities were reluctant to open up trading to outsiders, though Clay got the impression the VIP list for this place was even more exclusive than Liberty. "Well, I believe I should be on the guest list."

"Oh yeah! Definitely," he exclaimed, as if Clay was silly to even ask. "Mr. Watson himself said that you are welcome to come here anytime."

Clay walked up to the gate but it was still locked.

"Forgive me," the guard said as he unlocked the gate and opened it. "Here I am yammering away..."

"Thanks," Clay said as he walked through the gate. He stopped just as he passed through, trying to recall the gatekeeper's name. "Derrick, isn't it?"

"Yes sir," the young man said with a tilt of his head. "Enjoy your stay."

Clay leisurely made his way over to Watson's house. He watched as various folks busied themselves with chores and tasks for the day. It was simply amazing to see such things. It was commerce: a carpenter sanding down a beautifully crafted hutch; an older woman delivering fresh eggs to a family; a young boy playing jacks on the porch with some of his pals while their mothers sat in rocking chairs knitting, talking amongst themselves. It was as if he had stepped out of a wasteland right into the 1950's. Most everyone that made eye contact with Clay either smiled or said hello—a bit of a warmer welcome than last time, though the situation was substantially different.

He walked up to the porch and Matthew stepped outside, greeting him at the top step.

"Hey Clay, good to see you again. What can I do for ya?"

"I'm here to see Mr. Watson. I have some things he might be interested in," he said as he turned his body slightly to reveal the backpack.

Before Matthew had a chance to respond, a voice from inside interrupted, "Well, hello there, Clay,"

Watson said boisterously. "What brings you this way?"

"Thought I would take you up on your offer to do some trading."

"That sounds good to me," Watson said as he pushed the storm door open and walked out on the porch. "Let's head on over to the store then, shall we?"

All three of them left the porch and walked down a small dirt path that went between various buildings. It was set up like a miniature downtown street.

Watson was a man in his mid-sixties, and was relatively fit for his age, but despite his physical stature, he still walked a bit slowly. Clay didn't mind. Life for him usually meant moving fast. Slowing down and being able to enjoy a moment was always appreciated.

"It's quite a nice little community you have here," Clay said with admiration.

"Thank you. It's my land, but the folks here," he said as he gestured towards the people who were out and about, "are the ones that make it a community."

"So, how many live here?"

"A hundred and sixty-two."

"Actually," Matthew interjected, "a hundred and sixty-three."

Watson smiled. "Deborah have the baby?" Watson asked.

"Yep," Matthew smiled. "A baby boy. Elijah."

Watson returned the smile. "So, a hundred sixty-three it is. We have a lot of good folks living in this town. Many of them came here with their bachelor's degree in political sciences or liberal arts from those fancy schools up in Boston or out in California. I tell ya, some of them couldn't even fry themselves an egg when they got here. And now..." he paused and looked around, "I bet you couldn't pick one out of a line of career farmers," he said proudly.

Clay did a quick glance around—Watson wasn't lying.

The store was a small addition on a barn and was about twenty-five feet wide and twelve feet deep. A bell hanging just above the door bounced around as they walked in. It reminded Clay of an old meat market his family used to frequent.

A larger, middle-aged woman came from a doorway behind the counter and saw the three standing there. "Good afternoon, Mr. Watson," she said before busying herself with some small tasks around the store.

Watson walked behind the counter and assumed the role of the clerk. "So, what have ya got for me today?" he asked.

Before Clay responded, the bell above the door rang again. Jeremy walked in and greeted everyone. When he noticed Clay, he walked up to the counter and acted as if he had been there the whole time. He nodded at Clay to carry on.

Clay lifted the bag onto the counter top; a weighty thud followed. He could tell Watson was curious. Trading was an essential way of life now, but it was always exciting to discover what someone was willing to put up for trade.

Clay pulled things out of his pack one at a time. First came the ammo: 200 rounds of .38 Special. He had a revolver that shot the ammo, but he seldom used it. It was never a good fit for him, but he kept it anyway as a rainy day gun. He had a fair bit of ammo for it, so the 200 cartridges weren't a big loss. He continued to pull some various items out of the pack, including the nice tool set he had found at the mechanics. He had piqued Watson's interest already, but he was saving the best for last. He watched for Watson's reaction as he removed the last item.

Watson stepped back and stood in awe. "Son, is that what it claims to be? Or are you just teasin' me?"

"Not teasing, sir."

Watson took the big, plastic red can from Clay and removed the black lid. To his astonishment, it was still sealed. He grabbed the tab on the foil seal and started to peel it back.

"Hey now," Clay said with a stern but joking voice. "You open it you bought it."

Watson tore it back and inhaled deeply. The sweet aroma wafted through the room like a Columbian breeze. Even Jeremy closed his eyes as he savored the whiff.

They haggled back and forth for a little bit, but the advantage was all but Clay's after Watson opened the container. Ordinarily, Watson was a shrewd negotiator, but after smelling coffee grounds for the first time in three years, Clay had the deal in the bag.

"Margaret," Watson called for the middle-aged woman who had wandered to the back during negotiation.

"Yes, Mr. Watson?" she said as she peeked around the doorway.

"Would you be a dear and get our friend here three quarts of milk, a block of butter, a pound of cheese, two dozen eggs, and a few vegetables?"

"Yes sir," she said and promptly left.

Clay was elated. He felt like he had just made the deal of the century. Everything he traded he either had more of, or not much use for, and neither he nor Megan really cared for coffee. They had a small can they would dip into from time to time should the need arise for a late night, but they had both learned how to operate without caffeine. It was a finite resource that they only used when they needed a jolt. The last time Clay had sipped on a cup of joe was six months ago when he had thought somebody followed him home and was convinced they would try to attack. He had already been up for thirty-six hours and didn't want to go to sleep. Megan thought he was just delusional. She was probably right, he eventually conceded.

The woman came back with the items. It was going to be tricky to carry everything back home, but it would be well worth it. While he was trying to figure out how best to pack everything in his bag, the bell above the door jingled again.

"Clay?"

He didn't need to turn around to know who was there—the voice was unmistakable—but as he did, he smiled, "Kelsey, I was hoping to run into you."

She walked over and gave him a hug. Jeremy glared at the them both before walking to the other side of the store to look at the new goods Margaret had just set out on the shelves.

Kelsey and Clay chatted for a few minutes until Watson, looking at his watch, inserted himself into their conversation. "I gotta run here, kids, but before I go, Kelsey did you have anything for me?"

Kelsey reached into a pouch hanging off her side and pulled out two nine volt batteries. Watson took them from her and dabbed his tongue on the two terminals; he made a funny face and pulled it away quickly. He repeated the same thing on the other battery.

"I found them yesterday on my way home."

Watson nodded, "Do you want credit, payment, or trade?"

"Payment's fine."

Watson pulled out a little pocket-sized notebook and wrote something inside.

"So, Clay, I was getting ready to head out and do some scavenging. You interested in joining me?" Kelsey asked.

Clay had planned on scouting the area anyway, but having Kelsey to chat with would make it much more enjoyable. Excited to hear her request, Clay responded, "That sounds great! Just let me grab my stuff and," he paused as he stared at his purchase. "Uhm."

"No problem," Watson answered the question Clay hadn't asked. "I'll have Margaret put your stuff back in the ice box. You just let her know when you are ready to retrieve it."

"I owe you one," Clay said.

"Y'all be safe," Watson said as he walked out the door.

****

Clay and Kelsey wasted no time and headed south to check out a few buildings of interest that she had spotted on one of her trips a few weeks back. They started with an old ma-and-pa gas station but turned up empty-handed. The veterinary clinic was the same story, which surprised Clay. Usually he could find *something* in such a large facility, but no such luck this time.

They decided to cut their losses and head back to the farm. They took a different route back and came across a roller skating rink. In its prime, it was probably the place to be for the small town of— according to the sign they saw a mile back—a population of 752.

The long, windowless brick building was consumed by creepers, vines, and any other plant that could latch on to the masonry. The cracking white and purple paint revealed the faded red color of the raw bricks beneath. At the far end was a small overhang covering a double-door entry. They stepped through where windows once made up the door and eased their way in.

They walked down a short, declining hallway and turned on their flashlights as they lost light from the doors. It was an ominous sight to behold, like something out of a horror movie. Clay could almost hear the sound of children's laughter and swing music as kids and adults alike did the limbo on roller skates. Trash and debris littered the rotting wooden floor; several planks had started to bend upward.

Big, dark buildings like the rink usually yielded some good finds. With low visibility, even in the daylight, scavengers usually missed valuable items. Clay and Kelsey began to search slowly and thoroughly.

"So, what's the deal with Watson?" Clay asked.

"What do you mean?" Kelsey asked as she crouched down to sift through some trash on the floor.

"Well, the two times I've met the guy he's been as nice as can be—probably more so than any other person I've met in a long time. The whole place just seems great. Yet, you don't really seem to like it there."

Kelsey shrugged, "Yeah, I mean it's nice and all, but..." she trailed off.

"But what?"

"It's complicated."

"How so?"

She sighed, reluctant to share. "About a year and a half ago, I was coming through the area with Dakota. We were on the brink of starvation. We had been on a long stretch of road, heading towards Oklahoma, and there were very few places to search for food. I had no way to hunt for food—not that I was finding any animals to hunt anyway. So, we just toughed it out. But we both had reached our breaking point. I was just about ready to collapse when I heard a cow.

"I practically sprinted up the small hill off the side of the road and came to a barbed wire fence. There were three or four of 'em there. So big; so much food. I was out of my mind to try and kill the thing with my knife. After I tried to slit its throat, it knocked me down and took off, screaming and crying and scaring the rest of them away. I had put Dakota down near the fence, and when I got back to her...that's when I met Watson."

"I don't imagine he was too happy with you," Clay said.

"No, not really. He only butchers the cattle when it's absolutely necessary, and I made it necessary for that one," she paused as she picked up a nickel and stuffed it in her pocket. "I *am* grateful, though. Most folks would have just shot me on the spot for doing what I did. At least he's letting me stay there and work off the debt—as insurmountable as it is."

That's true, Clay thought. Without rule of law, many people settled even petty crimes with execution. Killing a man's cattle was by no means petty, either. Although he could understand more clearly where Kelsey was coming from and why staying there wasn't as pleasant of an experience as it seemed for others, he also thought it was very generous for Watson to give her an opportunity to settle the debt, not to mention she had a warm place to sleep and access to food for her and Dakota.

"How much more do you owe?"

"I don't even know anymore," she said, sounding a bit frazzled. "I used to keep track but it's a lot, so I just stopped doing the math."

Clay could tell she was getting worked up talking about it, so he stopped with the questions. The whole thing made him feel uncomfortable, but he wanted to know more. Perhaps, with time, she would open up to him about it.

They had finished searching the rink, finding a couple things of value. They moved to the other side of the building to check some lockers that had long been emptied. The concession stand was the same story. Everything in the main area had been picked clean.

As they made their way to the back of the large room, they came up to a pair of industrial doors; they were riddled with dents, scratches, and even a few bullet holes. Clay grabbed the handle; it was still locked. If it was still locked from the inside, there was a good chance what was in there seven years ago was still there now.

He observed the efforts made by countless people in the past and wondered how on earth he was going to break through. It wasn't like cracking a safe, and without any tools, it was going to be near impossible.

They searched around to see what they could find. Clay brought back a roller skate and began to hammer on the handle, but the skate gave way long before the door. Clay thought about drilling it with a couple of rounds from the AR-15, but it was getting late and Screamers could already be out. They didn't need to draw any unnecessary attention to themselves. They had just about given up when Kelsey had an idea.

"See that?" she said pointing her flashlight at a vent on the wall near the ceiling.

Clay looked at it and wondered if she could fit. It couldn't have been more than two feet wide and probably eighteen inches high. He knew for sure *he* couldn't get through.

"You're crazy," Clay said.

Kelsey smiled at him, "Come on. Give me a boost."

Clay positioned himself in front of the wall and linked his fingers together. Kelsey stepped on his hands and stood up straight. Clay grunted from the weight as he lifted her a bit.

"You trying to tell me something, Clay?" she said jokingly.

"That I need to work out more."

"Good answer."

Kelsey pulled a small fixed blade out of a sheath and began to pry at the vent. The screws put up no fight at all, and the vent popped right off. Dust and other particulates exploded off and rained down on Clay.

"Wish me luck," Kelsey said as she did her best to push off of Clay's hands and pull herself up through the opening."

The vent was merely a hole in the wall and not connected to any sort of ductwork. He heard her fall to the floor below followed by a loud clatter and hissed profanity.

"You okay?" Clay shouted as loud as he dared.

"Yeah, I'm fine. Just not one of my more graceful moments. Glad no one saw it," she said with a chuckle. "Let me see if I can find my way to those doors."

Clay returned to the doors. He began to pace back and forth as the minutes ticked by. He started to worry. If anyone was back there, he had no way to get to her. She was on her own. He should have given her a gun.

After a few more unsettling minutes, he heard some noise from the other side and saw light dancing beneath the doors. "Kelsey?"

"It's me," she replied.

Clay heard the door unlock, but Kelsey couldn't open them. After a couple of rams with his shoulder, Clay had burst through causing Kelsey to stumble backwards. She was covered in dust with cobwebs clinging to her hair; she looked like an extra in a campy horror movie from the 70's. She had a big grin on her face.

"You're never going to believe what I just found back there!"

Chapter 10

Kelsey shut and locked the doors and led Clay through the series of hallways. He could hardly contain his excitement at all the rooms that were just begging to be searched. Finding such an undisturbed place had become rare and was like coming downstairs on Christmas morning to all the gifts under the tree.

They walked into a break room. It was relatively bare but not ransacked. It appeared as if the owner had taken everything himself and then locked up—perhaps hoping to reopen someday.

Kelsey practically skipped across the room to a closed door. She grabbed the handle and turned around to look at Clay.

"Are you ready?" she asked before she swung open the door.

Clay's mouth hung wide open, "Are you serious?"

Kelsey gave him a friendly punch to the shoulder. He looked at her, still stunned, then smiled.

It took a while for it to sink in. They stood in the doorway of the supply closet, staring inside. Clay was afraid to blink, lest when his eyes reopened the closet would be empty. But it was not empty. It was quite full. There were two large boxes of individual potato chip packs, several boxes of candy, and a couple twelve-packs of soda.

"Unbelievable," Clay said while staring at all the goods.

"So, what do ya say? Fifty-fifty?" Kelsey asked.

"Sure," Clay said as he walked over to the goods, still thinking a good, hard pinch was in order.

He picked up a case of his favorite caffeine infused citrus soda, a box of candy bars, and a dozen or so bags of chips and carried them to one of the tables in the break room.

"The rest is yours," he said to her.

Kelsey gave him a perplexed look. "What? That's not even a quarter of what's there. Why?"

"I imagine Watson will pay well for this. It's a good score, not one I ever thought I would find. Heck, all that," he pointed to the goods he had set aside for himself, "is more than I ever imagined I would find."

Kelsey's eyes began to well up, her voice got shaky, "Clay, no, this is as much yours as it is mine. You have people who count on you to provide food."

"Bah!" Clay said and waved his hand. "It's all chemicals, sugar, and starches. Hardly what I would call actual sustenance."

"Yeah, but they can bring comfort..."

"That's true," he said, "which is why I didn't give you *all* of it. My family and I will enjoy that plenty. The rest will benefit you much more than us."

"Clay," she said softly, "I don't know what to say." She reached out and hugged him. "Thank you."

"You're welcome. Just don't let Watson get 'em for cheap. He nearly fainted when he smelled the coffee I traded him. He knows the power of creature comforts like this, and he will be able to mark them up quite a bit in his store.

Kelsey smiled warmly, gave Clay another hug, and pecked him on the cheek. "You're so sweet."

He found himself at a loss of words after the friendly kiss but managed to stammer out, "You're welcome."

They figured it was going to take at least two, maybe three, trips to take everything back to the ranch. They were only about seven miles away, so it would be easy to finish tomorrow.

They scavenged the rest of the rooms in the back area finding quite a few smaller items, but nothing that could measure up to the discovery in the break room. Clay picked a few things for his family and then donated the rest to Kelsey's debt.

Exhausted, they set up camp in the manager's office which had a love seat along one of the walls. They split a chocolate bar before settling in for bed. Kelsey lay down on the loveseat, her legs dangling over the armrest. She used her jacket as a blanket and fell asleep quite quickly.

Clay sat in the manager's chair and propped his legs up on the desk. Much to his surprise, he wasn't all that uncomfortable. Taking a cue from Kelsey, he draped his coat over his upper body and tucked his arms in. Unlike the last time they had been together, Clay had no trouble sleeping...until he heard the noises.

It was early in the morning when the loud thud had come from down the hall. Startled, Clay nearly fell out of his chair when he heard it.

"What was that?" Kelsey said in a panicked whisper.

Clay was already on his feet heading for the door, his rifle at the ready. "Stay here," he said, "I'll go check it out. If something happens, just hide under the desk," he said as he handed Kelsey his pistol.

She acknowledged his command by standing behind the desk.

The sounds continued, echoing through the otherwise silent building. Following the audible trail, it took him right to where he had expected—the same doors they couldn't get into earlier that night.

He heard three or four voices on the other side. Not Screamers. Although Clay couldn't understand what they were saying, their calm chatter distinguished them from the babbling psychopaths he had expected. Most likely just a group scavenging for food like him, but that didn't make them any less of a threat.

The crashing sound intensified as the men began alternating blows on the door in an attempt to weaken it. Suddenly, there was a heavy impact that caused enough of a gap from the door frame for Clay to see their flashlights coming through between the doors. He raised his rifle and took aim. He thought about firing a warning shot or two, but that might just cause them to respond in kind, and he had no idea what he was dealing with on the other side of the heavy steel doors. Plus, he would lose all element of surprise should they successfully breach.

"I've almost got it," one of them said loud enough for Clay to understand.

Anxiety with a hefty dose of adrenaline shot through Clay's body as he waited. Despite the chill in the air, a bead of sweat rolled down his forehead and on to the tip of his nose. The gap in the door seemed to increase with each successive blow. Clay wrapped his finger around the trigger, squeezing ever so slightly. He felt the pounding of every heartbeat in his head. They were almost through.

Silence.

He heard one of them shush the others. What was happening? Something wasn't right.

"Screamers!" one of them shouted.

Clay listened from the other side of the doors as the group of men were brutally slaughtered with frightening efficiency by the Screamers. It felt as if the massacre went on for hours, when in reality it was mere minutes. The screams eventually hushed; the cries fell silent. And after Clay was able to shake off the horrific sounds, he returned to the office.

Kelsey nearly shot him when he returned. Even she had heard some of the screams from the attack and was terrified she had been listening to her new friend being murdered.

"They're gone," he said as he returned to the chair.

Neither of them could fall back to sleep after the attack. They both wanted to get out of there and get back to Watson's, but the last thing they wanted to do was run into a group of Screamers now. So, they both pretended to sleep until dawn.

Morning took forever to arrive. Clay noticed how ironic it was that it always came too quickly when you were sleeping well, but not fast enough when you anxiously awaited it's arrival

They dumped the bags of chips and candy bars into a couple of trash bags. Clay took the cans of soda out of the box and put them in his backpack along with his cut of the snacks. They hid the remainder of the goods the best they could, seeing as the locked doors were all but compromised. They would return a bit later to retrieve the rest.

They walked back out into the main room and saw the remnants of the battle that occurred early in the morning. Almost perfectly centered in the roller rink was a massive pool of blood. Too much blood for any victim to survive. Markings and crude drawings surrounded the pool, which was common to see at a Screamer's kill site.

Even though Clay was preparing to shoot those same men himself, he couldn't help but feel sorry for their demise. It was one thing to be shot and killed; it was something entirely different to be hacked to death.

Clay and Kelsey headed for the exit. They both felt a huge weight roll off their shoulders as they were greeted by the fresh air outside. They arrived back at Watson's in less than two hours. As expected, he was quite enthusiastic with what Kelsey had brought him, and offered her a fair price on the whole lot. Kelsey was grateful to Clay—more so than she could ever articulate. Watson's offer was so generous that they decided to leave the rest back at the roller rink. They dubbed it their "rainy day" stash.

Clay decided to get a jump start and head out early so he wouldn't be racing the clock to get home before dark. As Kelsey said goodbye, she gave him a kiss on the cheek—not a peck, but a real kiss. She stepped back and smiled, thanking him for all that he had done for her. He kept his composure until he left the property, then he couldn't stop smiling. Even though a kiss on the cheek was hardly an act of romance, it made him think that perhaps she had some feelings for him too.

The pair had decided to meet up every Thursday to scavenge and barter together. Clay was thrilled; it gave him something to look forward to each week—at least until winter hit.

The trip home was uneventful, exactly how Clay liked it. He saw home in the distance and began taking the evasive path. He tried to never walk the same exact route twice, but after a few months, he realized how impossible of a task that would be long-term. Still, he tried to always be random and elusive each time he came home.

Clay saw Charlie sitting on the steps on the fourteenth floor landing. "What are you doing down here?" Clay asked.

"It's quieter here," he said and tapped his book.

Clay knew exactly what he was talking about; he had gone as far as the basement to get some quiet time of his own. The stairwell could still get noisy, especially as the kids headed to the roof to play, though after Michelle's accident, both Megan and Clay made it a concrete rule that there was to be no playing in the stairwell itself.

"You at a good stopping point?" Clay asked. "I'm gonna need your help with a couple of things."

"Sure!" Charlie said enthusiastically. The kid loved to learn whatever Clay was willing to teach him.

Clay swung by the kitchen and handed Megan the loot. Her eyes got wide, as if she had just witnessed a miracle. Without saying a word, Clay left. He was nearly halfway down the hall when he finally heard Megan's excited shriek. He smirked as he imagined the animated dancing she was likely doing while no one was watching.

He rounded the corner and saw Charlie standing in front of the armory door. Though he had been entrusted with the combination to the lock, he still was not supposed to go in without Clay unless it was an emergency.

"Ready to do some reloading?" Clay asked.

Charlie was confused. Clay had shown him how to reload when they had gone to the shooting range and wondered why they were going over that technique again. Had he been doing it wrong?

They walked inside and up to the bench where Clay cleared up the misunderstanding. They were going to reload bullets. He could tell Charlie was apprehensive at first, but after Clay showed him how it was done, Charlie realized that when done properly, it was a safe process. Anyone unfamiliar with the procedure could easily think it was dangerous. Even Clay thought so until his dad showed him.

Smokeless gunpowder wasn't quite as volatile as most people thought. Holding a match to a small pile of it for a brief moment wouldn't ignite it, though that was not something Clay ever recommend doing. The real danger to reloading, especially in such hazardous times, was the finished product. Not enough powder would drastically reduce the effectiveness of the bullet and most likely cause the gun to jam as it cycled the next round. Conversely, too much powder could rupture the barrel, causing all sorts of damage to the gun, as well as the person holding it. Improper overall length of the cartridge could also cause jams. Those kinds of details were the difference between life and death and why Clay always double-checked every single step.

He went through the process a couple of times, explaining very carefully what he was doing and how he was doing it; from depriming, to trimming the cases, to seating the bullet—and most importantly, powder measurements. Charlie picked up on it quickly. They began to load the V-Max bullets Vlad had traded to Clay. He trimmed some of the brass while keeping a close eye on Charlie's work.

"Perfect," Clay said giving him a slap on the shoulder as he finished a few rounds. "This is a very important skill to have."

"Is all your ammo reloaded like this?" Charlie asked.

"Not all of it, but a good deal of it. Most of the factory loaded ammo is for the shotgun, the .22, and your .30 carbine," he said pointing over to Charlie's rifle leaning up against the wall. "Oh, and the .38 special, too," he added.

"Why don't you reload those?"

"Well, I don't have the dies for the .30, I don't have *any* of the tools I need for the shotgun, and you can't reload the .22 caliber."

"Why not?"

"The .22 is something called rimfire which means that the primer is essentially built into the shell. You can't just pop the used primer out and put a new one in like you can with those," he said pointing to some of the rounds Charlie had just finished loading.

"Oh, neat!" Charlie said genuinely and smiled. "I like learning these things, Clay."

Clay returned the smile, "I like teaching them. You're a good student."

Charlie's smile faded as his thoughts got deeper, "I wish my mom could see how much I've learned and see how responsible I am."

Clay put his arm around Charlie and gave his shoulder a squeeze, "I think she knows and *is* very proud, Charlie."

"I never knew my dad," Charlie said as he seated a primer into the case Clay had just trimmed. "Mom said he had died saving a bunch of people in war."

"Sounds like he was a brave man."

Charlie nodded. "I think he would be proud of you, Clay" he said.

"Me?"

"I think he'd say that you are doing a good job raising his son."

Though Clay had thought of himself as a father figure to these kids, Charlie's statement brought a whole new perspective to their situation. He and Megan were raising kids that weren't theirs. Every single one of them once had a mother and father, and now Clay and his sister had taken over those roles. It was both humbling and frightening.

Clay snapped out of his thoughts as Charlie pulled down on the lever to deprime a shell and heard a snapping sound. "Oh no!" Charlie shouted, "What did I do? Did I break it?"

The sound was a resounding yes to Charlie's question. Clay looked; the die had indeed broken. He examined the case and saw it was zinc-plated steel, not nickel-plated brass like he thought it was. More importantly, it was Berdan primed, not Boxer, which was why the die broke.

"Crap," Clay said with frustration.

Charlie's eyes watered up, "I'm sorry, Clay. Please don't be mad."

Clay's frustration turned to guilt as he looked at the remorse on Charlie's face. "Charlie, it wasn't your fault."

Charlie wasn't convinced.

"Here, take a look," Clay held up the steel case and shined a flashlight into it. "You see those two little holes next to the primer hole?"

Charlie nodded.

"That means its Berdan primed. We can only reload a shell using Boxer priming, which means there's just a single hole for the primer to sit in. It's *my* fault for not pitching the case when I was sorting through."

Charlie was relieved that he wasn't at fault but was still upset for Clay. He could tell that it was bad. "Can you fix it?"

Clay stared at the broken die for a moment and shook his head. "Maybe if I was more of a gunsmith or even a handyman, but I just don't know enough about this stuff."

They tallied up the rounds that had been loaded. 273. Clay took 125 of them and put them into a plastic bag. He would still honor the deal he had made with Vlad and hoped he would be able to find a replacement die somewhere. It wasn't unheard of to come across them for trade, but it was rare and *always* expensive.

It was close to six. Clay figured Megan would have dinner ready soon, so they cleaned up and made their way back to the other side of the building. Charlie went to his room, and Clay found Megan in the cooking room stirring a pot.

"What's wrong?" she asked noticing Clay's long face.

"One of the reloading dies broke."

"That's not good," she said then lowered her voice. "Charlie?"

He sighed, "No, it was my fault. I got lazy with my sorting."

Megan added a few ingredients to the pot and asked Clay to hand her a packet of salt. "Can you find another?"

"Well, it's not as if I can run down to Cabela's and pick up a new one," he said and paused for a moment. "Though I know Uncle Ted had at least two sets of dies...I wonder if he's even still alive?"

Ted was a family friend who had adopted his title as uncle before Clay was born. He was a little off the deep end when it came to conspiracies. Though he often spoke of legitimate issues that most people should have been more concerned about, Ted always found ways to spin them with crackpot theories that removed any credibility the original discussion might have held. Clay remembered his dad having to go over to his house several times one year to calm him down when he got really riled up about some laws that had passed. Clay had been to his house quite a few times, but his dad never let him go there alone. It wasn't that Ted was a bad man, but his unbridled passion to find an ulterior motive for every event in the headlines was not something his father wanted Clay subjected to. At least not without a buffer.

"Now, that's a name I haven't heard in years," Megan said, "but Clay..."

"I know," Clay replied.

If Clay really pushed himself, he could make it to Uncle Ted's in two days, maybe three. He lived just a few miles from the house Clay and Megan had grown up in. Screamers were just one of a handful of murderous gangs that set up camp in the area. The terrain was also a major challenge; fissures, massive sinkholes, and collapsed bridges were just some of the headaches for a traveler going through. There was a reason why Clay avoided going east. However, the vast amount of land combined with the relatively low population did make it one of the lesser scavenged areas, increasing his chances of finding food and supplies. It was tempting to go, but it was an awfully dangerous trip, especially for something that, while important, was not essential.

Megan finished cooking and began to pull the bowls out of the water they had been soaking in since lunch. "Can you go round up the kids?" she asked.

Clay nodded and walked over to the craft room where Tyler and Blake were in the corner, feverishly working on a collaborative comic book. He thought back to days when he was their age and remembered doing the same thing. The girls were all along the wall, recreating scenes from a nature magazine with water paints. Clay left the room and got Charlie who still looked upset about the broken die. Lona was already helping set the tables, and Bethany was in her playpen, doodling with some crayons. Everyone was accounted for.

They all sat down and held hands while Clay blessed the meal. The eating had commenced before Clay had even finished saying amen. Everyone had brought their appetite to dinner, and those that expected seconds were sorely disappointed with Megan's response. Clay also would have liked another helping, but Megan was doing the right thing. She had already started rationing conservatively for the daunting winter ahead. The kids wouldn't ever miss a meal, but their requests for seconds would go unanswered, especially since several of them would only eat a few additional bites before getting full.

After he finished dinner, Clay stood up and walked over to the kitchenette. None of the children really took notice as they talked across the table. He opened one of the upper cabinet doors just enough to reach in and pull out a couple of candy bars that he quickly hid behind his back.

"Watch'ya got, Clay?" Sarah asked.

Sarah's question sparked all sorts of speculation amongst the other children.

"I've got a treat for you all, tonight," he said as he held up two chocolate bars.

Only about half of them truly grasped what he was holding. The others had heard of the mysterious 'candy bar' before, but couldn't recall ever having one. Once the realization set in, the kids went bonkers with excitement, several of them dancing and skipping around the break room. The atmosphere was contagious, and even Bethany began rocking in her playpen.

Clay split the bars up and handed them out to each of the kids. It was only then that he realized it was probably a mistake to give them their first taste of such pure sugar in years just before bedtime. He looked over at Megan, expecting a scowl, but her eyes were closed as she set sail into a chocolate paradise. Each nibble on the sweet chocolate was followed by a sigh of delight.

Clay had decided he would not partake since he had split one with Kelsey the night before. Plus, watching the kids' faces was a treat in itself.

Per Megan's request, the kids ran off to get ready for bed. The screams and shouts echoed down the halls as they discussed just how delicious their dessert was. Megan cleared the tables, then snuck a sip of the milk in the fridge. She tossed a dish towel onto the counter and placed her hand on her hip, "Ya know what? Those calories were too good to burn off with cleaning. I think I am just gonna go put the kids down and go to bed myself."

Clay nodded. Megan worked harder than anyone he had ever met. Being a stay-at-home mom was a thankless job in a civilized world; it was downright brutal now. She had more than earned a night off.

She turned and opened the cabinet door and pulled out the chocolate and bags of chips and handed them to Clay. "You should probably lock these up in your room."

"Good idea," Clay said. "Don't want the kids getting into these, huh?"

"Yeah," she said with a sly smile, "it's not the kids you'd have to worry about."

Clay laughed, "Oh yeah, I forgot what kind of chocolate fiend you used to be."

She flicked his arm and left the room to get the kids ready for bed.

Chapter 11

"I can't sleep," Charlie said.

Clay had been drifting in and out of consciousness, but was fully awakened by Charlie's statement. "Why not?" he grumbled.

"Too excited!"

"About what?"

"I've never been to a store like this before."

Clay hadn't thought about it from Charlie's perspective. The idea of walking into a room full of goods that were for sale could be exciting for someone who had never been to such an establishment. Over the years, Clay's feelings had evolved. The curious thrills of what the shopkeeper might have in stock were slowly replaced with angst-filled wonder. Would they have any medicine? Or perhaps a replacement for the die that had broken two weeks ago? To someone like Charlie, it was more of looking at all the stuff somebody else had and less about finding specific items that he needed.

"Well," Clay said followed by a long pause, "the sooner you go to sleep, the sooner morning will get here, which means the sooner you will be able to see what Vlad has."

Earlier that day, during their travels to Liberty, Clay and Charlie had to hide from a sizeable group of men in the area. Clay had mixed feelings about running into them. On one hand, it was another teaching opportunity for Charlie. On the other hand, they had arrived at Liberty much later than expected, and Vlad had already closed up for the night.

Vlad had always offered Clay a place to stay for the night, so they let themselves in and found their way to a vacant room. There weren't nearly as many people there as last time, so Clay found a nice two-bed room.

"I'm trying," Charlie said. "It's just cool, is all."

After a few minutes of silence, Clay started doze again, only to be dragged out of his slumber with yet another question.

"Do you like her?"

Clay sighed, "Like who?"

"Kelsey. Do you like her?"

Clay was already regretting that he had mentioned her to Charlie. "Yes, I like her."

"Do you love her?"

"Seriously, Charlie, go to bed."

"You do!" the onslaught continued.

He and Kelsey had quickly grown close. Each time they met up, Clay cared for her more. They had become good friends—more than friends to Clay, but he could tell she was always a little reluctant to venture down that road. He could see that she cared for him, too, but she would always change the subject any time Clay steered the conversation that way.

The fact was, he *did* love her. It hadn't even been a month since he first met her, but he couldn't do anything to change the way he felt. The answer to Charlie's question was yes, but he wasn't about to talk to a thirteen year old about it.

"Go to bed, Charlie," Clay said and turned over in bed.

Charlie had more loaded questions, but decided not to rock the boat. Instead, his mind switched gears, and he thought about all the things that he might find on the shelves in the morning. After a few minutes, he started coming up with some more ideas for a story he'd been developing in his head over the last year. Clay had kept him so busy over the last few weeks he hadn't had much time to continue writing. But he knew the long winter ahead would afford him plenty of time. He hoped to have it finished before the thaw; perhaps Vlad would sell it in his store. As he tried to think of a name for the protagonist, he drifted to sleep.

****

"Come on, Charlie, time to get up," Clay said as he shook Charlie's shoulder.

Charlie groaned and pulled the blanket over his head.

"Hey, you were the one who wanted to stay up all night, gabbing away like a girl at a slumber party. This is the price you pay," Clay said as he yanked the blanket off Charlie.

Charlie protested again, but got up and got ready anyway. They quickly collected their things and headed to Vlad's shop.

"Clay," Vlad greeted them as they came through the door. He then turned to Charlie, "Welcome to Vladimir's! I will be with you in one moment."

Vlad was already in the middle of wheeling and dealing with a local, so Clay and Charlie poked around the store. Charlie was enthralled with the inventory. Most trading posts had a specialty or focus and would pretty much stick to that. Vlad's, however, was a mixed bag. Though he certainly had a heavy emphasis on weaponry, medicines, and other high ticket items, he never turned down a trade for an item he thought could be of any value—from clothing to children's toys, first aid supplies to books—the latter immediately drawing Charlie in.

Clay saw Vlad shake hands with the local man who then left. "Charlie, I am gonna go talk with Vlad, I want you to pick out something for Bethany's birthday tomorrow. Also, see what else you can find that might be helpful for us, okay?"

"Okay," he replied absent-mindedly, his gaze locked on the bookshelf.

Clay and Vlad chatted, mostly about the imminent freeze. Vlad also mentioned some rumors he had heard about small groups of soldiers and FEMA workers traveling around, handing out food and first aid. Clay wasn't buying it. It had been radio silence from all government agencies for far too long for the rumor to be believable.

"Sounds like a bunch of bull, to me...Or worse..." Clay said.

"I feel same way, my friend," Vlad replied.

Both men had encountered more than their fair share of scams in the past seven years. Most of the time, people would be out some food or supplies. Other times, however, rumors of relief efforts had more sinister motives.

Charlie walked up and put a few items down on the counter, including a small giraffe stuffed animal.

"For Bethany?" Clay asked as he picked up the slightly worn-out plush.

"Yeah, I think she'll like it."

In addition to the giraffe, he had also brought some bandages, a few packets of powdered drink mixes, and a bag of mixed beans and rice. Clay looked it over and thought his choices were good, but a bit conservative. He walked him back out to the shelves, and they picked up a few more items. Clay reminded him of what they brought to trade Vlad and that what Charlie had picked out was worth less than their trade goods, especially since Vlad did not have the neck sizing die he was looking for. Clay stressed that Vlad, like most traders, was a tough negotiator, and that Charlie was going to have to stand his ground. That made Charlie nervous.

After looking around for a few more minutes, they returned with some more items. Most notable was a relatively new pair of shoes for Megan, who had been wearing the same pair of sneakers since they had moved into the building. She was always on her feet and deserved shoes with a bit more cushion. They also found another fiction paperback book they were both equally excited to read.

Vlad looked over the deal and shook his head, "I am sorry, but this is not fair trade."

Charlie looked up at Clay who nodded. The young man gulped and took a deep breath. With all the courage he could muster, he replied "You're wrong. It's more than a fair trade." His squeaky voice trembled as he dove head first into the world of bartering. With Vlad taking a second look at the trade, Charlie began to list several reasons why he felt the trade was indeed reasonable.

Vlad took a step back and scratched his head as if he was pondering the deal. The fact was, Vlad and

Clay had done business so many times they knew exactly what the other would view as fair and what wasn't. Negotiations seldom happened between them, and if they did, it was usually on high ticket items.

Vlad looked over and Clay gave him a wink. He knew Clay would keep the deal fair, but he was to be stubborn so that Charlie could learn to haggle. And after nearly fifteen minutes of back-and-forth with quite a convincing performance by Mr. Bezrukov, the young negotiator had finally made a deal with the Russian. Clay was impressed by Charlie's efforts, even Vlad was almost convinced to throw in something extra by his resounding arguments. Charlie and Vlad shook hands, and the goods were exchanged.

"Great job, Charlie," Clay said to him.

Charlie smiled brightly; his confidence never higher.

"So," Vlad said, "you will be back before winter, yes?"

"I don't think so, but you can never know for sure these days," Clay said and stuck his hand out.

Vlad took his hand, "Have safe winter, my friend. Will see you in spring, then."

"You, too, Vlad. Tell that beautiful daughter of yours I said bye."

"I told you, I never let my Olesya date a sabaka like you," Vlad said as he chuckled. "I joke, of course."

Clay had heard him use that word a lot, but he didn't know what it meant. He suspected, however, it was unlikely to be a flattering word.

"Yeah, well, I'd probably kill myself if I had a father-in-law like you, anyhow." Clay quipped back.

Charlie interrupted the laughter. "Clay's already got a girlfriend, anyway."

"Is that so?" Vlad said curiously.

"Nope, it's not so. Have a good winter, Vlad." Clay turned and looked back at Charlie. "Move it," he said as he pointed to the door. He wasn't mad at Charlie, but he had to brace himself for a long winter with Charlie prodding about Kelsey.

They made their way through a few of the other shops, looking for opportunistic trades. There wasn't much, though they did pick up a few packs of crackers, and they found a small amount of wheat at Short Stop before heading back home.

On the way home, Clay was able to take down two rabbits with his collapsible .22 rifle he always had in his pack. When they came across another rabbit, Clay handed the rifle to Charlie. Even though Clay talked him through the shot, the inexperienced hunter still missed. He was embarrassed and upset. Clay tried to encourage him with a pun.

"You missed him by a *hare*, Charlie" he said, laughing at his own joke.

Charlie didn't laugh.

"You'll get it later," Clay said.

They arrived home just before sundown. It was the first time Charlie had to make such a long journey, and he still had the stairs to look forward to. Just another burden that came with the job.

Everyone already had dinner, so Clay and Charlie scarfed down what Megan had set aside for them. It was cold but delicious nonetheless.

Charlie excused himself and headed for his room, the new book in hand.

"So, uhm," Megan said as she sat down next to Clay. She stammered over her words; she was nervous. "Do you think you can get another quart or two of milk?"

Clay glared at her through squinted eyes. "What did you do?"

"I may have stolen a sip, or fifty, over the past two days, and now I don't have enough left for the dinner."

Even though he had not planned on going to Watson's in the morning, he wasn't mad at her. Megan was the most selfless person he knew. Her sacrifices and efforts to help others were unparalleled. She almost never took time for herself or indulged in anything like that. She deserved a break every now and then.

Plus, Clay didn't mind the opportunity to possibly see Kelsey again.

Clay sighed loudly and sarcastically, followed by a smile, "Yeah, I'll take Charlie there in the morning. Should be home in time for you to get Bethany's birthday dinner ready.

Megan leaned over and hugged him, "Thank you, brother."

She stood up and walked towards the door.

"Hey, Megan," Clay said, catching her just as she got to the doorway.

"What's up?" she asked.

Clay grabbed his pack off the floor and flung it on to the table. He unzipped one of the pouches and said, "We picked something out for you."

She walked back over to the table, and Clay presented her with the new tennis shoes. She stopped in her tracks and gasped. She covered her mouth with her hands, and tears began to stream down her face. She had never asked for new shoes, but desperately needed them. Some days the shin splints were so painful that she would have to wrap her ankles up just to make it through the day.

She didn't say anything; she found that she couldn't. It was such a kind gesture—one that meant more to her than anything else in recent years. She took them from Clay and held them close to her chest. "Thank you," she squeaked out before turning to leave.

The next morning, Clay and Charlie headed to Watson's. Charlie was unusually quiet during their travels. Clay attributed it to the exhaustive past couple of days. He did manage to find enough energy to tease Clay about Kelsey. Clay warned that he'd be charging the battery banks all winter if he kept it up. Charlie over-dramatically gulped and stopped talking.

The gatekeeper let them through without any delay. Clay and Charlie went straight to the store. Margaret, again, was behind the counter. Clay wondered if she was the only employee at the store since she had been there every time he visited. She was pleasant to deal with, though, and not a very tough negotiator—at least compared to some of the others Clay had been up against in the past. Clay let Charlie handle the negotiations; he did quite well. Clay expected to just get two quarts of milk, but Charlie also managed to finagle a half dozen eggs out of the deal. His experience at Vlad's was already being put to work.

Once they had the milk, they stepped outside, and Clay briefly chatted with Derrick as he passed by. Derrick had warmed up to Clay after the awkward first encounter they had at the gate. He was a good kid, though only about three years younger than Clay. Their conversation was interrupted by Jeremy, who informed Derrick he was needed at the stables.

"Yes sir, Mr. Hatfield," Derrick replied before turning back to Clay. "Take it easy, Clay," he said as he headed towards a field behind the little town.

Jeremy nodded at Clay before continuing about his business. Clay felt the cold shoulder from Jeremy, who didn't try to hide it.

Clay kept his eye out for Kelsey as they were meandering back towards the gate. He didn't want it to be too obvious he was seeking her out, though. Fortunately, he spotted her as she was coming through the gate.

"Hi, Clay!"

"Good morning, Kelsey," Clay said with a smile. She gave him a quick hug and then looked down at Charlie, "Now who is this handsome young prince?"

Charlie blushed and looked down at the ground.

"Kelsey, this is Charlie. He's my right-hand man these days."

Charlie worked up enough courage to look her in the eyes and managed to say hello.

Kelsey could see the boy had a crush, and she exacerbated the issue by giving him a kiss on the cheek. "It's a pleasure to meet you, Charlie."

Charlie froze and then looked at her, "uh...uh-huh," is all he could utter.

Clay smiled and then looked at Kelsey. "So, you coming back from a scavenge?" he asked, gesturing to her bag.

"Yeah. Unfortunately, there's not much to show for it."

"Well, hopefully we'll have better luck on Thursday," he said, his way of subtly reminding her of their recurring 'date'.

"I wouldn't miss it."

After chatting for a few minutes, she gave Clay a kiss on the cheek, and they went their separate ways.

"Safe travels," the gatekeeper said as they left.

"So," Clay said a few minutes into the journey home, "you have any more jokes for me about Kelsey?"

Charlie looked embarrassed and didn't say anything. After a few minutes, he spoke up, "She's *really* pretty."

"Yep."

Clay was keenly aware of Charlie's awkward position, and kindly dropped the matter.

About halfway home, Clay spotted some hogs across a field. It was a little late for them to be out, but with winter coming and food scarce, even the hogs seemed to be scrambling to prepare. Clay detached the LaRue from the sling around his neck and handed it to Charlie.

"Remember, this ain't the .308—your shot needs to be perfect. Aim just behind the shoulders."

Charlie took the rifle, and they quietly approached the hogs as they sifted through the dirt. There was no wind to speak of, and they were within fifty yards; it was an ideal shot, even for an inexperienced shooter. Charlie rested the rifle up against a tree and looked through the holographic sight. It provided no magnification, so the hog's entire body nearly fit within the grainy red ring. After missing the rabbit yesterday, Charlie was very nervous about another failure. He silently recited the steps Clay had taught him, and he squeezed the trigger.

"Nailed him!" Clay shouted.

Charlie exhaled loudly and then cracked a smile. The adrenaline had kicked in and now, as if a dam of energy had burst, he had returned to his normal self. He handed the rifle back to Clay, and they made their way over to the kill. Charlie took a few moments to admire his first hunt. It was a clean shot; right through the lungs. The swine had dropped instantly.

"That's a good, clean kill, Charlie," Clay said.

Concerned with time, Clay field dressed the hog as quickly but efficiently as he could. He told Charlie what he was doing, but the more in-depth, hands-on session for Charlie would have to come later.

Charlie didn't mind, actually. Of all the things he wanted to learn, butchering a pig wasn't really one of them. He realized the importance of that knowledge, though, and would be ready to get his hands dirty when the opportunity came.

It was about an hour before sunset when home came into sight. All either of them wanted to do was get home, clean up, and go to bed, but they still had a party to attend. It wasn't that they weren't excited, but they had easily covered over sixty miles in the last three days, and the exhaustion was taking a toll, especially on Charlie, who hadn't done that much walking in the last year—maybe two.

Despite being so close, they still had an extra half hour of walking to do, playing cloak and dagger near the building. Clay was tempted to just ignore protocol for the night and go straight home, but he didn't want to teach poor discipline to Charlie.

As Clay and Charlie rounded the corner of a nearby building, they were surprised by a man walking towards them. Clay quickly reacted, shouldered his rifle, and took aim. The other man had also put Clay in his sights.

"Well, this is some déjà vu," the man spoke.

Chapter 12

Megan had everything prepared for dinner; she just needed to add the milk and throw it in the oven. *Where are they?* She wondered. *If I don't get this thing cooking soon, the birthday girl will fall asleep before she is able to eat her special dinner.* She chided herself for overindulging on the milk Clay had brought home last time.

Megan heard the banging on the door and jogged down the hallway to let the boys in.

"Hey sis, look what the cat dragged in," Clay said and stepped aside.

"Geoffrey!" Megan shrieked and hugged their old friend. "It's so great to see you!"

"Likewise," he said and hugged her back.

It had been nearly a year since they saw him last. Clay was particularly happy. He really missed having another guy closer to his own age to talk to. Not to mention, the two had become close friends after he joined their group.

"I almost killed this clown as we came around the corner," Clay said as he slugged Geoff on the shoulder.

"Please!" Geoff protested. "I had my sights trained on you before you realized I was there. Plus, I have the scatter gun. I wouldn't have missed from that distance," he said and held up his fancy tactical shotgun.

The two kept one upping each other as they walked down the hallway. Megan took the milk and eggs from Clay then went back to work on dinner. Charlie, still bitter with Geoff for leaving, decided to make sure the batteries were fully charged for the night.

The kids came out to see what all the commotion was about and saw Geoff standing in the lobby. Lona, Paige, and Maya knew Geoff from before. Tyler had only been part of the group for about a month before he left and barely remembered him. The rest of them had arrived afterwards but were still excited to meet him. They had all heard stories that included him, and now they had a face to go with the name.

"Five minutes!" Megan shouted from down the hall, "Go get cleaned up."

The kids stormed off and headed for the washroom to clean up from the day. Clay and Geoff sat down at the table in the kitchen and did their best to catch up, talking loudly as they competed against the shouting and horseplay nearby. Megan stood next to the table and chimed in when she wasn't excusing herself to check on dinner.

"Ruth sends her best," Geoff said as he pulled two loaves of bread out of his bag. "They are fresh baked. Well, fresh when I left last week, anyway."

Megan held the sourdough up to her face and squeezed it. The cracking sound was crisp and pronounced. A good bread sounded as good as it looked.

"You know what? Now that we have some more eggs, I think I'll make some French toast in the morning," she said with glee. She practically skipped over to the fridge and placed the loaves inside. She returned with some water for Clay and Geoff then went to serve dinner. Lona came in holding Bethany who was fading by the minute. It was already a half hour past her usual bedtime.

"There's the birthday girl!" Clay said as he got up to go hold her. "Are you excited for your special dinner?"

Bethany looked around and saw everyone pouring into the room for the meal. She looked back at Clay and emphatically nodded which generated laughter around the room. Just then, Megan came back holding more plates than she should have been carrying.

Everyone in the room was eager to dig in. The macaroni looked delicious; it reminded Clay of Thanksgiving with the family. And even more surprising was that it tasted every bit as good as it looked. With the exception of replacing the noodles with ramen, it looked almost exactly how the cookbook had presented it.

Megan was a decent cook, especially given their present situation. But she was never into culinary arts before, at least not like her sisters. Michelle and Emily were *always* helping with dinner each night while Megan would study. Once their mother had died, Michelle took charge of preparing food for the family. Emily took the death of their mother the hardest and couldn't bring herself to cook anymore. She never touched a pot or pan the rest of her short life.

Megan looked anxiously around the room as everyone ate, "Well, what do you think?"

The kids all shouted their unanimous approval. That was no surprise to Megan since they liked just about anything she sat in front of them, especially when made with ingredients that hadn't been pumped with chemicals to lengthen shelf life. She glanced over at Clay, seeking his endorsement.

"It's actually *really* good," he said as he forked another bite into his mouth.

She smiled and her shoulders dropped as she relaxed. It was always a big deal for her to have everything turn out perfectly for the birthday dinners; this had been her biggest success to date.

"So," Clay said as he chewed his food, "I guess you followed the recipe this time, huh?" He couldn't help but to dish out some brotherly ribbing.

Megan replied with a sour face and continued eating. They all ate their fill; there were no leftovers. When it was time for gifts, all signs of Bethany's tiredness had faded away. She was energized by all the excitement in the room. The kids had all made crafts or drawings for her. Each one she giggled at and shook around with enthusiasm. Tyler was particularly excited to see her enjoy the toy car he had made from random materials he had found.

Charlie looked over, and Clay nodded. He left the room and promptly returned with a shoebox. He walked up and placed the box in front of Bethany on the table. "Here you go, Bethany. Happy Birthday!"

Entertained with the bright orange cardboard box, she hadn't noticed she could open it too. Charlie, unable to resist the urge, reached over to start lifting the flap. Bethany caught on and flipped it up the rest of the way.

She wrinkled her brows as she carefully studied the contents inside. "That!" she said excitedly and pointed at the toy.

"Go ahead," Charlie said. "It's for you!"

Bethany reached in and pulled out the small plush giraffe. She stared at its yellow, smiling face as she studied every fiber. Suddenly, she pulled it up to her chest and squeezed it tight. With a firm grip around the animal's neck, she brought it up to her face as she sucked her thumb. Megan said it reminded her of Linus from Charlie Brown. Clay and Geoff were the only ones who understood the reference.

The late dinner meant no playtime afterwards. Megan told the kids they had to go get ready for bed right away. They all said their goodnights to Clay and Geoff and scurried to bed. Clay and Geoff cleaned up the disaster the break room had become while Megan went through the bedtime rituals. Charlie, normally the first to volunteer to help, quietly slipped out of the room, which did not go unnoticed by Geoff.

"So, what's the deal with Charlie?" he asked. "He still seems pissed at me."

Clay shrugged, "He feels like you abandoned us."

Geoff was silent.

"I tried to explain, but he just—he's still a kid. He'll understand why you left some day and realize you did what you needed to do," Clay said.

Geoff nodded and finished clearing the table. When Megan returned both of them could see the exhaustion on her face. However, she had not seen Geoff in quite some time and knew he'd most likely be leaving in the morning. So she forced herself to stay awake while they continued to catch up.

"Both of you sit down. I'll finish cleaning tomorrow," she insisted.

They all sat and sipped on some water.

"So, what made you decide to up and walk all this way?" Clay asked. "Word get out that Megan was actually going to cook a decent dinner?"

Megan smacked his arm.

Geoff let out a chuckle before responding. "Well, first of all I wanted to tell you guys in person that I am going to be a father."

Megan jumped out of her chair and squealed like a girl in junior high. She clapped her hands rapidly and gave him a hug. The sudden outburst of excitement—a stark contradiction to her body language just seconds before—startled both Clay and Geoff.

"Congratulations," Clay said warmly, but in much more control of his emotions. "That's great news!"

"So how far along is she?" Megan asked.

"The doc thinks about four months, but he can't be entirely sure."

"Y'all have a doctor?" Clay chimed in.

"He was Ruth's mom's doctor. He retired about a decade ago and has a small plot of land a little west of us. He's a good man; always willing to help. He's pretty old, so we try not to pester him with small issues, but obviously this is pretty big," he said with a large grin, still in a bit of disbelief himself.

Megan excused herself and went over to the fridge. She poured some water and came back with some flavor packets—the post-apocalyptic champagne. "It's time to celebrate!"

Clay and Megan toasted their old friend, and they all drank up. Megan stood up from the table and collected the cups. "I hate to do this, but I need to get some sleep. Geoffrey, it was so great seeing you, and I am so excited for you and Ruth! I hope to meet her one day."

"Hopefully sooner rather than later," he replied.

Megan smiled and congratulated him once again. "Goodnight, we'll see ya in the morning," she said as she walked out of the room.

Geoff turned back to Clay. "Ya know," he continued as if the conversation hadn't been interrupted, "I've been talking with Ruth's father and brothers recently. They know all about you and Megan, what you guys are doing for these kids. He wanted me to tell you that there is a nice little chunk of land with your name on it, should you be so inclined."

Clay was stunned. Such a generous offer from a man he had never met, a man that knew only what Geoff had told him. It was an offer he would love nothing more than to accept, but it was far from a cut and dried situation.

"Wow!" Clay replied, "I don't really know what to say."

"You could say, 'Sure, Geoff, I would love to come out there and own a piece of land that is as close to perfection as one can find in the world these days.'"

"If only it were that simple. Northfield is what, eighty miles away?"

"More like ninety. And it *is* that simple. You guys move there, and we all get to hang out together again, like the good ol' days."

Clay shook his head.

"And to be honest, we could sure use the extra help, too. Cliff is getting up there in age, and he hasn't been the same since Ruth's mom died. Her oldest brother, Michael, does what he can to help, but he took a bullet to the leg last year and doesn't get around too well anymore." Geoff stopped for a moment to lean back in his chair. "I know this might sound like me asking for a favor, but it really isn't my intention."

Clay knew it wasn't some scheme to get extra work hands. If it had been anybody else, he might have been skeptical, but he knew that Geoff was true to his word when he said that. He was looking out for a friend, and he knew that Clay wasn't the idle type, anyhow. He desired to work. The thought of resting all day rarely occurred to Clay. It was one of the most dreaded things about winter for him; there was never enough to do.

The offer was indeed tempting seeing Watson's ranch reaffirmed his desires to get out of the aging tower and move to a proper homestead where they wouldn't have to worry about a rogue tremor toppling their home; a place where the kids could run around in an actual field instead of the rooftop jungle gym; a place where they could trade in their twelve-by-fifteen greenhouse for acres of crops; a proper fireplace and a wood burning stove didn't sound all that bad either.

Clay found himself daydreaming about such a life, but the logistics of his situation would not allow for him to just pick up and move, no matter how much he coveted the thought. Traveling that far on foot would take *at least* twice as long with the kids. It would take a half dozen or more trips just to transport their belongings, which was just an absurd thought. Many of their possessions would need to be left behind, something Clay was reluctant to do. And then, of course, there was Kelsey, who would be too far away for Clay to visit. Of all the excuses not to go, severing ties with her was near the top.

Before Clay could reply, Geoff continued, "Just think about it, okay? Obviously, it's not realistic to think that you could do that before winter anyway, so we can continue this conversation after the thaw. Sound good?"

"Well, like you said nothing can happen between now and winter anyway, but..." he trailed off. Geoff gave Clay a hopeful look. "I'll give it some serious thought."

That answer was satisfactory enough, and the two continued to talk long into the night. As the conversation closed down, Geoff engaged Clay about a different opportunity.

"Do you still happen to have that Bulgarian beauty?" he asked.

"Yep," Clay replied, "I attempted to trade it to Vlad a while back, but he wasn't offering much for it. I tried selling him on the fact that it was a pre-ban AK-47, but he said that 7.62x39 was just too hard to find anymore. I couldn't really argue with him on that. I swear, though, I saw a tear rolling down his cheek when I left with it in my hand. Obviously, it's a bit nostalgic for that ol' Ruskie."

"Do you still use it?"

"I believe you were living here the last time I fired that thing. It's collecting dust in the armory. I like it, but without ammo, it has no practical use for me anymore."

Geoff lifted up his shotgun and placed it on the table, "Care to make a trade?"

Clay looked at the small, unique shotgun lying in front of him. It was a KSG-12. It wasn't exactly the flashiest looking shotgun, but the concept and design was nothing short of brilliant. It was around two feet long and had dual, side by side magazine tubes, allowing for seven shells in each tube. It was certainly a distinct design that others tried to imitate, but none were able to match its quality before it was banned.

"Can I take a look?" Clay asked.

"Go right ahead."

Clay picked it up and pressed it into his shoulder, taking aim at an old corkboard that still had fair labor and discrimination posters tacked up. Shotguns were not really Clay's thing, but they had their purposes. And having more than a dozen rounds of buckshot to hurl towards a hostile certainly gave it quite an edge over the typical break barrels most people had.

"Why don't you want it?" Clay asked.

"It's not so much that I don't want it, but at this point, I would prefer having a nice battle rifle to use. I've come to learn that having a short barrel scatter gun out on a farm isn't quite as useful as I thought it would be. Ruth's father must have a dozen or more long barrel shotguns, both pump and semi-auto."

"They don't have any extra rifles?"

"They have an extra SKS or two lying around, but it's the cheap Chinese crap, not exactly something I want to trust my life to. Plus, I remember really loving that AK."

Clay thought about it for a moment, "So, what about ammo? Obviously, I don't have any."

"Oh, don't worry," Geoff said. "Her dad and brothers all went in and bought a pallet full of spam cans before the import ban took effect. They still have at least twenty of those things lying around. Still sealed."

"All right, then" Clay said. "It's no use to me anymore, so let's do it."

They got up and walked down the hall to the armory. Even though he didn't use shotguns all that much, he was happy to help out a friend. Besides, as short and light as the KSG was, it could become a weapon to love. It was certainly more practical for him in the urban area than the common twenty-eight-inch barrel shotguns, though most folks did saw them down to a much more manageable length.

"Still four, twenty-nine, six?" Geoff asked.

"Won't be after tonight," Clay replied jokingly.

"Just the way it was when I was in here last," Geoff commented as he walked into the room. "Except there's a lot less here," he said gesturing over to the reloading bench.

"Yeah. It's been almost impossible to find components these days."

"I imagine everything's drying up."

Clay nodded. He walked over to the wall and removed the AK-47 from the rack. He hadn't lifted it up in probably two years or more; it had a nice weight to it. Unlike most AK-47s, it was a milled receiver, not stamped. It felt more like an AR-15 than an AK-47, at least until the trigger was pulled.

He handed it to Geoff who immediately inspected it and looked through the iron sights a few times. "Yeah, let's do this," he said with a smile.

Clay fished around some boxes for a few minutes and finally found the extra magazines. "I have three polymer mags, and four steel mags, plus the one that's already in it."

"Perfect," Geoff said.

Clay picked up one of the magazines and saw it was loaded. There were only twelve rounds; it must have been his "just in case" magazine. He handed it to Geoff. "Well, hopefully you won't need it, but at least you will have it in case you run into some trouble on your way home."

Geoff took the magazines and stuck them into his bag. He then reached his hand out, "Thanks, Clay."

Clay shook his hand, "Eh, it's a pretty even trade, really."

"No, I mean thanks for—I guess I never thanked you for taking me in. You and Megan—if it hadn't been for you two—I know I wouldn't have made it much longer."

Clay was touched by the kind words, even a little choked up, but he didn't want to show it, "You would have been fine. You had this slick shotgun and knew how to use it."

"Yeah, I never told you this but...I was drier than a desert when we faced off against each other."

Clay laughed, but the fact was if it had been an aggressor instead of Clay, Geoff probably wouldn't have survived that day. Clay quickly pushed that 'what if' scenario out of his mind and smiled at his old friend. "Likewise, buddy. You helped this family out more than you'll ever know."

There was an awkward moment when neither spoke a word, at which point, Geoff cleared his throat and deepened his voice, "So, uh, yeah man, back to guns and stuff."

Clay also deepened his voice, "Yeah, and beer and girls and stuff. *Manly* stuff!"

It was humorous to them both that even though the world as they knew it had ended years ago, they still worried about sounding girly and getting emotional over conversations like that.

It was silent again until Geoff spoke up, "I've actually never had a beer. You?"

Clay shook his head. "Even if I found one now, I don't think I'd be drinking it."

They continued ribbing each other to compensate for the sappy moment they had just shared and began to pack up. Clay set the shotgun down on the reloading bench and made sure he didn't miss any accessories that went to Geoff's new gun.

"Hey," Geoff said to Clay as they were leaving the armory, his face serious, "I want you to think about my offer. I think you, Megan, and the kids would love it there."

"I told you I would...You nag."

"Night, bro," Geoff said as he walked to his old room on the other side of the building.

The next morning Geoff collected his things and headed home. He planned to make a pit stop in Liberty for the night and then finish the remainder of the journey, stopping wherever he could find a secure shelter. It was not an easy voyage even for an experienced traveler like Geoff. Clay knew it would be a nightmare to do that with several children. In fact, he wasn't sure it could be done without severe risk. A fussy baby or a night terror is all it would take to attract a whole slew of Screamers.

True to his word, though, he would think about it over the winter, but he knew it would be less thinking and more about trying to convince himself the reward outweighed the risk. Losing just one person during the journey would be completely unacceptable to Clay. With them having a safe enough setup already, he was struggling to find arguments for the move.

Chapter 13

"You're late," Kelsey said standing in the middle of the dark bay of an old fire station. She was bouncing on her tiptoes to combat the frigid morning temps.

"Sorry," Clay said with a hoarse voice, "Tyler was sick all night, the poor kid."

Kelsey was sympathetic. She knew what it was like to take care of a sick kid and was thankful that Dakota hadn't been hit by anything this year except for the occasional sniffle. Kelsey found it endearing how much Clay cared for those kids. He never acted as if they were a burden, nor did he do the bare minimum just to get through the day. It was clear that they were very important to him. It was a remarkable quality for such a young man, especially with children that weren't his own blood.

"Are you ready?" Kelsey asked as she rubbed her hands together to try to generate some heat.

"Let's hit it."

The sun had just started to rise as they left, and twenty minutes later, it was bright enough to see the welt under her eye.

"What happened?" Clay asked protectively.

She reached up and tenderly touched her cheek, "What, this? Well, I guess you could say, 'Angry colt: one, clumsy girl: zero'," she said with a wry smile. "I'm fine, though. Don't worry about it.

Clay didn't want to drop it, but he did.

"So, where are we headed?" she asked.

Clay hadn't really thought about it. With Bethany's birthday party, Geoff's unexpected visit, and sick kids around the house, he hadn't had time to plan out the trip like he normally would. They would just have to wing it even though it was not a good trip to play by ear; they both agreed it would be the last one of the season. It was nearing the end of September, and there had already been a couple of dustings of snow in the last week. The opportunities to scavenge were all but gone, and they both needed a good score to help them through the winter— especially Clay—as they were running a bit leaner on food than he had anticipated. Growing kids gradually start to consume more food, which was something Clay always forgot to take into account.

"Honestly, I'm not sure. Any ideas?"

"Well," Kelsey said and thought for a moment, "let's just start walking, and we'll see where we end up."

Hardly a plan, but Clay didn't have a better suggestion to offer. So they just continued walking the direction they were already headed. They walked by a few neighborhoods they had had some success with a couple weeks ago, but knew it was pretty skimpy to be spending much time there. They decided to keep going in search for some more fertile grounds.

They eventually found themselves in an equestrian subdivision: a wealthy, gated community with half million dollar homes and several acres between houses. Though the dilapidated houses were slowly being reclaimed by nature, Clay could envision how it must have looked when it was filled with people. It was the kind of place he had desired to live someday. He grew up on a small ranch with a little more than five acres. He loved his childhood home and missed it more every day, but he never wanted to have that kind of place for his family. He still wanted the privacy and land his old house had offered, but something more modern. The gated community he stood in had been the perfect balance.

The neighborhood was a giant loop, eighteen houses in all. Most of them had been trashed; a couple had even been burned down. There was something menacing about the neighborhood, though. Clay had spent the last several years wandering around a 200 square mile radius and had seen the exact same chaos time and time again: entire neighborhoods ransacked; businesses and shops looted; the stench of death never far away. It was all too common, yet there was something different about this place. As he thought about it more, the hair on his neck stood up. It felt as if the souls of the residents still dwelled there, trapped in a world that no longer existed. He didn't believe in such things as ghosts, but he couldn't shake the threatening vibe that was almost smothering him. The feeling got worse when he watched a tire swing swaying eerily in the breeze, kept together by just a few fraying strands. He looked over at Kelsey and could tell she was uncomfortable too.

Clay and Kelsey spent the majority of the day carefully searching one home after another, taking about an hour to clear each house. They found small amounts of useful items here and there.

As they approached a house about halfway through the neighborhood, they decided to call it quits for the day and claimed the house as their own for the night. The solid oak front door was wide open, the lock still intact. Whoever abandoned the house hadn't bothered to lockup, allowing looters to walk right in.

The inside was just as impressive as the outside: high vaulted ceilings, some places twenty feet high; hardwood floors throughout the first story except for a nice tile in the kitchen; a fireplace in the living room that acted as a dividing wall for the dining room so that both rooms could enjoy the crackling heat. It was beautifully designed. Clay was somewhat bitter that he would never get to enjoy such luxury.

Just off the kitchen was a walk-in pantry that was larger than his childhood bedroom. It looked the same as every other pantry he had seen in the last several years. Barren.

With not much luck downstairs, they wandered upstairs to continue their search and look for a place to hunker down for the night. As they reached the top of the stairs, they found themselves in a large, open room. Directly in the middle was a full-sized billiard table. A dusty cue ball sat atop the decaying green felt. Almost perfectly centered on the table, it felt as if it had been carefully placed there.

Clay walked into one of the bedrooms and saw the walls had nearly been covered with posters. Years of exposure to the elements from the broken windows had all but faded the water damaged images, but there was just enough visible to see that most of them were of the various branches of the military. Army, Navy, Air Force, Marines. All divisions were represented. It was common décor for a young boy's room. Hanging just above the bed was a cracked picture frame. Inside was a letter signed by S.J. Eisenberg, Secretary of the Navy; next to the letter was an imprint of the Navy Cross, but the medal itself was absent. The letter was dated just three years before the eruptions. Clay surmised it had been written to the boy's father.

Under the bed, Clay found a shoebox with some toys in it: a few action figures—little green army men—and several metal cars. Clay was excited with the find; the boys would have a great Christmas this year. He dumped the contents of the box into his pack and went to see how Kelsey was faring in the next room.

He walked inside and was greeted by copious amounts of pink. It, too, had posters throughout, but in contrast to the other room, they were mostly of baby-faced 'tween singers. There was a four-poster bed with a hanging fabric that was so tattered it looked more like a spider web than a bed canopy.

Kelsey was leaning against the bed, but not quite sitting on it. She was looking at a fashion magazine and shaking her head. On the cover was a woman who was more Photoshop than human, one of those women who was in her thirties but still acted like a bratty fourteen year old.

"Can you believe the crap in here?" Kelsey said as she flung the magazine towards the wall.

"Can't say I've ever read one of those."

Kelsey was upset enough that she picked the magazine back up just so she could throw it again. "Lies," she said. "It's all lies. Telling little girls that in order to be beautiful you have to look like this, act like that, say these things..."

Clay could tell this was about more than just a magazine.

"Sorry," Kelsey said as she sat down on the bed. "My Aunt Cassandra was one of those people who had a monthly subscription to a half dozen magazines just like this." She picked up another off the bedside table. "When I was a kid, she would enter me into beauty pageants, make me go to photo shoots on a monthly basis, and was constantly having me do auditions for commercials and TV shows."

Clay knew the type. A good friend of his from school had a mother just like that, though his friend didn't seem to be bothered by it like Kelsey was; she liked the attention she got from it. He also saw how much it changed her before she had even gotten into junior high.

"My mother never really cared much for the idea, but my aunt had her convinced that as soon as I landed my first modeling contract, the days of food stamps and public transportation would be behind them; it'd be nothing but limousines and fine wine. You know, the sweet life." Kelsey sighed as she rubbed her eyes with the palms of her hands. "But as a result, I wasn't allowed to just be a kid...By the time I was ten, I felt like I had a fulltime job on top of school."

"That sucks," Clay said compassionately.

Even though what Kelsey's aunt had done was deplorable, Clay could understand, from a vain worldview, why Kelsey's mother allowed it. Kelsey was stunning. Even as she stood in a decrepit room, her face covered with layers of dirt and soot; her hair pulled back; and wearing clothes that were stained six different colors, she was still gorgeous. Clay thought all she would need to do is run a comb through her hair, and she could be on the cover of that same magazine. He contemplated telling her that, but wasn't sure if she would be flattered or insulted with the comment.

They eventually moved on to the master suite and quickly decided it would be home for the night. The master closet—which was the size of a small bedroom—would be the ideal spot. No windows would expose them to the cold, nor would their lantern draw attention from those who might be lurking around outside. It also provided them with just one direction to cover. It was about as perfect a spot as they were going to find.

Clay dragged the boy's mattress into the closet and then fetched a few blankets. Kelsey lay down and drifted to sleep. Clay sat down on the floor and leaned his back against the wall opposite the door. He laid his rifle across his lap, ready to defend them on a moment's notice. He did some reading by flashlight until it ran out of juice. Not wanting to wake Kelsey up from winding it back up, he closed his eyes and, soon after, sleep arrived.

Morning came, and they moved on to the next house in the neighborhood. Kelsey found a half-used tube of antiseptic ointment. Clay offered to trade her for it, but she gave it to him instead.

"After all the things you've done for me, Clay, it's the least I could do for you," she told him.

Clay was deeply appreciative of the gesture. That kind of generosity had all but gone away in the world. It was just another trait he admired about her.

They finished searching the rest of the houses by early afternoon and decided to head back to the fire station. An hour or so after they left, they heard a distant rumble in the sky; a storm was heading their way.

It was in the mid-forties, and the temperature seemed to be dropping by the hour. Being exposed to rain in temperatures like that could be deadly, especially when it would easily drop to freezing before midnight.

Since they were heading straight into the storm, Clay stopped walking and pulled out a map and compass. After he got his bearings, he realized they were only a few miles from the cabin; the fire station was more than double that. The cabin would be going out of their way, but it would also be moving away from the storm. If they kept a decent pace, they might even get there before any rain fell.

Clay pitched the idea to Kelsey, and she agreed it was probably the best option they had. He folded the map and placed it back in his bag before they moved out.

The wind rapidly evolved from a light breeze to powerful gusts. The storm was closing in as they headed into the cabin's neighborhood.

About a mile or so from the cabin, Clay stopped dead in his tracks. Kelsey also stopped and looked back at Clay, then turned to see the pack of mangy, feral dogs in front of them. They were all past the point of starvation, their ribs clearly visible from twenty-five yards away. Clay and Kelsey remained frozen, as did the dogs. It was like a duel in the Old West. Who would flinch first?

"Don't move," Clay whispered calmly.

"Uh huh," Kelsey said. Her heart was pounding.

Clay ever so slowly moved his hand down to his side and eased his pistol out of the holster, never breaking his stare with the dogs.

He could hear their growls from afar, a sound that shot fear through his body like a jolt of lightning. With their hackles raised and their bodies lowered, it was clear they would attack.

"Get ready to take this from me," he said and shifted his eyes towards the pistol.

Kelsey barely nodded.

As the dogs crept closer, the growling intensified, becoming more vicious, more desperate. It was time to act.

"Now," Clay said.

He tossed the pistol up into the air, a decision he made at the last second that Kelsey had not been prepared for. The gun fell to the ground, and Kelsey scrambled to pick it up. The decision to toss the gun was calculated, and it paid off. The extra milliseconds he gained allowed Clay additional time to aim and fire his rifle, neutralizing the middle dog in three quick shots. The other two dogs broke away from their fallen friend and went opposite directions from each other. They both ran in a big circle and made their way back around towards Clay and Kelsey. Clay took aim at the dog on his side and opened fire. He shot eight times before he was able to catch the hindquarters. The dog spun around like a top. The canine tried to get up and continue with the attack but collapsed from the injury and began to wail.

Clay heard gunshots to his right. Kelsey had been shooting the pistol but to no avail. She had emptied her magazine in a hurry with nothing to show for it. He swung his body around and found Kelsey was blocking his shot. "Kelsey, out of the way!" he shouted. She leapt to the side, and Clay shot multiple times. An unsteady hand combined with the dog's movement made it a hard target. One of his rounds ricocheted off the ground and lodged into the dog's gut. It wasn't enough to stop the ravenous mongrel, though, and it lunged at him.

"Clay!" Kelsey shouted from a few feet away.

The dog snapped at Clay and clamped down on his forearm. Clay grunted in pain but immediately pushed his arm further into the dog's mouth causing it to break its grasp and stumble back. It made a second attempt to attack but was greeted by the tip of Clay's boot. The dog yelped and fell to the ground. The animal wasted no time getting back to its feet and turned around for its final assault. But it was too late.

A well-placed shot to the head dropped the dog immediately. Blood gushed from the wound causing Kelsey to turn her head away. Whimpering from one of the nearby challengers prompted Clay to retrieve his pistol from Kelsey. He changed out the magazines and closed the slide. He walked up to the wounded pup who, moments ago, acted like Cujo, but now looked no more threatening than a puppy. The dog was panting heavily, its backside matted in blood. Clay felt sorry for the dog. It wasn't much more than skin and bones and just acting on instinct.

He raised the pistol and promptly put it out of its misery. He probably did all three a favor by ending their desolation. It wasn't the first time Clay had to kill a dog—the first being the family pooch, near the end of the second winter—but it was never a pleasant experience.

Kelsey walked over and asked the question Clay had already asked himself, "Can you eat them?"

"You *can*," he said and then looked a bit more closely at the body, "but I wouldn't take a chance on these three. They look to be a breeding ground for diseases. Plus, we'd be lucky to get ten pounds of meat from all three of them. It's just not worth the time or risk."

Kelsey nodded. "Are you okay?" she asked as she pointed to his arm. She felt guilty for not inquiring about his arm before asking about the food.

Clay felt his arm and flinched, not realizing just how tender it was.

"Are you bleeding?"

"I don't think so," he said, uncertain if the dog had actually punctured skin or not. If it had, he was probably as good as dead, but that was a problem to deal with later.

Clay felt a drop of rain hit his face, and the wind picked up even more. He looked up at the sky and knew there wasn't much time.

"Take two minutes and help me pick up all the shells you can, then we need to go. Let's hurry!"

They found about half the shells and then jogged the last stretch to the cabin. The rain began to increase over the last quarter mile, getting them just wet enough to give them chills, but not completely soak them.

They reached the cabin, and Clay lifted up the heavy mat in the garage and then opened the door in the floor. He motioned for Kelsey to go through and then followed her.

Kelsey was shivering and trying to warm herself by rubbing her arms. Clay lit two candles, and Kelsey sat down on the creaky bed. In an effort to try and be prepared for anything, Clay had a spare change of clothes packed away in one of the boxes in the corner. He opened it up and began to haphazardly toss things onto the floor to get to the bottom of the container. He pulled out a pair of jogging pants and a fleece sweatshirt and turned back to Kelsey.

"Here," he said and handed her the clothes. "Not exactly hot out of the dryer, but they aren't wet."

Kelsey snatched them from his hand and began to take off her shirt. Clay turned around and faced away from her as she changed. All he heard was the rustling of clothes and chattering teeth.

He removed his heavy coat and pulled up the sleeve of his shirt. He could see the impressions from the dog's teeth on his arm, but as best as he could tell, it did not actually break the skin. A wave of relief flooded his body as he realized just how different his night would have been had he seen blood.

"Okay," Kelsey said, "I'm finished."

He turned around and saw her sitting on the bed in the dry clothes, her wet clothes in a pile on the floor at the foot of the bed. She was still shivering and trying to warm up. Clay picked up the blanket lying on the bed and wrapped it around her. He crouched down in front of her and rubbed her arms vigorously. After a few minutes, the shivering stopped, but he found himself continuing to rub her arms: softer, slower.

Their eyes locked. Beads of water were dripping from the tips of her hair, her lips a tinge of blue and still quivering. He stared into her deep, green eyes— their faces just inches apart.

"I love you, Kelsey."

Chapter 14

Seconds felt like days as Clay waited for Kelsey to say something. Anything. She remained silent. Her expression, a mixture of shock and confliction, did not instill confidence in Clay. He had never uttered such words to a girl before; he had never had such feelings to share. Even though what he said was true, he was stunned he actually said it. He continued to wait for a response, growing more and more anxious. She drew a breath.

"Oh, Clay," she said and closed her eyes. She was silent for a few more seconds, then put her hands on his face and kissed his forehead.

Clay wasn't experienced when it came to romantic relationships, but it didn't take an expert to know that her action was not congruent with his words. Clay had laid it all out on the table, and she had walked away.

He slowly leaned back and ended up sitting on the floor, his head lowered in defeat. Kelsey began to cry softly.

"I am so, so sorry Clay," she said with a remorseful sincerity.

She longed to hear him say those words, even from the night they met. She thought at first those feelings were a result of Nightingale syndrome: a stranger came to her aid, saved her life, and treated her with the utmost respect; he was chivalrous in a way that had all but died even before civilization had ended. The amorous attraction did not diminish, though. Over the following weeks, each time they went out, she felt as if their relationship grew stronger. Despite the romantic feelings both had for each other, a friendship developed first. Clay had even told her at one point that he viewed her as his best friend, dethroning Geoff from that role. Clay was not perfect—nobody was—but he was as close to perfection as anyone she had met. Which is why she desired, with all her being, to reply with the same three words Clay had just spoken.

But she couldn't.

Unfortunately, as perfect as Clay was, her life— dark times from her past, some not so long ago—was not worthy of someone like him. She had tried to convince herself otherwise time and time again; that maybe she could be good enough for him. She had even dreamed about this moment. She dreamed she could verbalize how she truly felt. Yet, the day had finally arrived, and it would not turn out as it had in her fantasy.

The room's silence was broken up with the intensifying rain pounding on the garage roof from above, the occasional crack of thunder providing an ambience fitting for the mood. Kelsey leaned forward and put her hand on his shoulder. His initial reaction was to pull away, but he knew that such an action would only do more harm to their friendship. Despite the pain of rejection, he did not want to lose her as a friend.

He eventually looked up at her and simply asked, "Why?"

Though the two had grown so close over the past month and a half, Kelsey omitted various parts of her life she was too ashamed to tell him—memories she had willed herself to forget, despite them creeping into her thoughts on a daily basis. She wanted to bottle them up once more and shrug off his question. But she knew she owed him an explanation. He had to know why. Besides, she figured she knew how he would respond, anyway. It might ease the blow to both of them if she just told him.

She took a deep breath and held it. Her mind was at war over whether or not to open that door. She didn't know why it would matter, really. Whether he knew it or not, she had no intentions of them becoming anything more than friends. Perhaps if he knew, their friendship might even be stronger. She finally worked up the courage and began to speak, revealing a window into her past. Her memories consumed her, her words flowed easily as her mind's eye recalled the darkness.

****

It was the year after the ash fell. The previous winter had been brutal, and by that point, the electrical grid had become unstable at best. The economy was in shambles, a devastatingly high unemployment rate. Those fortunate enough to have jobs were mostly employed by the federal government to sift through the rubble and ash across the country. Everyone else was working to try and find a way to rebuild. It was a fruitless effort, however, and slowly the entire nation began its descent into a perpetual state of chaos.

Kelsey and her mom had run out of things to trade. Their food supply was all but gone, and their little house on Franklin Street no longer had power, water, or gas. With winter coming, there was no other card to play except to pack up and leave. They would have to walk to a train station in El Paso in hopes of heading to Fort Worth to live in one of the FEMA camps that they had heard about on the radio.

Like most people, Kelsey and her mother made that a final resort. Nobody was particularly eager to go live in a government run refugee camp with tens of thousands of other people, but desperate times were upon them. By the time they reached El Paso, the trains were gone. They, along with dozens of other families, waited for days for the next train. It never came.

After a week, they decided to start heading east on foot. Even at the age of thirteen, Kelsey knew they were never going to survive the season walking across the western half of Texas. She was well aware that that winter would be their last.

They had made it as far as Odessa, walking along I-20 when they heard a distant rumble, a sound that was becoming less and less common. The vehicle was traveling towards them and quickly went from a blurry spec to a large, roaring SUV approaching them in a hurry. It slowed down, eventually coming to a stop.

"Looks like you two could use a ride," a man said out of a half-rolled-down window.

The temperatures outside had continued to plummet. Kelsey's toes were numb; her fingers felt as if a thousand needles were jabbing her relentlessly. She had always been told not to talk to strangers and *never* get into a car with one, but she realized it couldn't be any worse than the alternative.

"Please, Mom?" Kelsey asked.

Her mom didn't put up a fight, and they climbed into the SUV. The man indicated for Kelsey's mom to get in the front seat.

The man stuck is hand out, "Name's Denny."

"Victoria," Kelsey's mom replied and shook the man's hand, "and back there is Kelsey."

"So where are you two headed? Maybe I can help get you there."

"Trying to get to Fort Worth, but we missed the train."

"Fort Worth? Well, I'm afraid I can't take you all the way out there," the man said as he cranked up the heat to help thaw his passengers. "From what I understand, the trains stopped running out of there anyway. Something about several bridges being damaged or collapsed between DFW and Abilene. I guess some of those six pointers last month took their toll."

Victoria sighed.

Without saying anything, the man threw the car into gear and slowly pulled back onto the road. He did a sharp U-turn and headed back in the direction he had just come. The SUV was quite elegant. Kelsey had more legroom than she thought possible, and all of the leather seats were heated. The cabin was filled with a heat she hadn't felt since the last Texas summer before the eruption. It was blissful.

"Well, I'll tell you what," the man said. "It looks as if you folks have had a rough few weeks and are in need of a place to stay." The man looked over at Victoria who simply nodded. "I have a place just east of Midland. It's a pretty large house, and I have plenty of food, water, power and—"

"You still have power?" Victoria interrupted.

"Have a few large generators and enough diesel to last another six months or more, and the solar panels can at least keep the necessities after that."

Kelsey was elated. Victoria was skeptical, but the prospect of soaking in a nice hot bath again clouded her judgment. She quickly snapped back to reality and realized this wouldn't come without a catch.

"Thank you, Denny, for your generous offer, but we don't have any way of paying you, and I wouldn't feel right just living there rent-free."

"Well, there are a couple of other families that are staying there as well. They help out around the house in various ways to earn their keep. It's a nice arrangement, and I think you two would fit right in."

Victoria's shoulders lowered; she cracked a smile for the first time in months, "That sounds wonderful...Well, I can, of course, cook and clean. I'm also a fairly decent seamstress. To be honest, we didn't have much of anything *before* the eruption, so we're used to making things last longer than they should," she said with a smile.

"That sounds good to me," he said and placed his hand on her leg, giving a gentle squeeze. "As long as you're contributing like the others do, then you may stay as long as you like."

Victoria swallowed the lump in her throat and forced a smile. "Great!"

She fought back the tears and kept up the charade of excitement. It wouldn't be the first time she had joined the world's oldest profession. A few months ago, she had made a deal with a man for a can of beans and a small packet of almonds. She felt utterly numb afterwards, but she did what she had to do to keep her and Kelsey alive. That night, when they were able to have their first bite of food in nearly four days, she all but forgot about the dreadful morning she had endured.

If what Denny said was true, though, then she and Kelsey would fare much better this time around. She thought it might even be possible to give Kelsey a better life *now* than she did before.

When they arrived at the house, it was even better than either had imagined. The inside was almost uncomfortably warm, as it was in the car. Denny showed them around and introduced them to the other families who were staying there. One by one, each of the women introduced themselves and their children, first Leslie, then Nadia, and finally Jackie. It was abundantly clear that Denny was the only man in the house. There were two boys, though, but neither had even hit puberty yet. Victoria had a pit in her stomach when she realized she and Kelsey would essentially become part of a polygamist family. She thought about taking Kelsey and leaving when a fourth woman came out from another room. She was, by far, the youngest of the group and couldn't have been a day over twenty-one. In her hands was a large platter displaying a plump goose.

"Oh my, I didn't realize we would be having company," the woman said and quickly put the tray down to introduce herself to the new arrivals. "My name is Crystal. Welcome!"

Victoria and Kelsey gawked at the perfectly cooked bird sitting just a few feet away. Any contemplation of leaving the house had been forced out of their heads by the succulent aroma filling the room.

Over time, Victoria and Kelsey settled in, and life almost seemed normal. The winter months were cold, but for the first time in over a year, they didn't go to bed each night with the fear of not waking up the next morning. There was no shortage of food, just as Denny promised. Victoria appreciated the strong friendships that quickly developed with the other women which were something she hadn't had since her sister Cassandra had died.

Denny spent most of the days out trying to find food, supplies, and other stranded people. He brought home another family a few months after Victoria and Kelsey—a woman named Yolanda and her son Robert. Then, a few days after their arrival, they were gone. Denny acted as if they had never come home with him; he just went about his business like every other day.

Victoria's trepidations when summoned to the bedroom gradually faded. Denny continually provided for Kelsey and her and acted—most of the time—like a husband to her. She came to accept that he *was* her husband and she was one of his wives. She realized the more accepting she became of this new life, the easier things would be for her and Kelsey, and she was right.

Over the next year, the families grew closer together. With five women and twelve children, the household was always up to something. Once the diesel ran dry, many of the amenities were reduced, but even so, they still had daily TV watching times— Denny had looted an old library and had thousands of movies—as well as heated water, plenty of food, and even their monthly square dancing in the large open living room. It was a single-family community within a home. It was strangely pleasant.

****

Kelsey looked at Clay, her eyes swollen and red, tears streaming down her face, "But then everything changed."

"What happened?" Clay asked, a sick feeling panged his stomach as he started to postulate a conclusion in his head.

"One night, as I was getting ready for bed, my mom came and got me. She said that she and Denny needed to talk with me in his bedroom. I didn't think much of it at the time and went without question. My birthday was coming up, and I thought maybe he was going to do something special for me.

"When we got to his bedroom, they had me sit on the bed and Mom..." Kelsey began to lose her composure and had to cry for several minutes before continuing. "She started talking to me about being a woman and pulling my weight for the family and that because Denny had been so good to us and had provided us with so much that I needed to...to lay with him.

"I didn't understand what she meant at first, but then she walked out of the room, and it became quite clear what she had meant." Kelsey broke down again.

Clay rubbed her shoulders but could sense she didn't want to be touched, so he stopped.

"I remember hearing awful, terrible screams in my head. Screams I wanted to cry out loud, but I don't think I ever made a sound. I blocked out almost everything about what Denny did to me that night, but the thing that still haunts me to this day was hearing my mom weeping just outside the door. I kept hoping she would come in and rescue me from him, but she never did.

"I didn't leave my bed the whole next day. I was defiled. I was worthless. I thought over time I would get over it and things would return to normal, but not even a week later I was taken to his room again, and then again the following week, and the week after that..." she said as she wiped away tears from her face with the sleeve of the sweatshirt.

"Kelsey, I am so...so sorry." It was all Clay could say. He knew there were no words which could provide consolation to such malevolent actions.

As if Clay hadn't said anything, Kelsey continued. "One day while the rest of the family was outside, I came in for a drink of water and heard my mom talking with Denny in his room. She was pleading with him to stop forcing himself on me. That it wasn't right and was slowly killing me. She wasn't all that far off with that statement. I had many nights when I thought about dragging a blade across my wrist.

"But Denny didn't care. And when my mom grabbed his arm as he walked away, he turned around and smacked her with the back of his hand. She cried and held her face; I remember seeing blood pouring out of her nose. I'll never forget what Denny said to her after that. 'So you are going to start telling *me* how things should run here? How about I send you and your skank of a daughter back out into the cold? You think things were bad when I found you two? It's ten times worse now. Or how about I just deal with you like Yolanda? Maybe that would be the easier thing for me to do.'"

Kelsey slowly shook her head; she stared blankly at the floor as she found herself lost in a nightmare. She continued, "I walked back outside to the rest of the family. The kids were playing some games while the other women were washing clothes. I didn't know if Denny treated any of the other girls the same way or if it was just me. I felt completely dead inside and had no one to talk to about it. My mom was too ashamed. Over time she could barely look at me.

"Less than a year later, I told my mom my stomach hurt. It didn't take long to figure out that I was pregnant."

Clay's eyes widened, which caused Kelsey to snap out of her long stare. "Dakota's not your sister, is she?"

Kelsey shook her head.

"My mom told me to keep it a secret, not to tell anyone in the house, but after another month or so I started to show and we couldn't keep telling Denny I was just under the weather. One night my mom told me that she was going to tell Denny. I couldn't bear the thought of listening to that conversation, so I went to my room. On my way to bed, I grabbed a paring knife from the kitchen and put it to my wrist. I had finally psyched myself up enough to follow through when the door opened. I only saw Denny's silhouette standing in the doorway. I hid the knife under my pillow.

"He shut the door, locked it, and walked over to the bed. He told me that my mom said I was 'sick' and that he was going to fix me up. He had a plastic prescription bottle in his hand and tapped out a pill. 'Take this, and you'll feel better in a few days.'

"Just a few minutes before he came in, I was ready to take my own life, subsequently ending the life of my daughter. But when Denny tried to force me to take that pill, I no longer wanted to die. I was no longer making decisions that just affected me but affected my daughter, too. Despite how much my mom loved me, decisions she made had driven me to the brink of insanity, and I knew that *I* would love my child more than that.

"When I first resisted taking the pill, he tried to convince me it was just going to help me feel better. At first, he was calm, reassuring that everything would be okay, but the more I resisted, the less patience he had. Finally, he was able to get the pill in my mouth. I managed to break free from his grip and spit the pill in his face, and that really pissed him off. The sound was so loud I don't know if the ringing in my ear had been from the slap or the sound itself."

Kelsey began to weep again, attempting to finish the story but couldn't spit out a coherent sentence. She slid off the bed and dropped to her knees, burying herself into Clay's chest. Clay wrapped his arms around her and held her close.

"He grabbed my neck and began to choke me. That's when I slid my hand under the pillow and grabbed the knife."

Kelsey sat up and took a deep breath in. She slowly exhaled through pursed lips before continuing. "I stuck the knife straight into his stomach, and his grip on my neck loosened right away. He tried to take the knife from me, so I stabbed him again. I was able to kick him off the bed, and he hit the ground hard. I remember hearing him moaning in agony as I jumped off the bed and ran out the door.

"My mom shrieked when she saw me come out, blood all over my clothes. I am not sure if she was shocked with the sight of her daughter covered in someone else's blood, or that I had just potentially taken away her meal ticket.

"I remember vividly each and every face that watched me, soaked in Denny's blood, as I ran down the hall, through the living room, and out the front door. I heard screams and cries from inside the house as I jumped off the front porch, heading into the frigid evening. Nobody tried to stop me, not even my mom."

Kelsey sighed deeply as if a huge burden had been lifted from her. Clay was shocked: not with what she did; but rather that somebody did that to her. That someone put her in that situation, giving her no alternative but to fight back. She fought to save her life, to save her daughter's life, and Clay would never fault her for that.

"Kelsey, you did what you had to do to protect yourself and Dakota. You did nothing wrong."

She shook her head. "Maybe, but what he did to me... he tainted me!"

"That's *not* your fault."

"Maybe not, but it changed who I was. Clay, after that day, I was dead inside. Dakota was the only thing that kept me going. My desire to protect her, to provide for her, and give her a life that I had lost took priority over everything else. Denny forced himself on me, but since I left, I have willingly walked a similar path to ensure Dakota's well-being."

Clay gazed at her but didn't know how to respond. She could see sadness and anger in his eyes—an anger that wasn't directed towards her but at Denny. She had dumped a lot on him, and it was all still sinking in.

"And *that* is why you and I can't be together, Clay. I am no good for you. You deserve a girl who can give you *all* of herself, not just the shattered ruins.

Clay was silent.

"I have wanted to tell you about this ever since we met. I see how you look at me, Clay, and I would be lying if I said it didn't make me feel more alive than I have felt in years, but I just can't let myself be with someone who would treat me better than I deserve. I can't; I won't." Her eyes were heavy and bloodshot. Her shoulders dropped. "I'm really tired," she said as she lay down. "Can I rest some?"

"Of course," Clay replied.

He watched as she turned her back to him and faced the wall. He covered himself with a sheet and laid down on the cold, hard floor. Neither fell asleep right away. Kelsey thought about Clay's response. It wasn't what she had been expecting, and it certainly didn't make her feel any better. If anything, she felt worse.

Chapter 15

He saw her sitting on the floor of a child's bedroom filled with toys. The room, furniture, and toys were all charred black, as if they had been run through an incinerator. Kelsey was wearing a bright yellow dress, like something a princess in a fairytale would wear. She had her knees to her chest and was crying, rocking herself. He tried to talk to her, but he couldn't. She looked at him and whispered, "Please stop. Don't hurt me."

Clay tried to tell her he wasn't going to hurt her, but his voice could not find his lips. He walked closer to her, and she scooted across the floor. Ash and dust stirred around her. By the time she reached the corner, her dress was as black as death itself.

"Please, don't," she cried. "Stop it!" she shrieked.

He crouched down in front of her and leaned towards her. She reached for a roller skate that was lying on the floor nearby, but it crumbled in her hand. Without saying a word, Clay watched in horror as he grabbed her by the throat. "No!" he heard himself shout inside his head, but still said nothing. Kelsey's hand slid up the wall as she struggled and gasped for air. Her hand began smashing the wall, and fragmented pieces started dropping to the floor. Clay watched as she continued to hit the wall not realizing that she had drawn a knife and had thrust it into his stomach with all the strength she had left.

He fell backwards and hit the ground with an intense impact. Kelsey stared lifelessly at him, her hand still clinching the knife. "Kelsey!" Clay finally shouted with a clear, audible cry, but it was too late.

The boundaries of his vision pulsated with a creeping darkness, with every contraction of his heart, so too did his vision fade. Then darkness.

He awoke suddenly. His body was trembling, and he wasn't sure if it was from the awful visions in his head or the cold room. He quickly rose to his feet and ran up the stairs, flung the door open, and found his way to the corner of the garage just in time to vomit.

His shaking intensified from the heaving; he leaned against the rotting two-by-four framing of the garage as he tried to pull himself together.

"Clay?" Kelsey said, her head sticking out just above the floor. "Are you okay?"

He turned to look at her, concern covered her face. "Yeah, I'm okay. Guess I just ate something bad yesterday," he said with a weak smile. "I'll be back down in a minute. We should probably get ready to head out, anyway."

Kelsey returned to the room. In her absence, Clay attempted to spit the awful taste of the bile out of his mouth and force the horrible dream out of his memory. He couldn't remember having a dream as surreal or emotional as the one he just experienced. He wasn't sure what to make of it. Was he watching things from Denny's perspective? Or was Clay the one killing her? The whole thing had played some terrible games with his mind. At that moment, he hated Denny with an unrivaled passion. Clay started to hope that Kelsey did kill Denny that night. But part of him hoped she hadn't so that, perhaps, Clay would be able to pay the sick and twisted man a little visit someday.

Clay was weak and still hadn't moved; he heard Kelsey climbing back up the steps.

"Here," she said and handed him a canteen.

He took a swig, swished it around in his mouth, and then spit it onto the floor. He took some smaller sips that he swallowed, followed by some larger gulps. "Thank you."

Kelsey looked at his ghostly white face and knew it wasn't just bad food. His eyes looked as if they were screaming in torment. Not even realizing it, she leaned in and wrapped her arms around him. His body was shuddering fiercely, and his breathing was hurried. She rested her head on his shoulder and rubbed his back with her hand. Clay hugged her back. Neither spoke.

They both went back downstairs and packed up their things. Clay's color returned to normal, but he was still awkwardly quiet. She wanted to ask him what that episode was all about but didn't want him to relive whatever had him so distressed. Besides, she had a pretty good idea what was plaguing him.

Clay walked to the stairs, still without a word.

"Hey," Kelsey said to him gently. Clay stopped halfway up the stairs and turned to her. "Really, are you okay?" she asked.

Right then, like the rage of a tornado dissipating into the sky, the anger in his eyes faded, and his body relaxed some. He grabbed her hand and gave a gentle squeeze, "Yeah. Yeah, I'm okay."

"Okay," she responded with her sweet smile.

Clay stepped into the garage and then helped Kelsey up. "Thank you," she said to him, stroking the back of his hand with her thumb.

The door on the side of the garage wouldn't open; the heavy rain quickly froze as the temperatures dropped. It took three good shoulder rams from Clay to open it. Even though the light of the sun seldom punched through the constant haze, the dusting of snow and ice on the ground made the world a lot brighter. Clay was kicking himself for forgetting his sunglasses.

As the day wore on, Clay's thoughts slowly shifted from the darkness that had intruded on his sleep. His mood improved with each mile, and Kelsey could tell.

As they approached the firehouse, Clay stepped on a slick surface and took a tumble down a slight incline. As soon as Kelsey knew he wasn't hurt, she laughed hysterically and mocked how he tried to catch his balance before falling. She eventually walked over to help him up but also slipped. It was Clay's turn to laugh, but instead, they laughed together as they both lay on the frigid ground, enjoying a much needed, light-hearted moment after such a cold, dark night.

After they gathered their composure, they decided to eat lunch before parting ways. Clay told her about Geoff's offer and how tempting it was. "So what's holding you back?" she asked.

He gave her a quick glance before he looked down at the ground, "Nothing, I suppose," he lied. She heard his unspoken answer.

They finished eating and double-checked to make sure they both had all of their new things. They walked outside and stood in front of the decaying fire station.

"So, I guess this is goodbye for the next five or six months," she said with an exaggerated frown, sticking her lower lip out.

"Yeah, I guess so."

Clay was discouraged with the thought of her absence from his life for nearly half a year, even if they were only going to be just friends. It had already crossed his mind to try and travel to see her during the winter months. There are a few days each season when it creeps into the mid-30s, and if there isn't much snow on the ground, it's actually not too bad to travel in. He was hoping for multiple days like that this winter.

"Well," she said as she stood on her toes to kiss him on the cheek. "Be safe this winter." She turned to walk away.

"It doesn't change anything," Clay spoke up sheepishly.

Kelsey stopped abruptly. She turned around and looked at him baffled. "What doesn't?"

"What you told me last night. It doesn't change how I feel about you. If anything, I love you more."

Kelsey put her hands over her mouth. "Clay," she said walking back to him, "I can't even begin to tell you how hard it is for me to hear you say that. It's not because I don't want to love you back, but it's because I won't let myself."

"Kelsey, please just—"

"No, Clay," she cut him off. "There's someone better for you out there. I wish I were her," her eyes got watery, "but I'm not."

She put her hand on his face and stroked his cheek with her thumb. She opened her mouth to say something, then closed it and smiled. "Goodbye Clay." And with that, she turned and walked away.

****

A trip that should have taken Clay an hour and a half took almost three. His pace was slow; his mind occupied. He was fortunate not to run into anyone along the way. He probably wouldn't have noticed them even if they had walked right up and said hello.

After two knocks, the door opened up.

"Hey Maya," Clay said, expecting to see Tyler. "You taking over Tyler's post?"

"Tyler's sick," she said. "His tummy hurts."

Clay had forgotten. "Well, I know Megan will make him all better. She's good at making owies disappear, huh?"

Maya held up her arm and pointed to a bandage on her elbow. "Yep, she is the bestest!" she said with a smile.

Clay closed the door and walked down to his room to drop off his gear before heading to the kitchen. His eyes widened, and he gasped. "What happened?" he asked, his voice stricken with panic and confusion.

Megan was emptying the freezer chest. Several towels were on the floor, soaked with blood and juices. She looked over at him, "Clay, we have a big problem!"

"No kidding!" Clay practically screamed.

Megan had two piles of foods. She began putting one of the piles back into the freezer. Clay concluded the other half would be getting pitched. The pile going back in was frighteningly smaller than the other.

"I walked in to fix breakfast, and there was this awful stench," she said motioning around the room. "I looked around and saw the giant puddle under the freezer."

He walked over and helped her load the remaining food back into the freezer. It was mostly venison and vegetables. One of the rabbits he had bagged a few weeks back with Charlie had also managed to stay frozen at the bottom of the pile, as did about five pounds of the hog. There was around twenty pounds of meat left in addition to whatever was in the freezer above the fridge. Even if Megan got very creative, that might last a month into winter.

Clay sighed heavily and shook his head. The unthinkable had happened. He was kicking himself for not being more diligent. Usually he would pop the freezer open every two or three days just to make sure that everything looked okay. Not just to make sure it was still frozen but also to check for freezer burn. However, in the past month, he had gotten lazy about it. Never having any issues with it in the past, it was one of those trivial tasks that had become overlooked and forgotten. Ironic how it might just cost them everything.

"Did it break?" he asked.

Megan shook her head, "Unplugged."

"What? How?"

"A few days ago, I had a really bad migraine and had to lie down. Lona volunteered to run things, which she did very well. Unfortunately, she doesn't keep quite as close of an eye on Bethany as I do."

Clay could see where this was going and knew there wasn't really going to be anyone to blame.

Megan was ill; Lona tried her best; and Bethany was a curious toddler.

"Listen, Clay, you *cannot* mention this to Lona. It would crush her."

Clay agreed and added, "We shouldn't mention this to anyone right now. Let's get this food into a trash bag, and I'll bury it. Then, first thing in the morning, I'll head to Watson's and see what I can come up with."

"I hope you can work something out. Clay," she said with a tremble in her voice, "I'm really scared this time. The last time we went into a winter with this little food..." her voice trailed off, and she began to cry.

She buried her face into Clay's chest, and he gave her a reassuring hug, "It's going to be okay. I'll take care of it. I promise."

Megan was comforted by his promise and quickly pulled herself together before any of the kids saw her and began worrying too. Megan was always calm and collected. Most of the kids only saw her cry when the group lost someone.

"I need to go get lunch started. It should be ready in about thirty minutes."

Clay nodded, but he wasn't hungry. All he wanted to do was go to bed, but he first had to take the trash bag downstairs and bury it at least a mile away. Then he needed to get some things together to trade with Watson. He knew he would need to up the ante to get food so close to winter.

Clay skipped lunch in lieu of sleep. He was physically and emotionally drained and slept through the afternoon and all through the night, only waking for about an hour to eat some leftovers from dinner. He woke up around 7:30 A.M., got ready and left, only saying bye to Megan because he happened to pass her in the hall. Every minute counted, especially this time of year. Since he had a feeling he wasn't going to be walking back with a hundred pounds of meat, he assumed Watson's wasn't going to be his last trip before winter settled in.

He arrived at Watson's and made a beeline for the shop. It still hadn't even reached forty degrees, and it was half past noon—not a good sign. Even though he very much wanted to see her, Clay decided not to go looking for Kelsey. He needed to deal with Watson, and then head out.

"Well, howdy there, Clay," Watson said from behind the counter. "I wasn't expecting to see you here again until spring."

"I wasn't expecting to come, but I'm in a bit of a jam."

"Well, what can I do for ya?"

"How much meat do you have for trade?" Clay asked in desperation. He was not optimistic from Watson's expression.

"Well, to be honest with you Clay, I don't really have any for trade. Usually I wrap up that kind of bartering at the beginning of September and start preppin' for winter."

Clay explained what happened, and as heartbreaking as the story was, it had little impact on Watson's stance.

"Please, Jake, I really need your help on this one."

There was a look of hopelessness in Clay's eyes that matched his voice. Watson begrudgingly conceded, "All right, son, but you better have some good trades."

Clay pulled out the last container of coffee they had. Watson's eyes got big, nearly as big as the first time Clay brought coffee.

"As much as I love coffee, I lived without it for years before, and will eventually have to live without it again. I'll give you five pounds for it, and that is more than that coffee is worth right now. What else do you have?"

Clay threw an oblong shaped pack onto the counter and unzipped it. He pulled out a Ruger 10/22 Takedown and assembled it for Watson.

"Well, I'll be! I haven't seen one of these in ages. But you know that this gun is worthless without ammo. I haven't seen a .22 long rifle cartridge in probably three years now."

Clay took off his backpack and plopped it on the counter as well. The loud thud made Margaret—who was organizing some items on the other side of the room—jump.

"How many do you have?"

"Three and a half bricks."

Watson nodded, "I tell ya what. For the rifle, ammo, and coffee, I can give you fifteen pounds of beef, and that's the max I can do."

"Jake, come on, fifteen pounds isn't gonna cut it. That wouldn't even last one person halfway through winter, and this gun is worth so much more."

"Sorry, Clay, but I gotta make sure that people around here can eat too."

This time, Watson had the advantage. Even though he wanted what Clay had, he was willing to let Clay leave with it. Clay, on the other hand, wasn't leaving without something.

Clay slumped his shoulders and nodded. "All right."

Watson promptly went to the back and packed the meat into a small plastic cooler with some ice, a courtesy few people received from Watson. He returned with the cooler and something in a small plastic bag, "Here's your beef," he said and put the cooler on the counter. He handed Clay the plastic bag, "I feel for you Clay, I really do, so I wanted to give you a little something extra. Sorry it's not more."

Clay looked inside and saw a whole frozen chicken. He stuck out his hand and said, "Thank you, Jake."

He said goodbye to Watson and Margaret and left for home. He had just been screwed, and knew it, but he left with a lot more food than he arrived with. He was going to miss that 10/22—a gift from his father on his thirteenth birthday. He still had another brick of .22 back home and a drop-in bolt carrier group that would convert his AR-15 to shoot .22LR. It would have to do.

On his way home, Clay kept a watchful eye for game, but there was nothing worth shooting. He hadn't seen any large game since Charlie bagged that hog. That worried him. He did see a rabbit, but he only had the .308 with him and wasn't going to waste a shot on something that would likely be vaporized upon the bullet's impact.

He returned from his trip and went straight to the kitchen. Megan was already there sitting at the table and sewing some torn clothes.

She noticed the cooler and bag in his hands. "What'd you get?" she eagerly asked.

He opened the cooler and pulled the chicken out. She was elated to see poultry, something they hadn't really had in quite some time. Overall, she thought Clay had a good trade, though she didn't quite understand the significance of parting with the .22 rifle.

The extra meat would provide some buffer, though, and afforded Clay some time to come up with a better long-term plan. But, even with Watson's food, they had no chance of surviving the long winter.

Clay plopped down in the chair across from Megan and leaned back. With blank eyes, he stared up at the ceiling.

Winter, as stressful and mentally draining as it could be, provided Clay opportunities to get physical rest. Trips out were held to a bare minimum and close to home. Usually by this time of year, he had all of his affairs in order and would be able to take a few days to recover from the busy weeks prior. But life seldom went as planned.

"I've gotta go east," he said.

"What? Why?"

"There's nothing around here to hunt, and east is the only direction I haven't really scavenged before. Plus, I can swing by Uncle Ted's. Who knows? Maybe he's still alive and can help us."

Megan's worried look didn't exactly motivate Clay. Going east was a bad idea even in the best of weather. The dangers were numerous, and the frigid winter compounded the risk. Not only had Clay never traveled such a distance alone, but he had never really been out traveling in October. The thought of going was daunting to say the least, but he was out of ideas.

"I'm leaving first thing in the morning."

Megan knew further objection would be fruitless and continued sewing while Clay went to pack. He had no idea what he was going to take; he had no idea what to expect. He started by attaching an extra magazine pouch to his vest and loaded them up for a total of six extra AR magazines, instead of the usual three. A look down at his boots with at least a half dozen holes in each told him extra socks would be essential. He grabbed smaller items—such as matches, tinder, and food—and rolled them up with the socks to save space and keep the items as dry and protected as possible. He filled his hydration pack and retrieved a few extra bottles of water. Megan had given him a few packets of powdered sports drink mix which would be crucial for replenishing lost electrolytes, even in the middle of winter. He also had rolled up a thermal sleeping bag which he tied to his pack. It was bulky and added a couple extra pounds of weight, which was why he didn't typically bring it along for his normal travels. But traveling in winter was anything but normal.

Aside from that, he had his normal every day carry (EDC) items: first aid pack, emergency rations, extra boxes of ammunition, and survival supplies. He laid his supplies out on the conference table and glanced over them; it didn't feel like it would be enough. He wanted to take more, but he had to travel as light as he could. It was going to be at least four solid days, maybe more, of hiking to reach Ted's place. Then he'd have to try and scavenge, and if he were lucky, track down some food. He needed to keep plenty of room in his pack for any food he might be fortunate enough to score.

He walked over to make sure his MP3 player was charged and then heard a knock on the door.

"Hey Clay," Charlie said. "Can I come in?"

"Sure, Charlie, what's up?"

Charlie walked over, his rifle slung over his shoulder; it was always on him, which Clay liked to see. He looked at all the items Clay had laid out on the table, "You're leaving again, aren't you?"

Clay nodded. He realized that he hadn't really taken much time to spend with Charlie since Bethany's birthday. For that matter, he hadn't seen any of the kids very much. He knew that Charlie was concerned, especially now that winter had begun, but he didn't have the time or energy to feel bad.

"Look, Charlie, I am going to be gone for a while. Two, maybe three weeks."

Charlie looked down at the floor, "Oh."

Clay didn't want to say it, but knew he had to be blunt. "I am not going to lie to you about this...you're old enough to know that there's a chance I might never come back," he said solemnly.

Charlie, still looking down, nodded.

"I know there's still a lot that I haven't taught you, and hopefully we can pick up right where we left off when I get back, but I need to know," Clay interrupted himself, "Charlie look at me." Charlie slowly raised his head and locked eyes with Clay. "Can I trust you to take care of the family?"

"Yes sir," Charlie said with a mumbled voice, but clear enough to understand.

Without saying anything else, Charlie left and returned to his room. Clay wanted to sit down and talk with him more, but he had to get things ready for the morning. Megan had dinner ready around five and gave Clay twice the amount he would normally be served. He didn't like that she used more food on his behalf, but he needed every bit of energy he could get while he still could. He went back to his room shortly after and lay down in bed. He started reading a book he had actually read for a book report some years ago; it was as boring now as it was back then, and as he had hoped, it helped him fall asleep quickly. Despite his angst, he slept soundly.

Chapter 16

Charlie rubbed his quads as he sat in his bed, utterly exhausted from the past forty-eight hours. Clay had postponed his trip to tie up some vital loose ends that he had neglected to take care of first. He enlisted Charlie to help share some of the workload. They spent nearly twelve hours yesterday carrying water from a nearby stream into the parking garage at the bottom of the building. They carried back 200 gallons in various sized containers over the course of fifteen trips. The stream was a mile and a half away with some inclines on the return trip when their load was at its heaviest. And with every trek back, they had to play their cat and mouse game before going home, adding at least an extra half mile to the journey. Charlie was thankful that they didn't have to carry the water up the sixteen flights of stairs. Two years ago, Clay had installed a pulley system in the elevator shaft that could haul up fourteen gallons at a time. It was one of the many tasks Clay did on a weekly basis which gave him an intense upper body workout. While Clay was gone, however, it would be up to Charlie to hoist the water from the garage and filter it for consumption.

Charlie winced as his thumb slid over a tight knot in his thigh. He was empathetic towards Clay who was leaving dark and early in the morning and would be walking over sixty miles in the next few days. An intimidating task in pleasant weather; a nightmare in the winter.

He looked down at the watch on his wrist and saw it was pushing midnight. Clay had given him the watch earlier that morning. It was one of those watches that was powered by light and didn't use a battery, which turned out to be a pretty important feature in recent years.

Unable to sleep, he made his way down to the armory to clean and oil his M1. Clay had lifted all of Charlie's restrictions of coming and going from the armory. He had more than proven himself responsible. His free access was a privilege and trust unlike any other from Clay, and Charlie took that honor seriously.

Satisfied with the near-white patches coming out of the bore, he cleaned up and began to reload some 9MM bullets. It wasn't the first time he had done it on his own, so he dove right in, confident but careful.

About an hour into it, the door opened.

"You're up early," Clay said as he approached the bench.

"Haven't been to sleep yet."

Clay gave him a surprised look but understood the angst Charlie was feeling. All of the responsibility that rested on Clay's shoulders would be transferred to this young man for the next couple of weeks, perhaps indefinitely. Nobody felt good about the trip, and the fact that Clay was leaving even later than he had planned made everyone a bit more nervous. Winter's first big storm always came randomly in early October, and it had yet to come. They had hoped it would hold off over the next two weeks, but that would be the latest start to the winter since the ash began to fall. No one was optimistic about that possibility.

Clay randomly selected three bullets from Charlie's "finished" pile. He reached for the calipers and measured each of the three bullets. "One point one-two-five," he read off the measurements on each of the bullets. "Spot on there, Charlie. Good work."

Charlie cracked a tired smile, "Thanks."

Clay started moving about the room to collect some items while Charlie continued to reload.

"You should have left back when you said you were going to," Charlie said.

Clay continued to sift through some boxes on the floor. "That would have been irresponsible for me to do."

Charlie shrugged.

"Charlie, it's my responsibility to make sure my family is cared for. If I had left, you guys would have run out of water before the end of the week. Then *you* would have had to go get all that water by yourself and haul it back." Clay walked over and put his hand on Charlie's shoulder, "And I know you would have done it too. You're a hard worker, Charlie, and I have no doubt you will step up for our family while I am gone. But it would have been unfair for me to leave you that and everything else I should have taken care of weeks ago. It's not what I would expect from you, so I certainly don't expect it from myself. You get what I'm saying?"

Charlie shrugged his shoulders again, "Yeah, I guess."

Clay gathered the rest of his things and walked over to the door, "I'm heading out in about ten."

It was almost 3:30. Clay would be leaving while the Screamers were still out. It was a calculated risk. He wanted to get as far as he could before the first night. Trying to cross Devil's Canyon was foolish to do once the sun went down, and if he didn't leave soon he wouldn't have enough daylight left to get across.

Charlie cleaned up, slung his rifle over his shoulder, and locked up. He heard Clay and Megan whispering in the kitchen as he stumbled towards his room. Clay was scarfing down a big plate of eggs to fuel up for the journey. It would be his last hot meal for quite some time.

Clay ate the last few bites of the eggs, followed it down with a glass of water, and then stood up, "Welp, time to head out."

Charlie and Megan followed him to the stairwell. His pack was leaning against the wall next to the door filled to the brim with supplies and food that he would likely go through before reaching his destination. He grunted as he picked it up and threw it over one shoulder and then the other. He grabbed his LaRue and placed the sling over his neck and shoulder.

Megan's eyes had started to well up, and she wrapped her arms around his neck and pulled him down to give him a kiss on the cheek. "*Please* be careful, little brother," she said as if he was considering otherwise.

"I will do my best," he said before shifting his attention to Charlie. "All right, dude. You're the man here. I expect you to keep everyone safe. This is your fortress; defend it at all costs."

"Yes sir," Charlie said assuredly.

Clay stuck out his hand and firmly shook Charlie's, then gave him a tap on the shoulder. He looked back at Megan. "You're in good hands, Megs," he said and then winked at Charlie.

Megan scoffed, "I *hate* that name."

"I know. I can't believe I forgot that I used to call you that. I'll be sure to do it more often, now," he said with a chuckle.

"Don't be such a jerk!" she said as she slugged him on the shoulder. "Now get out of here before Charlie and I make you stay."

Clay gave a lazy salute and started his descent to the bottom of the building. Megan locked the door behind him.

"I am going to try and get back to sleep before Bethany wakes up," Megan said to Charlie. "You should go back to sleep, too."

He nodded and returned to his room. It took him another hour to fall asleep, but, once he did, he slept like a rock.

Charlie opened his eyes and would have guessed it was around six had he not seen the muted light of day coming through the filthy windows in his room. It was almost 2:30, and he was surprised he had slept in so late. Charlie couldn't remember the last time he woke up so refreshed, but he had a busy day ahead of him, what was left of it anyway. He thought about just taking it easy for the day and start working hard tomorrow, but he remembered that Clay didn't do that the last two days. And now, Charlie was filling those shoes. He knew he needed to set a good example for Tyler and Blake.

Megan was in the kitchen cleaning up from lunch. Bethany was napping, and the other kids were in the craft room.

"Good morning, sleepy head," Megan said with tired eyes.

Charlie gave a halfhearted wave and looked around for something to eat. Megan handed him a bowl of stew, one of his favorites, though it was missing the carrots. The taste of beef was a nice change from the typical venison stew.

He quickly ate the chunky soup and finished it off by drinking from the bowl as if he was slurping milk after cereal. With no time to waste, he immediately got to work. The first thing he did was stretch his quads by pedaling the battery bike for about fifteen minutes to bring it back to a full charge. Last night had been relatively warm, only dipping into the upper thirties, so they didn't use the heater much. The solar panel would take care of the minor electrical use throughout the day.

As Charlie was heading to the armory, Tyler came running down the hall in tears. "Tyler, what's wrong, buddy?" Charlie asked.

"S-S-S-Sarah punched me," Tyler cried, his lower lip quivering.

Sarah came running down the hall to give her side of the story, "Only because you stole my red crayon!"

Charlie had them both come over to him. He knelt down in front of them to talk to them like Clay would, except when Charlie knelt down, the kids stood taller than him, so he stood back up. "Sarah, you shouldn't've hit Tyler. You were wrong to do that," he said with an effort to imitate Clay's voice. "And Tyler," he added, "you were wrong to take her crayon without her permission. That's called stealing."

Tyler was remorseful and nodded his head.

"While Sarah was wrong to hit you, her action was a direct consequence from *your* action, wasn't it?"

"Yes," he mumbled.

"All right," Charlie said as he put his left hand on Sarah's shoulder and his right on Tyler's, "I want you two to apologize and hug."

Sarah made the first move and squeezed Tyler tight. "I'm sorry for hitting you, Tyler," she said.

Tyler reciprocated and apologized as well. The two skipped off back to the craft room eager to get back to work. Charlie turned around and saw Megan smiling; she had observed the confrontation from down the hall. Charlie was slightly embarrassed and didn't know how to respond. He walked down the hallway towards her. "Kids!" he said shaking his head as he passed by.

Megan began to laugh loudly, "You're too funny, Charlie!"

It was good to hear her laugh, Charlie thought. Ever since the freezer had broken, Megan had been very quiet; she hadn't quite been herself. She tried to mask it, and maybe the other kids fell for it, but she seemed scared, and that worried Charlie. They both needed a good laugh.

Charlie decided to fetch some more water while the weather was still fair. He made two trips, lugging an additional twelve gallons back home. He would do that each day the weather allowed.

He took care of a few of the unfinished chores on the task list he had inherited from Clay. There was still plenty left to do, but he was exhausted, and he felt good with what he had accomplished. It hadn't been a tremendously productive day—he had slept through more than half of it—but he had marked off several things on the list, and that was way more industrious than what he originally wanted to do with his day.

Megan had dinner ready at the usual time, and Charlie quickly ate his portion. His body was yearning for more, but he didn't ask. He had gotten accustomed to the portion sizes Megan would dish out, but he had been burning significantly more calories the past few days than he had before. And with food as lean as it was, Megan had served even less than usual.

While Megan was going through the bedtime routine with the children, Charlie did a security check making a dreaded trip to the garage to ensure everything was locked and secure. It was a good thing, too; he had forgotten to put the wedge behind the door in the garage after Clay left. He was to remove it again in two weeks so Clay could get back in.

Back upstairs, Megan had finished reading and praying with the kids and was headed to bed herself. It had been a long day for her too. Charlie retired to his room as well and lay down in bed. He tried to sleep, but it didn't take. Though he was physically tired, his mind was reeling. He pulled out his journal and continued writing his book. He hoped to finish it by spring so he could take it to Vlad's with Clay to sell in his store.

****

"I saw him running this way!" a young man carrying a rifle said as he pointed down the road.

They had taken the bait. Clay had just been running in the direction the man was pointing, but he had double backed and was now hiding in a flanking position. He had no intention of ambushing them, though. Having already burned through a mag and a half laying down some covering fire just to get on the run, he didn't have the ammo to waste on an ambush. Clay also preferred avoiding a bloody gunfight that he would almost certainly come out on the losing end. He had almost died—twice—crossing Devil's Canyon, and he wasn't about to become victim to a bunch of boys playing commandos with real guns.

The man ran down the road, and six others followed close behind. After a few minutes passed, Clay slowly lifted the dumpster lid, made sure it was all clear, then pulled himself out. The alley was dark, nearly impossible to see from one side to the other. He took his time moving to the other end, being careful to avoid cans and bottles that pockmarked the asphalt like urban landmines.

He stepped out of the alley and started to cross the street when he heard the unmistakable sound of a Kalashnikov bolt being yanked back. He stopped dead in his tracks, then was illuminated by a flashlight.

"Hands in the air. Turn around!" the man ordered, though his voice nearly cracked in the process.

Clay complied and slowly turned to face two men. He was blinded by the flashlights, but he could barely make out that one of them was holding an AK-47, the other holding a pistol. It was hard to see, but it was obvious neither one was old enough to smoke, perhaps even drive a car.

"We should just kill him!" the one with the rifle said.

The other one overruled the idea. "What are you talking about? Anderson wants all intruders arrested and brought to him to be tried and executed," he said, as if there could be no other verdict than guilty.

"Dude," the one with the rifle said, "you're all about the rules, aren't you? It'd be so easy to tell everyone he pulled on us, and we had to put him down."

The one holding the pistol looked over, "And that's why Guthrie promoted me instead of you. Now go get Sergeant Phillips and the others. I don't have any zip ties on me, and Anderson would have a fit if we brought this clown in without shackles."

The man with the rifle grunted, displeased with being given orders by someone his own age, if not younger. He took off down the street in a hurry to catch up with the others.

"Now," he said returning his attention to Clay, "you need to *slowly* put your rifle on the ground and kick it over to me."

Clay reached for the plastic clasp on the sling and squeezed both sides causing the lower half of the strap to disconnect. The rifle smacked onto the ground with a loud clatter. Clay begrudgingly kicked it over to him.

The man took small steps over to Clay, keeping the pistol aimed at him and his finger on the trigger. "Any sudden moves and I shoot, got it?"

He started to reach for Clay's holster, but before he could seize the side arm, Clay grabbed the man's pistol and shoved it to the side. The man pulled the trigger, releasing a deafening bang that filled the otherwise silent streets. Clay's grip on the slide prevented the action from cycling the next round, rendering the semi-auto pistol inoperable until the jam was cleared.

Clay punched the man in the stomach before shoving him backwards. The young soldier raised his arm to shoot the gun unaware of the jam.

Click.

By the time he realized what had happened, Clay's pistol was aimed right at his head.

The man dropped his gun and put his hands up. "Please, don't kill me." His voice trembled with fear.

Clay heard shouting in the distance; he had to move quickly. After having the guard turn around, he knocked him out with a good shot to the back of the head using the handle of his Sig Sauer. The man fell to the ground without protest. Clay picked up his rifle and sprinted down the street away from the militia.

Running as fast as his legs would allow, Clay reached the end of the neighborhood in just a few minutes. He went around to the back of a nearby house, finding an unlocked door. He kept his flashlight off and moved stealthily through the first floor eventually making his way upstairs. It was an older house, likely built sometime during the Second World War, and each stair creaked and groaned from Clay's weight. He got to the top of the steps and cleared each of the rooms, determining that no one had lived there in quite some time.

Towards the end of the hallway, he saw the pull string for the attic. Pulling the ladder down was a much louder event than he would have liked, but it would be the safest place to hole up for the night. He climbed up the ladder and pulled the trap door shut.

Clay finally turned on his flashlight, illuminating the area. The musty loft was filled with boxes and other common attic fodder from the pre-eruption days. He was surprised to see that the attic was full of items that had some decent trade value. Clay recalled just how clean and pristine the house was, given that it appeared to have been abandoned for quite some time. The house hadn't been looted; none of the other houses on the street looked as if they had been, either. The area must have been well defended from day one, which explained the men's hostility towards Clay just for passing through. Most people didn't take too kindly to outsiders, but they usually didn't respond so aggressively, either.

As the night carried on, Clay gradually relaxed, and things in the neighborhood quieted down. He hadn't heard any activity outside in at least an hour, and figured the search party had finally been called off. He guessed that the people looking for him concluded that he was long gone when all the while he was going to be sleeping behind enemy lines for the night.

He started to go through some of the boxes in the attic, mostly finding keepsakes and family mementos. He hit the jackpot when he opened a box that had some clothing and, best of all, a relatively nice pair of hiking boots. They were a half size too big and fairly worn, but there were no holes in them and they claimed to be waterproof. Clay happily removed his old boots and laced up the new ones over a fresh pair of socks. What a difference that made to his morale.

He poked around a little bit more and discovered a box full of books. Most of the books were of no interest to him, but there was one that stood out as being very valuable. He blew the dust off of it and read the title: *The Survival Medicine Handbook* by Joseph Alton, M.D. and Amy Alton, A.R.N.P. He scanned through some of the chapters and saw that the book was packed with a mountain of good information and written specifically for scenarios when there was no functioning hospital nearby. Clay was amazed at what a good find that turned out to be and couldn't wait to give it to Megan when he got back home. She'd probably read through it at least three times before the end of winter.

He went through the rest of the boxes, but didn't find much else that he was willing to sacrifice the limited space in his backpack for. He did, however, find a hooded sweatshirt that he put on right away.

Exhausted, he found a couple of old blankets and created a makeshift bed. It was bitterly cold in the poorly insulated attic, but a fire would have been deadly in more ways than one. He created a small tent out of some sheets and strands of Christmas lights he tied to the rafters. It wasn't much, but it helped keep some of his body heat inside. He piled on as many blankets and clothing he could find and then climbed into the sleeping bag.

He woke the next morning chilled, but not nearly as cold as he thought he would be. The extra warmth from the sweatshirt and the thermal sleeping bag made a big difference.

He stretched and yawned. A plume of visible breath erupted from his mouth as he exhaled. He fumbled around to find his flashlight and then sipped on some water. He could see faint shafts of light pouring through various holes in the roof. It was still pretty early, so he quickly packed up and made his way down from the attic. After a quick search of the house, he left.

The patrolling guards were no slouches, but they were not on the same heightened state of alert as they were a few hours before. Through some patience and cautious movement, Clay was able to escape the town's boundaries without detection.

A few miles away, he ducked into a small pharmacy to get his bearings and noted on his map the town he had just left. He outlined the approximate boundaries and wrote inside "Devil's Den" since it was the first town he discovered after crossing Devil's Canyon.

While in the pharmacy, he looked around for anything useful. As expected, there was nothing except garbage caked beneath layers of dirt and mud. Pharmacies and gun stores were the hardest hit and always the most thoroughly picked through. Clay occasionally found something good, but they were often a bust. He did, however, find some packets of red pepper and parmesan cheese at the pizza parlor next door. Those would add a nice—and much needed—flavor to some of Megan's dishes.

As he left the pizza parlor, the flurries began to fall.

Chapter 17

Charlie stood in the front conference room—which had become his quarters for the duration of Clay's absence—and stared out the window. The snow was heavy and visibility worsened by the hour. When he had woken up he could just barely see the freeway right outside his window. Now, he couldn't even see the parking lot at the bottom of the building. It was a whiteout in every sense of the word; bad even compared to more recent winters.

"Charlie," Megan popped her head in through the door, "lunch is ready."

Charlie acknowledged her and then looked back out the window. Standing there, with his rifle over his shoulder and a solemn look on his face, he saw a faint reflection of himself in the window. Even he could see that he had physically matured over the last few months. He wondered what kids his age did before the eruptions. He could just barely remember playing a hand-held game system that his mom had given to him for his fifth birthday. He remembered enjoying it but couldn't recall a single specific memory about the times he played it.

Charlie watched as the wind whipped the snow in every direction. As the drafts shifted, he could hear the snow and sleet smack into the window like particles of sand hitting a windshield. The howling wind intensified with each gust, giving him chills from the eerie noise it produced. He was grateful to be out of the storm, safe and relatively warm in the shelter of the sixteen story office building. But he couldn't help but feel a pang of guilt that he stood inside while Clay was somewhere in the blizzard. The storm came in from the west, but there was no doubt Clay was already feeling the impact.

The sounds of hungry children scurrying to the lunch room snapped Charlie from the ominous trance of the blowing wind. He said a quick prayer for his friend and mentor before joining his family for lunch. The mealtime noise was a deafening myriad of conversations mixed with chomping and slurping that drowned out coherent thoughts.

The happy family banter was suddenly hushed by a loud crashing sound that had come from down the hall. Charlie leapt to his feet and darted across the room. By the time he had reached the door, he had his M1 chambered and the stock pressed firmly into his shoulder. Megan placed herself between the door and the children, her pistol tightly gripped in her hand.

"Stay here," Charlie commanded as he left the room.

He managed to sound calm and collected to Megan and the others, but his chest was thumping, and his muscles were tensed to the point of pain. As the adrenaline kicked in, he no longer noticed the muscle tension, but the pounding in his heart worsened as he approached the source of the sound. It sounded as if it had come from the arts and crafts room. He had his back against the wall and side-stepped the final few feet to the door. He got right up next to the door and rested his finger on the wood frame of the rifle just above the trigger. He swallowed heavily and spun around the corner only to be greeted by an arctic blast of air.

The floor-to-ceiling windows along the outer wall were the source of the sound. The center window had shattered. Charlie couldn't tell if something had hit it or if it had just become so weak over the years that the wind itself caused the destruction.

The window was tempered glass and was still in place, but it would only hold out for so long before the whole thing would come down. Content there wasn't an active threat to the family, Charlie fell back into the wall, and became mesmerized by the fractal pattern in front of him. Soon after, the adrenaline wore off, and he became shaky. He slid his back down the wall and sat for a few minutes.

"Charlie?" Megan said as she peeked through the door.

Charlie jumped.

"Sorry, I didn't mean to scare—Oh my goodness!" she said. "What happened?"

Charlie shrugged, "I think the wind broke it."

The damaged window, held together by film on either side of the pane, was waving in the wind like a crystalized flag. The room was no longer safe for the children to play in, and they both agreed they had to move the arts and crafts room elsewhere. There were plenty of vacant rooms, but none with lighting quite as nice as the current one.

Megan went back to the kids to ease their fears while Charlie moved all of the supplies into a room on the other side of the building closer to the children's bedroom. Once he had everything out of the old room, he closed and locked the door and used some duct tape and towels to minimize the draft. It wasn't perfect, but it was an effective temporary solution.

With two winters' worth of tasks to do, Charlie tackled the chore list for the day, which included repairing the busted solar panels. Again. He bundled up as if he were going on a long-term expedition in Antarctica.

Despite the added layers, the vicious wind pierced through his clothing with ease. The snow pelted the exposed parts of his face like thousands of tiny bullets, stinging without mercy. He fought against the intense wind and made his way to the panels. Struggling for his balance, he leaned unnaturally far forward to keep from being blown backwards.

Due to the delicate nature of the task, Charlie removed his gloves so he could utilize the agility of his naked fingers. In the frigid temperatures, he only had a few minutes of precise dexterity before his fingers became too numb to even grip his tools effectively. He made sure he had all the tools and equipment he needed, then stuffed his gloves into his pocket and began to work feverishly on the repair.

Charlie was able to repair the panel, but once he put his gloves back on, he started to feel the painful effects the cold had caused while his skin was exposed. He started to make his way back to the door and noticed the greenhouse, which had been tied down for the winter with tarps and bungee cords, was not secured. One of the cords had come unhooked and was flailing about like an unmanned fire hose. Charlie changed his course and headed for the greenhouse.

It took several attempts before he was able to wrangle the cord in. He stretched the cord down to one of the eyehooks Clay had screwed into the roof top. He took a step back to look for any other areas that might need to be addressed when he heard a loud cracking sound.

The cord had snapped, and the corner of the tarp was once again flapping in the wind. With no spare cords on the roof, he went back inside and headed for the tool room just across from the armory. He was walking down the hall when Megan rounded the corner.

Her eyes were wide, "Charlie!" she screamed, "What happened?" she asked while she ran over to him.

Charlie was confused. *What on earth is she talking about?* He looked down and noticed the blood all over his jacket.

Megan took off his scarf and ski hat and began to assess the wound. As Charlie's face warmed up, he felt the effects of the injury. The pain was most intense just to the right of his right eye. Megan took the scarf and put it on the wound and walked him down to the infirmary, which was a spacious private bathroom off one of the executive conference rooms.

She got some water and carefully poured it on Charlie's face then dabbed at the blood that was still leaking out.

"This is pretty deep," she said with concern. "It's going to need stitches."

Charlie played down the severity of the injury to Megan, but inside he was terrified. Surprisingly, he had never needed stitches before. He had no idea what to expect.

Megan fished around the cabinets for some sutures. Sterile sutures were few and far between, but they still had a few left that Clay had found at an urgent care shortly after the lights went out. Most of the time they just used butterfly strips, which were easier to find. Scars were never a concern, but Charlie's gash was too deep for her to feel comfortable just closing it with some tape, especially since it was reluctant to stop bleeding long enough to let the adhesive bond with the skin.

"Charlie, this is going to hurt...a lot."

Charlie looked at her and nodded, as if to tell her to get it over with. She wiped the gash with some rubbing alcohol on a cotton swab. He winced and grunted deeply. They had long since run out of lidocaine, so some ice was all the numbing he would get. She had him hold it up to his skin while she prepared the sutures.

"You ready?" she asked.

He nodded again.

She took a deep breath and curled the curved needle through his skin and began to close up the wound. Megan had practiced on an orange once when she first decided she wanted to get into the medical field. She remembered her dad's instructions as he stood over her shoulder and watched her work on her citrus patient. Since then, all of her practice had come from living patients, and she felt she had gotten pretty skillful at it over the years.

To Megan's surprise, Charlie barely made a sound the entire time. In fact, the worst of it was when she applied the alcohol, though his eyes were streaming the entire time. Megan had never had to have stitches without a numbing agent and couldn't imagine what Charlie must have been going through. He was even tougher than she realized.

"There," she said as she leaned back to examine her work. "All done. I think that'll do the trick." She grabbed a bandage from the counter and placed it over the cut. "You're so strong, Charlie. I would have been crying like a baby if that had been me." Charlie cracked a brief smile as she continue, "Well, if I had to guess, you will have a scar, but chicks dig scars anyway, right?"

Charlie chuckled quietly and got up out of the chair. He was a bit woozy from the past hour and sat back down. Megan wasn't at all surprised by his reaction and helped him to his room to rest but not before giving him a snack and some water.

She left his room and went back to the infirmary to clean up the mess. After she finished, she reached into one of the cabinets and pulled out a bottle of vodka. Clay took a few shots of it whenever he needed more substantial medical attention. She pulled the top off and poured a small amount into a mug. She downed the contents in a quick gulp and cringed at its awful taste. She didn't know how anyone could drink the stuff straight out of the bottle, but knew that it was like water to more than a few Russians.

Returning the bottle to its hiding place, Megan went back to her day as if nothing had happened. The alcohol helped calm her nerves, but she couldn't stop imagining how different the day would have gone had Charlie been standing just a half inch to the right. A cut that severe would have been absolutely devastating to his eye. With no hospital to go to and no paramedics to call, Charlie likely wouldn't have made it through the week having sustained that kind of trauma. Luck was on his side today.

With the kids napping and Charlie still resting, Megan took the opportunity to have a good, hard cry. After a brief concert of tears and whimpers, she felt recharged; her shields were back up. She wiped her face and began preparing for dinner.

****

They say that death wears a black cloak and rides a dark horse—black is the color associated with death. But as Clay pushed through the torturous elements of the winter storm, he knew that death was, in fact, shrouded in white.

The gale force winds added to the already unbearable challenge. He was quite certain that some of the gusts could rival the winds of a hurricane. At times, he had to crouch down just to keep from falling over. And even then, his balance was shaky at best.

He had bundled up as best as he could, but it didn't take long for the cold to penetrate through his shabby clothing. Each step he took was accompanied by sharp pain that ricocheted throughout his body. It had been four hours since he had last seen a structure of any kind. He had probably passed a few buildings in that time, but visibility was down to less than twenty yards—all he saw was white.

He checked his compass to make sure he was still heading in the right direction. He was. He was in the right county, too, but had no idea how far he had traveled since leaving the pharmacy earlier. He was moving much slower now, taking one step for every four he took before the storm hit.

He felt vulnerable, like a baby bird that had fallen from the nest. He couldn't tell if he was alone or if he was about to walk right into a Screamer camp. His fear and anxiety grew with each step he took, causing him to become paranoid. Several times in the last hour he was convinced he heard someone talking to him, which caused him to drop to one knee and swing his rifle around, searching for a target that wasn't there. The paranoia was further fueled by the hypothermia which was growing more severe by the minute.

Night came quickly. The whiteout had turned to a blackout, and the intense pain from the cold still terrorized every part of Clay's body. He turned on his flashlight so he could see the few feet of ground in front of him. Normally, walking outside at night was a death wish, a danger magnified when using a flashlight. But if there was any silver lining to not being able to see anyone that might be around him, it was that they also couldn't see him.

Two more hours went by, and he still had not found a suitable place to camp. He could no longer feel his toes, and his fingers had been numb for hours. He was kicking himself for not stopping at the motel he passed when the snow really picked up. He thought he would be able to make it a few extra miles before things got too bad, and he did. Unfortunately, he was on a particularly long stretch of asphalt with fields on either side; no shelter in sight.

His flashlight danced carelessly ahead of him, piercing through the thick falling snow to illuminate the knee-deep blanket that had accumulated over the past eight hours. Suddenly, he saw a dark object protruding from the buildup. It was just barely visible but unmistakable. A fire hydrant! As he shined his light around more, he discovered multiple cars. He had found a road!

Clay walked until a large brick wall stood just a few yards in front of him. He could have cried at the sight of such a sanctuary but knew the tears would just freeze to his face, further exacerbating his pain. He found a pair of doors about ten yards down and tried to go in, but they were not only locked, they were also barricaded on the other side—not the best indication of an abandoned building—but there was no time to search out an alternative shelter.

He followed the brick wall in search of another entrance. There were elevated windows about every eight feet, but they were boarded up or blocked from the inside. Breaking through the barricade was off the table. If somebody was in there, they would almost certainly hear Clay forcing his way in. Not to mention, Clay barely had the strength to stand, let alone pull himself up through a window, which was almost five feet off the ground.

He eventually reached the end of the building and turned with the wall, following it around back. He maneuvered around some playground equipment before having to climb over a short chain-link fence. He barely made it over the top and then fell face first into two feet of snow. The blast of frozen powder to his face gave him a jolt of energy to press forward. He pushed himself up from the ground and trudged on.

Clay finally came to another set of doors, one of which was popped open just slightly. He cleared away the snow at the bottom of the door and pulled on the handle, but it only opened another foot before it wrenched to a stop. He heard the clanking of a chain bouncing off the metal door from inside. Clay shined his light in and saw there was also a wall of debris piled behind the doors. He noticed a distinct path in between the various pieces of furniture that had been stacked up. It was obvious that this was the occupant's point of entry. He took a good look at the door; it was not open very wide, but Clay thought it might be just wide enough to fit through.

He kept telling himself how foolish it was to break into a building as inaccessible as this one was. Somebody went to a lot of trouble to keep people out, just as he had done with his home. He also knew that someone going through that much effort to keep people out would probably not hesitate to blast any intruders who managed to get in. Ordinarily, he wouldn't take such an imprudent risk, but being mere minutes from a bitterly cold death, he decided it was worth it.

He took off his pack and sat it on the ground next to the door. He pulled the door open as far as he could, then crouched down and began to maneuver himself between the doors. He had to duck beneath the chain binding the two together, forcing him to stretch his body awkwardly. Clay's muscles felt as if each one had snapped in two, causing him to produce a noisy groan. Once he got past the door, he reached outside and grabbed his pack before lying on the ground to crawl through the barricade maze. He got about half way through before he had to stop. He was too big. *Whoever lives here must be tiny,* he thought to himself.

Able to eventually wriggle out of his coat and sweatshirt, he squeezed his way through, pushing his pack and coat ahead of him. Then, finally, freedom.

He stood back up and sighed deeply, which echoed around the large room. He turned his flashlight off and stumbled around until he found a door. Despite his best efforts, the room seemed to amplify the sound of his footsteps, so he unlaced his boots and carried them in his hand.

Clay thought he would never find his way out of the room, when suddenly his hand felt a series of light switches along the wall. He figured he was close to a door and felt around blindly in the darkness.

There wasn't a single light to be seen, and as such, he was unable to see his own hand in front of his face. Visibility was no better inside than outside, but at least the wind was no longer assaulting him.

Finally, he discovered a doorknob. He walked inside the room and closed the door so slowly that even he didn't hear a sound. He made sure the door had no windows. He took a gamble and turned on his flashlight for a quick burst to get a sense of the layout of the room. Though it was only on for about two seconds, Clay was able to see a couple of couches and a handful of chairs, a pair of vending machines, and several smaller square tables with some chairs. It was a break room of sorts, reminding him a little bit of home. It was as good a place as any to setup camp for the night.

As comfortable as the couch looked, Clay knew it would be smarter not to sleep in such an exposed position. He pulled the couch out a few feet from the wall and laid his sleeping bag down behind it, putting himself between the back of the couch and the wall. He climbed in and zipped it up. He pulled some hand warmers out of his bag, threw two down by his feet, and put another on the back of his neck. Slowly, his body started to warm up, but not without the excruciating pain that accompanied the defrost.

The accommodations were hardly ideal, but after the day he had endured, sleeping on the cold, hard floor of a break room, behind a rather putrid smelling couch, felt like a five-star resort.

Chapter 18

Daylight streamed in between the boarded up windows. The musty air of the break room filled Clay's lungs as he yawned and attempted to sit up, but every muscle in his body seemed to be on strike. He lay there staring at the water-stained drop ceiling wondering if he was actually going to reach Uncle Ted's or not. His mind wandered and eventually became curious about where he was and gave him enough motivation to exit the warmth of the sleeping bag.

He gingerly walked across the break room, around a partition, and into a short hallway which lead to some bathrooms and a supply closet. The men's bathroom came up empty, as did the supply closet, but the women's bathroom surprised him. His thorough search efforts paid off. Taped to the bottom of one of the toilet tank lids was a flat bottle of liquor, nearly three quarters of the way full. Clay wasn't much of a drinker, only the occasional sip here and there, but he knew this bottle could fetch a nice price. Finding alcohol wasn't exactly rare, but most of the bottles he ran across anymore were homebrews. Homemade liquor wasn't even on the same planet as pre-eruption booze.

He slid the bottle into one of the pouches of his bag and continued searching the break room. He found a box of maxi-pads in a cabinet just outside the bathroom doors. Only two left. He tossed them into his bag as well. Pads, while not sterile, made excellent bandages in a pinch. In fact, some soldiers actually carried them in their combat packs to help stop bleeding.

Satisfied no stone was unturned, Clay rolled up his sleeping bag and walked out the same door he came in. It was still dark in the hallway since it was an interior corridor, but there were large pockets of light on either end which provided a minimal level of lighting to navigate. The bulletin board and various fliers in the break room led him to believe he was in a school, and the lockers in the hallway confirmed it.

The hallway was silent with the exception of the howling wind and an incessant dripping sound that never seemed to dissipate no matter how far he walked. The whole building felt stale and unoccupied; he started to think no one actually lived there, at least not anymore.

Clay turned on his flashlight, which needed a few dozen cranks on the charging handle, and began to go through the lockers. He found a few random things that would have been useful, and had he been closer to home, he would have taken them. However, with limited space in his pack, he had to restrict his scavenging to more useful and essential items. After about fifteen lockers, he found himself debating on what was considered essential when he found *Our*

Lonely Past, the sequel to *The Remaking*, which he had just finished reading a few weeks back. He had no idea there was a follow-up, and couldn't believe he had found it in some rusty, old school lockers. He deemed the book was, in fact, an essential.

It had been an hour by the time he reached the other end of the corridor. He peeked between the boards covering a window and saw that it was still nearly a white-out. He had an uncomfortable feeling he'd be staying another night. It was frustrating, but the smart thing to do. If yesterday repeated itself, there would be no chance of him pulling through. It was a miracle he had survived; he wasn't going to push the limits again. Not voluntarily, anyway.

Clay found himself on the second floor going through each classroom with a fine-tooth comb. There wasn't much to discover; most everything of value had been taken. He did find some dry erase markers that the kids would enjoy and a small bottle of aspirin locked in a teacher's desk. Office supplies were abundant—rubber bands, paperclips, and thumbtacks could be useful back home. He bent over to pick up a pair of scissors on the floor when he heard a shriek come from down the hall.

He stuck the scissors into his pocket and ran to the other side of the room. With his back against the wall, he slid closer to the door. He heard hustled footsteps moving through the hall; two men began shouting. He leaned out the door and looked towards where the sounds had come from, but nobody was there.

It was obvious somebody was being chased—a young girl more specifically. Despite Clay's apprehension, he wasn't about to let a helpless child fend off two grown men. He didn't leave Kelsey, and he wasn't going to leave this kid. Clay readied his rifle and began pursuit.

He moved swiftly through the hall and kept his rifle in a quick-fire position. It wasn't long before he tracked down the sounds. He picked up the pace when he heard a loud crashing around the corner. As he turned down the next hallway, his rifle up and ready, he saw two men pounding on a locked door, one tall and burly, the other somewhat scrawny. The bigger man had an aluminum baseball bat in his hand, the other, a double barrel shotgun. They both had black bandannas tied around their left leg, just below the knee. Clay had seen those before. He got angry.

Whoever they were after was on the other side of the door. Clay didn't know if she was still in the room or had escaped elsewhere. He didn't want to risk collateral damage, so he opted for the pistol that would likely not penetrate the steel door behind his targets. Prioritizing the threat was easy, the man with the shotgun first, bat-man second. Clay took a breath to order them to stand down, but before he could say anything, the man with the shotgun spotted him. His eyes were wide; shock jolted across his face. Without saying a word, the man raised his shotgun, but Clay had already fired the first shot, striking him in the chest. He fired two more times just as the man pulled the trigger on the shotgun. The shot was wide, but so was the spread, and Clay caught a few pellets to the shoulder. At that point, the skinny man crumpled to the ground; he gasped for air as life escaped.

The pain in his shoulder had not yet registered in Clay's brain, and he immediately transitioned to the bigger man. The man charged him like an angry rhino, so Clay pulled the trigger, but there was no boom. The gun had failed to fully eject the previous shell and botched the cycling process. With no time to clear the jam, he reflexively dove to the side, *almost* avoiding the man's homerun swing. The bat tip made contact with his shoulder—the same shoulder—which he felt immediately, and sent Clay crashing into the floor.

The big man bounced off the wall as if it was the ropes in a wrestling ring and stormed back to Clay. Before he could do any more damage, Clay used every ounce of strength he had to push himself up and swing his leg. Clay's boot, steel tip first, crashed into the side of the man's knee with such a fury that the popping sound of his kneecap dislodging echoed down the hall.

The brute screamed in agony and rage as he dropped to the floor just a few feet away from Clay. With one arm, the man grabbed Clay's leg and yanked him closer. He continued to assault Clay's injured shoulder before delivering a nasty blow to the head. Dazed from the impact, Clay did little to stop the man from getting on top of him to connect several more punches. With the man now sitting on top of the barrel of the AR, Clay reached for the pair of scissors in his pocket. He swung with all his might at the man's ribs, but they did not pierce the thick coat he was wearing. The pressure from the impact, however, was enough to make the man sit up straight.

A brilliant flash from the doors lit up the dim hallway for a brief moment as a deafening boom echoed off the painted cinderblock walls. The man screamed, but only for only a moment before falling backwards, landing on Clay's legs. As terrible as the grizzly sight was, it was the sound that Clay would not soon forget.

Clay looked over to where the blast had originated and saw a small figure standing in front of the now open door, she had the shotgun aimed at him. He tried to free his legs from the weight of his attacker but to no avail. The girl walked over and stood over him. Clay raised his hands slightly, a gesture of submission, even though he knew both shells in the old break barrel were spent.

"Look, I was just trying to help," he said, gasping for air between words.

The girl was silent, her stare piercing like she was trying to read his mind and discern his true intentions. Clay closed his eyes and sighed deeply, more from the exhaustion of the scuffle than anything.

The girl lowered the shotgun and then laughed. "You were trying to help me? Seems like the other way around," she said sarcastically, years beyond her age.

She walked over to the lifeless body pinning Clay to the ground and began pulling on his arm. Her efforts were mostly ineffective, but it was just enough for Clay to maneuver his way out from beneath the hefty body.

He pulled a rag out from his pack and began wiping the blood off of his face. He flinched, realizing just how tender his head was. Another couple of shots like that, and he would have blacked out.

The girl picked up Clay's pistol which had ended up down the hall a good ways, and then searched the bodies. "That's what you get for coming into my house," she jested to the big man's corpse.

Clay found the one-sided transaction to be a bit creepy for a young girl, but everyone has their way of coping in the new world. He wasn't about to judge.

She walked back to the door and nodded inside, gesturing for Clay to follow. He was still shaking the cobwebs from his head after the vicious attack, so he hadn't even noticed she was now in possession of his Sig. He slowly stood up and stumbled his way through the door. She locked up behind them and led the way to the cafeteria which was where she lived. It was the innermost area of the building, and all of the obvious entries were ably barricaded. The only apparent way in or out was the door that they had just come through, and she had the only key. It was actually a pretty nice setup, all things considered. She had turtled herself into a relatively secure area, and Clay could see a few quick escape routes that she had designed in the event someone broke through. Smart kid.

"The name's Dusty," she said and extended her hand.

"Clay," he said and shook her hand.

Dusty walked over to a table stacked with clothing and other fabric and returned with a ratty old bath towel. "Here, take this."

Clay removed his rag which had become saturated with blood and took the towel from her. He pressed it against the gash over his eye and applied as much pressure as he could tolerate.

"So, what are ya doin' in my home, Clay?" she got right down to business.

"I was just about dead in the storm last night when I stumbled across the school—I mean you're home. I found the chained doors 'round back and managed to get in through your little maze."

"Yeah, and your tracks to the doors probably lured those two jackals in right behind ya."

Clay found it quite improbable that the tracks hadn't been covered by the dumping snow, not to mention *he* had barely fit through that entrance. There was no way Tons-of-Fun out in the hallway could have made it through. But he didn't argue. "I'm sorry about that. I wasn't really thinking. I had been traveling all day, and honestly, I really thought I was going to die last night."

Dusty put up a good façade. She acted as if she were as tough as nails—a little girl you didn't want to mess with—but she also wasn't completely devoid of compassion. She let her guard down a little. "That sucks," she said with the first sign of emotion since he met her, "I've been there before, so I know what you mean."

Clay finally managed to stop his bleeding long enough to apply a proper bandage with some help from Dusty. His face had already started to swell and turn several shades of purple. "Man, you look terrible," Dusty said as she examined his wounds. "He really got you good."

"Yeah. It feels like I stepped into the ring with Ali," Clay joked.

"You did what with who?" she replied.

"Never mind."

Dusty went to the kitchen and returned with some water. Clay guzzled it down in a hurry. "So, what's your story?" he asked.

"What's there to tell? My parents are dead; I'm not."

She kept her cards close. Revealing the past can allow an enemy to exploit a weakness, and she was keenly aware of that fact. She wasn't treating Clay like a foe, but he was not a friend either, and he didn't blame her for that. In fact, it was the right thing to do.

"So, what about you?"

Clay filled her in on some high level details, but, like her, was cautious not to reveal too much. It's not that he didn't trust her, but it was just how he did things. Never divulge more than necessary.

"So, how did you end up all the way out here? I've seen your area on a map before, isn't it like seventy miles away?" she asked.

"Not quite that far, but it's a pretty good hike for sure." Clay tossed back the rest of his water before continuing, "I'm out here looking for food and supplies."

"Hah!" she replied sharply. "Good luck with that."

"Well, you're surviving."

"I get by...mostly because I'm a good shot," she said proudly and nodded towards a lever action rifle leaning against the wall next to her cot. "If you're looking for stored foods, you can forget it. I haven't found a can of food in a year or more."

It was apparent she had been living in the school for quite some time: the way the building was locked down; her little home in the cafeteria; those things would have taken a lot of time, especially for a kid her age. He couldn't imagine how old she was when she had to start fending for herself with no one to care for her and no one to comfort her when the nightmares started. Yet, somehow she had prevailed. Maybe the 'hard-as-stone' act wasn't actually an act at all.

"Well," Clay said, "it's the only chance I have, so here I am."

The two chatted throughout the afternoon, waiting out the storm. It was evident that Dusty had not had someone to talk to in quite some time and was pleased to have company that wasn't trying to kill her. She started to warm up to Clay as the day went on, giving him some more insight into her background, but she remained guarded when it came to vulnerabilities.

She invited him to stay for the night since the conditions outside had only slightly improved from earlier. He thanked her for the hospitality and offered her dinner in return. Megan had packed him a half pound of beef that he kept in a small pocket on his pack. With temperatures never getting above thirty-five, there was little chance for spoilage.

"What's it taste like?" she asked.

"You've never had beef?"

"Both my parents were vegans before everything happened. I'll never forget the night we all had to split a can of pork-n-beans," she said nearly laughing. "It was either eat it or starve to death. My dad gagged, and my mom cried," Dusty said as she shook her head with shame.

How did this girl ever survive? Clay thought to himself.

"If my parents hadn't been killed over a couple of cans of fruit, they surely would have died when I took down my first rabbit; I ate almost half of it raw."

That bit of information shocked Clay. He had never been desperate enough to eat raw meat. Wild game, especially, came with risks if eating it uncooked. It was not something most people would do unless they fancied a rather agonizing few days leading to their death. Either she was embellishing the story a tad, or she was one lucky girl.

They built a small fire in a pot in the kitchen and sat it beneath the range so most of the smoke would go up through the vent. Clay browned the beef in one of the many pans lying around the industrial-sized kitchen and then served the meal: beef with a side of onion straws, the kind dumped on top of a baked casserole.

Dusty inhaled the food in seconds. She was clearly malnourished, but you wouldn't know it just by looking at her face. She had chubby cheeks—the kind that grandmothers could pinch for hours; freckles dotted all across her face; and dirty blond hair that had clumped together in more places than he could count. But she probably wasn't an ounce over sixty pounds.

"That... was incredible," she said licking the plate.

Clay looked down at his food; he hadn't eaten but half of his meal. "Here," he said and handed the plate to her. She stared at him like he was missing his head. "Honestly, I'm not all that hungry, plus I really should patch myself up," he said and pointed at his shoulder.

Dusty snatched the plate from him and began eating, making an effort to savor the bites a little more this time.

Clay took his jacket off and examined his shoulder. He was fortunate that the first barrel the scrawny man fired was birdshot. Had it been the other barrel—which Dusty unloaded into the bigger man—the buckshot would have been much more destructive to Clay. He observed four small wounds and several bruised spots. Birdshot notoriously lacked penetration, and Clay's extra layers stopped most from going through.

He retrieved a pair of tweezers from his first aid kit and requested Dusty's help once again. He tore open an alcohol swab, the last one in the kit, and rubbed it on the wounds. The alcohol burned.

Per Clay's request, Dusty brought a candle over. He stuck the tips of the tweezers into the flame for about thirty seconds then handed them to Dusty who already knew what had to be done.

Without fanfare or dramatic catchphrases, Dusty started digging into the wounds, fishing out each of the tiny pellets lodged in Clay's shoulder. The pain was intense, but at least he was feeling it, which was more than he could say for the two cold bodies out in the hall.

"Ow!" Clay exclaimed as she pulled the last pellet out.

"Don't be such a wuss," she said callously.

"You ever been shot before?" Clay fired back.

She tried not to grin, but couldn't help it. "No comment," she said as she handed him the tweezers. "There you go."

They both had an appreciation for the moment of camaraderie. It was especially a welcomed change of pace in Dusty's life.

She grabbed a towel and wiped the blood off her hands while Clay dressed the wound and downed some of the aspirin he had found in the teacher's desk. His head was already starting to pound, and it would only worsen.

Dusty apologized for not having another cot. She told him where he could find another, but it required leaving the cafeteria and returning to the gym. It was already dark outside, and he was not up for the trip, so he spread his sleeping bag out and got as comfortable as he could on the floor.

His body finally started to relax, and he began to doze off when Dusty, who had been silent for the past twenty minutes, spoke.

"So, what do you miss about the old world?" she asked.

Clay hadn't thought much about it recently. It usually made him think of family and that led him down a path of unnecessary grief and sorrow. "I miss the unlimited access to food and supplies," he said. "Even if the weather was bad, if I *really* needed food, I could find a way to travel; step into a toasty-warm store; buy what I needed; and then get back home to my toasty-warm house." He thought of the great ice storm around his eleventh birthday. He and his dad had to run down to Wal-Mart to pick up a few necessities, and it took nearly four hours to barely go fifteen miles. At the time, Clay thought life could not get any worse. Now, he laughed at his absurd, childish understanding of life back then.

"That sounds nice," she replied.

"It was. Something we all took for granted, though. What about you? What do you miss?"

She shrugged her shoulders, but it was too dark for Clay to see. "This is really the only life I know. I was only four or five when everything went to hell," she said, realizing that she had spent more days of her young life in a frozen wasteland than not. "I vaguely remember my uncle taking me fishing just before it all happened, but I might have dreamed about that. He worked for some magazine that sent him to hunt and fish all around the world, and then he would write about his experience."

"Now *that* would be a sweet gig," Clay said enviously.

It was quiet for a few seconds before she asked, "What don't you miss about it?"

That was a new one. Anytime people reminisced about the past it always revolved around luxuries and hobbies that no longer existed. Oddly enough, Clay had plenty of answers for that question too. "The blissful ignorance that captivated most of the population."

"Huh?"

"For example, most people cared more about celebrity gossip or trying to prevent the world from getting too hot..." he stopped to laugh at the irony of that statement, then continued, "People were never satisfied and constantly sought to find new ways to entertain and distract themselves from the realities of the world. Preoccupied with things that were utterly pointless wastes of time.

"Ridiculous amounts of people spent thousands of hours and piles of money to play a video game about farming, yet when the time came when knowing how to actually plant and harvest crops would be a life-saving skill, most could only hope that someone else would be willing to do it for them. Pretty ironic, huh?"

"Wow," she replied.

"That's just the tip of the iceberg, kid. People lived and died for their phones and computers. It got to the point where you really couldn't operate without one or the other. Everything was done on the internet." Clay had to detour for a moment to explain what the internet was before continuing. "From ordering food, to people letting friends in Europe know what movie they were watching, computers became the primary way to socialize.

"Our culture drastically changed in a very short time. There were no more family meals at the dinner table or lively discussions in the living room. Hours of outdoor play were replaced by kids glued to the television screen for entertainment. Moms traded the challenge of calling out the front door for the kids to come home for dinner for the challenge of getting them outside for some fresh air." Clay sighed deeply as he recalled many times when he had fit the same bill. He was an active kid and spent plenty of time outside playing sports or doing chores, but he often found himself glued to the screen as a kid, especially the final few months before the eruption.

Dusty was overwhelmed by what Clay had told her. The thought of clicking a few buttons and having food at your door a short time later sounded like science fiction. At one point in her short life, she went six days without a bite to eat. And before Clay shared some of his food with her, she hadn't eaten in almost forty-eight hours.

She was jealous of those who were able to live back in such a wonderful time. Overindulgence in food, round-the-clock entertainment, distractions with the flick of a finger—all things she would kill to have. Dusty could see what Clay was getting at, though. People had become so wrapped up with irrelevant trends and fads that most of them couldn't provide for themselves once the store shelves were empty. Her parents aptly demonstrated that mindset. They had been among the technologically addicted group that lacked survival skills. Their life of convenience and prosperity came at a steep cost.

Chapter 19

Clay woke up to the sound of a locking door. Since there were no windows in the room, it was nearly pitch black, but Dusty was carrying a flashlight. She walked over to a table and lit a few candles and a hanging lantern.

"I just looked outside; it stopped snowing. You should be able to leave today," she said.

Clay couldn't tell if she was just giving him a weather report or an eviction notice. It made no difference anyhow; he needed to get back on the move as soon as possible. He tried to sit up, but his body cruelly reminded him of the beating he took last night. He grimaced and fished for some pills to help with the swelling—this time some ibuprofen from his first aid kit which was getting a lot of use since he found his way into this school.

Dusty handed him his pistol, "Sorry, I forgot to give this back to you last night."

Clay took it. The shell was still jammed in the port which he promptly cleared. He vaguely remembered the last shot having a much weaker sound to it; an indication of an undercharge. He wasn't sure if it was his reload or Charlie's—it didn't matter.

He unzipped his bag and pulled out the book he found in the locker. "I grabbed this before I knew anyone lived here. I wouldn't feel right just taking it." He handed it to her.

"You keep it," she said and gently pushed the book back at him, "Barely know how to read anyway."

Clay wasn't about to let her have the bottle of liquor; he didn't feel guilty about hiding that from her.

"Is that a .22 over there?" Clay asked, pointing at the lever action rifle she had.

"Yep. It was my Grandpa's. Found it up in the attic with a box of bullets shortly after my parents died. It used to be my Grandpa's house, I doubt they even knew it was up there. My dad was terrified of guns. My mom said she knew how shoot them but never seemed interested."

"Where'd you learn to shoot?"

"The neighbor," she said with no further explanation.

Clay walked over to the rifle and saw there was only a few dozen rounds left in the brick sitting on the bedside table. He reached into his pack and pulled out a quart-sized Ziploc bag filled with various calibers of bullets. He began to sift through them, picking out a few.

Dusty gave him a puzzled look. She was by no means an expert in firearms, but she could tell there were at least a dozen different calibers in the bag, plus a handful of shotgun shells. "Sooooo, you just carry around a bag of bullets to guns that aren't actually with you?" she quipped.

As he plucked a few more cartridges out of the bag, he replied "If you're not always prepared, you're never prepared. My father told me that all the time as a kid. I never gave it much thought before, but now I never leave home without thinking about it."

"So, how does this help you prepare?"

"Carrying bullets—even for guns I don't have—has saved my neck more than once. You never know when it will come in handy," he said, dumping the handful of .22 cartridges into the nearly empty box. "And today, my preparations will benefit you," he said with a smile.

"Really?" she said with a genuine glow. "Thank you!"

"I know it's not much, but hopefully it will provide you with a few extra meals this winter." He looked over at the double barrel shotgun lying on a table across the room. "You got ammo for that?"

"I got four off the skinny guy, but that's it."

He walked over to the shotgun and verified it was a 12 gauge and then quickly picked out the shells from the bag. "Here ya go," he said and handed her six shells. "The green ones are buckshot, the blue ones are slugs—it's like one *really* big bullet."

She nodded and shoved the shells into her pocket.

Clay walked over to the door leaving the cafeteria and turned around, "I need to keep going east, but on my way back, I can swing by again. I can't promise the trip would be smooth, but I think you would fit in with the others back home. There are several other girls to play with, it's relatively warm, and we have food...usually."

She thought about it for a moment. "You and your family sound very nice, Clay, but the last time I trusted someone they stole all the food I owned and left me in the middle of nowhere. Don't take it personally, but I'm better off alone.

As much as he wanted to, he couldn't argue with that. She had been burned, and that's not something easily forgotten. "Then take this," he said as he reached into his pack once again and pulled out a bag of crackers and a can of pink salmon. He examined the can, "No bulges or leaks, so it should be good to go. I had one about a month ago. Not the best tasting dish I've ever had, but it was pretty filling."

Dusty was in awe with the generosity, "Why are you being so nice to me?"

"We live in a dark world, Dusty. A place where people kill over a can of food," he began to stammer over his words when he remembered how her parents had been killed. "We live in a time when people need to help one another more than ever. I can't undo what happened to your parents or what that family did to you, but I can show you that not everyone has crossed that line, yet. And if that gives you even the slightest bit of hope to cling to, then it's worth it."

Dusty was choked up but quickly fought back the tears, keeping up with her cold demeanor. "Thanks, Clay. Good luck on the rest of your trip."

Halfway out the door, Clay turned around. "One more thing," he said. "If you ever change your mind, I stop by an old library every Wednesday morning around 11:00. If you ever need a place to stay, you're always welcome," he said before giving her directions. "It was nice to meet you, Dusty. Take care."

****

The house was still standing, but just barely. The entire structure was slanted; the foundation riddled with cracks. The front half of the roof had caved in from years of heavy snow and no maintenance. With each step closer to the porch, Clay felt less confident he would find Ted. At least not alive.

He stepped up onto the old rickety porch, and his foot went right through the rotting wood, cutting his leg; he shrugged it off as little more than a scratch. Taking his next steps more carefully, Clay reached the front door. Clutching the handle of his rifle with his right hand, he pushed the door open with his left and walked in.

Aided by the slant of the house, the door swung open, crashing into the wall. He had to slog through nearly a foot and a half of snow across the living room to get to the other side of the house. He searched for Ted, but his efforts came up empty. Ted was long gone. At first, Clay wondered if perhaps Ted had left for a safer haven already, but then he started to wonder if he was over in the living room, buried beneath the snow. He hoped for the former.

Clay rummaged through the house and found absolutely nothing. He even had a hard time finding any of Ted's personal effects, which seemed odd. Perhaps he did pack up and leave after all.

He did another pass through the kitchen just to be sure he didn't miss anything—he didn't. Tired and feeling defeated, Clay fell back into the wall and slid down until he found himself sitting on the peeled linoleum tile. The whole trip had been a dangerous, fruitless waste of time—though, he did meet Dusty, which made him feel a little better about everything.

Clay stared blankly across the kitchen floor as he contemplated his next move. There were still plenty of areas in the county to search, but he wasn't feeling too optimistic about his chances. If he left right away to go back home, he would make it back on time, maybe a day early, but then the trip *really* would have been a waste.

As he weighed his options, something caught his eye beneath the dinner table—a row of linoleum peeling up at an odd place. He crawled on his hands and knees the few feet across the floor and started to pull at the cheap flooring.

It was a hidden door.

The combination lock on the door was thoroughly rusted through, but the dials still turned. Clay could probably break it with a couple of good blows from a rock, or if push came to shove, he could shoot it, but that was always a last resort. He started spinning the dials: eight-four-four—it was the day Ted's wife died; it also happened to be the day Clay was born. He gave it a couple of tugs, and it unlatched, sending a small cloud of rust-colored dust into the air. He decided not to move the dinner table, but instead, he opened the door as much as it would go and slithered in. The stairs went down about seven feet.

It wasn't a storm shelter or even a bomb shelter. It was a safe room, and considering that nobody had discovered it after all these years, it was a good one. Clay looked around the room, his flashlight landing on a clipboard hanging from the wall next to the entrance. It was a log of when Ted would leave the room and when he returned. His last sign-out was nearly three years ago; there was no sign-in.

The room was quite large. It made Clay's cabin feel like a tuna can. There was a bed, shelves, an ice chest, as well as some cabinets. Up against one of the long walls was a desk made from two-by-fours and plywood. Clay saw an open notebook sitting on top. He skimmed through it, looking at each entry title for anything that might help explain what happened to Ted. The entries were mostly fluff, almost seemed like he was just going out to get experience for the book he had started writing. The last page, dated the same as his last log entry, was short:

Winter has been exceptionally difficult this year. I am down to my last few cans of food and must remedy the situation. For the first time in eleven days, it's not snowing. I will take advantage of the good fortune and seek out some wild game. I hope luck is on my side, for if not, I believe this winter shall be my last.

The chilling words from a dead man renewed Clay's hope. There was food somewhere in the shelter. He started his search at the front of the room and gradually made his way to the back, leaving no empty can of beans unturned. He found several useful items along the way, but nothing edible.

He arrived at the freezer chest and hoped the food Ted had mentioned in the journal entry was not in there. Clay held his breath and flipped the lid open. He immediately slammed it shut and heaved— grateful he was operating on a mostly empty stomach. He wasn't sure what had been in there while the freezer still worked, but it would require a whole lab of scientists to identify now.

The awful smell filled every square foot of the room, assaulting his nose with each breath. He went back up the stairs to get some fresh air before continuing his search. He finally had success—a few cans of vegetables that were still good. He was excited when he discovered the can of pineapple but then saw that it was bloated and the outside was crusted with a substance that had oozed out months, possibly years, back.

He hit the jackpot when he searched through one of the tall metal cabinets along the back wall. A wave of euphoria rolled through him like a tsunami as he stared at two #10 cans of freeze-dried meat. The first one he grabbed was seasoned chicken, but it was nearly empty, just enough to feed the whole family for one, maybe two meals if Megan got creative. But the other can—diced turkey—felt heavy when he picked it up. He popped the plastic lid off and was shocked to see it was still sealed. He also found a smaller pantry can of dehydrated corn that also had yet to be opened.

It felt as if he had been fishing all day without a single bite, but then, just as he was ready to pack up and head home, he got the monster bite that landed him a catch he would talk about for years. The stress began to ease some. He felt rejuvenated for the first time since before he saw Megan emptying the winter's food from the freezer.

After he finished searching the rest of the room, he put all of his findings on the desk and examined each one. Colloidal silver was the first thing he found. There wasn't much left in the bottle, and he wasn't quite sure how to use it, but knew it had some medicinal uses, so he grabbed it. He also found Ted's .357 Python between the mattress and box springs. There were only two cartridges in it, so Clay took the last three out of his mixed bag of bullets and loaded them up. He also grabbed a single .38 special to give himself a full cylinder. He slammed the cylinder shut and examined the gun. Clay had never been big into revolvers, but this was a beauty of a pistol.

Unfortunately, though, there was no .223 die set. He had conceded that he would never find a replacement, and would need to come up with an alternative plan. Since the neck-sizer still worked on the broken die, he would just have to de-prime the cases manually. It would be much slower, but would still work.

Even though there were several hours of daylight left, Clay decided to call it a night. He had gotten very little sleep the night before—Screamers were living up to their name, keeping Clay on high alert all night long. Even though he had more scavenging to do in the area before heading home, he had already found more food than he realistically expected. He didn't imagine he would find much else in there—perhaps a few morsels of food here and there—but every bit would help.

He was still in awe with the score he found in the cabinet. The freeze-dried food had a shelf life of twenty or more years, it was very lightweight—especially after Clay had poured the contents into some plastic bags and stuffed them into his pack—and once rehydrated, it was quite filling. He remembered his dad bringing some on a weekend campout. It was one of his fondest memories. Just him and his dad along with a couple of fishing poles and hunting rifles. The fish weren't biting, and they didn't see a single animal worth shooting, yet it was a weekend that would remain in Clay's memory for eternity.

Though physically drained, Clay was mentally very alert and wasn't ready to go to sleep. He pulled out *Our Lonely Past* from his pack and began reading. After getting through nearly a quarter of the book, his mental fatigue matched his physical exhaustion, and he fell asleep.

He awoke to the sounds of cans and bottles falling to the floor. His heart was pounding as he scrambled to find his gun, but he couldn't remember where he placed it. Panicked, he pulled his knife out of a sheath strapped to his ankle; that's when he noticed the shaking.

The quake was the biggest he'd felt in a couple years, but he thought that was partly due to the fact he was several feet beneath the ground. Most of the times, he barely noticed tremors in the office building, but anything above a three in scale was perceptible. He couldn't be sure if this was just another tremor or a legitimate earthquake. As suddenly as it began, the trembling stopped, and with the exception of particles of dirt and debris still making their way to the floor, it was quiet.

It was a little after four in the morning. He felt refreshed enough, so he decided to just pack up and leave instead of going back to sleep. The jolt of adrenaline coursing through his body would have prevented much rest anyhow. Clay slung his pack over his shoulder, grunting with pain as the weight of the bag pulled on his gunshot wound. He made a mental note to change the bandages later in the day. He climbed up the stairs—they were so steep they were practically a ladder—and made his way to the front door.

He stepped outside and stood still in the vast darkness. The world was deafeningly silent; not even the whooshing of a distant breeze. With it being difficult to see and the snow absorbing most of the sound, it felt as if he was standing inside a padded meat locker. He felt exposed, but he traveled anyway, keeping his head on swivel and his finger never far from the trigger.

The sun finally crested the horizon about an hour and a half later, and he began to pick up the pace. The snow was no longer soft, and for the most part, supported his weight. Every now and then, however, he would hit a soft patch, and his foot would drill right through causing him to fall. Oh, what Clay would give for a pair of snowshoes, but those were about as common in Texas as surfboards were in Montana.

About three hours later, he found himself walking towards an old two story house in the middle of a field. It wasn't quite a farmhouse, but it wasn't a typical suburban residence either.

He walked through a substantial break in the hip-high picket fence and then around some towering oaks that were crusted with snow and ice. The trees groaned under the significant weight of the ice. Clay took heed of the ominous warning and made sure he didn't walk beneath any of the branches as he approached the house.

He walked into the house and wandered around aimlessly; nobody had lived there in quite some time. He glanced over the various nooks and crannies instead of his usual systematic examination of each room. He knew the house was empty, so he didn't bother wasting the time. That wasn't why he was there.

The walls in a few of the rooms were down to nothing but rotting timber. The ceiling had collapsed in multiple places, allowing Clay see through to the second floor. The floor looked as if a garbage truck had exploded in the middle of the house. The carpet—the few places it hadn't been covered with trash—was caked with mud and, in some areas, blood. It no longer had the texture of carpet, but rather closer to hardened paper mache.

He walked into a large room towards the back of the house. French doors that were all but destroyed would have framed the large backyard had it not been blocked off entirely from a big pile of snow sloping in. He turned and walked over to a door frame that lead to the kitchen and saw various lines etched into the wood. It was faint, but still there.

Colleen – Age 3.
Emily – Age 6.
Michelle - Age 7.
Clayton – Age 10.
Megan – Age 13.

Chapter 20

Memories played out in front of him as if he were watching a movie. In the kitchen, he saw his mom baking challah with Emily and Michelle. In the living room, he saw himself watching the playoffs with his father. No matter what room he was in, the past came to life and gave Clay some much needed respite from the usual thoughts plaguing his mind.

Despite the fond memories, his mind gradually turned to the final few days before his family left their home. It was still as fresh in his mind as if it had happened yesterday. It was early August, and there was a nip in the air but still warm enough to go outside without a jacket most days. Clay was in his father's recliner, dozing off to the soothing crackles from the fire. Megan was sitting on the floor a few feet away from the fireplace, using the light to read. Charlie was making airplane and gunshots sounds while he played with some toys Clay had dug out of the attic.

Michelle was in the kitchen cleaning up from dinner. After Emily had died, she started to withdraw from all unnecessary interactions with the others. She cooked, cleaned, and then typically spent the rest of the time in her room. It concerned Clay quite a bit, but he had no idea how to address the matter. He prayed it was just her way of coping and that she would eventually recover. Unfortunately, she went to her grave under the bondage of depression.

Ryan—a nine year old boy Clay had found wandering around a grocery store just a few weeks back—woke Clay to tell him about the bug he had just caught upstairs in his room when they heard the front window break.

Michelle shrieked and zoomed into the living room. Clay jumped to his feet, picked up a shotgun, and walked over towards the front door. Though he couldn't see the door yet, he could hear someone reaching through the broken window to unlock the deadbolt. He pumped the shotgun, the clacking sound was a universal message: "You best be leavin' right now."

Despite the blatant warning, the assailant unlocked the door. The entry opened to a small breezeway with paths on either side. To the right was a small study; to the left was the kitchen. Both directions circled around to the living room where the others were all hiding behind the couch. Clay readied himself.

As the door pushed open, Clay whipped around the corner and fired. To say the aftermath was a mess was an understatement. Clay's stomach sank at the sight, but the adrenaline suppressed his urge to vomit.

He heard footsteps outside fast approaching and saw out the kitchen window two other men running down the porch towards the front door. He slammed the pump back, then forward, and fired as the second man came in. The buckshot hit the man in the shoulder, causing him to spin around before he fell on top of his departed friend.

In anticipation of the third man, Clay cycled the next round and tightened his grip on the shotgun. He waited, but the man did not enter. Out of the corner of his eye, he saw the man peek through the kitchen window. Clay spun to take a shot, but the long twenty-six inch barrel bashed into the wall, causing him to accidentally discharge. The bandit took the opportunity to storm through the front door and charge Clay. Though he had chambered the next round already, the man smacked the barrel upwards and plowed into Clay, crashing them both into the oven. The man pulled a machete out of a scabbard and drew his hand back.

Clay closed his eyes as he prepared for his death when he heard a single gunshot, followed by eight more. Clay opened one eye and saw Megan standing on the other side of the counter holding a pistol. Even though the slide was locked back, she continued to pull the trigger. He looked down on the ground and saw the attacker lying in front of him, his clothes soaking up the blood from the three 9MM-sized wounds. He looked over at Megan who was still aiming the empty pistol, a terrified expression painted across her face. Charlie and Ryan were crying behind the couch while Michelle tried her best to sooth them.

After Clay snapped out of his daze, he picked up the shotgun and ran outside to make sure nobody else was coming. He saw silhouettes of several men waiting at the end of the long gravel driveway, looking towards the house. He raised the shotgun and rested his finger on the trigger. The men casually turned and walked away, except for one. He stood there glaring at Clay for several seconds after the others had left. Clay was tempted to shoot, but knew he had just the one shell left in the gun. Suddenly, one of the other men called him over. The man finally turned and walked off to catch up with the others, a slight limp in his gait.

Back inside Megan was comforting three hysterical kids while trying to manage her own anxiety. Clay hadn't even noticed the man he had shot in the shoulder had also died; he bled out on the floor. As Clay dragged the bodies out onto the porch, he noticed that all three of them had a black bandanna just below the left knee. He knew it must have been some sort of identifying mark of their group. The men looked more like Billy the Kid than a street gang. Without rule of law, society had truly regressed into the Old West.

As Clay stared down at the old, cracked kitchen tile, the grout still stained with the blood of the man Megan had killed that night, he wondered how things would have been different had they stayed and fought to protect their home. He often speculated if the decision to move was cowardly or strategic. Even though he could tell some of the men at the end of the driveway were armed with rifles, he thought with a little preparation and help from Megan that he might have fended off the group, instead of fleeing when they returned three nights later. After all, it was *his* home, not theirs. And yet, he just handed it over to them without a fight. Now, four years later, it sat vacantly as the elements slowly chipped away at it. The bandits came and went, like parasites that got their fill before moving on, in search for the next meal.

He thought back to the two men chasing Dusty. They were no doubt from the same group that had forced his family out of their home. Joseph Patrick—as Clay later discovered—was the head of the group. At one point in time, he was one of the county judges, but after things went belly up, Patrick gave up law and order in exchange for anarchy. Most of his henchmen were the very people he'd locked up just years before.

On more than one occasion, Clay heard tales told by refugees fleeing from Patrick's territory—tales of atrocities that were fitting of a horror movie. He heard one man say he thought Patrick and his men were worse than the Screamers. Clay didn't know if the man was being melodramatic, or if he was on to something, but Clay knew with certainty one thing about the judge: if they ever crossed paths again, Patrick would be dead.

As Clay walked to the front door, something on the ground caught his eye. He just barely noticed it as it was covered by the trash and debris. He crouched down and examined it more closely; it was an old brooch. It had belonged to his grandmother who passed it on to his mother. Megan—being the first born daughter—was next in line to receive it, but sorting through jewelry boxes after their mom's death just wasn't high on their priority list.

The return to his childhood home was a mixed blessing. Replaying the events that had transpired years before was painful, but finding the brooch made the whole thing worthwhile. Megan had cried when she realized she had forgotten to bring it to their new home. Now, Clay would have a chance to give her a surprise of a lifetime, likely to bring a smile that would stretch from ear to ear.

He turned around and took one last glance at his home for almost sixteen years and walked out.

****

Dusty was not kidding when she said there was nothing left to scavenge in the area. Everyplace he stopped came up empty. It was as if the entire county had become a landfill of useless junk. Even with the food he found at Ted's, it was going to be a really lean winter. He wasn't completely confident they would be able to make it, but the added inventory would at least give them a fighting chance.

He scouted for a warm place to sleep for the night, but no such thing existed in the wintertime. He had developed a rather painful cough since leaving Ted's house a few days ago and could do with a good night's sleep by a roasting fire. Unfortunately, between Patrick's gang and roaming Screamers, starting a fire anywhere would be too risky. The next best thing was a room without a draft, which he found in a bathroom at the back of an office supply store.

The snow had started to fall again the next morning. Though it was not the frozen tempest he had battled through on his trip out, it still complicated the journey, especially as he crossed back over Devil's Canyon.

He finally made it back to the highway that ran past the office building, a welcomed indication that he was about fifteen miles out. Tromping through the snow meant sluggish progress, but barring any unforeseen circumstances, he would be back in his own bed by tomorrow night. That comforting thought fueled him to press on, after every ounce of energy had long been depleted.

Clay's cough had worsened overnight and breathing had become more demanding, even when he was out of the elements. He just needed a hot meal and a couple days of rest, and he'd be back to normal.

His hotel for the night was Caldwell's Wings and Beer, a little sports bar next to a bunch of low-rise office buildings. Clay set up camp in the walk-in freezer off the kitchen. Because of its insulation to keep cold air in, it actually did a good job of keeping cold air out, and since it hadn't been running in many years, the inside was significantly warmer than the rest of the establishment. He placed an old spatula in front of the hefty steel door to prop it open just a bit so he wouldn't suffocate in his sleep. He also set up two noise alarms, one near each entrance to the kitchen that would allow him time to react should anyone come in behind him.

The freezer was quite comfortable, and he would have slept well had it not been for his persistent cough. His body ached as if he had spent the day as a crash test dummy. He still found he had more energy than he had in days, so he got back out on the road for the final stretch.

Gradually, throughout the day, the temperatures climbed, surprising Clay and providing a much needed break from the cold of the past few weeks. The temperatures were creeping into the forties and Clay started to break a sweat. These days forty degrees was the new seventy-two.

As Clay reached the top of a small incline, he saw a bobcat trekking through the snow about seventy-five yards away. There wasn't much meat on him, but every pound would help them endure the long, brutal winter. He dropped to one knee and raised his rifle. Keeping the reticle fixed on the large cat was proving to be a difficult task for his shaky hands. Finally, he fired, and the cat stormed across the field, quickly disappearing into the nearest tree line.

He stayed kneeling for several minutes as he lambasted himself for the squandered opportunity. His head was stuck in a fog, and his clumsy actions were proof of that. After several attempts to return to his feet, he finally got back on the move.

At last he saw the towering sanctuary in the distance. The haze concealed most of it, but he could just barely make out the profile of the building. Not a moment too soon, he thought, since every step he took felt like knives had been jammed into every one of his joints. The chilled breeze that had begun to intensify over the last hour wasn't helping matters either.

Clay's pace had slowed significantly, and he found himself taking short, but frequent breaks to catch his breath. One such break, he leaned up against a tree and howled in agony as he pressed his shoulder against the bark. Though his many layers of clothing prevented him from examining it, he knew his wounds from the birdshot had become seriously infected. He still hadn't changed his bandages, and wasn't going to bother now. The damage was already done.

With nearly five miles yet to go, and a fast approaching storm, he dug deep and pressed forward, doing his best to fight through the pain, but the pain proved to be a staunch opponent.

By the time the rain began to fall, his head was throbbing. His body had spent the last several days trying to tell him to rest, but like the 'check engine' light on a car's dashboard; he ignored it. The wintery mix had soaked him through and through in a matter of minutes. It was a blessing in disguise since his fever had spiked to dangerous levels and the cold rain was as effective as taking an ice bath. He took some ibuprofen for the pain and discarded the empty bottle. This also helped to combat the fever he was unaware he had.

About an hour later, he had made it to his street. He was walking through the road like a zombie; his brain on autopilot, nary a conscious thought to be found. He made his way directly to the building, no detours, no cloak-and-dagger.

****

Megan was on her way to the garage to load some water into the pulley basket. Charlie had faithfully hoisted water up every day for the past couple of weeks, which meant multiple trips to the basement. Since Charlie had developed a few painful blisters, Megan volunteered to give him a break.

As she swung around the landing on the twelfth floor, her heart stopped for a beat when she saw him lying on the next landing down. "Clay!" she screamed in a panic and ran down the remaining flight of stairs. "Clayton?" she asked loudly and pushed on his back, "Clayton, can you hear me? Answer me!"

No response.

She felt for a pulse which she finally found; it was weak. She put her palm on his forehead. "He's burning up," she murmured aloud.

"Charlie!" she shouted as loudly as she could, but nobody came. She ran back up the stairs, all the while shouting for Charlie's help. By the time she reached the fifteenth floor, she heard the door explode open. Charlie was already running down the stairs.

"Megan, what's wrong?" he asked frantically.

Out of breath, she gasped, "It's Clay!"

Chapter 21

Charlie was walking home from the library when he saw a lone fawn crossing the highway. The baby deer was frail; its rib cage protruded through the skin, and its posture was unbalanced. The poor animal was likely going to die in the next couple of days, perhaps even hours.

Charlie could tell he wouldn't be able to harvest much meat from it, but anything would be better than nothing. Despite the food they found in Clay's pack, there just wasn't going to be enough to last them the winter. Charlie had volunteered to skip a couple of meals a week to help stretch the pantry a little further; Megan did the same. Clay was barely eating as it was—Megan had a hard enough time getting him to take fluids, let alone chew and swallow food. It had only been a week since she found him near death in the stairwell, so she wasn't yet worried about his food intake so much as she was about hydration and staving off the fever. The antibiotics were helping, but she knew eventually she would have to find a way to get him to eat so his immune system could do the rest. In the meantime, however, Clay's lack of appetite also contributed to the efforts being made to conserve food.

The fawn stopped in the middle of the road and nosed around in a fresh layer of snow. It nibbled at a few things then moved a few feet away, repeating the same process. Charlie took his time and inched closer. He had Clay's LaRue, which was a superior weapon to the M1. Even though he had become quite a good shot with the old World War II relic, he much preferred the accuracy and ease of use the AR-15's optics provided.

Charlie crept closer, stopping about fifty yards out. He raised the rifle, took a deep breath, and slowly exhaled. He squeezed the trigger.

The deer dropped to the ground in an instant. It was a clean shot through the head. Charlie knew any shot to the torso could damage what little meat remained on the starved animal's body.

He quickly moved in and began cutting into the baby deer. Clay had not yet taught Charlie how to properly field dress game, so he did his best with what limited knowledge he had on the topic, which was mostly from listening to Clay talk about the similarities and differences of wild hog as Clay cleaned Charlie's kill the night of Bethany's birthday party.

There was even less meat than he had expected, maybe ten pounds at best. He put the meat into a bag and stuck it into his pack. He stood to his feet and turned to leave but was startled by a man who was approaching.

"Stay back!" Charlie ordered as he raised his rifle.

The man stopped and put his hands in the air. "It's okay, son. I don't want to hurt you. I just wanted to see if you could spare some of that meat you just took."

"Sorry, but this is mine," he said, then waved the barrel of the rifle to the left. "Now go on, and leave me be."

"I know it's yours; that's why I'm asking you, man to man. Can you please spare any? I have kids back home and we haven't eaten in days," the man pleaded.

The man's sunken cheeks and leathery skin suggested he was in his sixties, but Charlie doubted he was much older than forty. He wore tattered clothes that were two sizes too big and was missing three fingers on his left hand. Charlie genuinely felt sorry for the man, but he remembered one of the first things Clay had taught him. People are deceptive. The man seemed sincere, enough so that Charlie believed his story, but he struggled with the thought of giving a total stranger food when he wasn't even sure that his own family would be provided for this winter.

"I'm sorry, I-I-I just can't," Charlie reiterated.

"Please," the man said and started to move towards Charlie, his hands still in the air. "Just a couple of pounds."

"I said stay back!" Charlie said sternly and began to step backwards to keep the distance from the man. "I *will* shoot!" he warned.

The man continued forward, "Such a young boy ought not be making such threats," the man said.

Charlie kept stepping back as the man continued moving forward. "How about a trade?" the man asked, with a glimmer of hope in his fatigued eyes.

Charlie raised the rifle even more. His intense body language caused the man to stop. "I'm sorry, but

I am not interested in whatever it is you have," Charlie said.

"Just take a look; it's all I have to trade." The man moved his hand towards his coat pocket.

"Stop!" Charlie screamed.

The man reached into the pocket, and then suddenly the world went quiet for Charlie. He could hear the man trying to talk, but his voice was unintelligible. The man's expression was wrought with fear and shock. He stumbled forward a few feet before dropping to one knee. Charlie heard vague muffled coughs as he saw the man spit up blood, staining the untainted snow a dark crimson color.

Charlie looked down the barrel and saw smoke pouring out of the muzzle, his finger still on the trigger. His mouth hung open, and he began to tremble. Charlie looked back at the man whose life was fleeting. The blood from the bullet wound in his chest had started to seep through his many layers of clothing. The man removed his hand from his pocket, briefly clutching onto something small before reaching at his injury. He locked eyes with Charlie for a moment. There was no anger, no ill-will towards Charlie, only pity. Then, as if watching the final grains of sand slip into the bottom of an hourglass, the man's stare became empty, and his body toppled over.

Charlie remained paralyzed with shock. His brain was still processing everything that had just happened. Two minutes ago, he was cutting meat off a deer, and now he was staring at a man who had died at his hand. It was the moment Clay warned him about, it was the moment when Charlie was faced with that split second decision...

Suddenly, Charlie bent over and threw up what little food he had in his stomach. The stinging sensation ran all the way up his throat and out his mouth. He continued to heave for several minutes, but there was nothing left to come out.

After regaining his composure, Charlie worked up enough courage to see what the man had retrieved from his pocket. He instinctively thought the man was going for a gun or weapon of some sort, but it, in fact, was a pocket watch. Charlie picked it up and unclasped the cover. On the inside of the ornately engraved door was a picture of the man with his wife and kids. They were all smiling; they were happy.

Charlie snapped the watch shut and dropped it on the ground next to the lifeless body. Tears began streaming down his face which quickly froze to his reddened cheeks. "I'm so sorry," he uttered to the departed man before he turned and walked away.

He wanted to cry, he wanted to run home and have someone tell him it was okay, that he didn't do anything wrong, but he couldn't. Because he *did* do something wrong. He killed a desperate father who was just begging for food—all because he didn't want to share with the man. Charlie closed his eyes, hoping the whole thing was just a horrific nightmare that would cease as soon as his eyes opened again, but he knew this would be a nightmare that would torment him for life. In a split second, Charlie had destroyed the lives of this man and his family and perhaps even his own.

The walk back was long and arduous. It felt as if darkness followed him all the way home—a menacing feeling he could not shake. He walked into the kitchen with the bag of meat and handed it to Megan without saying a word.

"Charlie?" she asked, noticing the grim look on his face. "What happened? Are you okay?"

He kept walking towards the door. "I fed the evil wolf," he said and walked out.

Though his response was vague, she knew what had happened. She remembered what it was like to take someone's life, and was deeply grateful that she had not been forced to do it again. Justified or not, seeing another person die as a result of his action was not something easy to live with, especially at his young age.

She wanted to go talk to him but needed to tend to Clay. It was probably for the best. If Charlie was anything like her, he wouldn't want to talk. Right after Megan killed the man attacking Clay, all she wanted to do was lock herself in a room and cry for the rest of the day, but she didn't have that luxury and she didn't want to take that opportunity away from Charlie.

Megan walked into Clay's room with a tray of broth, water, and some stale saltines. He opened his eyes slightly when he heard her come in. His face was still sickly, but he had come a long way over the past few days. Short of an unexpected event occurring, it looked as if the worst was behind him, though he had lost a lot of weight and muscle which would make the remaining winter months that much more difficult for his recovery.

"Hey Megs," Clay said just above a whisper, "what's wrong?" He could see the concern on her face.

She sat the tray down on the conference room table and helped Clay sit up to eat. She handed him the soup which he begrudgingly sipped on. Megan sat down on the floor and leaned against the bed. "It's Charlie."

Clay gave her a look of concern.

She stared at the ground and fiddled with a strand of carpet that was coming undone. "He went to check the library and when he got back he... something just wasn't right." She paused for a moment and then looked at Clay, "I think he shot somebody."

Clay squeezed his eyes shut and sighed. He could relate, that first kill was brutal on his psyche. "But he didn't actually *tell you* that he killed someone?"

Megan shook her head. "No, but I could tell just by how he was holding himself, then he talked about feeding the evil wolf."

Clay knew Megan was right. Charlie had killed someone. He started to get out of bed, and Megan stopped short of pushing him back down. "What do you think you are doing?"

"I need to go talk to him," he told her.

"You are *not* ready to get out of bed."

"I don't care; I need to talk to him."

Megan pushed back once more, "Fine, I will go get him in a little bit and have him come to you, okay? But right now, he needs some time alone."

Content with the compromise, Clay eased back into his bed and sipped on the soup some more. Megan felt his forehead. It felt somewhat normal, a little cool if anything. The fever had broken yesterday and had not returned.

Clay thanked her for the food and turned to go back to sleep. Megan went back to the kitchen and divided the meat Charlie brought home into a few smaller chunks before throwing into the freezer. She fought the urge to go talk to Charlie herself, which was easy to do when every few minutes somebody was coming to her with a problem; a ripped shirt; a crayon that snapped in two; or a bump on the head. It was probably for the best she got sidetracked for several hours; Charlie needed space.

When she finally opened his door, she saw him lying on the bed, facing the wall. At first it appeared he was sleeping, but then she heard the gasp and sniffle.

"Charlie?" Megan asked softly, "Can I come in?"

He didn't respond, so she walked over and sat down next to him, waiting in silence. She rubbed his back for twenty minutes, listening to his sobs, without judgment. Finally, she asked, "Do you want to tell me what happened?"

He shook his head.

Careful to not bombard him, she waited silently for another few minutes before saying "Clay wanted to come see you, but I wouldn't let him out of bed. I promised him you would go see him. Can you do that for me?"

He broke his empty stare at the wall and looked over his shoulder at her and nodded.

She smiled and put her arm around him, "I love ya, Bub. If you need someone else to talk to, just let me know."

Megan left the room and gently closed the door behind her. She returned to the kitchen to prepare dinner. She prayed Charlie would get through this traumatic event in one piece.

Charlie eventually made his way to Clay's room and broke down as he explained what had happened. Clay was grieved with what the boy had to go through. He felt guilty for being bedridden and forcing Charlie to step up in his absence.

"He just wanted some food, Clay, and I killed him for it," Charlie said, his lip quivered uncontrollably.

"Charlie, this man put you in a very difficult and dangerous situation. How were you supposed to know if he was telling the truth or not? You were faced with a life-and-death decision that had to be made in the blink of an eye. If you hadn't shot and he *was* armed, I don't think we would be having this conversation right now..."

Charlie conceded, "I guess so. But if I had just given him some of the meat, this wouldn't have happened. It wouldn't have hurt us much, and maybe he would have just left me alone."

"Maybe," Clay said, "but maybe not. Maybe he would have tried to take advantage of your generosity and take everything from you. Even if he didn't have a gun, he still could have hurt you." Clay grunted as he sat up and rested his hand on Charlie's shoulder. He stared right into Charlie's eyes. "You made the decision you felt you needed to make, given the information you had. Learn from it, but don't let it destroy you."

"Do you think I did the right thing?"

Clay didn't know how to answer. On the one hand, from the sounds of it, Charlie might have reacted too quickly. On the other hand, Charlie was just a boy facing an unknown situation, alone, that could have just as easily left him dead. The fact was, Clay didn't know if he had done the right thing or not. How could he judge a kill or be killed situation without being there? In Clay's mind, Charlie was absolved. At the end of the day, however, Charlie's actions wouldn't be judged by Clay.

"I'll take that as a no," Charlie said with slumped shoulders.

"Silence doesn't always mean that, Charlie. I'll be honest with you, I don't know whether you were right or wrong, but I will say this... I probably would have done the *exact* same thing in your shoes."

Charlie felt better with that response, though it did little to remove the guilt weighing him down.

Clay prayed with Charlie, and they both wept for their own reasons. Clay asked God to bring Charlie peace. They prayed for the departed man's soul and for protection over any people that might have been relying on him as a provider.

That's when Charlie started bawling, begging for forgiveness.

Afterwards, Charlie went back to his room and skipped dinner. Neither Megan nor Clay bothered him the rest of the night. Clay, for the first time since leaving for his trip to Uncle Ted's, ate dinner with the family in the break room. He was very weak and nearly fell a couple of times, but the smiles from everyone at the table made the effort more than worth it.

He didn't eat very much, to Megan's chagrin. He had been laid up in bed for quite a while and was doing very little physically that warranted the need for much food. He knew his appetite would make a triumphant return soon enough, but until then, he would continue to eat small meals. He was glad that their dwindling supply of food would be able to stretch even further.

****

Nearly a month had passed since Charlie killed that man. Clay had almost fully recovered, but the muscle atrophy he had developed proved to be quite a hindrance. However, a few weeks of climbing stairs and hoisting water would revert most of that. He was relieved to be back on his feet and active again. He hated to be idle, especially with so much to do and so many counting on him.

He was fortunate to be alive, though. In a joint effort, Megan and the remaining supply of antibiotics slowly nursed Clay back to health. Of course, he was not thrilled to learn that they were less than two months into winter and had no more medicine, but Megan didn't have many options. He would have been a goner without them.

Clay was trying to hook up some new car batteries to the battery bank, but he was not having much success. Four of the batteries had already died and would no longer hold a charge; many of the others were draining much faster than they used to. It was a matter of time before they would all be depleted.

"I'm going downstairs to do a perimeter check," Charlie said standing in the doorway.

A week ago, someone tried to break into the garage, then again three days later, somebody had tried to get into the stairwell from the ground level. Neither were particularly uncommon, but seeing them happen so close together made Clay a bit more cautious. As a result, he decided to tighten up security with trips down there at least three times daily to see if anything felt out of the ordinary. He also reinforced the doors on the bottom three floors of the stairwell and garage.

"Do you need help?" Clay asked.

"No."

"All right. Can you load some more water onto the lift while you're down there?"

"Sure," Charlie said, then left.

Charlie had changed. He was no longer the boy who was eager to learn anything and everything Clay had to teach. The smiles and jokes had stopped too. Clay hoped someday he would go back to being the

Charlie they all knew, but killing a man takes a toll on even the strongest of people.

Frustrated with the lack of progress, Clay abandoned the battery project and went to the armory. He painstakingly popped the primers out of each .223 case by hand, using a punch and the bench. Charlie had finished reloading what bullets he had left for all the other calibers. He appreciated Charlie's initiative but was a little worried he did them all unsupervised while Clay was unconscious in his room. The overall lengths looked good; he just hoped the powder measurements were equally as precise.

Megan interrupted to alert him of a leak in the propane oven. After some investigating, Clay found a small hole in the aging hose going from the tank to the burner. He utilized some electrical tape and sealed the hole. It was a true patch job in every sense of the term, but it would hold for a little while longer. They would likely run out of propane before the end of winter anyway, so there was no need for an elaborate fix. It had been well over a year since Clay found a propane tank with any gas left.

After he finished patching the hose, Megan had a short laundry list of other things for him to do which consumed the rest of his day. Even with Charlie filling in for him while he was ill, the daily tasks and routine maintenance Clay usually handled had piled up. Now he needed to tend to them. He went through and prioritized and pushed a few things off until spring, like repairing the greenhouse; it would just be too difficult to do in the winter.

After sleeping for the better part of two weeks, and mandatory rest for the last month, he would spend the remainder of the winter catching up with his backlog of tasks as well as staying on top of his daily to-do list. It would be busy, but he was just happy to be alive to do them.

Chapter 22

Kelsey had just put Dakota down for the night and was preparing herself a cup of tea when she heard a light tap on the door.

It was Watson.

"Hi, Mr. Watson," Kelsey said with a quiet voice. "What can I do for you?"

"Ms. Lambert, may I come in?" he said, alcohol on his breath.

Before Kelsey could extend an invitation, Watson walked in and pulled out a notebook from an inside pocket of his coat. He flipped through some pages. Kelsey immediately knew what this was about, but wasn't sure why he was bothering her about it so late in the evening.

He finally settled on a page and began explaining some recent changes to her accrued winter debt. Kelsey mostly scavenged or ran errands for Watson as a means of debt payment, but the winter months provided very few opportunities to earn a wage. Ms.

Hawthorne, an older lady with whom Kelsey and Dakota stayed, had taught Kelsey some basic seamstress skills that provided Kelsey a small amount of income during the winter months. However, she was mostly idle so long as there was snow on the ground. This meant that she lived on a form of credit with Watson that deepened the hole she was already in. On average, Kelsey and Dakota would undo nearly half of what she paid off the previous year. At that rate, Dakota would be a teenager before they could escape Watson's imprisonment.

"So," Watson said with a tone that Kelsey knew meant bad news for her, "as you know this winter has not been kind to us. In fact, I think it's probably been the worst one we've had yet."

Kelsey nodded and knew where the conversation was going; it wasn't the first time.

"I'm not sure if you are aware, but we lost a good deal of our cattle this winter. Sickness, predator attacks, starvation; you name it. Of course, it was more than just the cattle, but that was obviously the biggest loss for us. I even lost poor Doris. Had that old girl twelve years and—"

"So, what is it that you wanted to tell me, Jake?" Kelsey interrupted, her patience running thin with Watson's rambling.

He gave her an icy stare, "I'd appreciate you not speaking to me that way, young lady. Respect your elders."

Kelsey wanted nothing more than to reach out and slap him across the face, but she had to swallow her pride and anger. She apologized, "Yes sir, you're right. That was very rude of me."

Watson's furrowed brows eased as he lifted the notebook. He handed it to Kelsey. "As I was sayin', I had to raise the prices on all the food in the store, and unfortunately, it is retroactive to the beginning of winter."

"That is total bull—" she raised her voice but was interrupted by another stern—and ultimate— warning from Watson about her manners.

"Little lady, I have a good mind to put you in your place for your behavior. *Don't* let it happen again or so help me..." Watson said then looked over Kelsey's shoulder as he heard a door open. "Evenin', Ms. Hawthorne," he said with a polite smile.

"Evening, Jake," Hawthorne said as she got a cup down from the cupboard. She poured herself some tea and sat down in her chair by the fireplace, making herself an arbitrator of sorts to ensure nothing got out of control.

"Mr. Watson," Kelsey said as calmly as she could, "this wipes out over seventy-five percent of what I brought you last year," she said, pointing at the notebook.

"I know, Ms. Lambert," he said, back to sounding formal and official, "but I'm afraid this is how it must be. I will keep workin' with you to try and get you out of this debt sooner rather than later. I should have some opportunities for you this summer to earn some extra wages."

Kelsey remained silent; her expression reflected the contempt inside.

"But look on the bright side," Watson said with gusto, "winter looks to finally be over, and you can get back to scavenging." He walked to the door. "Ladies," he said as he tipped his hat.

****

The sun was rising just as the farm appeared over the horizon. Clay thought he was going crazy when he saw a tinge of orange painted across the ground. Perhaps the ash in the atmosphere was starting to dissipate; though it seemed unlikely after the ruthless winter they had just escaped. The frosty grass crunched under his boots as he walked the final 200 yards across the field to the gate.

There was a fresh face at the gate, couldn't have been more than sixteen years old; he was not familiar with Clay. After a few minutes of explanation, Derrick walked by and instructed the young guard to let Clay in.

"Derrick," Clay said, "it's good to see you!"

The two shook hands and shared war stories about the ravaging winter as they walked towards the shop. The door was locked; it wasn't quite 6:30 yet. The two chatted while Clay waited.

"So, did you get promoted from gatekeeper?" Clay laughed.

"You could say that," Derrick said with mixed feelings. "We lost quite a few folks this winter along with more than half of our livestock," he said somberly.

"Oh, man, that's rough. Sorry to hear that."

"However, that opened up more than a few spots for wranglers, so Mr. Watson asked me to help them with the herds and some security detail," he said with a spark of excitement in his voice.

Clay was happy for him. He had always been friendly and helpful each time the two had crossed paths, and he had a sort of optimism about him that was rare to find anymore.

Margaret arrived, unlocked the front door, and walked inside.

"It was good to see you, Derrick." Clay said sticking his hand out.

"Likewise, Clay," he said as he shook Clay's hand. Derrick had started to walk away but quickly did an about-face, "By the way, I hope you aren't looking for food because I don't think Mr. Watson is trading any right now."

Clay's hopeful look washed away as he went inside only to be told the same thing by Margaret. They wouldn't part with a single pound. Watson arrived with Jeremy a short time later, and Matthew tagged along just behind them. Watson only reaffirmed what everyone else had already said.

"Clay, I can't spare anything. I wish I hadn't even given you what I did at the beginning of winter. Most of the cattle we lost had their meat spoiled or scavenged by predators. This is not a good time to ask me for a trade."

"Jake, please, I am begging you! You're not the only one who barely made it through winter. We have *no* meat right now; we're living off a dwindling supply of canned goods. I just need a little to get us through these first few weeks while—"

"I said no, Mr. Whitaker!" Watson snapped. "Look, I am truly sorry about your struggles, but it is none of my concern right now."

"Well, you *need* to make it your concern," Clay said sharply, shocked with his vague threat.

Jeremy slowly moved his hand to rest on his side arm. He looked at Clay, then over at Watson, who had a rather indignant expression on his face. Watson had a low tolerance for disrespect and viewed threats as one of the highest forms of derision.

"What'd you just say, son?" Watson said with a snarl.

Clay stammered over his words, both embarrassed and fearful for the repercussions that might follow such a threat—heat of the moment or not. "Look, Jake, uh Mr. Watson, I'm sorry. I didn't mean anything by that. It's just been a bad winter for us, and we are running on fumes. I just let my emotions get the best of me is all. I didn't mean anything by it."

"Nobody talks to Mr. Watson that way," Matthew chimed in for the first time since walking into the room.

Watson gave Matthew a disapproving glare before returning his attention to Clay. "I think it would be best if you went ahead and got on out of here. I don't have what you're looking for anyhow."

"I'm sorry," Clay said genuinely. "Thanks for your time."

Clay walked out the door and leaned against the wall just outside. He was still in shock over his reaction to Watson. The old rancher was an ally he couldn't afford to lose. He would have to do damage control later, once Watson had time to forget about the incident.

Even though the exchange—or lack thereof—with Watson went about as poorly as it could have, his mood lightened at the sound of Kelsey's voice.

"Clay!" she shouted as she ran across the muddy ground and into his arms. She had missed him over the winter, but seeing his face again made her realize just how much so.

Clay was thrilled to see her; he couldn't stop smiling. They quickly decided to head out on their first trip of the season.

"Ah!" Clay said, "I have a bag full of stuff I was going to trade to Watson that I need to drop off before I could go anywhere."

"Oh," Kelsey said, disappointment affecting her voice.

Clay looked down at his watch. It was only seven; still early in the day. "But, if you are interested in meeting everyone, you could come along with me and then we could leave from there."

Kelsey giggled, "That sounds wonderful! I would love to meet your family!"

Clay suddenly felt a tinge of apprehension with the invite, not so much about her knowing where they lived, but rather that she was going to meet everyone. Though they were not anything more than friends, the whole thing was akin to bringing a date home to meet the parents.

Kelsey ran home to grab a few things before heading out. Clay noticed Jeremy had been lingering nearby, as if to keep an eye on Clay for the remainder of his visit, so he told Kelsey he would wait for her outside the gates.

Kelsey walked out of the gate with a small, empty backpack hanging from her shoulders and a bounce in her step. "Ready?" she asked.

The two talked almost the entire hike, quickly recapping their winter experiences—though Clay left out quite a few details about his—and then gradually transitioned to more historical talk—like what they preferred on their pizzas and classic television shows. Clay brought up *Saved by the Bell,* but Kelsey had no clue what that was. He tried explaining it to her but realized how dull the early 90's television show sounded.

The building came into sight and Clay pointed it out to Kelsey.

"You live in that building?" she said.

"Yup. Been there four, almost five years now." Clay looked over at her and saw that she was a bit winded, which was to be expected after five to six months of inactivity. Even Clay was huffing a bit.

He went through his usual OPSEC routine but was not as stringent with his path and movement as he usually was. It made sense to Kelsey after he explained why he did that, and it made her appreciate the fact she didn't have to take such precautions whenever she went home.

It was about 11:30 when they finally entered the garage. "Ever use a Stairmaster?" Clay asked with a grin.

Kelsey's legs were burning by the sixth floor; she was exhausted. The thought of hiking the rest of the day after the climb was daunting, but as they reached the top of the stairs, her legs weren't bothering her as much as her stomach. The nerves Clay had been battling with all morning had now struck her as they approached the door.

The door opened, and they were greeted by Tyler who was all smiles. He skipped down the hallway yelling about Clay and Kelsey's arrival. Erica stormed down the hall and practically jumped into Clay's arms. She was more leery of Kelsey than Tyler, but that was just her nature.

Several of the other kids bombarded them as they reached the lobby, all eager to find out more about Clay's friend. Kelsey was overwhelmed. She remembered Clay saying they had ten children staying with them, but it didn't quite resonate with her just how many that was. The noisy kids became even too much for Clay to handle, and he asked them to go back to playing. The kids scurried off in various directions like deer after a gunshot.

Just as the kids ran off, Megan came out from the kitchen, still in her pajamas with a dish towel slung over her shoulder.

"Hi there," Megan said with a nasally voice. "I'm Megan, Clay's older sister. Sorry, I know I must look like a train wreck. I'm feeling a bit under the weather right now, so please don't be offended if I don't shake your hand."

"Not offended at all, and I don't know what you're talking about. You look lovely," Kelsey warmly responded.

"I like you already," Megan joked which got a chuckle out of the three. She turned to Clay. "Bethany has been asking for you all morning. I think she's waking up from her nap if you want to go say hi."

"Sure," he said heading towards his door, "I'm gonna drop my pack off in my room real quick, and then I'll head that way."

As Clay was walking to his room, Courtney darted across the lobby at him. Clay swept her off the ground and threw her up in the air before tickling her. Kelsey smiled at the priceless moment and saw yet another dimension to Clay. She had already witnessed his selfless demeanor on multiple occasions, but the way he interacted with the kids and the way he provided for his family...It was a quality unlike anything she had ever seen.

"He's really good with them, isn't he?" Kelsey commented.

"Yes, he is. The kids love him to death. And you know, I'm kinda fond of him too...sometimes," she quipped and tapped him on the shoulder as he walked back past them on his way to Bethany's room.

"He's definitely a sweet guy," Kelsey added.

"I don't know what we would have done without him," Megan said.

Kelsey tilted her head.

"He didn't tell you what happened over the winter?"

"Just that he came down with a pretty bad cold or something," Kelsey replied.

"That's what he told you?" Megan asked. "That's the understatement of the century."

"How bad?"

"Well, to put it bluntly, there was one night when I started thinking about how I was going to tell the kids..." she said, tears began to invade her eyes. "He was in really bad shape for a while. It's nothing short of a miracle that he's still with us."

Kelsey covered her mouth with her hand and gasped. Her eyes also began to fill up, especially when she found out that it happened because he went out for food after winter hit. Clay's devotion to his family, which mostly consisted of children he had not known very long, was awe-inspiring.

Clay returned to the lobby. Bethany was on his back, her arms wrapped around his neck. He introduced her to Kelsey, and as expected, she was quite shy. She quickly hid herself behind Clay's legs as she peered out to observe the visiting stranger. Kelsey found it simply adorable. It made her miss her own daughter.

Megan went off to make lunch with what little food they had left. Clay and Kelsey joined them, though they both ate from Clay's plate. Kelsey enjoyed watching the family interact. Though she was an only child, her mom's family was large, and it reminded her of holiday feasts over at her grandmother's house.

It was approaching 12:30, when Clay tapped his watch. "We gotta get moving."

Clay went to retrieve his rifle and pack from his room, and Kelsey used the time to say goodbye to the kids. As she reached the door, Megan stood there with a smile on her face.

"Kelsey, it was so nice to finally meet you. Clay has talked so much about you. I hope to see you around here more often," Megan said.

"I would really like that," Kelsey said. She hugged Megan who at first tried to resist but then hugged her back. It had been a while since she had interacted with a woman that close to her own age.

"Hope I'm not contagious," Megan said with nervous laughter.

Clay returned with his gear, said goodbye to Megan and the children, and started walking down the hall with Kelsey. As they rounded a corner, they spotted Charlie heading their way.

"Hi Charlie!" Kelsey said excitedly.

Charlie walked by and gave an emotionless nod. He was a different person from the sheepish young man she met on the ranch just before winter. His face was hardened, his eyes like stone. She knew the pain that accompanied such a transformation. She looked to Clay to ask, but decided not to.

Going down the steps was much easier on Kelsey's legs, but she still felt the burn in her quads. As they walked out of the garage, they were greeted by a crisp breeze that was almost refreshing. Clay turned around and locked the door. He spun back around and almost walked right into Kelsey. She didn't move.

"Whoa!" Clay said as he stumbled back to avoid running into her. "What's the matter?" he asked.

She stared at him with a conflicted expression. There was so much she wanted to say, but she didn't know where to begin, or even if she should say anything at all. Seeing Clay after months apart made her realize she couldn't deny the feelings she had for him and watching him with the children upstairs comforted her. He had an amazing heart. Charlie's hardened expression was a reminder of how quickly things could change and every moment she denied herself with Clay was a missed opportunity. Her thoughts were tangled and her words were lost. She kept opening her mouth to talk but didn't speak. Concerned, Clay tried to comfort her with his hand on her shoulder, "Hey, are you—"

She grabbed his face and kissed him passionately; it was a moment Clay had dreamed about since the instant he met her. But now that the moment was here, it was inexplicably better than anything he had imagined.

She slowly pulled away, one of her hands remained on his face. Her eyes began to tear up. "I hate you," she said doing her best to suppress a smile.

Clay's head was swirling with an array of emotions, but her comment had him completely baffled. "Uhm, what?" he said.

"I hate you because you make it impossible for me not to love you," she said. Her smile finally cracking.

Clay was still stunned. "I'm confused. Does that mean you love me or you hate me?"

She laughed and stood up on her toes and answered his question with another kiss.

"I'll take that to mean you don't hate me," he said with a smile.

"Come on," she said as she walked up the ramp, glancing back at him over her shoulder.

****

Kelsey and Clay found themselves about seven miles east, close to Devil's Canyon. Clay had spotted a couple of locations that looked promising but did not explore on his way to Ted's. He didn't know why, but he just felt the area was ripe for the picking, and he was right. Though not as good as the score they found in the skating rink, they did find quite a few useful items for bartering. After explaining to Clay what Watson had told her the night before, they agreed that all food related items would go to Clay, all non-food items would go to Kelsey to put towards her debt.

"You know, you really should just leave. The more time I spend around the guy, the less I am liking him," Clay said.

"I wish I could."

"So do it!" Clay stated emphatically, "I can help."

"It's not that simple, Clay."

Clay sighed with frustration. He could tell there were unpeeled layers to the situation that he knew little about. He wanted to ask why but left it alone. He hated seeing how unhappy she was. More than that, he hated that she was in bondage to this man.

He reached over and grabbed her hand, stroking her palm with his thumb. "Well, no matter how long it takes, I'll be here every step of the way. We'll get you out of there."

Kelsey smiled. She didn't understand why, after all the wrong she had done in her life, that she had been so blessed to have a man like Clay love her so much. But she no longer cared. She had revealed the skeletons of her dark past, and he still loved her. It sent a warm feeling through her body, despite the chilled air.

After Clay told her about the walk-in freezer at the sport's bar, they decided to stop at another restaurant for the night to camp out in the freezer. It was quite a bit smaller, but that just caused their body heat to warm up the space faster. Though winter had ended, the temperatures still dipped into the thirties some nights, and it was anything but pleasant to sleep in. The freezer was comfortable, at points, even a little cozy. Clay slept near the door while Kelsey slept behind some empty boxes near the back. If someone were to peek in, they wouldn't even know anyone was there at first glance.

Clay slept better than he had in years. Kelsey's words the day before still had not fully sunk in. Though he had only known her for a shade under eight months, six of which were holed up in their homes fourteen miles apart, he knew she was the one for him. Even when she rejected him, he knew it was not a matter of if but when. Once he figured out how to get her squared away with Watson, he was going to marry her. There was a small 'church' in Liberty that would be a perfect place for a wedding.

"Clay," Kelsey said towering over him, her flashlight aimed at the ceiling to provide some level of light in the freezer, "it's almost seven. We should get going."

Refreshed, they got back on the road. They started heading back to Watson's, stopping anywhere that looked promising along the way. Most places they found small, miscellaneous items that would barely make a scratch in her debt, but every proverbial penny counted.

The majority of their finds went to Kelsey's efforts. They did find a small bag of peanuts, but Clay gave them to an older woman they came across near the highway; she looked like she was on her last leg. He had never seen someone so appreciative in his life, which made him all the more confident he made the right decision giving her the small amount of food. Based on her sickly appearance, Clay knew she wouldn't likely last another night. But at least she wouldn't die with a completely empty stomach.

Clay and Kelsey also found the game *Twister* in the attic of an abandoned house. It was still gift-wrapped with a tattered bow on top. *To Shelby, Love Mom,* the tag read. Kelsey insisted Clay take it back home to the kids; he didn't argue. He knew it would be hilarious to watch the children, most of them for the first time, play a game like that.

They reached Watson's by night fall. They came in and headed for the shop when Jeremy stopped them. He looked disapprovingly at the couple who didn't even realize they were holding hands. "Where have you been?" Jeremy said rather rudely.

"I can come and go as I please; I don't need your permission."

"As head of security for the community, I would appreciate a little heads-up if you are going to be gone all night. It's the courteous thing to do," he said.

"When have I *ever* done that?" she retorted.

"Relax, Jeremy," Clay said, receiving an evil stare in return. "We were out scavenging, and night came faster than we had anticipated. That's all."

"Is that all?" he said as he glanced down at their clasped hands. "Well, I have some things to take care of. If you're planning to go to the shop, don't bother; Maggie closed up already," he said and walked away towards Watson's house.

"What's his deal?" Clay asked.

"He's had a thing for me ever since I got here. I've never felt the same way and have been quite clear about it."

His hostility towards Clay made a little more sense after Kelsey's explanation. Plus, after what Clay said to Watson yesterday, it probably just added to Jeremy's resentment. The sooner Kelsey and Dakota got out of there, the better.

"Well, clearly he just wasn't persistent enough," Clay said with a victorious grin.

Kelsey gave him a playful slug on the shoulder followed by a kiss on the cheek. "Don't be *that* guy, Clay."

"Never," he replied.

Daylight had escaped the sky, and Clay knew he would have to stay in town for the night. He was not comfortable with that idea given how edgy Watson and Jeremy were acting, but there was no way he would travel that late in the evening. "Are there any rooms in town I can rent for the night?" Clay asked.

"No, not really. Besides, you don't need to rent a room. You can stay at my place for the night. Well, it's not really my place. It's Ms. Hawthorne's, but she won't mind. I've told her about you."

"Ms. Hawthorne?"

"She was the only one that would put us up when we first arrived. She is the sweetest lady I've ever met. She watches Dakota for me while I am out, which is pretty much days at a time as you know," she gestured towards the land beyond the fence of the farm. "We wouldn't have made it without her. She's kind of like a second mom to me, and Dakota thinks she's her grandmother."

They walked along the dirt paths and made their way to Hawthorne's hut. It couldn't have been more than six hundred square feet in size. Inside was a living room/dining room/kitchen combo which had a roaring fireplace in the middle. Towards the back, there was a wall with two doors, one at each end.

"Hello there, young man," a voice greeted him from the kitchen area. "You must be Clay. Kelsey has told me so much about you."

"Ms. Hawthorne," Clay said and shook her hand.

"Oh, please, call me Bev."

Kelsey went through the door on the left to check on Dakota while Clay and Hawthorne chatted. Hawthorne used to run a haven house for young women in San Antonio for quite a few years. She retired from the job about two years before the eruption, then moved literally just down the road from Watson's farm. She had met Watson at a farmer's market a few months later. Barely making it through the first winter, she knew she wouldn't be so lucky the next time around. When she walked to Watson's farm in an effort to trade a few measly items for some food, Watson did one better: he gave her a safe place to live. She had been there ever since.

"So, what was Watson like before all this?" Clay asked.

"Oh, he was a real peach. Always willing to lend a hand, even to a stranger like me. He'd always throw in an extra couple ounces of beef for Athena, my pitbull, every time I bought from him. He was such a genuine man." Clay looked a bit surprised, especially considering his last interaction with him. "But," she added, "once the supply trucks stopped coming to the stores so frequently, people started becoming more and more desperate. One night, about a year after the eruption, someone tried to steal some of their chickens, and Lenore—Jake's wife—confronted the men," her eyes started to glisten in the fire-lit room, "and those men shot her dead. They killed a sweet ol' woman so they could steal her birds." Hawthorne dabbed a handkerchief under her eyes. "And you know what's really sad about that? Lenore was the type of woman who would have just given those chickens to someone if they truly needed it."

Clay couldn't imagine losing a wife. The thought of losing Kelsey—let alone a wife of many years—

was almost crippling anytime the idea crept into his head.

"He's just not been the same man since. I can see that he tries, and some days I think he genuinely is back to his old self, but it seems to me those days are few and far between anymore."

Kelsey came back out, and the conversations took a more pleasant road for the remainder of the evening. They sipped on tea and laughed late into the evening. It was a nice break from the discouraging reality that waited just outside the little shanty's walls.

Around 11:00, both Hawthorne and Kelsey retired for the night. Clay slept on the handmade lumpy couch with a nice warm quilt that Kelsey had sewn herself. He had no trouble falling asleep to the crackling sounds and bursts of warm air the fire emitted. He could get used to such luxuries again.

Chapter 23

Clay woke to a blurry face staring down at him. He blinked his eyes a few times and saw the little girl observing the strange man that was sleeping on her couch.

"Hi," the little girl said as she waved.

"Hi," Clay responded as he cleared his throat. "You must be Dakota."

"My name is Dakota, what's yours?" she said, not hearing what Clay had just said.

Clay chuckled at the girl, "My name is Clay, what's yours?" he added, continuing the game.

"It's Dakota, I already told you that!" she said with laughter. She held up a ragged looking plush doll close to his face, "This is Boo. You want to hold her?"

"Uh, sure," Clay said as he sat up on the couch. He rubbed his face with his hands then took the doll. "She's pretty," he added.

"Mmmm hmm," Dakota replied, very much aware of that fact.

Something caught Clay's eye on the other side of the room, and he looked up to see Kelsey standing in the doorway, watching the adorable interaction with a serene smile painted across her face. It had been years since she met a man who cared about children the way Clay did. It seemed like ever since the lights went out, children were a burden instead of a joy. Kelsey knew first hand there was an added layer of stress having to care for a child in this world, but she wouldn't trade it for anything in her life, both present and past.

Dakota put her finger right in front of Clay's eyes. "You got blue eyes," she said with excitement.

"You're a smart girl," Clay said.

"I know that," Dakota replied.

"Not very humble, either," Kelsey said from across the room, drawing Dakota's attention.

"Mommy's awake!" she said as she dashed across the room and into Kelsey's arms.

Kelsey walked over to the kitchen and fixed breakfast for everyone. Dakota was going on about helping Hawthorne—Mimi, as she called her—feed the rabbits. Hawthorne was doing it as a favor for Watson since the woman who normally tended to them had passed away over the winter.

Clay noticed Kelsey looked a little under the weather. "You okay?" he asked her as Hawthorne cleared the table.

"Yeah," she said softly. "Just a bit of a headache; don't think I drank enough over the last few days."

"Come on! Come on!" Dakota shouted as she jumped up and down and pulled on Hawthorne's hand.

"All right dear, hold your rabbits," she said with a chuckle. "Clay, it was lovely to meet you. Safe travels back home."

"Likewise, Bev. You take care."

The two left, and Clay helped Kelsey back to her room. He fished some ibuprofen out of his bag and handed them to her. She chased them with a large glass of water then lay down. She closed her eyes and got comfortable beneath the covers. Clay kissed her forehead which motivated a smile.

"Love you, Kelsey," he said, but she was already asleep.

Clay gathered his things as quietly as he could and left. Before leaving the ranch, he decided to stop by Watson's place. As he approached the porch, Jeremy stepped out the door and began questioning him. Clay grew impatient.

"Jeremy, with all due respect, this does not concern you. I'm here to talk to Mr. Watson."

Jeremy's irritation was not subtle, and he walked up to Clay with a furious look in his eye, but before he could say a word, they were interrupted.

"It's okay, Jeremy," Watson said on the other side of the screen door. "Let him in." They all sat down in the front room where Clay had first been introduced to Watson. "So, what brings you here, Clay?" he said then took a sip of bourbon—it was five o'clock somewhere.

"Well, I just wanted to apologize for my behavior the other day. I was out of line for my comment. I was just a bit stressed trying to get us back on our feet after the winter. Still, it was no excuse for me to say what I said. So..." As Clay reached into an outer pocket of his pack, he noticed Jeremy tense up, so Clay moved slowly, as to not startle him. "I wanted to bring a peace offering," he said as he pulled out the bottle of liquor he found in the school.

Watson leaned forward in his chair and took the bottle. He looked it over, the faded label offered no hint to Clay as to what brand, but Watson recognized the shape. He unscrewed the cap and gave it a sniff. "Ahhh, I haven't smelled a *good* Tennessee whiskey in quite some time." He downed the rest of his bourbon and poured just enough of the whiskey to cover the bottom of the glass. He tossed the drink back and swashed it around in his mouth. He clinched his jaw and exposed his teeth as he swallowed the strong drink. "Well, I've certainly had better but not anytime recently." He held up the bottle to Clay, "Thank you. Apology accepted."

Jeremy stood up, eager to escort Clay out. Clay stood up with him, but didn't move. "There's something else," he said. Watson gestured for him to continue. "When we first met, you had asked what it would take to get this rifle," he said tapping the side of his LaRue.

Watson recalled and laughed as he remembered the dialogue, though it was a little less humorous after the exchange he had with Clay earlier—peace offering or not. "You find something other than my life?"

Clay nodded. "As I understand it, Kelsey has a debt to you."

"That's right," Watson said.

"The rifle for the remainder of her debt."

Watson immediately shook his head, "I'm sorry, son. As nice as that rifle is, it ain't worth what she owes me."

"I have at least a thousand rounds of ammunition back home and a couple hundred more that I still need to reload; throw that in as well."

He still declined. "Even if you had five of those rifles I still wouldn't. I value her contributions to our little community too much," he said with a subtle smirk.

"Why do you care so much about her debt anyway?" Jeremy interjected.

"Once again, Jeremy, not your concern," Clay said, his eyes remained fixed on Watson.

"Well, it *is* my concern," Watson said, "and I am rather curious myself."

Things were certainly not going how Clay had planned. Watson seemed quite infatuated with the rifle before the winter, yet was not even willing to entertain the trade now. Clay looked over at Jeremy, then back at Watson, "I just don't think it's good for a girl to be indebted to anyone."

"I see," Watson replied. There was an awkward silence for several seconds before he picked up the bottle and looked at Clay with a sardonic smile. "Well... Thanks for the drink, son," he said then nodded for Jeremy to escort Clay out of the house.

Clay gave him a derisive stare as Jeremy reached out to grab his arm. Clay jerked his arm away and walked over to the door before he stopped and turned around. "My father always had a saying: 'A man leads; a coward dictates.' I guess we know which category you fall into."

Watson shifted his jaw, then forced a sarcastic smile. "You have yourself a good day, Mr. Whitaker."

Clay walked out the door and off the porch. Jeremy continued to chaperon him to the gate.

"Bye-bye, Mr. Clay!" the voice of a child shouted.

Clay turned to see Dakota and Hawthorne on their way back the from rabbit pen. Clay halted, much to Jeremy's chagrin, and chatted with Hawthorne for a moment. "Could you do me a favor and pass on a message to Kelsey?"

"Of course."

"Tell her that we'll meet at the usual time and place next week, but I might be a little late."

"I sure will, Clay."

"Thanks," he said to Hawthorne before looking down at Dakota. "Bye-bye!" he said and waved.

Dakota ran off back home; Hawthorne trailed behind.

Jeremy continued to follow Clay to the gate. "I think I can manage from here," Clay snapped.

"Zachery," Jeremy said to the young gatekeeper.

"Sir?"

"Please notify me immediately if this man comes to the gate. He will need approval from me or Mr. Watson before entry, understood?"

Jeremy's orders angered Clay, but it was not at all surprising. He probably would have done the same thing if he were in Jeremy's shoes, but of course, he wouldn't be the power-hungry tyrant Watson was in the first place.

On his way back home, Clay checked some snares that he and Charlie had set up last week. They hadn't captured anything since they set them up, but that was about to change as Clay discovered two out of the fifteen traps had done their jobs. One of the rabbits, in particular, was quite fat and would be perfect for a tasty stew. The carrots Megan had planted just as winter started to ease were looking promising. A trip to Liberty would hopefully give them the rest of the ingredients needed, and then they would have a nice, fresh home cooked meal, the first in what seemed like ages.

Back home, the hallways were quiet. Nobody opened the door, so Clay had to climb up the executive elevator from fifteen to sixteen. The fifteenth floor once held the main offices for the law firm that owned the building; sixteen was where the big wig lawyers that ran the company usually stayed. Clay didn't know why they needed an elevator that literally went up one floor, but it made a nice alternative entrance for him in cases like this. And since it was only about twelve feet he didn't have to worry about falling to his death climbing up through the shaft.

He pried the doors open and stepped out into the lobby next to his room. It was eerily quiet at first, but then he saw Lona come out of the kitchen with a bowl.

"Hey Lona."

"Hi," Lona replied with a very soft-spoken voice.

"Where is everyone?"

"It's nap time for the littles. The others are on the roof. Not sure where Charlie is. Megan's in bed, so I am bringing her soup," she said catching Clay up to speed.

It was hard for Clay to comprehend Megan being in bed in the middle of the day. She must really be feeling terrible. Like Clay, it was her nature to work until she could work no more. She always said she slept better when she worked hard and could think about all she had accomplished in the day as she fell asleep.

Clay put the rabbit meat in the freezer, dropped his things off in his room, and made his way to the roof. He played tag with the kids for a little while then began fiddling with the greenhouse which he should have fixed already. Fortunately the damage was minimal, and he was able to make the repairs in less than an hour. It would have been faster had he not been "it" a couple of times, requiring a brisk chase around the rooftop.

The access door to the roof opened and the rest of the kids came out fresh from their afternoon nap and ready to play. The sound of laughter and playful screams filled the air; it was such a pleasant sound.

"She's awake if you wanted to talk," Lona said to Clay as she followed the last of the kids outside.

"Thanks, Lona."

Clay made his way down to Megan's room. She looked as bad as she sounded.

"How ya doing?" Clay asked.

"I'm fine," she said, but fine sounded a lot like 'find'. "Just a really bad cold."

"I am heading to Liberty in the morning. If I find any antibiotics, I'll do whatever I have to—"

"Antibiotics won't work," she cut him off. "It's a cold. It's all viral. All I can do is treat the symptoms, and let my body do the rest."

Clay told her about the rabbits, and that brought a smile to her face. Canned beans and freeze-dried meat kept them alive, but the taste sure left something to be desired. She couldn't complain, though. If Clay hadn't found those #10 cans, they would have starved long before the thaw.

"Get some sleep," he said as he walked backwards to the door. "I'll swing by later and check in on ya."

"Thanks," Megan said and then rolled over, cocooning herself in the ratty old blanket. He looked over at a box that acted as her bedside table and saw his mother's brooch. He had totally forgotten he'd found it, and Megan assumed he brought it back for her. Correct in her assumption or not, Clay was disappointed he didn't get to see the look on her face when she discovered it.

After spending some time running back and forth gathering various goods to take to Liberty, he rounded up the kids—including Charlie—and had them follow him to the fifteenth floor, which had a rather large, empty room. Curiosity struck most of the younger kids as to what was in the box Clay was holding. Murmurs of what it might be began to dominate the conversation. Charlie, Lona, and Blake remembered it from before the eruption, but the others were clueless.

Clay set the box down on the floor and began pulling the contents out. The children watched with great anticipation. Once the mat was set up, Clay flicked the spinner. They had all come to the same conclusion: it was a game. Board games had started to become quite rare as technology continued its death grip on traditional means of entertainment. Who wanted to bother rolling dice or moving small metal figurines across an actual board when one click of the mouse could do it all for you with goofy sounds and exaggerated animation? Bouncing your thimble past go to collect your money had become a thing of the past, even before the quakes. Clay thought about how sad that was and recalled some of his fondest memories of the family was the weekly board game night. No cell phones, no computer, no technology other than music from the stereo; great times. So to find one that was still in the cellophane was quite the discovery.

Clay got four of the kids on the mat and explained the rules loudly so everyone, including those waiting for their turn, understood. The four on the mat started jumping up and down with excitement, begging for the game to commence.

"Are you ready?" Clay asked as he flicked the plastic spinner. "Right hand, red!" he shouted.

The children laughed and giggled as their bodies became more contorted with each spin, crisscrossing each other for the proper color. After just a few calls, the kids started to fall, and Maya came out triumphant. Despite holding out for a while, even Charlie began to have fun. It brought a tremendous relief to Clay when he heard Charlie laughing as he reached over Tyler with his right foot to hit that green circle. It was as if the damage done to the young man was temporarily repaired.

The game was a success, and Clay couldn't imagine a better way to start the warmer months. Even though it had been one of the hardest winters the family had experienced, and food was still a concern, Clay savored the moment and pushed all his worries out of his head. Though there were some close calls, they had *all* made it through the harshest of seasons, and he was grateful for that miracle.

For dinner, Lona made the rabbit stew which everyone—even Erica who was appalled at the thought of eating a cute little bunny—enjoyed very much. Lona was quite the chef; the meat was cooked perfectly.

"Lona," Clay said above the chattering children, "this is the *best* stew I've ever had. *Ever!*" The emphasis clearly indicating that he included before the eruptions too.

She smiled bashfully and looked down at her plate; her cheeks slightly reddened. "Thank you," she said with a soft voice.

Lona was a beautiful young girl. Her smile could restore life to a dead plant; yet, there was a void in her eyes that cried from a dark past. Clay had seen that same look in Kelsey's eyes, and he knew whatever Lona had gone through before they took her in was devastating. He hoped it was nothing like what Kelsey had experienced, but for all he knew, it could have been worse. She never had a willingness to share such details of her past, and Clay never asked. He just made sure she knew that if she ever needed someone to talk to, he was there.

Clay took some stew to Megan's room. Both of them were iffy about her eating a heavy meal when she felt so lousy, but the incredible aroma that filled the tiny copy room was too powerful for her to decline. She took her time eating it, both to ensure her stomach wouldn't sour and also to savor each bite.

After chatting for a few minutes, Clay went back to his room and packed the things he had gathered for Liberty. Good bartering items were starting to become as scarce as food. He began picking everyday items they used around the house, balancing the fine line of necessity and luxury. He had been so focused on finding food and meds that he hadn't realized how low they were running on high value barter items that the family had no practical use for. He sighed heavily as he put his MP3 player and headphones into his pack, realizing how much he would miss the hours of enjoyment it provided. That sacrifice emphasized his need to set a precedence on stockpiling more barter items, in addition to finding food. Just another task to consider when prioritizing.

Chapter 24

Clay squeezed the trigger, and the sharp crack from the rifle disrupted the otherwise still morning air. As his vision regained focus, Clay could see the tip of the motionless antlers sticking up just beyond the tall grass. He could hardly contain his excitement. He gave the usual ten minutes before he cautiously approached the animal and finally got a good look. It was a nine-pointer. How it managed to survive long enough for that kind of growth without catching a bullet seemed impossible, but the fact that Clay capitalized on the kill was a downright marvel. It was a much needed victory for Clay—a morale boost as much as the physical nourishment the meat would provide. He was in the right place at the right time.

It was still early in the morning—he didn't have to meet Kelsey for another four hours—so he took his time harvesting the meat. He took the hide, which always fetched a fair price with traders, and stuffed it into a separate trash bag. He guessed more than fifty pounds of meat in all. The deer, combined with the food he was able to get in Liberty a few days before, would last the family quite some time. Immediately, Clay felt as if a colossal burden had been lifted from his shoulders. He considered trading a few pounds to get some dairy, but was apprehensive whether or not Watson would still be interested in doing business with him. The last two times he attempted a trade, both parties walked away angry with each other; the relationship had become quite strained. It bothered him that Kelsey and Dakota were tangled up in that mess, and he wanted nothing more than to get them out of there and put that place in the rearview mirror, even if it meant the loss of a good trading post.

After collecting everything of value from the trophy buck, he packed up and made his trip home. The haul, which was close to seventy pounds everything included, was hardly noticeable. His renewed energy from the kill was greater than he could remember, and he barely felt the added weight.

On the trip home, he decided he was going to make venison burgers. It would take several pounds of meat—a bit of a splurge—but it would indeed be a celebration. Plus, many of the kids, as well as himself, were looking quite underweight since winter ended. A good hearty meal would do a lot of good for the family. He would invite Kelsey for the meal too. It would cut into their scavenging time, but Clay thought she would enjoy the classic American cuisine.

Clay was robbed of his excitement when he reached the garage door and saw the padlock lying on the ground, broken, and the door hanging wide open. He swiftly moved down the ramp to the door, his Scout rifle at the ready, and entered the garage. He swung the rifle to the left, then the right, clearing the room. He stashed his pack of food in a dark corner and made his way to the stairs. His hopes that someone had broken in but not found their way to the stairwell was dashed when he saw muddy boot prints that trailed off by the second floor. The prints suggested there were at least three people, but he couldn't be sure there weren't more.

He darted up the steps as fast as he could, his mind raced as rapidly as his heart. Of all the years they had lived in the building, Clay had never once been in such a vulnerable position. It was uncharted territory for him, and he had no idea what was waiting for him.

He had reached the sixth floor when he heard the first shot ring out, followed by a hail of gunfire exchanged for several seconds before he heard some shouting and a door slam.

Charlie!

Clay ran even faster. As he reached the twelfth floor landing, he saw a man on the ground leaning against the wall, a devastating wound to the head. He didn't recognize the man, but it was clear that Charlie had gotten the drop on the group.

There was blood leading up the stairs, and Clay was hopeful that Charlie had wounded one or more of the other assailants. Clay followed the trail up another flight and through a door into a large open office pit. The attackers were scouring the room in search of Charlie. Their attempts to lure him out with promises not to hurt him were unsuccessful. Had it not been for the gravity of the situation, Clay would have found it funny that the group was actually using such a tactic.

The office space, which was a sea of cubicles and filing cabinets, provided Charlie with a plethora of places to hide. It also gave Clay plenty of cover to sneak across the massive room without being detected. Towards the center of the office, he approached a man who was searching a series of partitions. Though the room was somewhat illuminated from the windows, the man clicked on a flashlight to look beneath the desks. Clay could hear at least two others on the other side of the room that took up nearly the entire floor and another man searching a row of private offices by the windows.

Clay laid his rifle along the edge of a cubicle wall and crept towards the man searching beneath the desks. Staying low and keeping his hand on his holster, he slowly bridged the gap between him and the stranger. He was just two desks down when his hand moved from his pistol to his knife. Removing it from the sheath, Clay grasped the handle firmly in his unsteady hand. It was a small blade, not even four inches, but it was razor sharp and extremely light. Clay was just outside the cubicle the man was searching. He waited.

"Got anything, Taylor?" a man on the other end of the room shouted.

"Just staplers and paperclips, Silas," the man in the cubicle shouted back.

Clay remained still and did his best to suppress his anxious breathing. The man walked out of the cubicle, and Clay sprang up like a jack-in-the-box, grabbing him by the face, covering his mouth, and pulling him down to the ground on top of him. Before he realized what was happening, Clay swung the knife around and drove it deep into the man's chest. The muffled cries were brief, but horrific—a sound that would haunt Clay for life. Within seconds, the man's body relaxed and Clay noticed his chest had stopped moving.

He rolled the body off of him and peeked over the short walls to see if anyone had noticed. They had not. He returned the knife to the sheath and retrieved his rifle. The other two men that had been searching the large room were much closer together, and Clay was certain a similar take down would be impossible. If he hadn't missed anybody, there were three men left. If he played his cards right and if the execution was flawless, he could dispatch both men and move back into hiding before the last could exit the private offices.

The man they called Silas headed towards a hallway at the far end of the room while the others continued to search the cubicles. With Silas out of sight, Clay crept towards the remaining bandit in the large room. He had to act fast because the man searching the offices was checking the last one.

As Clay stalked his next target, gunfire erupted from the hallway. Clay's target started running towards the action, weaving in and out of narrow hallways formed by the cubicle walls. Clay popped up and took the shot.

The sound of the powerful .308 Winchester dominated the other gunfire which caused a pause from down the hall. Clay's shot hadn't been fatal as the man he hit was on the ground screaming. But the impact was catastrophic.

With no time to retrieve and chamber a new cartridge, Clay threw the sling over his shoulder and reached for his Sig. He ran towards the man he had just shot, who was still howling in pain, and considered a mercy kill. With only twenty-five pistol rounds, however, and at least two other armed men to engage, he couldn't waste the time or ammo. He picked up the wounded man's shotgun as he passed, and headed for the hallway.

Clay leaned around the corner of the wall. About fifteen feet down, the hallway turned, providing the two robbers with decent cover. One of them continued to exchange fire with Charlie at the opposite end of their hallway; the other was peering around the corner, waiting for Clay. Their eyes met briefly before the man moved back behind the corner. Since he wasn't shooting, Clay suspected that he, too, was low on ammo, if not completely out. Clay swung his body around, then immediately back to get behind cover. The aggressive move caused the bandit to leave his cover and blast both barrels of his shotgun towards Clay. Several pellets struck the wall near the corner causing an explosion of fragments that peppered the side of Clay's face. It stung, but the bigger concern was his blurred vision from the drywall dust and debris.

Knowing the man had to reload, Clay whipped back around and responded in kind, unloading both barrels at the corner of the wall the man was hiding behind. He dropped the shotgun and took his pistol back out. He emptied the magazine in a flash and had the next one ready to go by the time he dropped the depleted one. With a fresh mag chambered, Clay began to run down the hallway.

"Let's go!" one of the men shouted followed by the sound of feet tromping down the hallway.

As Clay rounded the corner, he raised his pistol and took aim. Between his fuzzy vision and the heavy smoke in the air, he could barely make out two silhouettes fleeing. Clay rapidly pulled the trigger until the slide locked back. He hit one of the men for sure, but they both escaped to the stairwell on the opposite side of the building than they came up. Clay chased after them, but by the time he got to the stairs, they were already down several floors, so he halted his pursuit.

He inserted his last magazine and holstered his pistol. He rubbed his eyes in a feeble attempt to clear the haze when he heard Charlie.

"Clay!" a faint cry called out.

"Charlie!" Clay yelled as he ran back in and discovered the boy laying on the floor a few feet from the hallway. Clay had run right past him and hadn't realized it.

The sight was dreadful. Charlie was already coughing up blood, and his breathing was labored. An expanding pool of blood encompassed the shell casings that littered the floor around him.

"Are they gone?" he asked before giving a fluid-filled cough.

"Yeah," Clay said and knelt down next to him to examine the injury on his stomach. Silas was carrying a revolver, so Clay assumed it was a .38 or .357. But after looking at the size of the hole, he was thinking bigger. "Hang in there, Charlie. I'm gonna get you upstairs, and Megan will patch you up, okay?" Clay said as calmly as he could.

Charlie gave a subtle nod. His pale face was a grim backdrop for his dark brown eyes. Clay slid his left hand beneath Charlie's head and his right under his legs and carefully picked him up. Charlie's groans were brief as he could not sustain the energy to cry. As Clay walked up the steps, he began shouting for Megan.

"Clay?" Megan screamed from the other side of the door, "Is that you?"

"Open the door! Charlie is hurt!"

The door launched open, and Megan jumped out, her knuckles were white from clutching her pistol. She saw Clay holding Charlie, both of them covered in blood, all of which was Charlie's. "Charlie! What happened?" she cried.

"They shot him!"

Megan holstered her pistol, pushed the door all the way open and held it, giving Clay as much clearance as possible. "Get him to the infirmary!" she ordered.

Clay carried Charlie to the infirmary and lay him on a conference table that would serve as an operating table. Charlie's eyes started to close as he drifted in and out of consciousness. "Charlie!" Megan cried, "You need to stay with us, stay awake, okay? Can you do that for me?"

His eyes were barely more than a squint; he attempted to acknowledge her but couldn't.

"What do we do?" Clay asked frantically. "What do you need me to do?"

Megan paused for a moment and started stammering over her words. She was still battling the cold that had been plaguing her for the past week, and her head was in a deep fog. She didn't have experience dealing with such severe trauma, let alone while ill. Her mind was swirling, and she froze up.

"Megan!" Clay screamed, snapping her out of her daze.

"I'm sorry, Clay, I'm trying! I-I-I just can't think straight," she said with frustration. She looked over at Lona who was standing just inside the door, blocking the view from the other kids watching from the hall. "Lona, I need you to find every single towel or rag you can find and bring them back here right now!" Lona tore off down the hallway revealing the other kids who were sobbing just outside the door. Megan grabbed the only towel in the room and put it on the wound, pressing down firmly. "Clay, get me the med bag and vodka from the cabinets in the bathroom."

While applying pressure with her right hand, she checked Charlie's pulse with the other—it was weak.

Though she didn't have a functioning sphygmomanometer, she knew his blood pressure was falling. Maya began to cry hysterically from the door, adding to Megan's stress. "Blake, get them away from here right now!"

Blake was the next oldest after Lona and Charlie, but since he and Courtney were the newest to the group he had never really been given much responsibility. "Where?" he asked with a tremble in his voice.

"I don't care!" Megan shouted, causing them all to flinch. "Just get them away from me right now!"

The kids stormed off; the cries and sobs faded. Clay returned with the bag and vodka and set them on the table just above Charlie's head. "Now what?" he asked.

Megan instructed Clay to take over for her, keeping pressure on the wound while she started to pull out tools and equipment from the bag. The towel had quickly saturated with blood. He looked over at Megan, but her expression didn't have the reassurance he was looking for.

Lona returned, her arms filled with an assortment of towels and clothing, a lantern sitting on top. It was quick and incredible thinking for such a young woman—the room was dimly lit, especially for surgery, and it would be crucial for Megan to have proper lighting to work.

Lona turned on the lantern and held it up while Megan examined the damage more closely. As soon as Clay removed the towel, blood gushed out of the hole. The wound was just above and to the right of his belly button.

"Clay, can you lift him up a little bit? *Very* slowly and *very* carefully."

Clay obeyed and lifted him, causing Charlie to give a fading moan. Megan leaned down and saw an exit wound, which was what she was hoping for. She was ill-equipped, both in training and tools, to be digging around in his stomach looking for a hunk of lead. Even so, Charlie was facing an uphill battle at best. Judging from the angle of the exit wound, she was confident no major organs were hit, but he was losing a lot of blood—too much blood—and she couldn't be sure of the extent of the damage inside.

Clay looked at her hoping for good news. "The bullet went through, which is good, but," she started to shake. She looked at Charlie then back at her brother. "Clay, I just don't know what to do," she whispered, hoping Charlie didn't hear. Without advanced medical imaging, Megan would have to feel for any internal damage. Though she had read many medical and trauma books, there was no substitution for hands-on experience, of which she had none. There was a real possibility she could do more harm than good, and she knew with certainty that it would put Charlie through a tremendous amount of pain. Making a decision, she reached over and grabbed the bottle of vodka and told Clay to reapply the pressure.

She dumped some vodka on her hands and rubbed them together. She started to pray aloud. "Dear God, please give me wisdom and steady hands. Let me find nothing wrong."

"Amen," Clay added.

Megan turned and looked at Charlie who was narrowly conscious, "Charlie, honey, this is going to hurt more than anything you could imagine," she said with tears streaming down her face, "but I promise, it won't hurt for long."

Charlie's expression was almost indifferent to her words. "Am I going to die?" he whispered.

"No, Charlie," she said, feigning a smile, "you're going to be just fine," she said as she stroked his hair, knowing she was probably lying. She looked over at Lona and had her move to where Clay was standing and had Clay move to the other side of the table. She wadded up a rag and told Charlie to bite down hard when he felt the pain.

Megan motioned for Clay to lean across the table. "You're going to need to hold him down," Megan whispered into his ear.

An ominous silence filled the room which was broken when Megan took a deep breath. She removed the soaked rag and inserted her fingers into Charlie's abdomen. The initial scream was deafening and caused everyone to cringe. His back arched and his legs kicked as Clay struggled to keep him pinned. Charlie clenched down on the rag in his mouth and gave a deep, throaty groan. Then silence.

"Megan! What happened?" Clay asked distraughtly.

Megan checked for a pulse. It was weaker than before, but still there. "He passed out from the pain. Now shut up! I need to concentrate," she said. Frustration permeated her voice, not so much with Clay, but because her mind was drawing a blank. She struggled to recall anything from the books she had read cover-to-cover numerous times. She decided to just start feeling around, hoping she would know if something wasn't right. Suddenly, her studies rushed back to her mind as if she had the book open on the table right in front of her.

The anxiety in the room was palpable as Megan felt around inside his stomach; the occasional sound of blood slushing around her fingers broke the silence in the room. After several minutes of exploration, Megan slowly removed her fingers and placed a fresh towel on the wound.

"So, is he okay?" Clay asked.

"Well, a bullet just punched through his stomach, so no, not really, Clay," she said, instantly feeling remorse for the cold, cynical response. She sighed heavily. "I'm sorry," she said shaking her head. "The fact is, I just don't know. I couldn't find anything wrong other than the obvious. It doesn't look like it hit any major arteries, and there are no organs in the area, but the shockwave from the bullet could have done damage that I just can't know about." Megan had Lona take over applying pressure, and she cleaned her hands with one of the towels, but it did little good. "If he were in a hospital, I'd say his chances of living would be fair to good," her face went grim, "but he's not in a hospital."

"What are you saying?" Clay asked.

"At this point, any number of things could happen, but my immediate concern is blood loss." She motioned around at the bloodied towels all over the table, as well as Charlie and Clay's clothes. "That is a *lot* of blood. How much did he lose downstairs?"

Clay recalled the bloody scene and remembered it being a good amount, but then again he wasn't sure what qualified as "a lot" in medical terms. "I don't know for sure."

"I need to go see," Megan said.

The two left the room, leaving Lona to keep pressure applied to the wound. Before heading down, Clay grabbed his AR-15 and extra magazines.

Clay walked into the large room and cleared it before motioning for Megan to come in. Though Clay wasn't expecting resistance, he didn't want to be surprised. Megan walked in holding her pistol with unsteady hands.

They walked the same path Clay had taken, stepping over the body of the first man Clay took out with the knife. Up ahead there was a large blood stain on the floor where he had shot the man with the Scout, but there was no body. Clay raised his rifle and had Megan stay back while he went down the hallway. He found the man on the other side of the room where he had found Charlie. The bandit had tried to make an escape but gave up just a few feet from the stairwell. Clay felt a pang of guilt that the man had suffered as long as he did, but those feelings quickly dissipated when he turned around and saw Charlie's blood.

He called Megan in, and she immediately started to cry.

"It's a lot, isn't it?"

She nodded briskly. "This is not good, Clay," she said as she moved her hands to the top of her head, unconcerned with the blood getting into her hair. She looked over at the body on the other side of the room, his back ravaged from the .308 that tore through it. "Is that him?" she asked, almost hopefully.

Clay shook his head.

They stood in silence for a moment as they both felt the weight of the situation sink in. "I should get back upstairs," she said, wanting to leave the scene.

Clay crouched down and picked up the M1 carbine from the floor. Charlie's blood had soaked into the wooden stock, staining the old rifle an eerie dark brown. The sight was more than Clay could handle.

As they walked back up the stairs, Clay asked, "So, you said that blood loss was the immediate threat. If he manages to survive that, what's the long term concern?"

"Well, obviously we're in a not-so-sterile environment. God only knows how many germs and bacteria he picked up in the last hour. Short of a miracle, he's going to get an infection of some sort; we need antibiotics."

Back in the infirmary, Lona was still holding the towel. Megan took over and started dressing the wound with more appropriate gauze and bandage since the bleeding had finally slowed.

Clay was frightened with how pale Charlie appeared to be, but the kid was a fighter, and that gave Clay hope. "Okay," he said, "I am going to load up and head out to get antibiotics. I think I remember Watson saying he had some."

"You think he'll trade with you?" Megan asked.

"Let's hope."

"Okay. Be safe, Clay."

Clay left the infirmary and gathered some supplies before heading downstairs. He put on a different jacket—one that wasn't covered in blood—and headed out. When he got to the basement, he remembered the food he had stashed in the corner. Despite the urgency to depart, he knew that allowing the food to spoil was not an option, and he went back upstairs to drop the meat off in the freezer, further adding to his exhaustion.

****

He arrived at Watson's a little after 3:00 in the afternoon. He had brought half of the venison with him to trade; it was all he could spare. Even though he did not hesitate to take what he thought he would need, it was still a gut wrenching decision to take several weeks' worth of food away from the family just for some antibiotics. He just hoped Watson would be willing to barter.

Under strict orders from Jeremy, the young gatekeeper was forced to hunt down the head of security before allowing him to enter. Minutes felt like hours as Clay attempted to wait patiently.

The gatekeeper returned with Jeremy. "What do you want, Clay?" he asked with an edge in his voice.

"Jeremy, you can go back to hating me another time, but right now I *really* need to make a trade with Watson."

Jeremy could hear the desperation in his voice, like a parched child begging for a glass of water. He sighed and nodded for the gatekeeper to let him in. "I'm going to take you over to the shop, if they don't have what you need, we turn around and you walk right out with no stopping to chat with your girlfriend or anything else, you got it?" Clay didn't attempt to argue and graciously thanked him as he walked through the gate. They strolled through the makeshift town at a casual pace set by Jeremy. "What's got you all wound up?" he asked.

Clay locked his eyes on the shop just a few hundred feet away, never bothering to look over at Jeremy. "We were attacked this morning. One of our kids was shot."

Jeremy was shocked. He then noticed the blood on Clay's shirt just beneath his jacket. "Dear God. I'm sorry, Clay." Jeremy's demeanor towards Clay softened, and there was a bit more insistence in his walk. Jeremy didn't like Clay much, but that was more about his relationship with Kelsey and less about the abrasive dynamic between Clay and Watson. As Watson's employee, Jeremy had to be defensive and leery of threats to the old man. As an individual, however, he didn't fault Clay for his hostile attitude towards Watson. The old man just had that effect on people.

"Is he going to be okay?" Jeremy asked.

"I don't know yet, but that's why I am here. We need antibiotics."

Jeremy reached for the door and held it open for Clay, then followed him inside. Watson was on a stepladder in the middle of hanging a shelf on the wall. Matthew stood right next to him, holding some nails and brackets. Watson turned to greet his customer, but his smile turned sour. "Oh, it's you. What do you want now?" he asked as he started pounding a nail into the wall.

"Look, Mr. Watson, I know we had a bit of a falling-out, but I am *begging* you, please make a trade with me today."

Watson finished driving the nail into the wall and placed the hammer down on the top platform of the ladder. He stepped down and walked over to Clay and forced a smile. "Well, what do you need?"

"I need antibiotics...whatever you've got, please!" The despair in Clay's voice matched his expression.

"Well, that's a mighty tall order, son. That's the kind of stuff I reserve for the people of the town or my closest of friends. You currently reside in neither camp."

Clay glared at him, his eyes pleading for help. He reached into his bag and pulled out the venison. "This is about twenty-five pounds of venison, harvested this morning. It's all I've got. I know you guys are stretched thin for food too..."

Watson let out a single laugh. "Son, that ain't gonna amount to squat with a town this size. You might as well hang on to that," he said, insulted with the offer. "However," Watson continued, "perhaps we can finally make a deal on that rifle of yours."

"Come on!" Clay raised his voice. "You know as well as I do that this is worth far more than the medicine."

"Value is subjective, son. You *need* the medicine, and I *want* the rifle. Notice the difference in our situations." Watson gave a baleful grin, as if he were savoring the moment. "That's my offer, Clay, take it or leave it."

Clay was seeing red. Watson's true nature was revealed as he exploited Clay's dire circumstances. The thought more than once crossed Clay's mind to take advantage of the fact that he had a semi-auto rifle with just three targets, and he suspected that Matthew didn't even carry a gun. He was surprised and disappointed in himself for even considering such an act, which made him all the more deflated with the whole transaction.

He knew that Watson had him beat, and there was nothing to be done about it. He slid his hand over the receiver of the rifle and gave it a couple of taps. He unsnapped his pouches and began stacking the fully loaded magazines onto the countertop.

"I've got Amoxicillin or Ciprofloxacin," Watson said, stumbling over his pronunciation of the latter.

Just before Clay had left home, Megan had told him a specific drug that would be best for Charlie's situation. He couldn't remember the exact name, but knew it was neither of the options Watson had. She had told him anything would be better than nothing, so he went with the Amoxicillin, a name that was familiar to him. Watson headed to the backroom to retrieve the antibiotics when the bell above the door jingled. Watson stopped and looked back.

"Hey, Doc, whatcha need?" Watson asked.

Clay shifted his weight to try and hide his frustration over the delay. Seconds counted, and he needed to get back home with the medicine.

"Running quite low on a few things," he said as he held out a small sheet of paper.

Watson walked over and took the list, giving it a quick glance. "All right, I can get a few of these things now, but I'll have to send some people out to look for the rest."

Doc nodded.

"Oh, one more thing," Doc added, once again stopping Watson just as he was about to go into the back room. Clay gave off a less than subtle sigh. "I need a bottle of ibuprofen. Once the morphine wears off, Silas is going to have a pretty bad day without some form of pain management."

Shock ripped through Clay's body as Doc's words echoed in his head.

Did he just say Silas?

Chapter 25

The sun was descending, and Clay still had at least another ten hours ahead of him. He had been unable to think straight since he grabbed his things and left Watson's without saying a word—and without the antibiotics. He had been betrayed in the worst kind of way. At moments, his body trembled as he writhed in anger; at other times, he shuddered in fear. Would he be able to have any luck finding meds in Liberty? How would he respond to Watson's aggression? Did Watson even know what happened? How did they know where he lived? Thinking of the possible answer made him sick to his stomach.

It wouldn't have been inaccurate to describe Clay and Watson's relationship as unstable. What had started off as a promising business relationship—something that could have evolved into the kind of dynamic between Clay and Vlad—had quickly gone south. Backhanded threats only made matters worse.

Despite it all, Watson would never have sent men after Clay. Would he?

An unsettling silence filled the air. The frigid temperatures, in addition to the absence of sound, sent a chill down Clay's spine. It felt like the calm before the storm. And not five minutes after the sun fell behind the horizon, he heard the Screamers announce their presence. Stopping, hiding, or evading was not in Clay's game plan. Anyone or anything that attempted to delay his arrival at Liberty would not get a warning—as if the nomadic psychopaths would ever heed one.

Clay loaded a magazine filled with XM855's. The full metal jacket with the steel core would make light work of the body armor most Screamers sported.

It didn't take long before Clay had his first encounter. The two savages had already spotted him and were racing his way by the time he saw them. There was just a hint of light filling the sky that allowed Clay to see them well enough to be confident with his aim. The red holographic sight illuminated brightly against the dark backdrop, making it easy to lock on to his target. The first shot rang out, and the man on the left face-planted into the ground, his body sliding across the asphalt several feet before coming to a stop. The second man, unconcerned by his comrade's death, continued his sprint. Firing two more shots, Clay watched as he suffered the same fate as the first.

The skirmishes continued throughout the night. Normandy Creek lived up to its reputation that evening as Clay burned through nearly two magazines by the time he reached the other side of the small forest. Even though it was dark, he knew he had dished out a significant amount of carnage and suspected the stream ran heavy with blood that night.

The Screamers stopped coming around 3:00. There were no more sightings, no more attacks, not even a distant scream. It was as if they all got the memo that Clay wasn't messing around. It was almost unnerving to be out so late and *not* hear sadistic shrieks.

About a half-hour before dawn, Clay's body was ready to quit. He had already been awake for twenty-four hours, and on the move for most of that. Despite his fatigue, he pressed forward; Charlie's life depended on it. His pace was slow, but he did not stop.

He pondered how many lives he had taken over the past few hours. He couldn't be sure but suspected that it was more than double the amount he had taken since his first kill at age fourteen, perhaps even triple. He contemplated whether or not what he did tonight was self-defense or murder. He never gave any of those men a chance to retreat and in many cases, never allowed them to get close enough to inflict any harm. Yet, he knew if he hadn't shot them from afar, he would have just had to do it up close. He quickly flushed the thoughts out of his mind; one problem at a time.

He began to rub his bleary eyes and let out a big yawn when he heard a shriek come from the left. The impact felt like what could only be described as being blindsided by an all-pro linebacker. Clay took several nasty blows to the face before he was able to kick the man off. Operating on instinct, Clay rolled over and pushed himself up on top of the man. The man swung his fist and struck Clay numerous times but was unable to stop him from pulling his pistol out. Clay jammed the barrel up to the man's temple and pulled the trigger.

If the sound was any indication to the mess the jacketed hollow-point had left, Clay was glad it was still too dark to see the destruction.

Before Clay recovered from the attack, another man came storming from ahead. Still sitting on top of the corpse, Clay raised his pistol and fired four rounds at the screaming silhouette. He wasn't sure which shot did him in, but the man fell silent. Clay took a few minutes to collect himself before he got back to his hike. The surge of adrenaline fueled him to move at a cautious jog. He was still another two hours away.

The rest of the journey, as he hoped, was uneventful. Once the morning came around, the Screamers vanished—almost as if they were on a time clock, and at 4:30 every morning, they punched out.

As Liberty became visible in the distance, Clay picked up the pace even more. When he arrived at the gate, he was happy to see the usual gatekeeper who let him in even though he was a bit wary of the blood on Clay's clothing. Clay noticed the look.

"There's a few less Screamers the world has to worry about," he said trying to make light of a very harrowing night.

The gatekeeper gave a disconcerted smile. "Glad you came out on top."

Without saying another word, Clay hurried over to Vlad's shop.

"Clay! I cannot believe it's taken this long to come and visit your old friend! How did you fare this winter?"

As Clay approached the counter, Vlad saw a battered, bruised, and bloodied man standing in front of him.

"Vlad, *please* tell me you have some antibiotics," Clay asked hopefully.

Stunned, Vlad's face got long, and he shook his head, "I am sorry, my friend; it has been rough winter."

Clay's shoulders dropped. He rubbed his face, then ran his fingers through his hair. The fleeting optimism he had for the trip was now completely gone. "I suppose none of the other stores in town have any either, huh?"

Vlad saw the despair in Clay's eyes. He wanted to give him some hope, but he knew better. He shook his head again, "I do not think so."

Clay sighed deeply. After everything he had been through, after all the men he killed just to get there, it was all for nothing. Clay screamed vehemently as he smashed his fist down on the countertop, startling Vlad—a feat few men had accomplished.

The store was silent. Olesya peeked around the corner to see what was happening. She had never seen Clay so upset before.

Resigned to the fact that he wasn't going to be able to get his hands on antibiotics, Clay plopped his arms down on the counter and rested his head on them.

"I'm sorry, Vlad," Clay said, regretful of his outburst. He was anything but in control of his emotions at the moment. He stood back up and tried to regain his composure. Breaking down and calling it quits wasn't going to get Charlie the medication he needed.

Vlad wanted to ask who needed the meds, but he did not want to add to Clay's anguish. He simply reached across the counter and gave Clay a squeeze on the shoulder. There were no words of solace that could ease the distress Clay was experiencing—Vlad knew that firsthand.

Clay sensed someone walk up behind him. He hadn't even noticed that someone else was in the store with him, which made him all the more ashamed of his reaction.

"It's Clay, right?" The man asked.

"Yes," Clay said with a gravelly voice. He turned and instantly recognized the face.

The man shook his hand and continued, "I'm—"

"Barry Shelton," Clay interrupted. It was the mayor. He felt even more embarrassed now.

"That's right. I remember meeting you several years ago. I've heard a lot of good things about you from the folks in town. You are well liked here, I gather."

Clay gave a crooked smile. "Thanks," he said with little enthusiasm, not really in the mood for compliments.

"I'm sorry for the small talk. Obviously, you're in a bit of a tough situation, and it sounds like you are in need of some antibiotics, right?"

Clay perked up, his demeanor flipped. "Yes! Do you have any for sale?" he asked eagerly.

The man nodded towards the door, and Clay followed him outside, forgetting to even say bye to Vlad. The pair made their way across the town and ended up inside one of the nicest homes in the entire neighborhood.

Shelton led him through a giant, open living room and over to an office at the rear of the house. The layout and quality of construction reminded him a lot of the houses in the equestrian estate that he and Kelsey had been through just before winter.

Shelton unlocked a massive gun safe and opened the double doors revealing a small arsenal inside. To say his collection of firearms was impressive would be an understatement. Many of the rifles, most of which were pre-ban, appeared to be in good working order. Clay may have had a whole room devoted to his firearms back home, but this man had more quality guns just in the left side of his safe than Clay had in his entire collection.

The upper right portion of the safe had another smaller safe inside, a separate pistol safe that he had bolted in for additional security. Shelton opened that, too. Inside was an assortment of goods: jewelry and other precious metals, some photos, documents, and a few bottles of pills.

He pulled out one of the bottles and handed it over to Clay. "Should be full," he said.

Clay was dumbstruck. Why would this man give up his own private stash for a complete stranger?

"Go on," Shelton said, shaking the bottle slightly. The sound of the pills bouncing around the plastic container was a heavenly sound to Clay's ears.

Clay took the bottle and saw it was Penicillin, another name he was familiar with. "Thank you," Clay said with a weary voice. "Here," he said as he started to pull his gun sling over his shoulder. "Take this."

Shelton grabbed Clay's hand and gently pushed his arm down, lowering the sling back over his shoulder. "That won't be necessary. As you can see, I am quite situated with firearms," he said as he waved his hand towards the open safe. "The good Lord has been kind to us during these bleak years. I wouldn't feel right making you pay in your time of need."

Clay was speechless. He noted the stark contrast between this man and Watson, who just yesterday was attempting to rake him over the coals. The mere thought of Watson infuriated Clay, but Shelton's act of generosity quickly diluted the rage. Still unable to speak, Clay just looked at the man with glassy eyes and a smile.

"You're welcome," Shelton said, not needing to hear the words.

Clay gave Shelton the twenty-five pounds of venison he had planned on trading for the medicine. At first, Shelton declined, but once Clay explained that the meat would likely spoil before he returned home and he would rather it be put to some good use in Liberty, Shelton graciously accepted.

After a firm handshake, Clay walked out of the house and made his way to the front gates. He was tempted with Shelton's offer to let him rest for a few hours before heading back home, but Clay couldn't allow himself to rest. Not until he returned home with the medicine.

Hindsight is twenty-twenty, though. The journey was taking considerably longer than he had planned. Even though his mind was racing, his body was beyond fatigued and night had ambushed him. Having checked his gear before departing Liberty, he knew that he didn't have the means to face onslaught after onslaught like he did the night before. The best option—the *only* option—was to seek shelter. An apartment just above a small corner store about a half mile off the highway would have to do.

****

Clay was up at least every hour checking on the time, eager to get back on the move. Each time he woke up, his mind would terrorize him with images of Charlie lying in a pool of blood, crying for help.

Inevitably, his train of thought led him back to Watson. How could he have done such a thing?

He sat up and arched his back, trying to stretch his muscles out. Though the bed was soft and comfortable, Clay had grown accustomed to sleeping on a hard mattress that was several years past its prime. He continued to work out some tightness for a few minutes before he got out of bed.

It was around 5:30 and still dark outside, but there was a glint of light pouring over the horizon that no doubt would evolve into a beautiful sunrise, even if diffused by an everlasting layer of ash suspended in the atmosphere.

He leaned over and hoisted his pack up onto the bed and began to unzip some pockets. He blindly felt around until he was able to find some food. It was stale and nearly devoid of all flavor, but it would provide him with some much needed fuel for the rest of his journey.

The food made his mouth feel dry, so he unscrewed the lid to a bottle of water and downed the remaining contents. He was about four hours from home, so dehydration wasn't really a concern. He wiped his mouth with his sleeve and tossed the disposable plastic bottle onto the bed. He slung his pack over his shoulders, grabbed his rifle, and was on his way.

It was just bright enough outside to see the body in the middle of the road. It was about a hundred feet away, and to the best of Clay's recollection, it had not been there when he arrived the night before. The bedroom he stayed in was right next to the street. He hadn't slept heavily and would have heard a commotion outside. Did this person just collapse and die in the middle of the road? Or was this one of the many tricks the Screamers used to lure unsuspecting victims into their web of brutality? Clay observed the body from a distance—from the looks of it, a middle aged woman—and determined she was dead. The urgency to get home overpowered his curiosity, and he walked the opposite direction keeping a tight grip on his rifle.

Shortly before noon, he could see home. Even though it was visible to everyone within several miles, it had always been a safe haven for the family. There were always the random scavengers poking and prodding, but the mere sight of a man holding a battle rifle sent any nosey strangers scurrying like cockroaches when a light turned on. *Now.* Clay thought, *it's over.* The tower, a once cogent fortress, seemingly impenetrable by any opposing forces, had fallen.

Clay began to wrack his mind for reasons why Watson would attack. He still couldn't even know for sure Watson *did* know. Even though he was something of a mayor of the town, that didn't mean people living there wouldn't run off and do their own thing. Watson certainly had some unflattering qualities about him, but was he the type to send a group to attack a family just trying to survive? Despite his efforts, Clay couldn't stop thinking about it.

Those thoughts led to a difficult question: how did those men know where they lived? It was possible it was just a coincidence; it wasn't like they lived in an underground bunker in the middle of the desert. They were in an area that regularly had others coming through. Clay felt sick as he started to speculate.

Was Kelsey Involved?

He could come to terms with the idea of Watson sending a group of armed men to his house. What he couldn't grasp was Kelsey telling Watson where they lived. There had to be another explanation, something he was missing. The more he dwelled on the thought, the more anxious Clay became. His stomach was in knots, and the mere thought of Kelsey's betrayal wrenched his gut like a vice.

He quickened his pace as he turned onto his street. He made a beeline for the building—no use in the cloak and dagger games anymore—they wouldn't be there much longer anyhow. He went in through the garage and made a mental note to secure the door later. The lock was damaged beyond repair, and he would need to find another one to replace it.

By the time he reached the top floor, he was gasping for air like a fish out of water. The physical and emotional toll that had been hammering his body over the last two days was nothing short of catastrophic. The fact he made it all the way up without stopping was impressive. Before he could knock, he heard the door creak open, a rifle muzzle the first thing coming through.

"Who goes there?" a young voice barked from the other side.

"It's Clay," he said, gasping for air between each word.

The door slowly opened, and Blake was on the other side holding Charlie's rifle; the bloodied stock still had a slight sheen to it. He did his best to hide his emotion, but he was never really good at acting.

"Is Megan with Charlie?" Clay asked, straight to the point.

"She's in her room," Blake replied then closed the door, immediately locking it up.

Clay walked briskly down the hall towards the lobby. He reached into his pack and pulled out the antibiotics, glancing at the label but unable to understand much of the text. Megan would know how to make the most of it. Or at least he hoped.

He walked up to her door and had already started to talk. "I got it!" he said excitedly. "It's not exactly what you were wanting, but it was the only..."

He saw Megan sitting in the bed with a tissue in her hand. She looked up at him with eyes that had no more tears left to shed.

Clay immediately dropped to the floor. "No..."

Chapter 26

"You can't keep avoiding this conversation, Jake." Jeremy said sternly.

"I don't see why you are so upset," Watson replied. "The attack didn't really concern you."

"It doesn't concern me?" Jeremy shot back angrily. "I am your head of security. You don't think something like this is worth mentioning to me?"

Watson walked across the room and pulled a bottle of booze off a shelf behind his desk. He sat down in the chair and began to pour the whiskey into a glass that was already on his desk; he had several more off to the side. Watson tilted the bottle towards Jeremy in an effort to calm him down.

"No, thank you," Jeremy said with an edge in his voice.

"Have a seat, Jeremy," Watson said gesturing to a chair on the other side of the desk.

Jeremy reluctantly complied and took a few deep breaths while Watson pounded back his liquor.

"Look," Jeremy said with a much calmer tone, "you put me in charge of security here at the ranch. While my responsibility lies within the boundaries of your property, factors from the outside effect how I do my job."

Watson didn't debate his point. Instead he popped the top off the bottle and refilled his glass. "I've sent Silas and his men out on many raids in the past without saying anything to you. What's got your panties in such a twist this time?"

Jeremy shook his head. "This is not like the other times. For starters, you've mostly gone after groups we've observed from afar, not people with a direct connection to our town, let alone someone we've traded with here at the ranch!" he raised his voice, but quickly calmed himself down before continuing. "And secondly, you've never gone after someone with the kind of firepower Clay has. Someone like him could inflict a lot of damage on our community if he ever had a reason to. And Jake, you just gave him a *really* good reason."

"And you think he knows it was us?" Watson asked.

Jeremy was amazed at Watson's naivety at times. "Well, the fact that he left without saying a word *and* without the medication he was willing to give up his rifle for," he paused for a second to let things sink in. "Yeah, I'd say the chances are pretty good, Jake."

Watson stood up, his imprint on the chair faded away as the cushion gasped through the worn leather. He walked over to a large bay window that stretched from floor to ceiling and looked out towards the gate. The sun was setting, casting a swath of dull colors across the sky. He sipped on his drink and stood in silence as he had made a habit to do each night.

"I didn't tell you where Clay lived just so you could storm the palace and pillage anything of value," Jeremy added.

"So why *did* you tell me?" Watson asked.

"It's my job to report any pertinent information to you. Clay had," he stopped to correct himself, "*has* the potential to be a security risk to the community. In the event he became aggressive, you would have the necessary information to retaliate. I just didn't think *we* would strike first."

Watson downed the rest of his glass and returned to his desk to pour one last drink before putting the bottle next to the others on the shelf. It was the same bottle Clay had given to him as a peace offering. The irony was not lost on Watson.

"So, why did you follow them anyway?" Watson asked as he walked back to the window.

Jeremy knew Watson was just trying to make him uncomfortable and redirect the conversation. He remained silent.

"Was it because he stole your girl?" Watson said as he stared out the window. He could see Jeremy shift awkwardly in his chair in the reflection of the window. "Of all people, I didn't expect *you* to be so upset about this. Heck, if Silas hadn't been so incompetent, your competition would be out of the picture."

Watson had succeeded in making Jeremy uncomfortable...and angry. Despite the age difference, Jeremy did have feelings for Kelsey. Strong feelings. And it was true that he really didn't like Clay all that much, if for no other reason than Kelsey seemed infatuated with him, but that didn't justify what had happened.

"Listen, Jeremy. I do apologize that I didn't fill you in on this one. I really thought Silas and his men would handle things more...professionally."

"Silas is an idiot!" Jeremy snapped.

Watson shrugged, "If you're looking for an argument on that one, you're gonna have to find another tree to bark up."

"For crying out loud, he shot a kid!" Jeremy added.

"The kid shot one of his men, first," Watson fired back.

"Any person with a shred of humanity would have retreated at that point. They were on that boy's property, all of them armed. Wouldn't you have shot too if you were in that kid's shoes?"

Watson turned away from Jeremy and looked back out the window. Darkness had overtaken the colors in the sky as the sun became obscured by the horizon.

Jeremy wasn't finished with the verbal lashing. "And Jay wasn't the only one to die, was he? Because Silas doesn't know when to back down, Taylor and Sullivan didn't come back either, did they?"

As if Jeremy hadn't spoken, Watson continued to gaze out the window in silence. He wasn't happy that the situation had unraveled so chaotically. *Silas isn't an idiot so much as he is a monster,* he thought. Still, if what Jeremy was saying was true, Watson and the rest of the town could be at risk.

With a deep sigh, Watson gulped down the rest of his drink and turned back to look at Jeremy. "So, what do you suggest we do now?"

Jeremy's solution would be to personally hand Watson over to Clay and let nature take its course. Obviously, that was not the type of advice Watson was seeking, so he just shrugged his shoulders. The only type of resolution Watson wanted to hear ended up with Clay on the losing end of a gunfight.

Jeremy did not like Clay, but his reasons were truly unfounded. The fact was, Clay was a decent man. Even when he threatened Watson, Jeremy didn't really blame him. Watson is holding Kelsey and her daughter as prisoners in a sense. If he had been in Clay's shoes, he probably would have done the same thing. In his position on the ranch, Jeremy could have helped Kelsey and Dakota escape numerous times but opted not to for his own selfish reasons. A sense of self-loathing flooded his mind at that moment.

"Well?" Watson asked.

"Pray he doesn't retaliate."

****

Numb. It was the only word that described Clay's state of mind. Even he wasn't sure if he was filled with anger or sorrow, rage or despair. His mind would abruptly trigger random memories for split seconds at a time, like a scene from a horror film designed to startle the viewer's every sensation. It was terrifying, yet strangely calming, which only added to the anxiety.

The ranch was already visible in the distance; sporadic candlelit windows in the twilight of the evening made the makeshift town easy to spot from afar, like metropolitan cities seen from earth's orbit. The fading light in the sky gave Clay a sense of invisibility. He was further concealed by the nearly waist-high grass he was walking through. His eyes were fixed on the small town a few miles ahead, but his mind focused on just one person.

He reached a small cluster of trees just off the dirt road leading to the ranch's entrance. He was about 200 yards from the gate. He rested against the trunk of one of the trees and kept his eyes focused on Watson's house. The windows were dark. Clay would wait. Wait all night, if he must.

As his breathing returned to normal from his hike, he searched for a prime position amongst the group of trees. It didn't take long before he discovered a large split in a sapling at just the right height. He glanced through the scope and had a clear line of sight to Watson's house, which at that point, was almost entirely veiled in darkness.

He reached into his pocket and pulled out a box of cartridges. The bullets were some of the more expensive back in the day. Known for powder accuracy to one-tenth of a grain and hand-inspected bullets, the ammo was what both competitive shooters and law enforcement used. Long ago, Clay chose not to use them until he ran out of reloads and lower quality factory ammo; it seemed like a shame to waste such precision on a hunt when his own loads did the trick just fine. However, Clay decided that should such a need arise, he would use them instead of the reloads. That time was now.

Clay opened the bolt and slid the cartridge into the chamber. As quietly as he could, he closed the bolt and was ready to fire. He *really* missed having a magazine, especially given his present situation. Even though he suspected he would only be able to get one shot off anyway, at least having the option to quickly cycle and make a follow-up would give him some peace of mind. With only one bullet and no time to chamber another, there would be no room for error. His aim must be true.

He rested the rifle in the splitting tree trunk and waited, staring at the silhouette of the old farmhouse contrasted against the dim sky.

A few minutes later, a large window on the second floor illuminated brightly, exposing Watson and Jeremy as they engaged in a heated discussion. Clay observed patiently as they bickered back and forth. Watson sat down and poured a drink. No surprise.

Seeing the old man again stirred a fury of emotions inside. Though he couldn't be entirely certain that Watson authorized such aggression towards his family, Clay knew in his gut that he was involved. And that was all the evidence he needed.

Then, as if fate had tapped Clay on the shoulder and said "You're welcome," Watson stood up and walked over to the window, his body almost directly facing Clay. He stood there with a drink in his hand while Jeremy continued to vent. Even though the Scout's scope had a low magnification, Clay was sure that he could not have been given an easier shot than what was presented right in front of him.

He estimated Watson's house was another hundred yards past the gate, so he guessed it would be around a 300 yard shot. For a human sized, generously backlit target, Clay was confident he wouldn't miss. He put the crosshairs towards the top of Watson's chest, just below his neck, to account for slight bullet drop. He tightened his grip on the rifle and moved his finger to the trigger.

He froze.

Clay began to tremble as his body wrestled with his conscience to squeeze the trigger. *Just do it, you coward! He deserves to die!* he thought to himself. Yet, he was no closer to pulling the trigger than he was before, nor was he any further away. He was in a deadlocked game of moral tug of war.

He grunted as he watched Watson walk away from the window and back over to his desk. Even with such a powerful round, a bullet going through glass could alter its trajectory significantly. Shooting a target a foot or two behind glass was not a big deal, but Watson's desk was nearly fifteen feet away from the window, making the chances of a strike nearly zero. Because of his hesitation, he might have missed his only chance for the night.

But much to his surprise, Watson returned to the window. Clay readied himself again, striving to overcome the whispers he heard in his head—warnings of the dangerous path he was on. As he tightened his finger around the trigger, Megan's pleas began to invade his thoughts.

Don't do this, Clayton. No matter how much you justify it to yourself, it will be murder! He heard her saying. *You are better than this.*

He had shrugged off any and all attempts she had made to stop him from seeking vengeance. She was right, though, and Clay knew that even before he left. There was no sense in trying to convince himself otherwise. But he didn't care. Charlie was dead, and the only thing keeping the guilty party from going unpunished was a two-point-three pound trigger pull.

Beads of sweat crept down Clay's face as his eye remained glued to the scope. *Why can't I do this?* He thought. His anger towards Watson was greater than anything he had ever felt before. When he left home, he knew if the opportunity to take a shot presented itself, then it would be done and over with. Clay would be on his way back home before anyone knew what had happened. Yet, as Clay learned, murder—even when seeking justice—was not so cut and dried.

Clay's convictions started to out-muscle his rage. His finger, although still resting on the trigger, eased slightly. With his left hand, he cleared away some of the perspiration building up around his eyebrows and kept a lock on Watson's chest.

Then he heard his voice. "Which will you feed?" Charlie asked as if he were standing right next to Clay.

Clay shut his eyes and removed his finger from the trigger. He rested his forehead on the top of the rifle still perched in the tree and sighed with relief. He felt regret for what he was about to do—what he still *wanted* to do. But he was thankful he couldn't go through with it.

Several minutes passed, and by the time he looked back up, the window was no longer glowing, and all activity had ceased. Clay was relieved the temptation was gone.

Once he was able to collect himself, he turned and left, stopping at a post office for the night before making the rest of the journey home early the next morning.

****

The climb up the stairs was more unbearable than ever. That was one appealing prospect about finding a new place to live—no stairs!

Megan was sitting on the stairs with a lantern just outside the door on the top floor. She had been up all night, waiting for his return. She looked even worse than he felt. Guilt sank in when he finally realized much of her stress lately had been brought on by him, and that made him feel even worse than he already did. It was bad enough that Charlie died less than an hour after Clay had left to get the antibiotics, but for the better part of two days, Megan had to take care of a house full of mourning children. She had no time to mourn herself because the children needed her to be strong for them. She didn't have it in her to do it alone, but Clay had given her no choice.

Then, once Clay had returned and discovered Charlie had succumbed to his injuries, she once again was left to handle everything on her own as her brother went off to seek retribution. Clay had been so self-absorbed that he had never taken into consideration the hell that Megan was going through. Judging by the empty expression on her face, he started to realize she was suffering more than he was.

She looked up at him and stared into his eyes, as if trying to read his mind. "Did you?" she asked, her voice barely above a whisper.

He shook his head.

She rose to her feet and hugged her little brother. It was the first sense of relief she had felt in the last three days. Megan bawled, pressing her face into Clay's chest. He wrapped his arms around her and held her tight. He hadn't heard her cry with such intensity since Michelle died.

The door opened causing both of them to jump from the loud and sudden noise. Lona leaned out to make sure Megan was okay. Clay nodded at her. Lona got the message and went back inside, doing her best to close the door without a sound.

Megan's sobs tapered, and the stairwell eventually fell quiet. She pulled away from Clay and saw a sopping mess of tears all over his shirt. She even managed to chuckle slightly when she pointed at it. "Sorry," she said as she wiped away a rogue tear.

Clay pulled the shirt away from his body and looked down at it briefly before letting go. "You do the laundry anyhow," he said with a smile.

Megan gave a small chuckle before taking a deep breath. Exhaustion had long set in, and she was running purely on adrenaline. Even so, she handled herself well and kept the big picture in view.

"Uhm," she said rubbing her eyes with the palms of her hands, "it's been nearly three days. There's already a bit of a smell coming from the infirmary, and it's only going to get worse. I think we need to get him buried soon."

That was the last thing Clay felt like doing at that moment, but he knew she was right. He nodded in agreement, and the two walked towards the infirmary. The odor of death had pervaded the hall, but it wasn't nearly as bad as Clay was expecting. He was grateful.

Clay gave Megan a moment to say goodbye and then wrapped an extra couple of towels around the body and proceeded to the stairwell. He was relieved that none of the kids with the exception of Lona were awake yet. He didn't want them to remember Charlie that way, wrapped in bloodied blankets and towels, being carried out by Clay.

He eventually made it outside just as the sun was rising. He struggled to carry both the body and a shovel, which made the journey to the burial ground all the more treacherous. While digging, Clay began to feel like he was trying to dig into solid rock. Each pile of dirt heavier than the previous. It took more than an hour to get the hole dug out, and it wasn't even close to six feet deep, but it would be sufficient for its purposes.

After sipping on some water and catching his breath, Clay picked up Charlie's body and carefully lowered him into the shallow grave. Sitting on his knees, Clay began to recall some of his fond memories of Charlie. To have *fun* in such perilous times seemed impossible. Yet, so often, Charlie and Clay would find themselves in such moments. Clay loved that kid like his own brother—he would be dearly missed.

Clay came to a stand and rested both of his hands on the top of the shovel handle. Staring down at the small excavation site, he prayed for God's mercy on Charlie, and strength for Megan and himself—something he had been severely lacking over the past few days.

Clay wiped his forehead with his arm and shoveled the pile of dirt back into the grave. "I'll see ya on the other side, dude."

Chapter 27

Clay awoke to muffled arguments just outside his door. About what, he was not sure, but before he could even sit up Megan had intervened, silencing the grieving kids.

He rubbed his face with his hands, slowly transitioning them to fists to rub his eyes. As he stared up at the stained drop ceiling of the conference room, he was surprised at how good he felt physically. He hadn't done much of anything since he had laid Charlie to rest four days ago. He mostly slept, and on occasion, if he was awake, joined the family for a meal. The days of sleep were as much for emotional exhaustion as for physical. Unfortunately, the state of his body and mind were not congruent.

He looked at his watch and saw how late in the morning it was. He immediately got out of bed and began to get dressed into the clothes Megan had placed on the conference room table the night before—black slacks and a black button-up shirt. He loathed wearing such attire, not because he didn't like dress clothes, but because wearing them only meant one thing.

Clay buttoned his shirt and brushed the sleeves in an attempt to flatten out some of the wrinkles. Megan went to great lengths to have the clothes prim and proper, but in a world without dryers and irons, there was only so much she could do. As he buttoned the cuffs, he heard the door open.

"You look nice," Megan said with a strong, healthy voice, a departure from the morning Clay returned from Watson's.

"Thanks," Clay responded looking at her, "You as well."

Megan looked down and examined the dress she was donning, one of the few she still had from her mother's wardrobe. It wasn't exactly a typical funeral dress, namely because of the bright floral pattern used. She had a dark dress she used to wear for memorials before Michelle's wake. It was then that she decided to wear something more vibrant, something that wasn't as dark and depressing as Michelle herself had become leading to her death. She said she wore the dress to celebrate life, not death: the life that Michelle had lived, the new life she was living. And for that reason, she would never again wear black to a funeral.

"Thank you," she said, then crossed her arms over her stomach and looked at Clay with sympathy. "How are you holding up?"

Clay was silent for a moment, trying to come up with a coherent response that would capture his mood. Nothing. All he could do was shrug.

She walked over and hugged him with one arm, tilting her head onto his shoulder. "Do you need to stay home? I can do the—"

"No," he interrupted and gently broke the hug to look at her, "I'll be okay. I can do it."

Megan wasn't sure if he was telling the truth or not, but she wasn't going to push the matter. Clay had developed a bond with Charlie unlike any of the other kids. In a house full of sisters, Clay had always wanted a brother, and Charlie had inherited that role. Even Geoff, who Clay considered his best friend, wasn't as close to Clay as Charlie had been.

As Megan looked into his bleary eyes, she wondered if he was grieving more for Charlie than he had for his own sisters—even his own mother. *Perhaps,* she thought, but then looked back and reflected on how she, herself, had responded to Charlie's death. It was only then that she realized that Charlie had joined the family only a few short months after the ash blanketed the sky. That meant they had known him longer than their own sister, Colleen, who died at the age of six.

More shouts from the lobby caused Megan to roll her eyes and sigh. She put her hand on Clay's arm. "We should go soon," she said.

"Yeah."

She left the room and stomped across the floor, chasing a few of the kids. "Blake, Tyler, go get your shoes on! We're leaving in five minutes!"

They both said "Yes, Ma'am," in near perfect unison and ran down the hall to fetch their shoes.

Clay walked over to a chest at the foot of his bed and knelt down. Spinning the dial on the padlock in a left-right-left motion, he unlatched it and lifted the top. Inside were mostly keepsakes from the family: his great-grandfather's purple heart; a photo of his father in his formal police uniform; beneath that was a picture of his father graduating from EMT school just two years later. All of the treasures within the chest usually spawned a flood of affectionate memories, but each one was carefully set aside as he dug towards the bottom of the trunk. Eventually, he found a letter sized envelope. He picked it up and stuffed it into his pocket.

He looked at all of the various items in the chest in total disarray. He wanted to neatly put them back in their proper place, but Megan would be coming to get him any minute, so he closed the lid and put the lock back on.

He heard the footsteps in the lobby heading his way, so he preemptively said, "I'm on my way."

The footsteps stopped, then started heading off in the other direction. Clay grabbed his rifle and slid a spare magazine into the oversized pockets of the slacks and met up with the rest of the family waiting in the hall next to the stairwell.

Some of the kids were taking it harder than others. Blake and Courtney hadn't known Charlie all that long. Clay thought perhaps their grief was more a product of the atmosphere. He looked over at Tyler and was pained to see his red eyes flooded with tears. Tyler, the boy who never stopped smiling, was shattered.

Lona didn't look any worse for wear. Clay had guessed her crying days were behind her. But as her eyes met his, he could see the pain; he could see the sorrow. *I hate you, Watson.*

Seeing everyone there, lining up to go mourn the loss of a dear friend and brother, Clay started to doubt himself for taking his finger off the trigger when Watson was in his crosshairs. He shuddered as the tidal wave of emotions once again smashed into him, bringing back unforgiving thoughts he wished would just go away. He knew he had done the right thing by walking away. He knew what Megan had said was true—it would have been murder—but he couldn't help but wonder how it would have felt if he had fed the other wolf.

Clay picked up Bethany, who was really too young to understand what was going on, but was feeding off of everyone else's emotions. She tightly grasped her stuffed giraffe, the one Charlie had given to her, and held it close to her chest as the group made their descent to the garage.

In the garage, the family stayed back as Clay unlocked and opened the door. He was startled as the door swung open, and he saw a figure sitting on the ground a few feet in front of him. He instinctively raised his rifle and took aim.

"Kelsey?"

She barely flinched at the intimidating sight of Clay with the rifle. "Clay!" she exclaimed with a smile. She turned her body and pushed off the ground with the palm of her hand and stood up. She had been sitting there for a couple of hours and hadn't realized how stiff she had become.

"Wow," she said as she looked at him, "You're looking sharp! Are you seeing someone else?" she said jokingly as she walked up and gave him a kiss.

The touch of Kelsey's soft lips nearly captivated Clay, but he pulled back and extended his arms slightly, creating some distance between the two.

"Hey!" she said, dissatisfied with the cold response. "What's wrong?"

That's when Megan leaned outside, pistol in hand. Kelsey immediately noticed her outfit too and was puzzled by the unusual attire.

Clay looked at her; his eyes were like piercing daggers. The last time they were together, all she could think about was how loving, kind, and gentle he was to her. Now, as he glared at her with contempt, it was all she could do not to flee.

The kids began to peek out, all dressed up in the same fashion.

"What's going on, Clay?" she said anxiously.

"We're going to a wake," he said before he turned to walk up the ramp.

"A wake?" she asked. "For who?"

Clay stopped and looked back. Megan walked by him, and the children followed. Kelsey took a second and looked at the kids as they passed by. She had a hard time remembering names and faces, but she immediately noticed who *wasn't* there.

"Charlie!" she gasped.

Clay started walking again, bringing up the rear of the group.

"Clay!" she cried, "I'm so sorry! What happened?" she asked as she followed him, hoping for an answer that didn't come.

Sensing Clay's fragile state of mind, Kelsey dropped back a few feet, and kept quiet. She followed the group to a small recreational center about two miles away.

As they reached one of the side entrances to the building, everyone but Clay stopped. He cautiously opened the door and entered alone, leaving the rest waiting outside. Megan handed Bethany over to Lona and retrieved her pistol—just in case.

Kelsey slowly made her way to the doors, stopping right next to Megan. "I am so sorry about Charlie," Kelsey said fighting back tears.

Megan awkwardly shifted her weight, unsure of how to respond. Though Clay had not said anything connecting Kelsey to the attack, Megan thought it was quite a coincidence that a short time after Kelsey visited their home, people from her camp came barreling through their doors.

"Thank you," Megan said, then paused for a while, looking down at the ground. She was fighting back tears; she had promised herself that she was done crying in front of the kids. "Charlie was…" a lone tear streamed down her cheek, "a great kid."

Kelsey noticed something was awkward with Megan. She didn't really know her all that well, but there was something she wasn't saying. "So…may I ask?" she inquired reluctantly.

Megan pushed away the tears with her fingers and formulated a response. "We were attacked by a group of men. Charlie died defending us."

Kelsey's hand covered her mouth; her eyes filled with tears. *What kind of monster would shoot a kid?*

"What did they want? Did you know them?" she asked.

Megan gave her a glare, one that sent chills down Kelsey's spine. "You'll need to ask Clay about that," she said with bitterness in her voice.

Kelsey felt a pit in her stomach from the icy response. She didn't know how or why, but knew that Charlie's death would not have occurred had she never entered Clay's life. Guilt started to spread throughout her body that caused her to tremble with remorse.

The door unlatched, and Clay gave the all-clear. The group slowly funneled in and walked down a long, filthy hallway to a door at the end of the corridor. Clay intentionally avoided eye contact with Kelsey as she came in behind everyone else. He shut the door and made his way down to the room at the end of the hall.

The doorway led to a large banquet room filled with round tables and folding chairs. Pictures, letters, and small trinkets filled up almost every inch of the tables, and the walls held the overflow. There was a stage set up at the very end which was clean, relatively speaking, compared to the rest of the room; there were no pictures or keepsakes. It was almost entirely empty except for a few more folding chairs and a couple of empty microphone stands.

Megan and the kids zigzagged through the tables and made their way to the front where they all sat down on chairs that had been neatly arranged to face the stage. Kelsey trailed slowly behind as she looked at some of the tables. The banquet room, from the looks of it, was a memorial of sorts to countless loved ones lost over the past seven years. It was hauntingly beautiful. Everything looked gracefully and intentionally positioned, as if nothing was out of place. Such a sight inside an unprotected building was unthinkable. It was almost as if the Screamers, scavengers, and other passersby observed the large room as hallowed ground and, for whatever reason, decided not to disturb the memories.

The whole thing was emotionally taxing on Kelsey, and she nearly lost it when she saw a picture of a little girl, not much older than Dakota, pasted onto a piece of paper. A note below the picture dated two years after the eruptions simply read:

> *My dearest Julia,*
> *I will never forget you. I will never stop loving you. For you made me a better person. Rest in peace, my beloved child.*
>
> > *Love always,*
> > *Mom*

The floodgates opened and the tears poured from Kelsey's eyes; she struggled to find her breath.

Clay walked by her as if she wasn't even there, further adding to her distress. By the time Clay had reached the front, Megan and the kids had already found their seats, filling most of the front row of chairs, leaving the two back rows vacant.

He walked up some steps on the side of the stage and moved to be centered with the chairs on the floor. He looked terrible. He looked frail, like he hadn't eaten in weeks, and his eyes screamed of defeat. He glanced over at Kelsey and cleared his throat, an invitation of sorts for her to take a seat.

Kelsey sat in the back row, putting distance between her and the grieving family. She looked up at Clay and mouthed, "Thank you." She wasn't sure why she was thanking him. Perhaps, it was because Clay gave her time to settle into her chair, or maybe it was because Clay loved her...or at least, he *had* loved her. She wasn't sure anymore. The thought exacerbated her grief.

"I have been thinking the past few days on what I would say to you all about Charlie," Clay said as he struggled to maintain eye contact with his audience. "The fact is, I don't have any words of my own..."

He stopped for a moment and looked down. His lip quivered as he wrestled with his emotions. He reached into his pocket and pulled out an envelope. Holding it up, Clay said, "I don't have any words of my own because I have a letter from my father that contains every word I need to describe Charlie."

Clay clumsily opened the envelope and reached for the paper inside. His hands were shaking profusely, turning a simple task into a challenge. Success followed, and he unfolded the single page, handwritten letter and skimmed over it.

The letter was written to Clay on his thirteenth birthday, only three months before the Cascadia fault line ripped. His dad had to work a double, but when Clay woke up, he saw a rifle leaning up next to his door with a red bow tied to the barrel. Taped to the side of the receiver was the letter he was preparing to read now.

Clay skipped over the personal salutation and got straight to the heart of it two paragraphs down:

"It is my deepest desire that you would become a great man. Not a man defined by our culture or by other men, but by our Creator. A man who is not remembered for his might, but," Clay paused for a moment as his eyes welled up, "by his sacrificial love."

Clay cleared his throat and continued, his voice stronger and deeper than before. "A righteous man is not remembered for the clothes he wore, but by how he wore himself. A righteous man is not remembered for his temper, but by his patience. A righteous man is not remembered for the woman he married, but by the husband he was. A righteous man is not remembered for his possessions, but by his charity.

"My son, each day the world grows darker. Things once called evil are now considered good, and things once good, now evil. We are told every day that we should live for ourselves; do what makes us happy. We are to be worshipers of self. Do not fall for these lies. A good man will put others first. A good man will give more than he takes."

Clay slowly lowered his arm down by his side, the piece of paper dangled between his finger and thumb. He continued from memory, "We live in perilous times, but I fear the true storm is yet to come. I pray in earnest that you would hold firm, even in your darkest hour. That you would not be discouraged or dismayed. I am proud of the man you are becoming, and I have no doubts about the man you will become."

Clay raised his arm, placing the letter above his head, "This letter was written *to* me, but it was written *about* Charlie." He folded the letter back up but kept it out of the envelope. "Even at such a young age, Charlie was a man. A *good* man. He lived to serve others. He desired to protect his family, and that's what he did. It's what he gave his life doing."

Cries echoed around the large room as Clay hopped down from the stage and walked over to a specific section of the wall. He stopped when he spotted a picture of his mother holding Emily right after she was born. There were pictures and other mementoes all around from the Whitaker family, both blood and adopted. A painful reminder of the storm his father had warned him about—a storm they were still enduring.

Clay tacked the letter to the wall just beneath a picture of Colleen. He reached into his pocket and pulled out a top. It was the only thing that got Charlie to laugh after Clay found him. Charlie would spin it on the kitchen table and let it drop to the floor. It was his favorite toy for many years, and even as recently as last month, Clay watched him spin it in his room.

Clay knelt down and placed the top amongst the other tokens the family had brought over the years to immortalize the departed. He stood up and stepped aside as the others followed suit. Some brought toys; others brought drawings they had made. They each whispered some sort of goodbye and moved out of the way for the next.

All eyes looked to Kelsey who was at the end of the line. She walked up and observed the little slice of the wall that made up the family memorial. "Goodbye,

Charlie," she said with her head lowered. She walked past the family and stood next to Clay.

They left the rec center and returned home. Nobody spoke a word the entire walk. It was almost painfully awkward. Kelsey wanted nothing more than to embrace Clay, to comfort him and hold him all day. Yet, she still couldn't even get him to talk to her. Her heart was breaking in more ways than one.

Clay opened the door to the garage, and Megan stopped at the door as the kids walked inside. "I'll see you up there in a little bit," she said as she glanced over at Kelsey who was standing a few feet away.

He shut his eyes and sighed. He dropped his shoulders and nodded. "Okay."

The door clicked shut; Clay turned around to look at Kelsey. He folded his arms and leaned against the door. His mouth opened a couple of times in an attempt to start the conversation, but he couldn't find his voice.

Kelsey walked over to him, her eyes locked to his. She could see it now. Betrayal. When she reached him, she put a hand on his waist and the other on his shoulder. She looked longingly into his eyes and gave him a gentle kiss. Clay wanted to fight it, he tried to fight it, but her compassionate touch disarmed him. He was worried perhaps it had disarmed him *too* much.

Wanting to respect his distance after the short embrace, she took a few steps back. "What happened?" she asked hoping this time he would tell her the whole story.

Clay took a deep breath and sluggishly exhaled. The kiss calmed him down enough that he was no longer angry. Now, he just wanted to know if it was her. He needed to know the truth. Her kiss reminded him that he still loved her, and even if she had told

Watson, he could forgive her with time. At least, he wanted to believe he could.

"Does the name Silas ring a bell?" he asked.

She grimaced and looked down at the ground. Just mentioning his name was enough for her to know what happened. It also explained all the fuss around Doc's office the week before. She just figured a trading party got attacked during their travels.

"Well?" Clay said with a little edge in his voice.

She nodded her head. "Yeah. It does. He's one of Watson's men. A mercenary or something, I suppose."

"A mercenary?"

"Jeremy's made some vague comments about him in the past. From what I gather, he and his men live on the far side of the ranch, and most days just go out scavenging, giving Watson some of the cut as payment for living on his property."

"That doesn't sound like a merc. That sounds like pretty much every person living within a community nowadays," Clay retorted.

"Well," she went on, "I know of at least one incident in the past where a group Watson was involved with had started scamming him. I don't know all the details, but apparently it had been going on for the better part of a year. So, once Watson found out..." she trailed off.

"Watson sent Silas and his men?" Clay finished her sentence.

"That's what Jeremy told me anyway, but he was drunk so I didn't pay much attention to it," she added.

Clay wasn't sure why, but the fact she brought up Jeremy made him uncomfortable. Perhaps the discomfort was more from the next question that he had to ask. "Did you tell anyone? Jeremy?"

"Did I tell anyone what?" she replied.

"Where we live! Did you tell anyone where we live?" Clay's shouting caused Kelsey to cower. His anger had returned tenfold, but it was against his wishes. One minute, he loved her; the next, he was so mad he couldn't see straight. He was a wreck.

"No!" she fired back, "Of course not, Clay. I would *never* do that to you! I know how important it is that the less people know about you, the better. I would never betray you like that." She tried to shake off the verbal lashing Clay had just dished out and keep her composure. She reached for his hand, but he quickly withdrew.

As soon as his hand had withdrawn, Clay reached back out and grabbed her arm, pulling her over to him. His tight embrace was both comforting and devastating at the same time. He sobbed inconsolably while they stood just outside the garage door. Charlie's death, the emotional toll it was having on the family, the prospect of moving out of the tower, not to mention the everyday worries he faced—the burdens had become too much for him to bear. He broke down.

Kelsey had never heard a man weep so loudly before. It grieved her deeply, and she would have done anything to take his pain away. All she could do, however, was to be there for him. Despite everything going on, she couldn't help but feel delighted to actually have somebody to be there *for.* Which is why it was all the more crushing when she heard Clay say, "I can't do this. I-I just can't be around you right now."

She looked up at him, pain shot across her expression. "What? What do you mean?"

"It's just too hard right now," he said clearly and stepped back, making himself cold and uninviting to her. "I want to believe you had nothing to do with this. The fact is, I think I *do* believe you, but you are, and forever will be, connected to Watson. I just can't deal with that right now." He stopped for a second as he wrestled with himself. He didn't want to say it, but he did. "So please, just go."

"Clay, please! Let me be there for you." She grabbed his hand, but he aggressively broke her grip, sending her arm swinging back towards her. "Please!" she said reaching for his hand again, this time successfully.

He gently squeezed her hand, then pulled away. "Just go." With his back still to the door, he reached behind and turned the handle. The door popped open an inch, and he moved out of the way as he opened it up. "I want you to know, Kelsey, that I did truly love you. I would have died for you..."

Did. It was amazing the devastation that could be caused by changing the tense of a single word.

"Take care, Kelsey."

The door closed.

Chapter 28

Kelsey arrived home late that evening. The trip back home took much longer than the journey there earlier that morning. Her morning had been filled with excitement, hope, and a fervent heart. But it was grief, anger, and despair that accompanied her back.

The gate to the ranch opened up. It was guarded by a young man wearing a cowboy hat and chewing on a piece of hay. "Howdy, ma'am," he said tipping his hat with a finger. His name was Toby, he was fifteen and was born in Cincinnati, a far cry from a Texas farmer before ending up on Watson's ranch. Yet, there he was, fitting every aspect of the stereotype.

"Thank you," Kelsey said, as she passed through the gate.

The young man promptly shut and locked the entrance and returned to his post a few feet away.

Kelsey was walking home when a persistent nag convinced her to take a detour by Jeremy's house. It was Tuesday night, which meant it was poker night and that he would be home. She prayed that Watson, who on occasion would partake in the gambling, wouldn't be there.

She tried to convince herself to just go home. She thought about a hot cup of tea and a warm bed to crawl into. She envisioned Dakota's sincere smile followed by a series of hugs and kisses as she walked through the door. Though her head was telling her to turn around, her feet kept moving forward.

The muffled sounds of a half dozen men playing cards, and likely drinking anything fermented, grew louder as she approached the house. She stepped onto the rickety porch and knocked on the door.

For a moment the laughter and noise continued, but then then she heard footsteps approach. Jeremy opened the door, snickering at a joke one of the men had made moments before.

"Kelsey?" Jeremy said with a surprised expression. "What are you doing here?"

Kelsey had the appearance of an orphan begging for food. She had her hands in her jacket pockets and was barely able to make eye contact with him. Her eyes were slightly swollen: the streaks of tears were evident by the lighter shades of skin on her cheeks where the dirt had washed away.

"Can we talk?" she asked.

Jeremy turned around and looked back inside and then back out at Kelsey. "Uhhh, yeah sure," he said turning around again. "Hey guys, deal me out for a couple of hands. I'll be back in a bit."

Grumbles and groans erupted from crass men who all looked like they had been working since before dawn. Jeremy waved his hand at the rowdy group and walked out the door.

They headed towards a pond a few hundred yards away, no houses around, and except for the occasional fishermen pulling in a couple of perch for the store to sell, there was usually nobody around.

Neither one had spoken a word since they left Jeremy's porch. The silence was uncomfortable for both. As they approached the banks of the pond, Jeremy finally broke the silence. "What's wrong, Kelsey?"

Kelsey didn't respond at first, she just looked out over the water and watched as the wind blew ripples across the surface, disrupting the indistinct glow of the moon. It was mesmerizing.

"I saw Clay today."

"Oh," he said. His expression was guilt-ridden. "How's the kid doing?"

Kelsey glared at him. "How did you know?"

"Well, Clay came here looking for medicine, and he mentioned one of the kids had been hurt pretty badly," he said, his voice unsteady.

Her glare evolved into a look of spite. She clenched her jaw and sighed deeply through her nose. "Do you know what happened?" she asked pointedly.

Jeremy nodded. "Yeah. I do."

Her eyes remained locked on him, though he avoided her scowl. She shook her head and in one swift motion raised her hand and slapped Jeremy's cheek with such a force she was certain she heard it echo off the distant trees.

Jeremy rocked his jaw side to side in an effort to shake off the surprisingly powerful blow. He brought his hand to his face and tried to rub the throb away. "I know you think I had some part in this, but I did not," he said.

She raised her hand again. "Liar!" she shrieked and swung again, this time Jeremy dodged her attack.

"Kelsey!" he said firmly, but quietly, "Watson didn't tell me a thing until *after* it happened."

AJ POWERS

Kelsey wasn't buying it.

"Look, I know you don't believe me," he said as if he was reading her mind, "but I swear to you, I had no idea that Watson was going to send Silas out there. If I had, I never would have told him where Clay lived." He instantly wished he could have put the words back into his mouth.

"How did you know where he lived?" she asked, anger surging through her voice.

"Well, uh," he stumbled over his words. He took a step back to avoid another attack. "A few weeks ago, Clay came here looking to trade for some food. The whole deal went south, so Clay left. That's when he ran into you and invited you over to his place. I heard the whole conversation, so I followed you two back." Jeremy sighed with regret. "I'm sorry, Kelsey, I let my feelings for you cloud my judgment."

"So you told Watson?"

"It's my job," he said with genuine remorse.

Kelsey was writhing with ire, but she did not raise her hand. She was worried if she tried to strike him again, she would not be able to control her rage and would likely end up on the losing side of the battle. Her head was muddled with so many emotions she could only think of one response. Flee.

She turned and started to walk away when Jeremy grabbed her arm and pulled her back. "Wait!" he said.

She tugged her arm to try and break his grip but was unable to. "Get your hands off of me," she said through gritted teeth.

"Not until you know something," he said as he eased his grip, but not enough to free herself. "I know you think that I am some crazy, obsessive creep that saw Clay as a threat."

She shot him a scornful look that confirmed his statement.

"The truth of the matter is, I *did* see him as a threat. Every time I saw you two together, I just wanted to go up and slug the guy. He had stolen you away from me, and there are few better reasons to hate a man than that."

Kelsey shook her head. "I thought you were trying to convince me that you somehow *weren't* involved in this."

"Let me finish!" he snapped back. She sarcastically gestured with her hand to continue. "As I was saying, I had every reason to hate him. And the way he started talking to Watson wasn't helping matters any. I had to at least be wary of his intentions," Jeremy's voice softened a bit: there was a touch of vulnerability within him. "Look, I know that you and I never had a chance. I have come to accept that, and when I saw you with him it was like flaunting my greatest desire in my face, knowing I could never have you. But then, he came to Watson, and tried to buy your freedom...I respected that and could tell he cares for you the same way I do."

Kelsey was moved with Clay's gesture—one he never told her about. To know he cared so deeply for her that he was doing everything in his power to free her and Dakota from Watson's grasp made her feel warm inside. It also made the sting of Clay's last words to her all the more painful.

"If I could go back in time, Kelsey, I would. It saddens me to know the kind of pain and damage I've inflicted, inadvertently or not. I would sooner lie in a shallow grave than repeat that mistake."

As mad as Kelsey was at Jeremy, she couldn't help but feel a little flattered with his devotion to her. Though she didn't want to believe him, she not only heard the sincerity in his voice but saw it in his eyes. He was telling the truth, and she found herself strangely comforted knowing that he had not been involved with the raid.

Kelsey accepted his apology with a nod, but wasn't ready to forgive him for what he had done. She searched her heart to try and find something that might offer him some form of comfort, but came up empty. She turned and began to walk away, stopping after only a few steps. "He's dead," she said without turning around.

"Who is?" Jeremy asked.

"You asked how the kid was doing. His name was Charlie, and he's dead."

Jeremy stood in silence. The weight of her words hit him like an avalanche. Charlie's blood was on his hands, and he had to live with that burden the rest of his life.

Kelsey continued walking away; Jeremy didn't follow.

She had stayed out later with Jeremy than she had anticipated, and by the time she got home, Dakota was already asleep.

"My, my Kelsey, you look exhausted," Hawthorne said as she handed her a cup of tea.

"It's been," she paused and took a deep breath, "a very long day," she said through an exhale.

"Well, I just put her down for bed. She might still be awake if you want to say hello," Hawthorne said.

Kelsey smiled. "Thank you, Bev. For everything."

"Of course, dear," she said as she lovingly patted the top of Kelsey's hand. "You and Dakota are family."

Kelsey sat down on the couch and reflected on the past twelve hours, thinking about how much her life had changed in that brief span. Hawthorne had fallen asleep in her chair as she read one of her books; it had become a nightly ritual for the aging woman. Kelsey grabbed a blanket from the couch, draped it over her, and kissed her forehead.

"Goodnight," she whispered.

Kelsey tiptoed into her room and over to the bed. Dakota was fast asleep, but tossed a little as Kelsey lay down next to her on the mattress.

Dakota sighed.

Kelsey pulled the little girl into a one-armed hug while gently stroking her hair with the other hand. As she thought back to the pain she saw in Clay's eyes earlier, she couldn't help but go to a dark place—to a place where Dakota no longer existed: a life without seeing her beautiful smile every morning or hearing her sweet little voice say, "I love you, Mama." The thoughts were crippling.

Her eyes welled up with tears, and it took everything she had not to burst into a good, hard cry as she decompressed from the emotional blitzkrieg she had endured throughout the day.

"Hi, Mama," Dakota whispered.

Kelsey squeezed her tight. "Hi, baby girl," she said, barely audible.

Dakota's muscles relaxed as she quickly drifted back to sleep. Kelsey would not allow herself to cry, but inside, all she could feel was pain, sorrow, and guilt. If Clay had not heard her cries for help months ago—had he not saved her life—then Charlie would still be alive tonight.

She tried to convince herself that it was her fault, that she was responsible for Charlie's death. It helped ease the pain of Clay's rejection earlier. She didn't believe it, though. Kelsey didn't believe in coincidences or fate. She knew these things were happening for a reason, and it didn't matter if Clay had saved her on that day or not. Their paths would have crossed at some point, regardless. She would still be laying right there, and Charlie would still be dead. She just hoped that, through it all, Charlie's death would somehow not be in vain.

Exhaustion set in and Kelsey's eyes became heavy. She kissed the back of Dakota's head. "I love you, Koty-bear," she whispered as she fell asleep.

****

The halls were finally quiet after an emotionally draining evening. A few of the children cried off and on for most of the day. Lona couldn't even eat dinner. Despite the grief, Clay suspected everyone would get a good night's sleep. Such turmoil can bring even the strongest of men to their knees.

Clay saw a dim light pouring out from beneath Megan's door. She was likely reading one of her medical books, second-guessing every decision she made with Charlie. Clay knew she did everything right, but she was her own worst critic.

Fighting the urge to go to bed, he made his way to the armory and cleaned his guns. In the past few days, he had done quite a bit of shooting, especially with his AR-15. Realistically, his guns never needed attention as frequently as he gave them, but he found it to be a very cathartic process, giving him some quiet time for his thoughts. Keeping the guns clean and oiled was also the best way to ensure reliability. Replacement parts would be near impossible to find.

As he fieldstripped the battle rifle with ease, he remembered teaching Charlie how to do just that. The kid was a fast learner, and after just a couple of step-by-step instructions, was able to disassemble and reassemble the rifle nearly as fast as Clay could.

Clay sprayed a solvent down the barrel and pulled a wire brush tip through with a flex-rod, followed by some more solvent and a few patches. His mind began to drift, and before too long, he was thinking about Kelsey. A mixture of joy and pain shot through his body, spreading like a poison. He *did* believe that she had never told anyone where they lived. In essence, she was absolved from the crime. However, he couldn't detach her from Watson. Why hadn't she told him about Silas before the attack? The fact was, she had no reason to tell Clay about Silas beforehand. And facts only matter once they matter.

He tried to push Kelsey out of his head, but he couldn't. He missed her. He missed the prospect of marrying her, spending the rest of his life protecting her and providing for her. He had looked forward to waking up to her glowing smile each morning. What wonderful days were ahead. Days of a future that no longer existed.

Even if he could reconcile with Kelsey over enough time, it wouldn't matter. The family had to move, and in all likelihood, it wouldn't be anywhere close by. Watson and his men were a threat. And even though Clay's family was attacked unprovoked, Charlie did kill one of Silas's men, and Clay took a couple out himself. He and Charlie had denied Watson's attempt at conquest, and that kind of bad taste wouldn't just go away. The only option to stay would be to somehow remove both Watson and Silas from the picture. That was an unlikely possibility.

As Clay dabbed a few drops of oil around the bolt carrier group, he wondered if life would ever be normal again. As normal as "normal" was anyway. Clay loved Charlie like a brother. His death hit harder than perhaps any other loss he had experienced, but the more he thought about it, the more he realized it wasn't just the fact that Charlie was dead. It removed blinders Clay had worn since the family first moved into the building. A naivety that caused Clay to let his guard down. There was no question that the world was a hostile place to live anymore, he never doubted that. For some reason, though, living in that building, more than a hundred feet up in the air, made him think their home could never be infiltrated. It was their tower of refuge, but as he learned through his toughest lesson yet, mere concrete and steel cannot hold evil at bay.

He reassembled the rifle and looked down the sights. He pulled the charging handle back a few times to ensure the bolt carrier group was seated properly and sliding smoothly. *Perfect,* he thought.

He put the magazine back in and set it on the workbench. He noticed a blue post-it pad sitting towards the edge of the bench. He saw an assortment of numbers scribbled down in Charlie's handwriting. Charlie had meticulously kept track of the rounds he had reloaded while Clay was sick in bed during the winter. How tedious it would have been to manually de-prime each case before loading, but such was Charlie's dedication.

Clay's grieving thoughts of Charlie were gradually shifting to ones more positive in nature. In the seven years Charlie was part of the family, he gave them all a lifetime of great memories. And even though his final days alive were among a darker period, he lived a joyful life in a world deprived of such things. Each and every day, he found a reason to get out of bed and did so with a smile on his face. Despite the circumstances around him, Charlie's outlook on life was something that would have a lasting impact on Clay.

He retrieved his rifle, turned off the light, and locked up the armory. He wandered down the hall, eventually finding himself in the middle of Charlie's room. It was dark and chilly, a fitting atmosphere. Clay walked over to a lantern and pressed the power button. The light chased away the darkness of the small room revealing a slice of Charlie's life frozen in time.

He stood in front of a bookshelf that was filled edge to edge with various novels that the two had shared over the years. Clay found it funny that a kid who never attended school—other than the candlelit classes taught by Megan—could read nearly twice as fast as him. It didn't matter, though, as Charlie always waited patiently for his turn to read the book and was eager to talk to Clay about each chapter.

Clay walked over to Charlie's bed which was little more than a desktop and a stuffed cot mattress. He sat down and immediately noticed an unnatural shape pressing up from beneath the mattress. He leaned to one side as he reached his hand under the mattress and fished around until he had the object in his grasp. It was a book. He pulled it out and saw it was a hardback journal. He opened to the first page.

Life on the New Frontier

It was Charlie's book, the one he had been writing. Clay remembered Charlie talking about Vlad selling it in his store after he finished. Clay wondered what it was about. Charlie had been tightlipped about the story and told Clay he could only read it once it was finished. He didn't know if Charlie had gotten a chance to finish.

He turned the page.

This is a story about a new world. A world that had been explored, conquered, and then lost. A world filled with evil men who wanted to destroy until there was nothing left to destroy. Men who killed just for fun.

When the few good people left had all but given up hope, a hero emerged from the rubble. A man of honor. A man who would restore order to chaos. This is a story is about a man named Clay.

Chapter 29

Hawthorne noticed the shake in Kelsey's hands as she struggled to keep a grip on the plate she was washing.

"You okay, dear?" Hawthorne asked. "You seem a little...antsy."

"I'm fine," Kelsey replied quickly, trying to mask her edge.

Hawthorne grabbed a broom and started sweeping around the small table; there was an excessive amount of crumbs beneath one particular chair. Despite the mess, it always made her smile because it reminded her of just how cute Dakota was when she ate.

CLANK! A mug slipped out of Kelsey's hand and smashed into the steel sink basin. To her surprise, it only chipped slightly around the base, still completely useable. Hawthorne stopped sweeping and looked at her again with a concern-filled expression.

"I'm okay, Bev," she replied quickly. After a moment, "I'm just not feeling all that well."

Hawthorne came over and rested her hand on Kelsey's shoulder, giving a reassuring squeeze. "You haven't been yourself since you got home last night. Is it about Clay? Is everything okay between you two?"

Kelsey forced back the tears and maintained her composure. "You know me too well," she said as she splashed a soapy plate into a bucket of water sitting in the middle of the sink.

Hawthorne gave a heartfelt smile, the kind of smile a mother would give. She slid her hand off her shoulder and down to Kelsey's arm, pulling her close for a half-hug. "I love you, Kelsey, like you were my own daughter. And a mother's instincts are never wrong—at least when it comes to her children."

The kind, loving words evoked a genuine smile from Kelsey, the first since she found out about Charlie. Hawthorne was indeed like a mother to her, the kind of mother she needed years ago—the type of mother that would sooner die for her children, rather than use them for her own gains.

"I won't pry any further," Hawthorne said, sensing Kelsey's reluctance. "Just remember, when you're ready to talk, I'm here for you, even if it means pulling me out of bed at three in the morning. Okay?"

Kelsey nodded, "Thank you," she paused for a second, debating whether or not she should say it, "Mom."

Hawthorne kissed Kelsey on the cheek and returned to sweeping.

As Kelsey finished up the last few dishes, her mind continued to wander. Not about Clay, or even Charlie, but about Dakota. Watson's ranch was no good for either of them, and she had no idea how she was going to be able to escape. She thought about going to Jeremy, but she was still so angry at him that the thought of asking him for a favor was repulsive. Not to mention she couldn't fully trust him, especially with something as dangerous as that.

She put the last dish back in the cupboard and dried her hands on a towel dangling off the counter. Hawthorne had found her way to her chair and was reading the same book as the night before. She was on the last few pages and would be looking to start a new one by the end of the evening.

"I think I am going to go lay down for a bit. Are you okay keeping an eye on Dakota?" Kelsey asked.

Hawthorne leaned to the side and looked out the window. Dakota was playing with a couple of children on the porch at the next house over. "No problem, dear. Go get some rest, sounds like you could use it."

Though she felt as if she hadn't slept in days, Kelsey was wide awake. Her mind was racing with the events from the past day, and with a very uncertain future ahead of her, she just couldn't seem to fall asleep.

The physical rest was nice, though, and she felt that was as important as emotional rest. About an hour later, she heard the stomping outside the bedroom door. The handle clumsily turned, and in came Dakota.

"Mama! Come look at what I did!" Dakota shouted with the kind of excitement only a three year old could have.

Kelsey smiled. "Okay pumpkin," she said with a raspy voice.

"I'm not a pumpkin," she said as she turned and skipped out of the bedroom. "Silly Mama! I'm Dakota."

Kelsey made fists and planted them on the mattress, pushing herself out of bed. She made her way into the living room where Hawthorne was hanging up a colorful painting that Dakota had made over at the neighbors. Kelsey had somehow not noticed the vibrant splashes of color that had made their way onto Dakota's overalls.

"It's beautiful, sweetheart! You did that?" Kelsey asked.

"Yup!" she said and nodded her head emphatically.

"You are quite the artist. Good job!" Kelsey said and crouched down with arms wide open inviting her daughter for a hug. Dakota joyfully obliged.

Kelsey decided to take Dakota over to the store for a treat: a token for a job well-done on the masterpiece hanging in the living room. She wanted peanut brittle. Watson had a small crop of peanuts— a glorified garden, really—so the peanut supply was not all that abundant and that made the brittle quite costly.

She reached into her pocket and pulled out a 1938 walking liberty half dollar she had found while searching through a bank last year. She held on to it for a rainy day. It wasn't about to buy her and Dakota's freedom, but it was good enough to use on something special when the time was right.

The time was perfect.

She got nearly twelve ounces of brittle. That was more than enough for the two of them, with plenty extra to share with Hawthorne. They stepped outside of the store, and Dakota was bouncing around, eager to try the sweet treat. Kelsey couldn't remember the last time she'd had some herself. It used to be one of her favorites, she only ever got it on her birthday when her mother would spend the few extra dollars it would cost to buy at the grocery store.

Kelsey snapped off a piece and handed it to Dakota. The little girl held it up in front of her eyes, examining every little crystallized imperfection. She took a bite and munched a few times. Her eyes widened, and her face lit up with joy.

"YUM-MEEEE!" she squealed with delight and started skipping around the dirt path as she took another bite.

Kelsey's heart melted with enchantment as she watched her daughter enjoy the candy. Oh, to be a child again! Dakota had certainly been through some rough times, but she was a genuinely happy child despite the lack of luxuries, the constant threat of hunger, and difficulties keeping warm for more than half the year. It was the kind of joy only the innocence of a child could bring.

Kelsey broke off another piece and handed it to Dakota.

"Come on, Mama. Let's go share some with Mimi!"

Kelsey was overjoyed and wished she could just freeze time and live in the moment forever. Life wasn't fair, though. In just a few hours, Dakota would be going to bed, and Kelsey would once again be faced with the daunting reality of her life.

She smiled as she watched her little girl run into the house calling for Hawthorne. This was a moment she really needed: A moment she was glad she could give to her daughter.

****

Kelsey gently closed the door to the bedroom. She had put Dakota down for the night a little earlier than usual, but she had to be somewhere, and she wanted to say goodnight to her. She *needed* to say goodnight to her.

She walked over to the kitchen table and pulled her jacket off the back of one of the chairs. It wasn't terribly cold outside, but the nights still had a tendency to get chilly, and she had no idea how long she was going to be out.

"It's a little late to be heading out," Hawthorne said as she tidied up from dinner. "Meeting Clay somewhere?"

Kelsey felt a pang in her stomach at the mention of his name. She still hadn't told Hawthorne what had happened, and now wasn't the time. "No," she said, trying her best to be nonchalant. "I just need to talk to Mr. Watson about some things."

The expression on her face told Hawthorne there was more to the story than that, but before she had a chance to ask, Kelsey continued.

"Bev, I uh…" she got a little choked up but reined it in quickly. "I need you to do me a favor." Kelsey almost laughed at her choice of words. A favor is when you borrow a neighbor's tool or ask for a glass of water. What she was asking of her dear friend would leave Kelsey indebted forever.

"What is it?" Hawthorne asked, concern in her eyes.

Kelsey reached into a pocket and pulled out a piece of paper, several times folded. She extended her arm and held it out for Hawthorne to take. "If something were to ever happen to me. If I…" she paused and took a deep breath, "If I don't come back home someday, *please* see to it that Dakota gets here," she said.

"You're worrying me, Kelsey? What are you *really* doing tonight?"

"Just promise," Kelsey insisted. "This is where Clay lives, and I know he and his family would take care of Dakota like one of their own." She wiped away a tear at the thought. She never imagined she could one day be separated from her little girl, but that reality lingered each and every day, regardless of the current events.

She knew that Dakota would be welcome with Clay's family. Even if Kelsey was no longer a part of his life, Clay would never hold that against Dakota. He had a kind and charitable heart; it was one of the many qualities about him that Kelsey had fallen in love with.

Hawthorne saw a distress in Kelsey's eyes, and it chilled her to the bone. She knew whatever Kelsey was planning to do was dangerous.

"Is there any way I can talk you out of whatever you're planning to do?" she asked, almost rhetorically, as she reached for the piece of paper.

Kelsey shook her head. "I love you."

Hawthorne slid the piece of paper into her back pocket, and the two hugged briefly before Kelsey broke away. She looked outside and saw how dark it was getting. "I really need to get going."

Kelsey walked to the door and opened it when Hawthorne stopped her.

"I hope this is not goodbye," Hawthorne said, a fierce shake in her voice. "I love you, Kelsey. Please be safe tonight."

Kelsey smiled warmly. "I will be," she lied and closed the door.

As Kelsey walked to Watson's house, she tried to come up with the right words to say. Watson was not easily flattered, so that would rule out a smooth, flirtatious conversation. Typically, at the end of the day, Watson just wanted to know how the bottom line benefited him. He was not an easy man to negotiate with, and if he became annoyed enough, bad things happened. Her mind wandered back to the black eye she had just before winter—the one she lied about when Clay questioned it.

Kelsey wondered if Clay's attempt to purchase her freedom was the real reason Watson had sent Silas. There weren't a lot of ways to please Watson, but countless ways to anger him, disrespect chief among them.

She felt inside her jacket pocket as she approached the porch. The knife was there. She had no idea how the conversation was going to go, or how on edge Watson would be after the attack on Clay, so she brought it just in case. She tried to convince herself it was a bad idea. The mere picture of Watson's face in her mind was enough to flood her with hatred; enough to want to kill him for what he did to Charlie, and what he was doing to her and Dakota. It would take a lot of self-restraint. Something she wasn't confident she had.

She knocked lightly on the door and after a few seconds passed, she saw a light flip on. He walked up to the door and looked out from behind the curtain. The sound of the deadbolt unlatching caused Kelsey to jump; she was on edge. She took a deep breath.

"Kelsey," he said, a slight agitation in his voice, "why are you on my doorstep at almost..." he looked at his wristwatch, "nine o'clock?"

"Mr. Watson, I know it's late, but I need to talk to you about my situation."

Watson rolled his eyes and shook his head. "This is a conversation we can have another time, darlin'," he said and began to shut the door.

"Please!" Kelsey said and wedged her foot between the door and the frame. "It won't take long; I just need a few minutes."

He furrowed his bushy eyebrows and let out a hefty sigh. *Not a good start,* Kelsey thought. She just needed to get in and calm him down; it wouldn't be an easy task.

"You've got five of them," he said and opened the door.

Kelsey walked in and immediately sat down on the couch. "Please...have a seat," Watson snidely jabbed at her etiquette.

Watson walked into the kitchen briefly before coming back with a glass of scotch. He didn't offer Kelsey anything. He sat down in the chair across from the couch and rested one hand on the chair's padded arm; the other cradled the small tumbler.

"Listen, Mr. Watson, I know we talked about this recently, but I've been here quite a while now. Nearly everything I find goes towards my debt, and yet I have barely made a scratch. I understand what I did was wrong, and it was very costly to you, but you can't keep me prisoner here forever," she said, nearly impressed with how well she articulated her thoughts.

"My dear, I'm not holding you prisoner. Remember, you are free to leave whenever you'd like," he said with a malevolent grin.

Kelsey became angered by Watson's reminder that *Dakota* was the one truly imprisoned by Watson. She hated him more than she thought possible. He was, in every regard, a monster. She had to keep her cool, though, or she would have no chance. "You *know* I would never leave without my daughter." She paused for a moment, trying to think of what to say next. "So, I guess we are at a bit of an impasse."

Watson raised his eyebrows. "An impasse? I don't think you know what that word means, young lady," he said with a chuckle.

Kelsey wrestled with her desire to jump over the coffee table in front of her and put the blade right up to his throat. She knew that would do no good right now, though. She couldn't let him know she knew anything about Silas's attack on Clay.

"Remember, sweetheart, this isn't some free ride you get while you pay off your debt. You have to earn your keep *and* pay your debt. It's how the world works," he said with condescension.

Keep it together, Kelsey. "I understand that, Mr. Watson, but it's really hard to make any headway when," she held up her hands and did air quotes, "*cost of living* here goes up practically every month."

Watson tossed back the remaining liquid in his glass and climbed out of his chair. "I'm sorry you don't like how things are run here, but it's just the way it's gonna be. Find a way to pay me what you owe me, and you and your daughter are free to find greener pastures." He turned to walk to the kitchen heading straight for the bottle on the counter. "I'm sure you can find some more...*creative* ways around town to earn a little extra," he said as he walked away.

Kelsey snapped.

She was so furious she couldn't see straight, and before Kelsey realized it, she was swiftly coming up behind Watson. She slid the knife out of her pocket and squeezed it tight; her knuckles lost all color. The world around her became a total blur; a spinning mess. Watson was crystal clear, however, and that's all that mattered.

He began pouring his drink and yelled something to her thinking she was still in the living room. His voice was muffled and the words sounded as if he were speaking a foreign language. She didn't know what he said, and she didn't care. Kelsey was tired of being Watson's slave. She was sick of him being a god in his own little patch of paradise.

And it was all about to come to an end. One way or another.

Kelsey raised her arm and quickly threw it forward. By the time she realized Watson had started to turn around, she was committed to the strike.

Watson swept his arm across his face to deflect the attack. It worked in the sense that it prevented a fatal blow, but Kelsey's momentum drove the blade deep into his triceps, about an inch above his elbow.

His scream was sharp and furious. He pushed Kelsey away then kicked her in her stomach. As she fell back, she yanked the blade out of his arm, yielding another scream.

The yell turned to a grunting through clenched teeth. He reached for his holster out of habit, but he had taken it off upstairs. Kelsey lunged at him again, set out to finish the job she had started, but Watson was able to grab her wrist and swing her into the counter. She struggled to break free from his grasp, but his strength outmatched hers. He lifted her arm up and then with all his might, slammed her wrist on the edge of the counter.

Kelsey let out a blood curdling shriek as the ferocious pain pulsated through her entire arm. The break was audible, and she knew the battle had just been lost. Her cries and whimpers yielded no sympathy from Watson as he beat her without mercy.

Eventually, the pain reached the point where it almost didn't exist. She wasn't sure if it was adrenaline or if she had taken so many blows that her body was shutting down. After a few minutes,

Watson grew tired and stopped. She could hear him panting, gasping for air like he had just finished a marathon. He hurled some insults at her, but her brain couldn't properly process the information.

She mustered enough strength to elevate her head; otherwise, she would have drowned in the pooling blood on the floor. Her left eye had swollen shut, and the right wasn't faring much better. She tried to move her fingers on the broken wrist, but that pain, the only pain that seemed to be present, was too much. What little vision she had was throbbing with each heartbeat; the world was getting darker.

No! She thought. *Not like this.* Kelsey thought of Dakota and Hawthorne. She thought of Clay and the life they might have had together. Even if such a thing no longer existed, it gave her motivation to keep going. It gave her hope.

Suddenly, Watson heard a knocking on the door. Somebody probably heard the scream. He looked and saw that Kelsey wasn't moving; he wasn't even sure she was conscious. The knocking persisted.

"Jake, it's Jeremy! Everything okay?" shouting came from the porch.

Kelsey tried to scream for Jeremy, but nothing came out. The pain was slowly throbbing back into existence.

"Just a minute!" Watson yelled while trying to clean the blood from his clothes with a dish towel. It was no use.

Watson looked around the kitchen, but found nothing, so he walked into the next room over in search of clothing. Kelsey took the opportunity to lift her head up and look around. She had no idea where the knife ended up. She found a weapon of opportunity, but before she could move, Watson's footsteps paraded across the floor back through the kitchen. He stopped and looked at Kelsey.

"What's going on in there, Jake?" Jeremy continued.

The old man sighed and left the kitchen, making his way through the living room to shoo Jeremy away. As he was reaching to unlock the door, he heard glass breaking from the kitchen. Watson stopped before he turned the deadbolt fully and darted back to the kitchen.

"Watson!" Jeremy shouted as he tried to open the door.

Watson rounded the corner and saw shards of glass on the floor and Kelsey facing away from him, leaning into the counter. He stepped quickly across the kitchen floor, holding Kelsey's knife.

"I am done dealing with you, little girl!" he said, gritting his teeth.

Kelsey spun around, holding Watson's bottle of scotch in her good hand. Using the momentum from her spin, she cracked Watson on the side of the head with the bottle.

The sound was even worse than when he had shattered her wrist. Watson stumbled for a moment before his eyes rolled back, and his body went limp. The old man fell to the floor and he made no attempt to break his fall.

Kelsey collapsed as well. The sound of a now nearly empty bottle of scotch clattered as it hit the ground still fully intact. She looked over at Watson. Her vision was too fuzzy to be able to tell if he was still breathing. She hoped he wasn't.

She heard Jeremy break the window on the front door. She knew he was close, yet it sounded as if he was miles away. Her heart rate slowed, and the darkness finally overcame her vision.

Chapter 30

She could hear a muffled voice. It was calling to her.

"Kelsey!" the voice yelled. It sounded as if he was shouting while being smothered with a pillow.

She opened her right eye briefly. The room was dark, yet the light from the hallway was still too bright for her. The voice got louder, slightly clearer. She wanted him to go away; she just wanted to sleep.

"Kelsey!" The scream was now deafening, perfectly clear.

She gasped as she woke up, immediately crying as the pain welcomed her back from her slumber.

"We have to get out of here, right now!" Jeremy said with urgency.

Jeremy wasn't just in the neighborhood. He had come for a meeting with Watson, Silas, and a few others. Silas would be there any minute, and asking questions wouldn't be first on his list of things to do.

Kelsey groaned in protest. She was tired and in pain; she didn't want to be awake.

"Kelsey, look at me, right now!"

She did her best to oblige. His face was just out of focus, as if she needed to slightly twist on the lens of a camera in order to restore the picture. Despite the blurred vision, Kelsey could see the grim look on Jeremy's face. She must look as bad as she felt.

"Can you walk?" he asked.

Kelsey knew the answer before she even attempted to try. Even though her legs had not taken the brunt of Watson's attack, she barely had the energy to speak, let alone run.

"Never mind," he said, frustrated with her delayed responses.

Jeremy picked her up and carried her out the back door. He walked as fast as he could while he cradled her limp body. They had gotten maybe a quarter mile away when he heard shouting coming from Watson's house. The windows on the first floor lit up one by one, and silhouettes could be seen moving about searching for the assailant.

This is real bad, Jeremy thought. There was no way Kelsey was walking out of there alive. He had to get her onto a horse, and even then, he wasn't sure she would be able to handle that. He had very little medical training, just basic first-aid knowledge, but enough to know she was in bad shape.

Jeremy and Kelsey were in the middle of a patch of high grass, one of many fields used to harvest hay. It wasn't but two feet tall, but it would be enough. He crouched down and gently laid Kelsey on the ground. "No matter what, stay quiet!" he ordered.

Some of the men were now outside checking around the house, their flashlights waving about like a rock concert. Unfortunately, the most likely route a fleeing attacker would take was the same one Jeremy had taken. It was his only option to avoid being spotted, but Silas and his men would be heading his way any moment.

The only way to keep Kelsey safe was to divert their search efforts—at least long enough to wrangle up a horse and get her out of there. Jeremy reached for a small pocket knife he always had on him and sliced it across his stomach and twice on his left arm. The pain was tolerable due to the enormous amount of adrenaline surging through his body. The self-inflicted gashes would explain the blood on his shirt from carrying Kelsey and would, hopefully, add a level of believability to his story.

"Kelsey, remember what I said," he spoke as loudly as he dared. "No matter what, don't move. I'll be back soon, I promise."

Jeremy took a deep breath and slowly exhaled. He pulled out his pistol and ran about fifty yards away. He turned and saw the flashlights heading towards Kelsey. He racked the slide on his gun and took aim.

"Hey, you!" Jeremy shouted as loudly as he could. "Stop right there!" Seconds later, Jeremy fired several times towards a cluster of trees a few hundred yards away. He couldn't really see them but knew they were there.

The first part of the plan worked, the flashlights were racing towards him, the men were shouting back and forth at each other. Within half a minute, the first had arrived.

"Don't move!" one of Silas's men barked at Jeremy.

Jeremy held up his blood-stained hands. "Don't shoot. It's me, Jeremy," he said while pretending to gasp for air.

By the time Silas reached them, Jeremy had dropped to his knees, putting on a believable performance that would back up his claims.

"What happened? What are you doing out here?" Silas asked Jeremy.

"I got to Watson's a little early for our meeting and saw someone in a mask attacking him. I chased him out this way," he said taking a few puffs of air before continuing. "He got me pretty good," Jeremy said tugging at his shirt, "and that's when he took off and I started shooting at him." He pointed out towards the trees.

"Michaels, take Hall, Garver, and Mueller and track that S-O-B down," Silas stopped for a moment, "and try to bring him back alive. I imagine Watson would appreciate the opportunity to have a chat with this man."

"Yes sir!" the men collectively said and began jogging towards the tree line.

"So, Watson's okay, then?" Jeremy asked, pretending to sound relieved.

"He was barely conscious when I got there. Doc's there now checking him out. Guess we'll find out soon enough if he's gonna make it," he said with indifference. He looked over at Jeremy and shined his flashlight on his stomach. "Looks like you need to go see Doc, too."

"Yeah, I guess so," Jeremy replied as he wiped his hands on his shirt. "I can help you guys out if you need it," he added.

Silas let out a laugh, sounding more like a grunt than anything. It was as if he was insulted by the notion that he and his men needed help from Jeremy. "No, I think we've got this under control."

"All right," Jeremy said. "I'll go check in on Watson. Just be sure to bring me up to speed later tonight."

Silas nodded and started moving in the direction his men had gone. Jeremy watched him for a few moments before turning and heading back in the direction of the house. Once Silas was no longer visible, he moved quickly over to where he had left Kelsey. She was still there, her eyes wide. She had finally snapped out of the daze she'd been in since Jeremy first discovered her in the kitchen.

"Jeremy!" she said as loudly as she could, which wasn't more than a whisper. "Is that you?"

He crouched down next to her. "Yeah, I'm here, but we need to move fast. They'll give up the search soon."

"Huh?" Kelsey said, clueless to what he was talking about.

"Never mind. We need to get to the stables."

He started to pick her up when she stopped him. "I-I-I think I can walk if you help me."

"Are you sure?"

She looked at him and nodded, "Yeah, I think so."

The pain was intense just laying still, and she imagined the hike to the stables would be nothing short of torment, but she knew Jeremy wouldn't be able to carry her that far. Not quickly, anyway.

Kelsey slowly rolled over towards her side and propped herself up with her elbow. If she felt that bad now, then she didn't want to think about how she was going to feel in the morning—if morning ever came. She groaned quietly as the agony jolted through every muscle in her body.

Jeremy quickly moved to her side and helped her to her feet. Though he only had just the faint moonlight to see, he saw the bruising already starting to form around her face.

"Ready?" he asked.

"As much as I can be," she said as she supported herself on his shoulder, keeping the other arm close to her body, stabilizing it as best as she could. The slightest knock on the wrist felt as if it were breaking all over again. It was excruciating, and she wasn't sure she would be able to suppress the screams.

They slowly made their way across the field and past the slaughterhouse. The smell was rancid, and it took everything in Kelsey not to throw up, but that could also be from the concussion. She breathed through her mouth and kept her mind focused on the task at hand: getting to the stables…about a half mile away.

"What happened in there?" Jeremy demanded more than he asked.

"I don't know…" she said, wincing with each step. With all her efforts focused on walking, having a conversation wasn't easy. "I remember talking to him about what I owe him," she said, racking her brain to try and remember what had occurred. "I remember being angry at him, and the next thing I know, I was trying to stab him. It gets a little fuzzy from there," she said.

Jeremy didn't respond. She was clearly the aggressor, but he couldn't convince himself that she was wrong in doing so. Watson hadn't exactly been subtle with taking advantage of the debt she owed. The 'interest' he was charging her—and all of the extra fees he tacked on—would have made even credit card companies sympathetic. She was never going to be able to square up on the debt, and Watson knew it. So did Kelsey.

Though he could never prove it, Jeremy knew that Watson had roughed her up more than a few times since her arrival. Watson never came off as the type of guy who would beat a woman, but he had a firm line when it came to certain issues, and Kelsey had skirted that line several times in the past. Once Watson got going, it was hard to calm him down. Jeremy wondered if Watson would have killed Kelsey had he not knocked on the door.

"Well, looks like you got the last word in, anyway," Jeremy said somewhat light-heartedly.

Kelsey wanted to smile, but even that would hurt too much. "Did I kill him?" she asked with mixed feelings.

"Doesn't sound like it. All the more reason we need to get you out of here before he's coherent enough to tell people what happened."

Jeremy and Kelsey stopped about a hundred yards away from the stables, hiding behind an old wagon that had once served as a decorative lawn ornament before being reactivated as a functional vehicle.

There was a single lantern just outside the stables. Jeremy couldn't see the guard, but knew there would be one there. After all, it was Jeremy's idea to have twenty-four hour security there. He turned to look at Kelsey who was resting on the ground, leaning up against the large wooden wheel.

"I am going to go grab us a horse. Stay put! I will come back to you," he said as he crouched down next to her. "We'll be out of here soon," he said with a comforting voice.

"Okay," she said, still trying to catch her breath. The journey across the field had taken a toll.

Jeremy jogged towards the stables, and as he got closer, he could see that no one was outside. Maybe they abandoned their post to help the search party. That's when he saw someone walk out the door.

"Hey Derrick," Jeremy shouted.

"Mr. Hatfield, is that you?"

Jeremy came out of the darkness, his face finally hit by the small lantern hanging on the outside wall. "Yes, it's me. I need a fast horse right now, we're tracking down Watson's attacker, but he got a good head start on us," he said, not even sure if the young man had heard about what was going on.

"But Silas told me to not let anyone check out a horse unless he explicitly gave the okay," Derrick replied.

"What? When did he say that?" Jeremy snapped back.

"When I heard all the commotion over at Mr. Watson's house, I ran over, and that's what he told me," the boy said, with a tinge of fear in his eyes.

"I don't have time for this!" Jeremy said, frustration radiating in his voice. "You take orders from me, not Silas. I am taking a horse."

Jeremy walked towards the door when Derrick blocked his path. "Sir, please don't put me in this position."

Jeremy stepped back a few feet and pulled his gun out, aiming right at the young man's chest. "You will step out of my way right now, or I will shoot you where you stand!" Jeremy was surprised with his immediate escalation of the situation. His reflexive response now put Jeremy in a 'do-or-die' scenario. His chips were all in, there was no turning back.

Derrick was terrified, but he did not move. He seemed to be more worried about what Silas would do if he let a horse get stolen.

Jeremy pulled the hammer back on his pistol. "Stand down, Derrick."

The kid stood his ground, and then he did what Jeremy was afraid he was going to do.

"Don't—" Jeremy shouted as Derrick reached for his gun.

Jeremy shot three times, each one a direct hit to Derrick's chest. The image of the boy's horrified expression would be permanently burned into Jeremy's memory. He kept the gun trained on Derrick as he fell to the ground. A fluid-filled breath escaped the boy's lips, then silence.

Jeremy felt a pang in his stomach for what he just did, but he would have to feel guilty later. Silas and his men had to have heard the shots and would be on their way.

He changed magazines on his pistol and holstered it. Reaching for the nearest saddle, Jeremy slung it on top of a horse and climbed on. He led the mare out of the stable and saw Kelsey limping her way towards him.

"I told you to stay put!" he hissed.

As Kelsey got near, she saw Derrick's body on the ground. She wanted to be shocked that Jeremy shot that boy who was on guard, but she couldn't find enough strength for sympathy.

"Here, let me help you up," Jeremy said as put his arm around her.

Getting her onto the horse was a much more difficult task than he thought. Every movement made her cry out in pain. Finally, after several attempts, she was up, clinging to the horse's neck like a log in a flood.

"Okay, watch out. I'm gonna—"

Shots rang out, striking the stable and spooking the horses inside. Jeremy looked over and saw a few shadowy silhouettes running towards him. He quickly smacked the horse's rear, and it took off in a rush. Jeremy pulled his gun out and took aim, but before he could acquire any targets, he heard footsteps behind him.

He turned around with just enough time to see the shotgun butt coming right at his face.

****

Kelsey woke up feeling like she had been hit by the *Titanic*. Aches and pains plagued her entire body. Her head throbbed relentlessly; the slightest sound exacerbated the pain.

She opened her eyes, and the first thing she saw was the splint on her hand. She wrinkled her forehead and could feel the various butterfly sutures keeping the lacerations on her head from separating. She saw that her arms were riddled with bruises and small cuts. What had happened? Where was she?

A noisy groan escaped her lips as she attempted to look around with little success. "Hello?" she said with a hoarse voice.

"Kelsey?" a voice called out from behind her. He walked around and leaned over in front of her, flashing a penlight in her eyes. "Pupil response has improved," he thought aloud.

It was Doc.

"Doc, where am I?" she asked before attempting to get up. She was tied to the chair. "What's happening?" she asked, panic creeping into her voice.

Doc wanted to ignore her questions. Watson would probably have him killed if he even spoke to her, but he still honored the oath he took nearly twenty years ago. "Kelsey, you're still on the farm."

Kelsey had presumed that much already. She wanted to sigh, but the pain was too great to inhale that deeply. "Why am I tied to the chair?" she asked.

Doc walked across the room, reached into his bag for a bottle of pills, and returned to Kelsey. Because her good hand was tied to the chair, he gave her a sip of water and then placed the pills in her mouth. "Take these. It's not much, but it will help with some of the pain."

She swallowed the pills before continuing her appeals. "Doc, *please!* Why am I tied to the chair? How did I even get here?"

Doc nervously looked around. He put his hands on top of his head. "Kelsey, how much do you remember about last night?"

She racked her brain trying to recall. She remembered just a few moments with Watson. "Not much, really. I remember who did all this to me," she said glancing at the injured wrist. "Other than that..."

"Well," Doc said, exhaustion in his voice, "Mr. Watson is claiming you attacked him, and he was just defending himself. Nobody knew what was going on for a while until Silas and his men saw Jeremy helping you onto a horse."

Jeremy! Is he okay?

Piece by piece, the events of the night started coming back together. She remembered Jeremy getting a horse from the stables. She remembered he killed someone in the process. Kelsey felt a pit deepening in her stomach as she considered the damage her actions caused last night.

"The guard at the gate was able to stop your horse, and you were brought to the infirmary," Doc continued. "To be honest, it's a good thing they did. Wherever you were going on that horse, you wouldn't have made it there alive," he said with a somber tone.

Kelsey wasn't sure if his comment was due to the extent of her injuries or the complete and utter vulnerable state she would have been in as she galloped through Screamer territory. Like a juicy cut of meat in front of starving pack of dogs.

She leaned her head back and closed her eyes. She finally got that sigh she was looking for. "Are they going to kill me?"

He was silent at first. "I don't know," he finally spoke. "I don't see why they would go through all the trouble of having me work on you all night if they were just going to kill you anyway."

That prospect frightened Kelsey more than if they just wanted her dead.

"What about Jeremy?" she asked.

He shrugged. "I honestly don't know. They never asked me to look at him."

Kelsey began to worry. Not about her dilemma, or even Jeremy's, but whether or not Hawthorne heard all the ruckus and was able to escape with Dakota. She began to weep at the thought of never seeing her daughter again.

Heavy footsteps tromped across the porch just outside, sending a jolt of fear through Kelsey's body. The door shot open. It was Silas.

"I need to talk to her," Silas said pointing at Kelsey.

"Okay," Doc said, "I'll just excuse myself."

"Don't bother, Doc. She's coming with me."

Doc interjected. "Silas, she has been through a lot, and her body is in a *very* delicate state. Moving her now is not a good idea."

Silas paid no attention to the doctor's professional opinion and untied Kelsey. She hadn't realized some of the pain she felt was from the tightness of the ropes around her abdomen. There was a genuine relief as Silas unbound her.

"Let's go," he said, grabbing Kelsey by the arm.

"Stop it!" she cried out.

"Silas!" Doc said, only getting a dirty look in response.

Despite her cries, Silas led her outside and put her on a wagon being drawn by two horses. One of Silas's men sat up front, reins in hand. Silas jumped in and sat next to Kelsey. "We're ready," Silas said to the driver.

The ride was slow and painful. Every bump and jostle reminded Kelsey of last night's beating. It was just before dawn, and most of the townspeople were still asleep. After a few minutes, the wagon turned off the dirt road and traveled in the grass heading towards the back of the property line. A short while later they came to the top of a small hill, and Kelsey could see a large barn barely illuminated by the diffused sun inching above the horizon. With nothing else in sight, she assumed that's where they were going.

Her assumptions were correct.

The wagon came to a stop. Without saying a word, Silas stood up and grabbed Kelsey's hand, forcing her to follow. Much to her surprise, Silas helped her get down from the wagon, but then quickly got back to marching her along directing her into the barn.

She had never been inside before—wasn't even sure she knew it existed. There was an unpleasant stench filling the air making the place all the more uninviting. As they came out into the main room of the structure, Kelsey saw two chairs in the middle of the floor. One was already occupied.

"Jeremy!" Kelsey shrieked. No response.

"Sit down," Silas commanded, pointing at the metal folding chair next to Jeremy.

Kelsey obeyed.

As Silas tied her to the chair, she looked over and noticed that Jeremy was still breathing, though he had been thrashed probably as badly as she had been, if not worse. Her relief was short-lived, though, as she heard voices from outside.

Watson.

The chatter drew closer, and Watson and a few of Silas's men appeared. Watson was walking a bit gingerly, his arm bandaged, and the upper half of his head dressed like a mummy with a faint trace of blood seeping through.

"Well, good morning, sweetheart," Watson said ominously, his speech slightly slurred. Kelsey didn't know if it was from alcohol or the trauma she inflicted. Perhaps a little of both.

She stared at the floor, trying to focus on a kernel of dried corn next to her feet. Gripped with a debilitating fear, she couldn't bear to look Watson in the eye.

"Wake him up," Watson said, waving his hand at Jeremy.

One of the men that came in with Watson walked over, lifted Jeremy's head and began slapping him quickly on the cheek. "Wake up, Cinderella!"

Jeremy's eyes were blood-shot; he barely had enough strength to hold his head up, not even enough strength to groan from the pain. He looked over and saw Kelsey, then Watson.

"Well, I just don't know what to do with you two," Watson said. "I mean, I can't say that I am completely surprised with your actions, Ms. Lambert. I've always known of your thankless attitude for my generous accommodations," he stopped and rubbed his head near where Kelsey had hit him. "And I kinda figured you hated me," he sneered. "Though I do admit, you caught me off guard with that little stunt of yours last night.

"*You*, on the other hand," Watson said, turning to Jeremy, "to say I am disappointed is an understatement. You have been my loyal friend for several years. You excelled in all of your duties for this community, and I trusted you with my life," he said shaking his head. "And now, you're no better than the brood of criminals outside these fences."

Jeremy started to drift from consciousness, but Silas revived him with a backhand across his already battered face. He still didn't scream.

"You frustrate me, son," Watson said, believable grief in his voice. "I just don't know what to do with you two," he reiterated.

A man from outside leaned into the main area and called for Watson. They all walked outside, leaving Jeremy and Kelsey bound to their chairs in the middle of the barn.

"Why didn't you just ask me to help you escape?" Jeremy asked slowly, forcing each word out of his mouth.

Kelsey wanted to say it was because she was mad at him for betraying Clay, but it was just as much pride as it was anger. She *was* upset with him, and the thought of turning right around and asking for his help seemed nauseating at the time. If only she could turn back the clock.

"I'm sorry about all this," Kelsey said. "I didn't think anyone else would get hurt..."

Jeremy tried to shake his head. "Don't be. You and your daughter deserve better than this. *I* should be the one apologizing to you."

What an absurd response, Kelsey thought.

"If I hadn't been so selfish, I would have helped you two escape months ago. I should have protected you from all of this, but instead..." Jeremy said as his eyes looked around the large wooden structure they sat in.

Before Kelsey could respond, the men came back in and walked up to Kelsey and Jeremy. Watson knelt down on the floor, resting his elbow on his knee. He looked directly into Kelsey's eyes, "Now, I need you to do something for me. You aren't going to like it, you may tell yourself that you won't do it, but you have to understand what's at stake here."

Kelsey glared at him with contempt. "I'm not doing anything for you!"

"Oh, I think you will," he said and turned around, nodding at a man standing just outside the door. The man stepped away for a moment before returning with the little girl.

"Dakota! No! Let her go, you sick monster!"

"Now, you *will* do what I say, or very bad things are gonna happen."

"Mommy!" Dakota sobbed from across the room, shattering Kelsey's heart like a dropped vase.

"Silas?" Watson said, maintaining his stare at Kelsey.

Kelsey looked over at Silas and saw him pull his gun out. "What are you doing? No! Stop!" she begged in vain.

Silas lifted the gun and pulled the trigger. Jeremy's head whipped back violently, a red mist erupted from the exit wound.

"Jeremy!" she howled, thrashing in the chair, ignoring the pain she felt.

Her anger turned to devastation, and she broke down into a turbulent cry. Watson tried several times to speak but found it annoying to try to talk over her cries. By the time she calmed down, Dakota and the man were no longer there. She wasn't sure if Dakota witnessed the execution. She prayed that she had not.

"Kelsey, look at me." Watson said, his voice eerily calm. "That man right there was like a son to me. Do you think I would hesitate for a second to do the same to you or your kid? Take some time to think about it, we'll come back and talk in the morning, see if you're more accommodating."

The men walked out and locked Kelsey inside with Jeremy's lifeless body on the floor next to her. She wept for hours. Jeremy had wronged her in the past, but he spent the last days of his life trying to right those wrongs. The remorse he expressed to her over the incident with Clay and Charlie was genuine. He wasn't a sociopath like Watson. Jeremy loved Kelsey even though she didn't feel the same way. And ultimately, he paid for that love with his life.

Kelsey sat awake all night, wondering what Watson wanted from her. Whatever it was, he knew she wasn't going to agree, and he preemptively struck fear into her heart.

What have I done?

Chapter 31

Clay sat there waiting like he did every Wednesday morning. It would likely be the last time though; he planned to have the family moved out by the end of next week. It was unknown whether or not Watson would try to strike again, and if so, when that day would come. If Watson were to send more men, Clay wanted the place to be empty when they arrived. The thought of torching the entire floor crossed his mind, incinerating any useful items his family would be forced to leave behind.

His stomach was in knots. Clay wondered how much longer he could handle the stress. How much more of the battering could he take in a world that was growing more relentless by the day? He struggled to remember how many loved ones he had lost over the past seven years. Dozens. The staggering number was a heavy burden on his shoulders that grew exponentially with Charlie's death. Somehow, it was different with Charlie. The others mostly died from illness—things outside of Clay's control.

A boy named Pete—who was not officially part of the group but an ally of Clay's—had been shot by a robber while he and Clay were scavenging a warehouse, but even that was different. Pete had been killed from a random attack by a desperate man looking for a way to survive. Such was life in the fallen world. Charlie's death, on the other hand, was an indirect result of Clay's actions. He wondered if he hadn't threatened Watson the way he did, or perhaps been more cautious in some of his decision making, if Charlie might still be alive.

As he looked around the mostly empty library, Clay wondered if he would ever be able to recover from the train wreck that had become his life. But he had to—his loved ones still depended on him. It was perhaps the only thing that kept him going, the only thing that held insanity at bay. But every man has a limit, and Clay felt that his was fast approaching.

He paced back and forth in front of the checkout desk, waiting for someone who would never come. His time there was never really wasted, though. Even though Clay found himself alone dozens of hours a week while traveling, the library afforded him protection so that he could actually lower his guard and just think. On the road, behind every stalled out car was a robbery waiting to happen. Behind every tree was a sociopath ready to kill. On the road, distraction was synonymous with death.

Clay walked up to a light box mounted to the wall. It was several feet in size and stuck out nearly six inches. The glass was caked with a layer of grime topped with several coats of dust. He had seen it before, but never paid much attention to it in the past. He used his sleeve to clean the glass, and after a few good swipes, an old colonial flag became visible. A replica no doubt but remarkable all the same. It was torn and artificially aged, riddled with stains. It was beautiful.

Clay thought back to the original settlers of the nation he had studied about in U.S. History class: how life in America back then, in many respects, was similar to life in the post-apocalyptic America. The colonists risked everything, including their own lives, to start a nation free from tyranny. Clay and his family faced many of the same risks each day, but not for anything as glamorous or significant as the birth of what would become the freest, most powerful nation on earth.

So many died, Clay thought to himself as he recalled some of the bloody battles of those days. But they died for something they truly believed in. They didn't just fight for survival; they perished so that future generations could live. And live freely.

That's when it hit him. Every day, Clay fought for something even more sacred than a great nation. He was fighting for life itself. He was defending the defenseless, providing for those in need. He was the head of this group he called his family. *That* was worth living for. It was worth dying for. It was Clay's calling, and it took his eyes resting on the tattered old flag to really understand the significance of his job.

With that epiphany came a second wind, bringing with it life and energy. Suddenly, the thought of starting over with a new home didn't feel quite so daunting. It was actually probably a good thing that the family was finally getting out of the tower. Though there were many fond memories made there over the last four years, there were also quite a few bad ones. Although fewer in number, the nightmares that occurred there greatly outweighed the good. He didn't like that Watson forced the matter, but Clay realized he was ready to go.

He looked down at his watch. It was 11:50. *Nobody's coming anyway,* he thought, so he decided to head out early. He had a couple of leads on some places just outside the county, and he needed to prepare to scout them out first thing in the morning. One such location was only a seven mile hike from Liberty, which was his first choice. Once he made a decision on the where, he just needed to work out the logistics with Megan on the how and when.

He considered breaking the glass on the light box, so he could take the flag, but decided not to. There was something almost poetic about seeing it behind glass, obscured beneath the grunge. Maybe it would provide another sojourner with some much-needed perspective as it had done for Clay.

Carefully stepping around collapsed shelves and flipped desks, Clay made his way to the exit. It was unusually bright, albeit hazy. He imagined that without the ash in the atmosphere, there would be a crystal clear blue sky hanging above. He could envision it.

Clay started walking when he heard a noise come from behind. He planted his foot into the ground and spun around like a door on a hinge. He whipped his rifle up and took aim.

"Howdy, stranger."

Clay slowly lowered the rifle. A grin painted across his face. "Fancy seeing you here. I thought you were a loner?" he joked.

Dusty smiled.

"Who else is going to save your butt when you pick a fight with a guy twice your size?" she quipped back.

Clay walked over and gave her a pat on the shoulder. "It's good to see you, kid," he said affectionately.

She gave him a hug and thanked him. Clay was glad to see her again. She looked even thinner than before. It had been a rough winter for everyone, but her appearance told an even harsher tale.

He reached into his bag and pulled out a couple slices of smoked venison. "Deer jerky?"

Before he finished the question, she had snatched the smoked meat from his hands and began scarfing it down. By the time she had finished the second piece, her eyes were watering. She looked at him like a puppy looks lovingly at its master, asking for another bowl of food.

"I don't have any more on me, but we have some more food back home," he said pointing in the general direction of the building. "You ready?"

Dusty nodded, and Clay turned to lead the way home. He was delighted Dusty had shown up. The whole trip to the library had done him a lot of good— a trip he initially decided he wasn't going to bother with, but a tenacious feeling in the back of his head made him go anyway. He was glad he did.

"So, where's home?" Dusty asked.

"See that big building there?" he said pointing at the tower up ahead.

"Yeah."

"That's it...for now."

Dusty tilted her head, as if to ask why he would say that.

Clay explained what had happened over the past few weeks, reopening some wounds that had just started to heal, but he felt obligated to bring Dusty up to speed.

"I'm sorry about Charlie, Clay," she said regretfully.

Clay knew Dusty had suffered as much loss as he had, perhaps even more, since she ended up alone for all those years. He wished that he had found her when she was younger so he could have protected her from the nightmares she had to endure. But then again, those nightmares, those traumatic experiences, shaped her into who she had become. And if there's an upside to such a life, it's how those horrible moments can reveal an underlying strength in an individual.

"So, where are we going next?" she asked, including herself in the equation.

"There are a few places I need to check out. Hopefully, we'll be ready to move sometime next week."

"Gotcha," Dusty replied.

As they walked into the small downtown area, Dusty stared up in awe at the towering structures. Even though there were only a few high rises, and all of them quite small when compared to the average skyscraper in a metropolitan area, Dusty was enthralled. She had never walked in the middle of any downtown before, not that she could remember anyway. The aging buildings were breathtaking, the dilapidation and overgrowth only enhanced the beauty.

"Wow," she muttered to herself as she imagined what such a place would have been like when it was filled with people who weren't trying to kill each other for food.

As they reached home, Clay warned her about the stair climb. Dusty brushed it off, as if she were a marathon runner about to tackle a 5K. Clay laughed at her overconfidence, giving her three flights before she would tire.

She held out longer than he thought. It wasn't until she got to the seventh floor that she stopped on one of the landings to gasp for air. She held her finger out to Clay, indicating she needed a minute. Putting her hands on her hips, she tried to satisfy the demand of her aching lungs.

"Breathe in through your nose and out through your mouth," Clay said before giving a demonstration.

Dusty looked at him with skepticism, but gave it a shot anyway. After doing it a few times, she felt noticeably better, though still needing to rest. "Thanks," she said during an exhale.

After another thirty seconds, she was ready to go and made the rest of the climb with no problem. Clay went a little slower for her benefit, and she was grateful. Clay knocked on the door at the top of the stairs, and Tyler answered. He was excited to meet Dusty and, as always, ran down the hall telling the entire floor of their arrival. A few of the other kids returned with Tyler and all said hello to the new arrival as they crowded around her. Some tried to hug her, others were just too close. Dusty was quite shy; her interactions with other kids had been limited at best. She tried to be sociable, but Clay could see the angst in her eyes.

"All right, everyone," Clay said holding his hands out and shooing the kids away, "give her some space. She's had a long trip and needs to rest."

The kids obeyed and backed off before turning to walk down the hall. Dusty released an audible sigh as the cushion of space between her and the others increased. Clay suspected that going from a life of isolation to a large family could be just as difficult a transition as the other way around. He would have to make sure to tell the other kids to be mindful of that.

As they entered the lobby, Clay pointed to his room. "Go ahead and drop your things off there until we find you a room, okay?"

"Okay."

"I'll be in there," Clay said, pointing to the kitchen where he assumed Megan was busy preparing a meal.

Dusty headed for the conference room while Clay went the opposite direction, heading to the kitchen. He heard Megan talking to someone. He figured it was Lona. As Clay walked through the door, he was already talking. "I've got someone I—" Clay stopped abruptly. His mouth hung open. "Ms. Hawthorne?" he said with both surprise and concern in his voice. "What are you doing here?"

She managed to muster up a slight smile, exposing a few missing teeth. Her left eye was swollen and bloodshot with a significant amount of bruising covering most of her cheek.

"It's about Kelsey."

****

Megan left and told the kids to stay out of the kitchen allowing Clay and Hawthorne to have an opportunity to talk in private. Clay was still in shock. He knew whatever was going on was serious; that much was clear. "What happened?" he asked, nerves rattled his voice. "Is she okay?"

"I don't know, on both accounts," Hawthorne responded. "She just told me that if anything ever happened to her to bring Dakota here. But, as you can see," she said holding her hand up to her face, "they weren't exactly okay with me leaving with the girl."

Clay sighed as he sunk back into the uncomfortable folding chair. He had enough troubling thoughts swirling around his head as it was, and now with Hawthorne's unexpected visit, life had just gotten infinitely more complicated. He tapped his finger on the table as he tried to process the words he just heard.

"She hadn't quite been herself over the past couple of days. To be honest, it happened after she returned from visiting you." Hawthorne adjusted in her seat. She felt awkard. "I know it's not my business, but did something happen between you two?"

Clay closed his eyes as a wave of guilt struck him. The last words he spoke to Kelsey before telling her to leave echoed in his head. Now, he wasn't sure if he would ever have an opportunity to undo the harm he inflicted that afternoon. Would he ever again be able to tell Kelsey how much he loves her? Or did she go to her grave believing that he hated her? The thought made him feel ill and furious at the same time.

He quickly brought Hawthorne up to speed about the recent events. Having to recount that twice in the last two hours was draining, but he didn't have time to be tired or emotional. He had to focus on the situation at hand; he had another decision to make.

"So, what now?" Hawthorne asked.

"I go pay Watson a visit," Clay said confidently. There was no question about it. He was going to the ranch.

Hawthorne smiled before grimacing. She was a tough old bird, but she had taken quite a lick by one of Silas's men. *What a coward!* Clay thought. Hurting a woman, especially one trying to protect a child, was the ultimate act of a weak man. It should have come as no surprise from a guy acting on the orders of an even bigger coward.

Megan came into the room and sat down across the table from Clay. "Lona gave Dusty some clean clothes and is now showing her around. She seems like a nice girl."

"She is," Clay agreed.

"So," Megan said as a means to jump into the conversation.

Clay looked at her with tired eyes. The past two weeks had felt like years, and he was struggling to find enough energy to get out of bed, let alone take on the daily demands of life. "Megan, we need to pack up everything we can carry and head to Northfield."

It was a terrible plan, but it was the best one he had. Taking Geoff up on his offer would be a no-brainer if it was just a day's hike away, but it wasn't. Realistically, with the kids and the supplies they would be bringing, it would likely take the better part of two weeks. With a group that size, most of which would be children, it was a risk Clay hated to take. To make matters worse, he wouldn't be traveling with them, at least, not at first.

He thought about just having everyone stay in Liberty until he could scout out those other locations, but his visit to Watson's farm later would not be a pleasant one, so they needed to be out of the area for good. Northfield was the answer.

Megan looked at Clay and wanted to argue, but she could tell he had already made up his mind. Clay was her younger brother, but at some point he stepped up and became the head of the family. She supported his role, and no matter how much stress it was going to put on her, she trusted his leadership.

"So, here's the deal," Clay said as he clasped his hands and rested them on the table. "We need to be packed and ready to go *tonight*. You and the kids will head to Vlad's first thing in the morning, and not a minute later," he said leaving no room to negotiate.

"Wait, *me* and the kids? Where are you going to be?"

"I can't leave Kelsey and Dakota there..."

"Clay, I don't know if I—"

"Yes you can. Besides, Blake is getting pretty good with that rifle, and Dusty has already proven herself capable. You guys will be fine. If you leave just before dawn, you should be able to make it to Vlad's by nightfall, but you'll need to move fast. Kelsey, Dakota, and I will meet up with you there," he said not knowing for sure if either were still alive. "You're going to have to push the kids pretty hard to get to Liberty in one day, so take some time to rest. If after two days we aren't there, you guys keep heading to Northfield, and we'll catch up to you there."

Megan was wrought with worry, more so for her brother's well-being than her own. She didn't feel good about it, but she knew there was nothing she could say or do that would stop him. She tried anyway.

"Can't we just wait here until you come back with them? It would give us extra time to pack, and that way, we could all go together."

"No," he shook his head. "If I walk out of there with Kelsey and Dakota, this will be the first place they come looking. You and the kids need to be gone long before that." Clay looked down at his watch. "And since I will be leaving for Watson's place in the next two or three hours, it's going to be cutting it close as it is. You *have* to leave in the morning."

Megan conceded. Despite Clay's emotions being wrecked, he was being methodical with his approach, and she respected that. "Okay, we'll do what we can to have everything ready tonight and head out first thing in the morning." She repeated his instructions. She looked over at Hawthorne. "Will you be joining us?" Megan asked. Hope filling her voice.

"Oh, I don't know, dear," the elderly lady said. "I am not sure my old body can make such a long journey. I would just slow you down."

"Well then let me change my question. Ms. Hawthorne, Bev, would you *please* join us?" she asked with a smile. Megan hoped she would say yes. Hawthorne was a sweet lady, and it would be reassuring to have another adult with her on the trip—someone who could help out with some of the children along the way and provide emotional support for Megan.

Hawthorne thought about it. The trip did sound quite intimidating and not one she thought she could handle, but where else would she go? Though she would have never believed it before yesterday, Watson might kill her for her disloyalty if she were to return. And she really did love Kelsey and Dakota as her own family. Living on a farm—far away from Watson—with Kelsey, Dakota, and the others didn't sound too bad. "Well, all right," she said with a grin. "I would love to join you."

Megan got up and went to tell the kids to start packing, bringing only what they could carry in their backpacks. Clay got out of his chair to prepare for the long night ahead of him when Hawthorne reached out and grabbed his hand.

"Keep her safe, Clay," she said.

"I will. I promise."

Clay walked down to the armory and collected a few vital things that Megan and the others would take with them. He hated that he was going to have to leave all of the reloading equipment behind, but it was all just too heavy to lug on the ninety mile trek. If he had more time, he would dismantle the turret and move all of the components to a hidden spot to retrieve later, but time was not on his side. He wanted to be at Watson's just after dark, and there was still a lot of preparation to do. Hopefully, the hidden door behind the vending machine would keep everything safe for a while.

After finishing up in the armory, Clay caught up with Dusty who was packing up the bag she had just unpacked.

"Sorry about all this," Clay said.

Dusty shrugged. "Don't be, I am used to being on the move. I get it."

"I am not sure what Megan told you, but I am not going to be with you guys for the first leg of this trip."

Dusty stopped packing and looked up at him, her expression demanded an explanation.

"Someone needs my help, so I am going to go help her first, and then we'll all go on together."

"Oh, okay," Dusty said somewhat indifferent as she continued to pack.

"There's one more thing," Clay said. "I need you to watch out for the others while I'm gone," he said as he lifted the LaRue's sling over his head. "You ever use one of these before?"

She shook her head.

Clay gave her a quick rundown of the functionality, how to aim, and how to load the magazines. Her familiarity with firearms made his demonstrations easy to understand. She took the rifle from him and laid it on the floor next to her bag.

"Thank you, Dusty. I'm glad you decided to join our family," Clay said and messed up her hair before turning around to walk out.

"Hey, Clay?" Dusty said, catching him just as he reached the door.

"Yeah?" he said as he turned around to look at her.

"Come back in one piece, okay?"

"I will."

Before Clay could leave, she added, "I mean, because I won't be there to save your butt this time, so you've gotta be extra careful."

Clay laughed and rolled his eyes. "You're never going to let me live that down, are you?"

She smiled, her round cheeks raised, causing her eyes to squint a little. She shook her head. "Nope!"

"Be safe, Dusty."

Chapter 32

"My patience is wearin' a bit thin here, Kelsey." Watson said as he circled around her like a lion stalking an injured gazelle. "You have everything to gain from this deal," he added.

Kelsey hadn't spoken a word since Watson had Jeremy executed right in front of her eyes. She had nothing to say to him, and she knew if she even tried to talk, Watson would find some way to exploit it. She remained silent, expressionless, staring forward as if she were studying a painting on the wall.

She had never entertained Watson's offer, not for a moment. If for no other reason than he couldn't be trusted. Any man willing to give a woman an ultimatum like that wouldn't think twice about lying. But even if he did keep his word, she would never be able to live with herself. She couldn't concede. She wouldn't. Even if it meant losing everything.

"I really just don't see what the holdup is, darlin'. It's simple. You get yourself over to Clay's, get him to

AJ POWERS

follow you, and then Silas and his men arrest Clay for murder. Then," he paused and gave her a friendly smile, "you and your daughter walk out of here, forgiven of all your debt." He stopped pacing and looked Kelsey right in the eyes. "Now, doesn't that sound like a fair deal? Think about it, you and Dakota would be free to go."

Unbound from her restraints, Kelsey fantasized about getting a second shot at Watson, but with an armed guard standing on the other side of the room, she would only succeed in getting smacked by the butt of the shotgun. Such an attempt would only bring more pain.

"Look, I know you think you're protecting your boyfriend by doing this, but it's only gonna get him killed." Watson paused while a sinister grin eased onto his face. "And he wouldn't be the only one."

Watson reached up and stroked Kelsey's cheek with his hand. His voice softened, and he transitioned away from sociopath to a caring grandfather seamlessly. "Darlin', this is the only way I can ensure Clay stays safe so he can be brought here to have a fair trial, the way we used to do things in this country."

What a load of crap, Kelsey thought. In the time she had lived on his ranch, not once did she hear of anybody accused of a crime having a fair trial. Watson was judge, jury, and executioner. "Fair trial? Just like the one you gave Jeremy?" Kelsey uttered without thinking.

That was stupid, Kelsey, she chided herself.

Watson was quite surprised by Kelsey's tenacity. He had grossly underestimated how difficult she would be to crack. Had he not been reveling in his successful attempt to get under her skin, he would have been offended by the first words she uttered during the interview. Watson saw a window of opportunity, and he knew just how to play it.

"I know I told you earlier that you had a week to decide, but wheels are in motion that I can't stop."

"Can't stop or won't stop?" Kelsey said.

"Doesn't matter," Watson replied.

Watson looked over at the guard and nodded for him to restrain Kelsey again. "You have until the morning to decide. After that, Silas and his men *will* storm that building with everything they've got. And it won't be pretty," he said shaking his head. "You have the power to stop a massacre."

The guard started walking her back to a makeshift jail cell when Watson spoke up again. "Kelsey, I've decided that you and your daughter are too much trouble to stay here on my ranch. So, one way or another, y'all are gonna be gone soon," Watson said with a serious look in his eyes. "It's up to you how that happens. Do what's best for your family. Don't sacrifice yourself or your daughter for this *boy* you hardly know. The decision is yours," he said as he opened the door, giving her one last glance. "Think of Dakota and the bright future she could have. If you are willing to give it to her, that is."

Watson closed the door and walked out with a grin on his face. He had gotten to her, and he knew it. The defenses she put up could only last so long, and he had finally broken through.

Doc was sitting at his desk in the corner of the infirmary as Watson left the cell. He glared as the old man walked by with a smirk of satisfaction visible even in the dimly lit room.

Doc wasn't stupid; he knew that they had been interrogating Kelsey for days. He didn't know what they wanted—he didn't want to—but he had never respected Watson so little since they met.

Watson walked to the front door and opened it. "Have a good night, Doc," he said without turning to look at him.

A gust of wind greeted Watson from the approaching storm. Bright flashes of lightning illuminated the darkened town, giving him a glimpse of Silas walking his way.

"Jake," Silas said as he approached, "we need to chat."

"What can I do for you, Silas?" Watson said as he began walking towards his house. "Do you have enough men yet?"

"That's what I wanted to talk to you about. I'm still a good half dozen short. Nobody's wanting to sign up to take on a kid with that kind of firepower for what you are offering," Silas said sternly. "It's barely more than what I pay my guys to take on an unarmed camp. You *have* to sweeten the pot."

"I don't think you'll need to worry about that, Silas." Watson said confidently.

"Did she agree?"

"Not yet," he replied, "but she will. I have no doubt about that."

Silas was annoyed. He didn't trust the girl to come through on anything, and he was never supportive of the plan in the first place. Despite his protest, Watson was convinced of his negotiating skills. "And what if she doesn't agree?" Silas asked with an edge in his voice.

Watson sighed. "How much more would you need?"

"Double for everyone," he hesitated for a minute. "Triple for me."

"Silas," Watson said shaking his head. "Sometimes you make me so irritated I could just kill ya."

Silas laughed. He knew he had that kind of effect on people, and he liked it. "So I'll take that as a yes?"

Watson stopped just in front of his porch and held out his hands, palms up, and felt the first drops of rain falling to the ground. "*If* Kelsey is not agreeable by morning, then yes, I will pay the men what they want."

Satisfied he had gotten his way, Silas told Watson goodnight and went back to retrieve his horse.

Watson walked inside and headed up the stairs. He needed a stiff drink to shake off the past few days—they were among the worst in recent times. He was just glad that after tomorrow those that had brought so much strife to his little town would forever be gone.

He walked into the office and flipped the light switch.

He never saw the lights come on.

****

Watson awoke a few minutes later to a throbbing pain in his head. He tried to reach up and wipe away the blood sliding down his face, but the rope wrapped around him prevented him from doing so. As his vision slowly regained focus, he saw who was sitting across the desk.

"Evening, Jake," Clay said.

"Clay, always a pleasure seeing you. What brings you to the neighborhood this fine evening?" Watson said casually, as if he had not just been pistol-whipped and bound to his chair.

"Sorry about the..." Clay said as he touched his own forehead in the same area he had struck Watson.

"I just wanted to make sure I had your undivided attention."

Watson clenched his teeth as he began to try and muscle his way out of the ropes, but to no avail. His Peacemaker was in the top right desk drawer, but it might as well have been on the other side of the house. Clay had tied him up tight. Surrendering to his current situation, Watson sighed and licked his lips. "So what do you want?"

"I just have two questions."

"Could I trouble you for a drink, first?" Watson said as he turned his head behind to look at his shelf full of various spirits. "Might make me a little more talkative."

Clay leaned back in the chair, one hand resting on the KSG-12 sitting across his lap while the other dangled off the edge of the armrest. "Why did you send Silas?"

"It's really quite simple, my dear boy. On more than one occasion, you disrespected me."

"I disrespected you?" Clay said in disbelief. "I disrespected you, so you sent a group of armed men to my house to kill me *and* my family, and then while you were at it, steal all of our stuff?"

Watson gave him an indifferent shrug. "We live in dark times, Clay. The kind of respect someone shows tells me whether I can trust them or not. And trust...Well that's the difference between an enemy and an ally."

Clay tried to come up with a suitable response, but he had none, so he allowed silence to hang in the air. Maybe Watson truly felt threatened by him. Or maybe he just found an excuse to take Clay's things. After hearing Watson give his side of the story, Clay no longer cared about the why.

The sound of the rain splashing off the window and a low rumble in the distance broke the silence that still lingered in the room. The quietness might have been awkward if Clay had not been so angry. He once again wrestled with his desire for revenge, but that wasn't his end game right now. At least not yet.

Clay shifted in his seat and leaned towards the desk, grasping the edge with his hand. "So, here's what's going to happen. I'm going to get Kelsey and Dakota, and the three of us are going to leave your little utopia, and you'll never see us again."

"Kelsey?" Watson questioned in a low growl. "That girl ain't worth all this, Clay."

"Good. Then you won't have any problem with telling me where she is so we can be on our way."

Watson shook his head disapprovingly. "What is it about her, Clay? I mean, I know she's pretty and all, but..." Watson interrupted himself. "She's damaged goods anyhow. I assure you, that little girl of hers wasn't brought here by a stork."

"I'm not worried about her past, just her future."

"I'm just sayin'. A girl like that is more suitable in a bordello. Save yourself the trouble, boy..."

Clay sat motionless, his expression hardened as Watson's words played back in his head. Before he consciously decided to, Clay sprang from his chair and planted a clean shot across Watson's face.

Clay flexed away the stiffness forced upon his knuckles by the blow to Watson's jaw. Blood began to trail from Watson's lip. He grunted through his gritted teeth and pursed his lips as he scowled at Clay. "Son, that was a very imprudent decision."

"Seemed pretty sensible to me," Clay said with a smirk.

"Yeah, I imagine it did," Watson replied before spitting out the blood that had collected on his lips.

"I'm not playing games here, Jake," Clay said as he removed his pistol from his holster and gently laid it on the desk, angling it towards Watson. "I'll give you one chance to answer my second question: where are they?"

Watson spit again, before he laughed. "Well, I hope you're prepared to man up, boy, because I ain't tellin' you squat," he said defiantly. He locked eyes with Clay, almost daring him to pull the trigger.

Picking up his gun, Clay stood up and walked around the desk. Walking past Watson, who braced for another blow to the head, Clay approached the shelf of alcohol and grabbed a bottle. He unscrewed the thin aluminum lid and held it up to his nose. He flinched as the potent smell burned his sinuses.

Clay looked down at Watson. "How about that drink?" he said as he splashed Watson in the face with the liquor.

Watson grimaced from the sting of the alcohol on his split lip. "What are you doing?"

"I wasn't kidding when I said you only got one chance."

Clay began to pour the bottle over Watson's head and then moved it over the desk. The bottle emptied, and Watson was sufficiently soaked. Clay dropped the bottle on the carpeted floor and walked over to the door. He stopped and turned around, brandishing a bright orange pistol.

"Wish I could say it was nice knowing ya, Jake," Clay said as he pulled the black hammer back on the flare gun and aimed right for Watson's chest.

"No!" Watson cried. "Fine! I'll tell you where they are. I don't want them here anyway. Just take them and be gone!" he said with a mixture of anger and fear trembling through his voice.

"Too late, Jake," Clay said.

"Please, no!" Watson began to sob.

Clay kept the gun trained on Watson's chest and sighed. "Fine, I will ask again. Where are they?"

"Kelsey is in a holding cell. It's in back of Doc's place, across from the shop."

"And Dakota?"

"Silas's camp, southern property line."

"You wouldn't be lying to me just to save your own skin, would you?" Clay said as he tightened his grip on the gun.

"No, I swear! I'll even take you there. Just get them and go!" The words rushed from his lips with an unspoken plea for his life.

Watson looked frightened, probably the first time in many years. The arrogant tyrant was in a position of power that seldom put him on the losing end of a battle, yet Clay had him weeping with no inhibitions. It was quite satisfying, probably more so than it should have been.

Clay lowered the gun as he approached the desk again. Having obtained the information he needed, he opened the gun, revealing the empty chamber inside.

Watson's eyes got big; he knew he had just been conned.

"Jake, if I was going to murder you, I would have done it the other night when I looked at you through my rifle scope."

Watson's muscles tightened up as anger surged through his body. "You son of—"

Clay threw another punch which quickly silenced the old man. Watson's head dropped to the desk with a loud thud. Clay hoped that he and the girls would be long gone by the time Watson woke up.

Picking up his shotgun that had fallen to the ground when he punched Watson the first time, Clay made his way to the front door. The storm had picked up while he was inside making the small settlement a sloshy ghost town.

After jogging the few hundred yards to the infirmary, Clay did a quick check for any activity. All quiet. He slowly climbed the few steps onto the front stoop and knocked on the door. After a few seconds, the door cracked open. A voice spoke. "Who's there? Are you hurt?"

Clay threw his shoulder into the door, sending the small bodied doctor back several feet before he fell to the ground. Clay raised the shotgun and pointed it at the man. "I don't want to hurt you, Doc. Just take me to Kelsey, and I'll be on my way."

Doc grabbed onto a nearby chair and pulled himself up from the ground. He started to walk towards Clay when a shout came from the back. "Doc? What's going on up there?"

Doc put his finger up to his lips. "Quiet," he whispered to Clay as he looked towards the back door. "Yeah!" he yelled. "Just tripped over my chair and dropped some files."

The man in the back didn't respond, and they heard the sound of a door slamming shut.

Clay looked at Doc quizzically.

"Look, I don't really know what's going on right now, but I know if she doesn't get out of here soon, Watson *will* kill her," Doc said. "The door to the jail is locked, but I can get the guard to open up."

Clay didn't want to trust him, but the look in his eyes was sincere. He didn't have much choice in the matter anyhow.

"Okay," Clay agreed.

"Follow me," Doc said and led him through a door into a mostly empty storage room. On the far side of that room was a heavy steel door. Even if Clay had tried to break through, it would have taken a very long time and a lot of loud noises.

Doc walked up to the door and turned to Clay who was leaning up against the wall next to the door, his shotgun at the ready. He rapped on the door a few times. "Hey, Hutchins, open up! I need to take a look at the prisoner, Watson's orders."

A loud clank sounded from the door, and then it opened up. The guard stepped back from the door and motioned for Doc to come in. "How come no one told me about this?" the guard asked.

"I'm telling you now," Doc replied.

Doc walked in, and the guard turned to follow. Clay came around the doorway and snuck up behind the guard. The man had no idea what was coming.

Clay swung his arm around the guard's neck, immediately applying pressure. The man began to flail his arms, pawing at Clay in a desperate attempt to ward off his attacker. As Clay reinforced his hold with his other arm, the guard's resistance lessened. Finally, his body went limp, and Clay eased him to the ground.

"Clay!" Kelsey tried to scream but only got out a whisper.

Clay ran over to the makeshift cell and tried to open it. Locked. He went back to the unconscious guard and returned to the cell with a key that opened the door. He swung the door open, and Kelsey immediately buried herself into his chest, unable to hug him with her hands cuffed behind her back.

He embraced Kelsey and held her close while she bawled. Moments before, she had prepared herself for the worst, but now she was being held by the man she loved.

He eased his hug and stepped back. A mixture of sorrow and anger flooded his mind as he looked upon her battered face. He managed to shrug off those thoughts and smile at her before giving her a brief but passionate kiss.

"We need to go get Dakota and get out of here," Clay said with urgency.

She eagerly agreed.

He had Kelsey turn around, and he examined the cuffs. The key ring he took off of the guard did not contain the key for the cuffs. Clay darted over to the guard and searched again.

"He doesn't have them," Kelsey said. "Only Watson and Silas have keys."

"Doc, do you have some paperclips, or something?" Clay asked.

"Uhh, yeah, I think so. Let me go check up front."

Before Doc reached the door, they heard the front door slam shut. "Hey Doc! Where are ya?" someone yelled.

Doc looked at his watch, "Shift change. He's early!" he said with a hushed voice as he shut the door to the room, careful not to latch it.

Clay had Kelsey and Doc move to the corner of the room while he stood a few feet behind the door. He raised the shotgun up and pressed the stock firmly into his shoulder. The footsteps drew closer but stopped just outside the slightly ajar door. Clay knew why the man hesitated, and it worried him. Any guard worth his salt would see that the door was open, even just a little bit, and know something wasn't right. Clay expected him to knock, to try and communicate with the guard inside. He didn't.

Instead, the guard waited on the other side, listening intently to try and hear anything happening on the inside. Several minutes went by; the anticipation was palpable. Clay just hoped the man hadn't snuck back out to get backup. Suddenly, the man kicked the door open and immediately met Clay's eyes. He slung his sawed off, double barrel up, but before he could put his finger on the trigger, Clay fired.

The explosive sound from the buckshot reverberated off the walls of the small room, giving everyone a terrible ringing in their ears. *Better than being dead, though*, Clay thought.

The guard had fallen straight back and was dead before he hit the ground. Double-aught buck to the chest from a few feet away wreaks a sort of havoc on the human body that Clay wished he could erase from his memory. The scene was gruesome, but unfortunately, necessary.

Clay racked the pump and chambered the next round. Anyone nearby would have heard that shot, even with the storm outside. They had to leave; no time to pick the cuffs.

"Kelsey, go sit on the bunk," he said pointing to the cot in the cell. She obeyed without question, and Clay followed her in. "You think you can get your arms out in front of you?"

"Yeah, I think so," she replied.

She lay down on the bed and lifted her knees to her chest. She grunted and grimaced as she tried to maneuver her arms down her back. The cuffs were putting a lot of pressure on her broken wrist, and it took everything in her not to scream. Clay helped wherever he could, and, in just a few seconds, her arms were in front of her. It wasn't ideal, but it would make traveling a lot easier.

"Okay, let's go," Clay said, helping her off the bed.

As they were leaving, Clay offered his hand to Doc. "Thanks for the help," he said. Doc took his hand and gave him a firm shake. "You should get out of here, if Silas or Watson shows up here..." Clay trailed off as he gestured to the bodies on the floor, though only one had expired.

"I'll be okay," Doc said. "You two be careful."

As the couple left the infirmary, they were relieved to see no one rushing towards them with guns drawn. Cautiously, they began their trek to the southern border of the property to retrieve Dakota and escape the ranch.

Chapter 33

The ground had quickly turned to slop, making it difficult to walk, especially for Kelsey. Clay reached out and put his arm around her waist, helping her keep balance and catching her when she slipped.

Time seemed to crawl as they traversed the slick, uneven terrain. Kelsey's angst grew with each step. Was Dakota safe? How were they going to get her out of Silas's place? Even if they were able to escape, where would they go after that? The questions, however, distracted her mind from the pain.

Neither of them spoke during the hike. The last thing they needed was someone hearing them before they reached Silas's camp, removing any chance of a silent infiltration and putting Dakota at even greater risk.

Leaving a trail of destruction wasn't in Clay's game plan. Killing the guard at Doc's was ill-fated, but compulsory. Fortunately, the damage was contained as it seemed no one heard the blast. They might not get so lucky with another surprise like that, so Clay needed to make every action intentional and precise.

As they walked up a slight hill, Clay suddenly stopped dead in his tracks. "What is it?" Kelsey asked with a whisper.

Clay remained silent as he stood motionless. Watching. Listening. Then Kelsey heard it, too. Voices.

"Get down," Clay said as he dropped to one knee, Kelsey did the same.

A few seconds later, the flashlights became visible. There were four of them dancing around as the men holding them slogged through the elements, traveling the opposite direction. With the group barely ten yards away, Clay and Kelsey remained motionless. Even though the visibility was poor, the strong beams from the flashlights were piercing through the dark rain with ease. All it would take was for one of them to shine the light in Clay's direction, and this rescue mission would turn into an execution. Clay's heart was thumping aggressively in his chest. He prayed the men would not spot them.

"I swear, if Hutchins doesn't have a really good excuse for not reporting back, I am going to kill him myself!" one of the men barked.

"Get in line behind me," another said, followed by laughter amongst the group.

Clay remembered Doc calling the guard Hutchins. The men were probably wondering why he had not returned from his prisoner detail. Clay was rife with worry. As soon as those men reached the infirmary, they were going to figure out what had happened and make a mad dash back to camp on high alert. Time was running out.

Clay and Kelsey allowed the men thirty yards or so before they continued their journey to Silas's settlement. Normally, Clay would have waited a little longer, but given the circumstances—increasing rain and a limited timeline—he opted to move. As they reached the top of the hill, Clay noticed a strong smell of burning wood and a faint light in the distance. They were getting close.

When the settlement became visible, Clay could distinguish three separate cabins and a couple of outhouses. Two of the cottages were dark, but the third shone with flickering firelight and rang with drunken laughter.

"I am going to go in for a closer look. Stay here," Clay said to Kelsey.

"All right," Kelsey replied. Even though there was nothing to hide behind, the darkness of the night, combined with the heavy downpour made her as good as invisible to anyone in those cabins. She crouched down, however, and kept low to reduce visibility even further.

Clay readied his shotgun, ensuring the gun was feeding from the buckshot magazine tube—he had loaded the other side with wax slugs he had made himself. Before leaving Kelsey, Clay handed her a pistol. It was Megan's FN9. He felt the additional magazine capacity might come in handy. "Only use it if you *absolutely* must," he told her while handing her a spare magazine.

He squeezed her hand briefly before he took off for the illuminated cabin up ahead. As he advanced to the building, he slowed his jog to a walk. Keeping the shotgun shouldered but tilted downward, he was ready for combat at a moment's notice. About ten feet out, Clay transitioned to a crouch and moved more stealthily. The sounds of clanking glass and laughter became clearer, more pronounced.

He finally reached the side of the cabin and put his back up against the wall. Staying crouched, he awkwardly side-stepped towards a nearby window. The noises grew louder with each stride. He heard some men joking around, accusing one another of cheating and other typical banter. It sounded like they were playing a game.

He reached the window and carefully peeked through the lower corner. He didn't see much. He ducked down and moved beneath the window to get a look from the other side. He saw three men sitting at a poker table. There were four empty chairs around them—probably for the four men that passed moments ago. He got a good look around the cabin; it was just one large room. No sign of Silas or Dakota.

Clay made his way down to the other side of the cabin and peered out from around the corner, making sure the path was clear. He ran over to the second cabin and quickly determined it was vacant. Dakota *must* be in the third. When Clay reached the cabin, he caught a quick glance through the window, but it was too dark to make anything out. There was no real evidence that Dakota or Silas were inside, but his gut was telling him otherwise.

The front door was the only viable way inside. The windows were too small for Clay to fit through— quietly anyway—and there was no back entrance. Clay was getting ready to walk into the unknown. He had no idea who might be waiting for him on the inside. He didn't know the layout of the interior, and worst of all, he didn't know if Dakota was even in the cabin. The dwindling time wasn't helping his anxiety, either.

As Clay moved to the front door, he looked over in the general direction of where he had left Kelsey. He couldn't see her, and he wasn't sure if she could see him. Between his nerves being wrecked and the frigid rain, Clay had trouble steadying his hands. He took a deep breath to calm down. He thought about Kelsey—safely in Northfield, free from Watson's oppressive reign. The exultant thought of her face was calming to Clay—he was ready.

The door was unlocked, something that surprised Clay. He opened it, taking great care to not make a sound. He stepped inside and closed it most of the way but leaving it unlatched. He quickly became chilled from his sopping wet clothes clinging to his body. Somehow he felt warmer outside where the sting of the pelting rain made him much less aware of the wetness of his clothes.

The room was dark—just a subtle glow from the dying embers in the stove—too dark to see. Clay had a flashlight but did not want to use it lest it draw attention to his presence. He waited just inside the door until a bright flash of lightning illuminated the room. It was brief, but it lasted long enough for Clay to take a mental snapshot of the room's layout. The last thing he needed was to smash his knee into a table and cause whoever might be inside to wake up.

Like Hawthorne's place, there were two doors on the back wall. Clay assumed each led to a bedroom, but he couldn't know for sure. There was only one way to find out. Carefully, he navigated around the furnishings from memory, using the sporadic flash of lightning to keep his bearings. He was able to stay quiet, only managing to bump into a single chair; it hardly made a sound.

With a small step towards the left door, the pounding in Clay's heart grew exponentially. The thought of Silas being asleep inside instilled an array of emotions, and not knowing how he would react when facing Charlie's killer, Clay worked to suppress them. He had to keep his cool. Even if he were to shoot Silas, Clay knew he'd then have to deal with the three men playing cards in the cabin just fifty feet away.

Clay quietly opened the door on the left. With his shotgun leading the way, he moved into the room and turned the flashlight on just long enough to see a small body asleep in the bed. Relief washed over him at the sight of Dakota. He didn't think Watson was the kind of guy who would harm a child, but he had his doubts about Silas having that kind of compassion. Not after Charlie.

Though seeing her brought respite, he knew they were still in danger. He had to manage to wake her without startling her, then leave the cabin, get Kelsey, and escape the ranch without anyone noticing—all before Watson regained consciousness. A daunting task to say the least, but finding her without being detected was a good start.

Kneeling next to the bed, Clay whispered in a barely audible hum, "Pssst! Dakota." He gently rubbed her back in an effort to ease her out of her slumber. Dakota jolted her body and went rigid. Then her muscles eased, and she turned her head to look at Clay.

"Dakota, it's me. Clay."

She rubbed her eyes but could see him no better than before. "Clay?" she said with a groggy voice. She wasn't loud, but she wasn't quiet, either.

Clay put his finger up to his mouth. "Shhhhhh. We need to be *very* quiet right now, okay?"

"Okay," she whispered, matching Clay's voice.

"Your mama's just outside. I am going to carry you out of here and we're going to leave, but I need you to be as quiet as a mouse, okay? Can you do that for me?"

"Okay" she whispered.

Clay put his shotgun down on the bed as he picked up the little girl . Holding her in his left arm, he reached down and grabbed the shotgun with his right. "You ready?" he asked.

"Mmmm hmmm" she said, still not fully awake yet.

Clay opened the door all the way and inched out of the room. He slowly made his away across the floor, trying to reverse the image in his head of the living room layout. About halfway across, he heard the sound of a revolver hammer being wrenched back.

"That's far enough," a voice from behind said.

Clay froze. His mind riddled with the various outcomes the present situation could have. None of them seemed very appealing.

The man turned on a lamp, and the entire room lit up. Clay was even closer to the door than he had realized. *So close.*

"Drop it," the man demanded.

Clay sighed as he released his grip on the KSG. Dakota jumped as the shotgun impacted the wooden floor.

"Now, turn around. *Slowly.*"

Clay complied.

"I'm glad we finally got a chance to meet. I'm Silas," he paused and stared Clay down. "I'm gonna go out on a limb here and assume you are Clay. Am I right?" he said with a grin.

Silas was just a few feet away, aiming a heavy-duty revolver at them. The large bore suggested it was a .44 magnum. A burst of anger shot through Clay's body as he realized it looked like the same gun Silas was carrying when Charlie had been shot. Silas's grip on the revolver was firm, his hand as steady as a surgeon's. His finger hovered just in front of the hair trigger, ready to complete the transaction.

Clay raised his free hand slowly into the air. "Listen, Silas, just let Dakota go, and you can do whatever you need to do to me. She's just a kid for crying out loud," he pleaded.

"I don't think you're in any position to negotiate," Silas said. He gestured to the floor with his pistol. "Put the girl down, and put both your hands up." He looked at Dakota. "And *you,* go back to your room!"

Clay crouched down, and gently let go of Dakota. She slid out of his arms and as soon as her feet hit the ground, she made a beeline for her room. She shut the door, jumped into bed, and put the pillow over her head. Her sobbing was audible to both men.

Silas stood still; his gun remained locked on Clay. There was a hate in his eyes that sent a chill down Clay's spine, the kind he usually felt when he heard the terrifying shrieks of the night.

"You know, I really just can't decide," Silas said with indecision in his voice.

"What's that?" Clay felt obligated to reply.

"Should I turn you over to Watson? Or just kill you right now. Of course, that's assuming you didn't go and kill Watson before you came here."

"So sorry to hear of your difficult dilemma," Clay said dryly.

Silas laughed. "I appreciate the sarcasm. It has made my decision much easier."

He straightened his arm holding the revolver and rested his finger on the trigger. "Nobody likes a—"

The sound of multiple gunshots fired from nearby caused both men to cower. The front window shattered and Silas grunted, grabbing at his neck.

Clay had no idea what had just happened, but there was no time to try and figure it out.

While Silas was reacting to the bullet that grazed his neck, Clay charged him, ramming his shoulder into Silas's chest. He picked the man up off the ground and slammed him into the back wall in-between the two doors. The air in Silas's lungs quickly escaped, leaving him gasping for a refill. Clay heard Silas's pistol hit the ground but had no idea where it landed.

Before Clay could react, Silas head-butted him and broke free. Clay's vision flashed as an excruciating pain soared through his head. His right eye quickly became impaired with the copious amount of blood pouring out of the gash just above his eyebrow.

Both men were stunned. Clay tried to clear his vision while Silas struggled to catch his breath.

"Silas!" a voice from out front shouted. "You okay?"

The men from the other cabin had heard the shots and were outside investigating. Clay darted over to the shotgun and picked it up. Just as he retrieved the gun, the front door exploded open and one of Silas's men came through. Clay fired, dropping the man immediately.

Clay turned just as Silas was rushing him. He knocked the shotgun out of his hands and landed several consecutive blows to Clay's face. Able to finally deflect one of Silas's attacks, Clay punched him in the shoulder where he had been shot two weeks ago.

Silas let out a booming roar; the pain only seemed to fuel his rage. Ignoring the throbbing pain that followed, Silas grabbed Clay and threw him into a wall.

Several more gunshots erupted outside.

"Contact!" one of the men screamed, and all of the sudden, it sounded like the OK Corral.

Kelsey.

While a war raged on outside, both Silas and Clay exchanged vicious hits, quickly wearing each other down. Clay took another swing, but his body was fatigued, and his punches were slow and sloppy. Silas evaded the attack and grabbed Clay's arm, throwing him to the ground next to the stove.

He pressed Clay's face up against the blazing cast-iron stove, causing a scream that was matched by the intensity of the pain. A surge of adrenaline and anger allowed Clay to overpower Silas, throwing him off. Silas stumbled back several feet before tripping over a chair. As Silas hit the ground, his eyes rested on the shotgun lying on the floor just a short distance away.

At the same time, Clay spotted Silas's revolver and scrambled to pick it up. As Clay spun around, gun in hand, he heard Silas pumping the shotgun.

The sound was deafening.

For a moment, Clay's eyes locked with Silas's. Fear and anger was all they saw in each other. Both men wanted the other dead, and for one of them, that moment had finally arrived. Suddenly, Silas's stare went blank. He dropped to the floor hard; he made no attempt to get up.

Clay was still aiming the gun where Silas had been standing. The smoke drifting from the muzzle quickly dissipating as it rose into the air. Clay's ears were ringing, and everything was slightly muffled, as if he were submerged in water.

Clay walked over to Silas and looked down at his dead body. He wasn't sure where he had aimed, and the recoil from the extraordinarily powerful cartridge was far greater than what he had anticipated, but the shot could not have been more ideal, right near his heart. It's why there was no last attempt to fire upon Clay, why there were no departing words. Silas was dead before he hit the ground.

The sound of approaching footsteps snapped Clay out of his daze. He looked towards the door just as it burst open.

Clay dropped down to his knees just as the man fired. The blast was high, missing him entirely, and devastating the wall behind him. Clay raised the gun and pulled the trigger. The hand cannon kicked back wildly once again; Clay knew his shot was off.

The man screamed as he stumbled back out the door. He tripped off the small step and fell backwards into the mud. He was clutching his shoulder and groaning in pain. Before Clay could stand up, a second man ran through the door. This time, Clay's shot was true, and the man dropped to the floor without protest.

Clay rose to his feet and quickly made his way over to the wounded man outside. He was struggling to get up off the ground when Clay came up to him and pulled back the hammer on the revolver. The man froze.

"Please," he said while still gripping his shoulder. "Don't kill me."

Clay kept the gun trained on him, not because he was considering an execution, but rather to prevent the man from trying anything foolish.

Clay saw Kelsey out of the corner of his eye. She walked up next to him and remained silent. Her expression was ice cold as she looked at the wounded man. Clay looked over at her and made sure she was okay before returning his attention to the man in front of him.

"Go," Clay said as he pointed back towards the front of the property, "and when you get there, you tell Watson what happened. You tell him that he brought this upon himself. You tell him that if he even *thinks* about coming after Kelsey again, he will share the same fate as Silas. Got it?"

The man didn't say a word. He just scrambled to his feet and ran towards Watson's. As his image faded to black, Kelsey turned and threw her shackled arms over Clay's head, and gave him a fierce embrace. She began to cry as the adrenaline wore off, and the full weight of the last ten minutes came to the surface. Despite the cold rain soaking them to the core, Clay wanted to stay in that moment forever. But time was not their ally.

"Is she in there? Is she okay?" Kelsey quivered, fear holding her from entering the cabin by herself.

He squeezed her tight, then eased her hands back over his head. "Come on," he said as he leaned towards the door, "let's go get your daughter."

Chapter 34

Clay exhaled deeply. The warmth of his breath bouncing off the towel and back into his face was incredible. He slowly transitioned the towel to the top of his head and began drying his hair before draping the cloth over his shoulder. He was still sopping wet, but at least his head was dry.

Kelsey was doing her best to warm up Dakota who was wrapped in a towel as well as a blanket. Despite the extra layers, Dakota was shivering like an Eskimo, and her lips were still a tinge blue. Kelsey lay her down in bed and placed another blanket on top of her.

"Get some sleep, Koty. I love you," Kelsey said with a warm smile that contrasted her frozen face.

It had taken them nearly five days to reach Liberty. After leaving Watson's ranch, they picked up a pack that Clay had stashed a few miles to the north and traveled as far as they could before hunkering down for the night in a convenience store. Between physical exhaustion and injuries, they traveled much slower than Clay had anticipated. The constant downpour didn't help much either. It rained nearly the entire time, only easing about three miles outside of Liberty. By the time they reached Vlad's, it had become little more than a drizzle.

Megan and the others had left two days before, according to Vlad, which meant they stayed longer than they were supposed to. He wondered how far they had traveled. The notion of getting a bit of shut-eye and eating some grub before quickly leaving to try and catch up with them was an idea that he was forced to abandon. Kelsey and Dakota were tired. *He* was tired. The thought of continuing the rest of the journey without some true downtime was unbearable at best. They would stay in Liberty for two nights and leave early on Tuesday.

Kelsey walked over to Clay as she tried to wring water out of her hair with the towel. The color was slowly returning to her cheeks. Her eyes filled with some life again. She rested her head on his chest and wrapped an arm around him. A sigh of contentment escaped her lips as she closed her eyes and held him.

Clay kissed the top of her head and gently rubbed her back. Kelsey giggled as she lived in the moment. She was in the arms of the man she loved, her daughter was just a few feet away, and Jake Watson was out of her life. It was the perfect moment.

"It just doesn't feel real," Kelsey said.

Clay looked at her quizzically.

"Me. Dakota. Being away from the ranch. It's like a wonderful dream that I worry I am going to wake up from."

Clay smiled and stroked her hair. "It's not a dream."

Kelsey broke away from the comfort of Clay's embrace so she could kiss him. "Thank you," she said before kissing him again.

A muffled "Ewww" erupted from beneath a pile of blankets on the bed, creating a humorous but awkward moment for the blushing couple.

Clay glanced down at his watch. It was nearly noon, but none of them had slept much since leaving the ranch. "Well," Clay said reluctantly, "I'm going to go back to my room to try to warm up some and maybe get some sleep. You should probably do the same."

Kelsey smiled. She was overwhelmed with total joy, a feeling she truly hadn't felt since long before the ash fell. "Yes...sleep sounds good," she said as her smile faded to fatigue.

Clay kissed her again, this time a quick peck as to avoid further commentary from the three year old on the other side of the room. "Sleep well," he said, then walked out the door.

He walked a few feet down the hall and went into his room. Vlad's "hotel" was completely vacant except for the three of them. It was strange having a house that large, that nice, and that warm all to themselves, even if they were just taking up two small partitions of a large bedroom on the second floor.

Clay stripped down to nothing and kicked his soaked clothes into the corner, creating a loud thwop as his pants landed on the floor. He would have to figure out how to dry them later since he neglected to pack a change of clothes. He was rather preoccupied before leaving the tower, and the foresight to pack such essentials didn't cross his mind.

He gave a sigh of relief as he plopped down into the cozy bed and buried himself beneath piles of sheets and blankets. He was finally dry and could actually feel himself start to warm up. He felt incredible. He felt...relaxed.

Gradually, the stress from the events of last week were melting away. Peace was creeping back into his thoughts, something that had been largely absent over the last month.

It didn't take long before his eyes got heavy and random thoughts began to zoom through his head, a sign that sleep was nigh. Suddenly, a knock on the door roused him from his tranquil state and startled him, he sat up quickly.

His first movement was defensive, but he quickly remembered where he was and his tension eased.

Another knock.

Clay cleared his throat. "Who is it?"

"It is Boris," Vlad said with a chuckle.

"Hang on," Clay said as he struggled to pull himself out of bed.

He grabbed the towel from the floor and wrapped it around his waist before opening the door.

Vlad was standing there with some folded clothes in his hand. He immediately joked about Clay's attire—or the lack thereof—which drew laughter from both men. Vlad was aware that Clay was trying to rest, so he got straight to the point.

"I forgot your sister gave me letter for you," he said as he held up a piece of paper folded multiple times. "She is very lovely girl, reminds me much of Olesya."

Clay nodded, "She's pretty awesome."

Clay looked down at the clothing Vlad was holding. "Oh, yes!" Vlad exclaimed, "I bring you change of clothing," he said as he handed them to Clay.

"Thank you, Vlad," Clay said with heartfelt gratitude. Vladimir Bezrukov was as good of a friend as one could have anymore. Clay examined the shirt and noticed it was a black button up, beneath that a pair of nice khaki slacks. "Is this what passes for lounge wear these days?" Clay joked, but was still grateful for some dry clothing.

"Did you notice activities at center of town when you arrived?" Vlad asked.

Clay thought about it, but couldn't recall. The tunnel vision was so bad by that point, he was surprised he found his way to Vlad's, much less notice things going on around town. He shrugged his shoulders, "Not really."

"Tonight is town feast Mayor Shelton hosts every year. Big event in middle of town. Food, music, dancing," Vlad said as he mysteriously produced a tie and held it out in front of him. "You two have fun."

"Wow," Clay said, completely caught off guard. "That sounds great and all, but we're not even residents here, so I—"

"Mayor personally ask for you to be there."

"Well, I would hate to be rude," Clay said, "but what about—"

Vlad interrupted again, "Do not worry about little girl. I have Olesya watch her. No problem at all. I keep an eye on them both; I have much to do in my store anyway."

Clay conceded, not that he had much of a choice in the matter. "Sounds great!"

"Festivities start at seven," Vlad said as he turned and walked back down the hall. "Enjoy, my friend."

Clay closed the door and put the folded clothes on a dresser up against the wall. He walked over and sat down on the bed and unfolded the piece of paper.

Clay,

We waited an extra day for you, please don't be mad. It was against my better judgment to leave without you, but I will respect your wishes and continue on anyway. The rain smocks you made for each of the kids last year are working great and allowed us to travel when the weather wasn't too severe.

I looked over a map with Vlad. I am hoping that we will arrive in Northfield by next Sunday, Monday at the latest.

Vlad and Olesya have shown us a great deal of hospitality. He is every bit as great as you mentioned and more. Please give him my deepest thanks.

Take care, little brother. We will see you when you arrive.

Megan
P.S. I'm proud of you.

****

After his fifth attempt to properly make a knot with the tie, Clay gave up and tossed it on the bed. He undid the top button of his shirt and left well enough alone. There was a dresser in his room which had a small mirror on top. Clay fiddled with his hair which was still damp from the bath he took fifteen minutes ago. He couldn't remember the last time he had soaked in hot water for that long. It was almost euphoric, and he caught himself dozing off more than once.

Unfortunately—probably for Olesya—the bottom of the tub was a disaster afterwards. He wanted to clean it out before he left, but he was already running late.

It had been years since Clay looked in a mirror for mere vanity. Such worries were laughable in the world now. But tonight was different. Tonight had Clay's stomach is knots, and he wanted to do everything he could to impress Kelsey.

He stepped back from the mirror for a wider view of himself. He brushed some lint off his sleeves and buttoned the cuffs. With a quick smirk of approval, he left the room and headed downstairs to meet Kelsey in the living room.

As Clay rounded the corner, he stopped just before taking the first step down the stairs. His mouth hung slack as he stared in awe at the beauty down below. She smiled at the unrealized compliment Clay was paying with his involuntary pause.

"Wow," Clay whispered, nearly in disbelief.

From the moment Clay met Kelsey, he thought she was the most beautiful girl he had ever seen. He knew that if he felt that way about her in a world such as the one they lived in, that she would be indescribable in less harsh circumstances. His imagination completely undersold the reality.

Kelsey's blush was camouflaged beneath some light makeup applied to her cheeks. She wore her hair up, her bangs framing her face. She was wearing a ruby shade of lipstick, and the dark lines surrounding her eyelids created the perfect accent to her beautiful green eyes.

It was then that he saw the dress. There was nothing special about the dress itself; it looked like the type of garment one would find at a thrift store, yet Kelsey made it work. She made it look stunning.

Without saying anything, Kelsey walked away from the stairs and headed into the center of the living room. Clay quickly made his way down the steps and walked over to her, giving her a kiss. "You look...beautiful."

Kelsey smiled. "Thank you," she said giving him a quick once-over. "You're not too bad yourself."

Clay noticed a clock on the wall and saw they were late. "Shall we?" he said as he stuck his arm out.

Kelsey hooked her arm through his. "We shall."

They walked outside and could hear the band warming up in the distance. Kelsey waved to Dakota who was playing hopscotch with Olesya. Kelsey's angst about leaving Dakota with a stranger quickly subsided as she saw the two interact. She trusted Clay, and Clay trusted Vlad; therefore Kelsey trusted Vlad.

Clay and Kelsey took their time getting to the feast. Though they didn't want to be late, they didn't want to rush themselves either. They casually walked through the neighborhood and decided to just arrive when they arrived.

They sat down at their table around 7:05. Clay noticed dozens of other people still straggling in and no longer felt so bad about being a few minutes late himself.

The whole setup was quite nice. The gazebo in the middle of town had been converted to a 360 degree stage for the band. A sturdy, albeit crude, construction of an elevated floor was built around the pavilion allowing for diners and dancers to move about without slipping in the mud. There were candlelit lanterns hanging all over the place, providing light and adding a romantic ambience. Each table had a bouquet of wildflowers and three candles, as well as a pitcher of water and some cups.

As the tables all around filled, Clay saw Mayor Shelton stand up in the middle of the gazebo. He welcomed everyone and thanked them for partaking in the annual festivities. After a short speech, he blessed the meal and gave the band a thumbs up to begin.

Not five minutes after the music started, Clay and Kelsey were served their dinner. On the plate was a generous helping of chicken drenched in a delectable gravy. Asparagus and mashed potatoes steamed on the side. It looked incredible, smelled delicious, and tasted divine.

Clay had to force himself not to scarf the whole thing down. Neither he nor Kelsey had eaten much in the past few days, but they both fought the urge to eat like animals and took small, reasonable bites. Kelsey closed her eyes as she chewed on the tender piece of chicken. It was cooked to perfection.

Clay looked on with admiration. He loved seeing her smile; seeing her happy. Kelsey was embarrassed as she noticed him watching her eat and ignoring his own plate which was cooling more by the minute.

"Sorry," Clay excused himself for his bad manners. "I can't help it. I just get lost in your eyes."

Kelsey swallowed her bite, "Well, when you put it all romantic like that and such," she said before taking a sip of water.

Clay pulled himself away from her eyes and returned to his food. He savored each bite, as if he were trying to study the taste like a food critic would. He was nearly finished with his plate when they were interrupted by the mayor.

"Good evening, Clay. I am glad you could make it," he said then turned his attention to Kelsey. "Why don't you introduce me to your lovely guest," he said.

Clay stood to his feet and shook Shelton's hand. "Mr. Shelton, this is Kelsey Lambert. Kelsey, this is Barry Shelton, mayor of Liberty."

Shelton shook Kelsey's hand, "Pleasure to meet you, Ms. Lambert."

"Likewise, sir," Kelsey replied. "And I just want to add how wonderful this all is," she said looking around at the party. "You are so kind to let us join you for this event."

Shelton waved his hand, "It's nothing. We look at Clay like an honorary citizen here. He is welcome anytime," he said giving Clay a pat on the back. "You as well, Ms. Lambert."

Kelsey smiled. "Thank you."

"So, did y'all get enough to eat?" Shelton asked.

"Oh yeah!" Clay said as he absent-mindedly rested his hand on his stomach. "Don't remember the last time I was this full."

Shelton looked over to Kelsey. She simply nodded with a smile.

"Good! Well I'll leave you two alone then. Y'all are welcome to stay in town as long as you need to. In the meantime," Shelton looked towards the dance floor as a few couples were making their way there, "enjoy the rest of your evening."

Shelton turned and walked away to socialize with some folks a couple tables over. The band started up again, and Clay saw the dance floor spark to life. It was an upbeat song that had people moving all around. Each couple had their own style of dancing, regardless of the tempo of the music. It was quite a sight to see.

Clay had never danced a day in his life—not unless he counted the ten minutes at the Junior High Spring Formal before his date got sick, and they had to leave. Though he didn't care about such things, he couldn't stop himself from asking, "May I have this dance?"

Kelsey smiled, "Absolutely!"

They moved in and out of the staggered tables and made their way to the dance floor. Clay knew, as the man, he was supposed to lead, but he didn't have a clue how. Before he made a suggestion, Kelsey put her arm around his back and rested the other over his shoulder.

She winced when her wrist bumped against his arm, but quickly suppressed the pain. She knew that with time it would heal, and she wasn't going to let it spoil the moment.

Careless of the type of music playing, Clay and Kelsey danced as if a sappy love song was filling the air. As their eyes locked, they became isolated in their own little world. There were no longer other people dancing around them. There were no Screamers preparing to terrorize the night. Buildings and other structures were not crumbling from years of neglect. There were no food shortages to worry about, or preparations for the long, harsh winters. None of those things existed right now. Just two souls, deeply in love, living in the moment.

Kelsey stood on her toes and kissed Clay passionately.

Life is good.

****

Back at Vlad's, Clay found himself sitting in an oversized recliner in the living room. Directly in front of him was a wall which once had a flat screen TV hanging from it—the mounting brackets were still securely in place. He closed his eyes and pressed into the back of the chair as it fully reclined.

He heard Kelsey coming down the stairs. She had traded in her dress for a pair of sweatpants and a baggy t-shirt courtesy of Vlad's department store.

"Koty's out cold; Olesya wore her out," Kelsey said as she came across the room to Clay.

She walked around behind the chair and began to rub one of Clay's shoulders. He thought nothing could have been more relaxing than the bath he had taken earlier, but he was wrong. After a few minutes, she moved her hand to the top of his head, running her fingers through his hair, and gently scratching his scalp. Clay's eyes became heavy.

Much to his disappointment, Kelsey removed her hand from his head. She walked around to the front of the chair and sat in his lap. Clay's disappointment was short-lived as she hugged him and rested her head on his shoulder. He felt complete, like the last piece of a puzzle being snapped into place.

They sat in silence, just listening to each other's breathing. It was soothing, and further prompted sleep for Clay. He felt the slightest of trembles go through Kelsey's body. He turned his head and looked at her. Her mouth was open like she wanted to say something.

"I was scared I would never see you again," she finally spoke with a wavering voice. "When Silas shot Jeremy, I," she paused, her bottom lip began to quiver as she replayed the horrible event in her head. She started to cry softly.

Clay pulled her in closer and gave her a gentle squeeze. He wasn't sure what to say to make things better. He wasn't sure there was anything that could be said. A traumatic event like that wasn't going to be washed away with a few positive sentiments. He, of all people, knew that. But still, he wished he had some magic solution to make all the nightmares disappear. There were few things harder for Clay than watching someone he loved be in such great pain and know there was nothing he could do to help.

"All I really remember is his eyes. His hollow, lifeless eyes that stared up at me from the floor." Her tears had stopped and her voice had calmed. "Jeremy wasn't the greatest guy in the world, but he saved my life that night," she said with reverence. It's how she decided she would remember him.

Clay had not been all that fond of Jeremy, but he agreed with Kelsey. Even though he had, in essence, been the catalyst for the whole mess, he didn't deserve to die because of it. Jeremy had not been the one that had ordered Silas and his men to attack. And if he was being truthful with Kelsey, he had no idea Watson was even considering such a thing. If Jeremy was guilty of something, it was a lack of sound judgment, not malicious intent. Believing that made Clay feel a little better.

Kelsey sighed, but then smiled as her mind snapped back to the present. She was in an upscale house protected from external threats. Her daughter was asleep upstairs, she was in a cozy chair holding Clay, and they were well on their way to the start of a new life—together. These warm thoughts were able to melt away the chill from the haunting images of her final days at Watson's ranch.

Clay felt a pang of guilt settle into his stomach. Kelsey and Dakota had nearly lost their lives; Jeremy *did* lose his—all of which might have been avoided if Clay hadn't been so harsh with Kelsey after Charlie's wake. He couldn't fathom what life would be like without her, and yet, because his emotions had controlled him like a puppet, he sent her back into the lion's den. He would have never forgiven himself if...He shuddered at the thought.

"Kelsey... Please forgive me."

Kelsey leaned back from his shoulder so she could look at him. "Forgive you for what?" she asked.

"The things I said to you...after Charlie's funeral...I didn't mean any of it."

She leaned towards him and kissed him. "I know that, Clay," she said with a smile as she returned to his shoulder. "Believing that you still loved me is what kept me going while sitting in that godforsaken cell." She put her hand in his and stroked his palm. "I believe everything happens for a reason, Clay. I may never know why, but I do know nothing is by accident."

Clay's mom had told him that very thing when he was younger. There was no such thing as a random event. Every experience had a purpose; every action had an impact. He believed it—for a while—until he watched his family die one by one while he sat on the sidelines, powerless to save them. He asked God many nights why He would allow such devastation, why He would allow him to carry such burdens. The idea that everything happened for a reason didn't quite sit well with Clay after that.

But, as he sat there holding Kelsey in his arms, he couldn't help but wonder if there was some truth to it after all. Though the past was chocked full of pain and sorrow, without those events, he knew he would not be where he was at that very moment: content, in love, and excited for the future.

And with that realization, Clay would never be the same. He never wanted to be the same.

It was love at first sight with Kelsey. He had never felt that way about anyone, and he knew that despite all the wrong in the world, with Kelsey by his side, things would be right. He felt completed when they were together, and the thought of being apart from her made him depressed.

Kelsey was starting to drift to sleep. Her eyes were closed, and Clay didn't want to wake her, but he needed to tell her what was on his mind. "Kelsey?" he asked while rubbing her back.

"Hmm?" she said with a vanishing voice.

Clay's heart was pounding—more so than he could recall even in the most intense of battles. He knew exactly what he wanted to say, yet he was unable to speak. He was crippled with fear, yet bouncing with excitement.

Kelsey was drifting fast. His voice and his thoughts finally reconciled. "Marry me, Kelsey," his voice barely above a whisper.

He sat in silence as he watched for a reaction. Her eyes were still closed; her expression remained unchanged. Clay could feel his pulse throbbing in his neck. Had she fallen asleep before he spoke? Was he going to have to find the courage to go through this moment all over again?

Then, he noticed a single tear collecting at the corner of her eyelid. After a moment, it grew large enough and slid down her cheek. Her lips slowly curled up, and her eyes fluttered open. She sat up and stared into his eyes.

The emotions swelling in her heart choked her response. More tears danced from her eyes as she responded the only way she could—an emphatic nod. After a kiss, a whispered, "Yes" escaped her lips followed by an elated giggle. She grabbed the back of his head and pulled him close. They kissed passionately until her voice returned.

"I love you, Clay."

****

Clay was up before dawn, packing for the rest of their journey to Northfield. Vlad, Shelton, and a few others from town had donated several goods to help with the second leg of the voyage. Both Clay and Kelsey were astonished with the continual generosity the community demonstrated. He would miss his frequent trips to the little town, but he vowed to visit at least once or twice a year in the future.

He zipped up his pack and checked a smaller backpack Vlad had given to him to help with some of the overflow of supplies. Everything was in order. His shotgun and pistol were fully loaded. His clothes were not only dry, but clean, compliments of Olesya. He felt utterly spoiled by the last two days; he would never be able to repay everyone for what they had done. He knew with certainty, though, that they didn't do it because they expected something in return. In mankind's darkest hour, their acts of humanity stood out all the more.

Clay and Kelsey had agreed they would leave around 8:00. It was 5:45, and Clay was finished with his pre-trip checks, so he decided to head out and take a stroll around town.

He always admired the all-stone façades the houses displayed. Unlike the vast amounts of cookie cutter subdivisions littered around the city, each house in Liberty had its own unique look and feel. This, coupled with the ad-hoc renovations that occurred post collapse, gave the neighborhood a one of a kind appearance.

The town was quiet with the exception of the occasional chirping bird or barking dog. Using the light from the solar powered street lamps, Clay made his way down the road to the gated entrance. He was surprised to see Mayor Shelton on duty with another armed man.

"Good morning, Clay," Shelton said before taking a sip of tea from his thermos.

"Morning, Mr. Shelton."

"I think you may be the only one who calls me that. Please, call me Barry."

"All right, Barry. What are you doing out here manning the gate?" Clay asked in such a way to imply Shelton's status in the community would discourage him from such jobs.

"Why wouldn't I?" Shelton replied.

Clay shrugged. "I dunno. You're a pretty important guy around town, and being gatekeeper can be a dangerous job."

"That it is," Shelton reaffirmed. "But there's a saying I've lived by for quite some time, 'Don't ask someone to do something you aren't willing to do yourself.'"

Clay nodded. "Yeah, I've heard that before."

"Before all this 'mayor' stuff, I was just another survivor, hoping to keep my family alive another day. Eventually, as our town grew and stabilized, a hierarchy of leadership was necessary. Not to cause separation between the people, but to keep the unity." Shelton paused to take another sip of his steaming tea from the metal canister. He smacked his lips as the liquid warmed him, and then continued, "Yeah, there are a few of us who have some authority around here, but the first rule was that no abled-bodied man was exempt from certain tasks, which includes me."

Clay had a whole newfound respect for Barry Shelton, if it were possible. It was why Liberty was the kind, generous, and prosperous town that it was. Not because of strong, defensible gates, or thriving crops and livestock. It was from a strong foundation of leadership that inspired each and every citizen to do their part. Not from the threat of force or intimidation, but from the desire to help their fellow man.

Clay looked out towards the horizon. The sky began to turn several hues of purple as the sun started its ascent. Clay thought about what Shelton said and realized good leadership is born and cultivated within an individual. It's not a skill inherited with a position of authority, but one that is learned—usually through trials and tribulations.

Though Clay hadn't asked for this life, it was the one he was given. Like Shelton, Clay too was just a survivor at one point. Then, over time, he became the leader of a small group of people who depended on him with their very lives—he became the leader of his family.

As the sun crept higher into the sky, Clay noticed he needed to squint a little more than usual. Had it been that long since he'd really watched a sunrise? Or was there something different? Then he noticed them. Rays of light punching through the layer of ash. He counted at least a half dozen of them casting in various directions. They were faint, but they were there. And they were magnificent.

And just like that, the rays faded to nothingness, and the sun returned to the hazy, floating orb in the sky he was used to seeing. Clay could once again glance at it briefly without hurting his eyes. He was still in awe with what he had just witnessed, and the expression on his face must have matched his thoughts.

"You saw it, too?" Shelton asked as he stood beside Clay.

Clay found that no words could appropriately capture his feelings, so he simply nodded.

"So long as there is hope, there's a will to carry on," Shelton said.

"Amen," Clay replied.

Epilogue

Kelsey walked out of the house and sat down in a rocking chair. A warm breeze wafted through the field, eventually reaching her on the front porch. It was a beautiful day, the third one in the past month. More and more, the ash in the atmosphere gave way to clearer skies, allowing direct sunlight to once again strike the surface of the earth. Dakota and some of the other children gasped in awe the first time their eyes observed the twinkling stars of the heavens. The moment brought everyone to tears.

As the breeze passed through, Kelsey closed her eyes and soaked it in: the sound of leaves dancing on the branches; wind chimes colliding; and children laughing as they chased each other through the rows of corn. It was indescribably beautiful.

She looked across a small field and watched as Geoff pushed Wyatt on a tree swing. He laughed and screamed with glee as he soared higher and higher. Ruth sat on the porch, rocking back and forth as she cradled Elizabeth in her arms, singing lullabies to the infant.

Twenty yards away, Megan and Lona were hanging laundry with Hawthorne. Kelsey could see Lona's smile from across the field as Blake took a break from chopping wood to bring her a bundle of flowers.

It was precious.

Kelsey picked up a glass of iced tea from a small table next to her chair and took a sip. Something so fresh and crisp still felt foreign to her palette.

Maya and Bethany darted out from the cornstalks, Dakota hot on their heels.

Dakota reached out and touched Maya's arm, "Tag! You're it!" she yelled as she did an about-face and made a mad dash back to the cornfield, laughing and giggling in between gasps of breath.

The farm was truly an oasis in the middle of a sea of devastation. A little slice of heaven. It was fifteen miles from the nearest urban area, which was little more than a few abandoned shops and a single fast food restaurant. This meant unwanted visitors were few and far between. With multiple water sources and fertile soil, there was no better setup a group of survivors could ask for.

Life was different for Kelsey now. Gone were the days of scavenging and bartering just to make a scratch in her debt. Now her time was filled with taking care of the kids, cooking, cleaning, and other household chores that many women would have balked at before the eruptions. Responsibilities that would have been mere inconveniences in the past were things she looked forward to each day. Not because she enjoyed the tasks themselves or that they were a service to her family—which they were—but rather because she had the *freedom* to do so. She no longer had to be away for days, even weeks, at a time to try and provide for Dakota. Instead, she could spend the mornings making breakfast, afternoons playing games, and the evenings reading bedtime stories. Clay gave her that freedom. He gave her renewed hope when she had all but given up. He gave her his life, and for that, she felt there was no woman more blessed than she.

Kelsey looked down and saw her thumb fidgeting with the ring on her finger. Even though it had been three years since Clay had given it to her, it still felt strange on her hand. She still wondered how Clay could have loved her after everything she told him, everything she had done. Though she knew it was through no fault of her own when Watson attacked Clay's family, she couldn't help but feel a pang of guilt for it. And she would gladly spend the rest of her life trying to make it up to him.

As she watched her daughter running through the field in the warm, fading sunlight, as Kelsey had done as a child, she was happier than she ever thought possible. It was moments like these that made life worth living in this unforgiving world. It was what Clay risked his life for when he rescued her and Dakota from Watson's tyrannical grip.

Kelsey gazed at the surreal colors washed across the sky, the sun dipping lower and lower, casting long, dark purple shadows across the fields. Another breeze flew across the porch, gently brushing Kelsey's hair across her face. Her eyes lit up, her smile widened as Clay came around the side of the house holding a stringer full of fish in one hand and a little boy holding the other.

"Gorgeous evening, isn't it?" Clay said as he started to climb the steps.

Kelsey's smile was as beautiful as the sunset. "It really is."

"Daddy,   taked me fishing!" the boy said excitedly.

"He did?" Kelsey said playing along. "Well that's because Daddy is a good provider, and we should always thank him for that," she said as she tickled the boy's foot. "Say 'Thank you, Daddy,'" Kelsey instructed him.

"Kankem, Daddy!" the little boy said.

Clay chuckled with the fumbled pronunciation. "You're welcome, Charlie," he said as he leaned down to give Kelsey a kiss. She ignored the fishy smell and enjoyed the moment all the same.

"I'm gonna go fillet these things and fire up the grill," Clay said holding the string of black bass up. "You want to help me, Charlie?"

"Daddy," the boy elongated the word with a whine. "My name is Chawalls."

"Sorry, *Charles*." Clay winked at Kelsey. "So, do you wanna help?"

The little boy contemplated for a moment before replying, "Umm, Okay!"

Clay put Charlie down and held open the screen door. The toddler stumbled through in a hurry. Clay looked adoringly at Kelsey who was watching Dakota run towards the house. Within seconds, she reached the porch and zoomed up the steps, giving Clay a hug. "Hi, Daddy," she said before stepping back from the offensive odor. She wrinkled her nose then looked over at Kelsey, then back to Clay. "You need a bath," she said with a chuckle in her voice. "You stink!"

"What?" Clay said with an exaggerated look of shock on his face. "You don't like the way I smell?" Clay said as he gestured for Dakota to walk into the house too. "Your mom doesn't mind it, why do you?"

Kelsey made a similar expression as Dakota, followed with a smile. "But I love you anyway," she said with genuine joy.

Clay returned the smile. "I love you, too," he said before he turned and walked inside.

Kelsey stood up from the rocking chair and walked to the front of the porch. She leaned over the banister and gazed out at the large property, taking in its scenic beauty. As the sun made its final descent below the horizon, she thanked God for this new season of life, a second chance in a world so harsh.

Before she met Clay, she felt unworthy of true happiness. The things she had done, the life she had lived, the pain she had inflicted—these were not the character traits of a woman worthy of the love and respect of a man like Clay. As angering as it was to hear, Watson hadn't been too off base with some of his backhanded comments about her. She *was* damaged goods; she was not whole. She could never give all of herself to anyone.

But Clay loved her just as she was. For some unknown, seemingly impossible reason, Clay loved her despite her dark past. And for that, she would be everlastingly grateful. She would love him until the day she died.

Because of Clay, Kelsey's past no longer mattered to her either. She was able to forgive herself—something she had not been able to do previously.

Though memories still plagued her from time to time, Kelsey's past no longer had the throttling grip on her it once had. The darkness that had dwelled inside her for years had disappeared. She was freed from the bondage of her past—a gift Clay hadn't even realized he had given her. Instead, Kelsey could think about the future; a future she could be excited about; a future she could be proud of.

"Thank you." Kelsey's whisper was carried away by the breeze.

She was free.

ABOUT THE AUTHOR

AJ Powers is an artist in the video game industry, working on some of the biggest franchises in the world.

He currently resides in Ohio with his wife Talia and their three children.

If you enjoyed this book, please consider leaving a review.

For more information on AJ, please visit
www.ajpowers.com

You may also join AJ's mailing list to keep up to date with the latest info on his books, free content and win prizes!
www.ajpowers.com/newsletter

You can also follow him on Facebook:
www.facebook.com/AuthorAJPowers/

26467043R00277

Printed in Poland
by Amazon Fulfillment
Poland Sp. z o.o., Wrocław